ISLANDS WEST

STORIES FROM THE COAST

Islands West

Stories from the Coast

Edited by

Keith Harrison

OOLICHAN BOOKS
LANTZVILLE, BRITISH COLUMBIA, CANADA
2001

Canadian Cataloguing in Publication Data

Main entry under title:

Islands west

ISBN 0-88982-198-4

1. Short stories, Canadian (English)—British Columbia*. 2. Canadian fiction (English)—21st century*. I. Harrison, Keith.

PS8329.5.B75I84 2001   C813'.01089711   C2001-910844-3
PR9198.2.B72I84 2001

We gratefully acknowledge the support of the Canada Council for the Arts for our publishing program.

THE CANADA COUNCIL | LE CONSEIL DES ARTS
FOR THE ARTS | DU CANADA
SINCE 1957 | DEPUIS 1957

Grateful acknowledgement is also made to the BC Ministry of Tourism, Small Business and Culture for their financial support.

BRITISH
COLUMBIA
ARTS COUNCIL
Supported by the Province of British Columbia

We acknowledge the financial support of the Government of Canada through the Book Publishing Industry Development Program for our publishing activities.

Published by
Oolichan Books
P.O. Box 10, Lantzville
British Columbia, Canada
V0R 2H0

Printed in Canada

Cover image courtesy of www.heffel.com

To Jo
For the love story

Acknowledgements

Thanks to Cedar Wallace, Kathy Linnman, and Beth Lowther for help finding books, to Hiro McIlwraith, Linda Martin, and Jay Connolly for help proofreading, and to John Lepage for help convincing Malaspina it should pay me money to stay away. —K.H

Contents

Introduction

HAVING PUT TOGETHER these compelling short stories by thirty contemporary writers, I began to hear voices in my head. I was being haunted by a ghost anthology of another few dozen writers who might have been present here—evidence of the uncontainable aliveness of story-telling on the British Columbia coast.

In choosing works for inclusion, I decided not to excerpt novels or abridge long stories. I wanted the formal completeness and separateness that is akin to the shape of islands. As well as imaging the form of stories, "islanded" describes many of this book's isolate protagonists, who are cut off by geography, culture, jobs, madness. Additionally, the title, *Islands West*, points to a frequent setting for these fictional pieces, although several stories make no reference to the watery world.

Given the variousness of story-tellers gathered here, patterns are hard to find. A few of these writers are internationally famous, others have considerable national reputations, some have been unaccountably neglected, and many are just emerging. The stories themselves range, on a map of British Columbia, from the southern tip of Vancouver Island to the northern coast—with links to different countries, continents, and hemispheres. The narrative structures of the individual stories also vary—perhaps most noticeably in their kinds of closures, which include the epiphanic and the open-ended. Language in this collection shifts from the seemingly casual to the elegantly formal. Modes of story-telling include slice-of-life realism, murder mystery, prose lyricism, reportage, comic sketches, barely fictionalized autobiography, and hallucinatory vision. Can variety be an identifying feature of short fiction on Canada's West Coast?

One perspective on this heterogeneity—or many-islandness—comes from the cross-currents of cultural history. If most of the written stories of British Columbia take English as their expressive medium, and many speak indirectly of European origins, then the emigrant literature that has emerged on the North-West Coast of North America has a tradition of discontinuity and disconnectedness. Even when fantasy transfigures the beauty of the coastal forest into Paradise Regained, this edenic wish necessarily belongs to an outsider. Malcolm Lowry in *Under the Volcano*, the only acknowledged fictional masterpiece written (and rewritten) here, shrewdly depicts Dollarton through the eyes of his main character as an unattainable northern paradise. In parallel to Lowry's rendering of the failed dream of an alcoholic, several of the authors in *Islands West* create protagonists whose paradisal longings collide with an alien reality. This pattern of dissonance and discontinuity has taken on new fictional energy over the past decades with writers of Asian ancestry using English to give imaginative shape to uprooted lives on this side of the Pacific. Estrangement, paradoxically, may be greatest for those who were not outsiders: the First Nations. In recent years, Native writers have begun to draw on very deep oral traditions of story-telling, and have with renewed voices and different angles of vision written of a West Coast that is home.

But the shifting, unexpected voices in *Islands West* tell of lives more particular, complex, and variable than cultural categories. The artistry is personal, and the diverse narrative styles, tones, and structures express individual sensibilities. Self-defined and one-of-a-kind, these stories are like islands.

To end on a fancy metaphor, this book is an archipelago— a sheet of water with many scattered islands—around which I hope readers will voyage with excitement.

Keith Harrison
Hornby Island

After the Season

Jack Hodgins

ABOUT FIFTY MILES up the coast past the end of all public roads, in a little bay where the wildest tides throw logs and broken lumber far up the land like spat-out bones, Hallie Crane ran a café and a small cabaret for tourists staying at the fishing camp. Although there was a wharf built well out into the bay so fishing boats could tie up without being smashed against rocks, and down in the curve of the shore there was a small gravel beach where the bravest American tourists could run in for a quick swim and rush out again, Hallie's place and most other buildings were perched up on the rock and looked as if a good wind would fling them right out into the strait. The café was so close to the edge it had legs straight down into the water and whenever Hallie wanted to go anywhere, down the slope to Morgan's boat rental or around the bay to the well, she had to walk on a rickety boardwalk that ran right past her door and hung out over the sea. Tourists kept life jackets on their children the whole time they stayed in the camp.

Hallie liked it well enough, at least in the summer. When the last tourists left in September she squinted up her two bright green eyes at them and told them it had been fun just having them around. "Now there'll be nobody here at all for the next eight months except Morgan and me." She had a grown family down-island where the grey ribbon of highway went right under their noses when they sat in their living room, and she could have moved down to stay with them any time she wanted if she was willing to keep off the bottle, but she never did.

She never went back, hadn't seen her own daughter for eight years. They told her when she left not to bother unless she could stay sober, and though she hadn't touched a drink now for two years she still hadn't got around to packing up and catching the boat out for the winter. She could imagine herself landing in on them easily enough, tall and straight and good looking as ever, and hear their shrieks of surprise: "What? You can't be old enough to be this baby's grandmother!" But oh yes, she was, she was fifty-one years old. She was tall and straight, could walk like a youngster on her long narrow legs, could tell a joke with all the youth she knew was still inside, could snap her eyes in anger or fun as sharp and quick as she ever could. She touched up her hair now, natural blonde faded out faster than any other colour. But her face, though it had added laugh lines around the eyes and the skin was drier than it used to be, was still striking, still pretty. She could see herself going back, could imagine the fuss they'd make, but every fall when the season ended a sharp cold fear inside told her to put it off for another year.

During the summer Morgan, who owned the camp and ran it practically single-handed except for Hallie's help, lived down in his rooms behind the boat house and Hallie lived in the back of her café. They treated each other like strangers, like employer and employee, like invisible beings. When he came into the café and sat with his hairy arms folded on the counter, he ordered coffee without looking at her. When she walked down to his place, picked her way along the boardwalk hanging on to the rail, to tell him the plumbing was plugged up or the toaster needed fixing, she walked in and out amongst the boats while she talked, touching them as if feeling whether the paint was good enough to last the season. But when the tourists had gone and Hallie had tidied up the café and the little cabaret room beside it and closed the shutters over the windows, she moved down the hill into Morgan's rooms, into Morgan's bed, and stayed there until the first lot of people arrived the next June.

Not suddenly. Not just like that as if they had been thinking about it all summer and could hardly wait. Every year she was a little surprised all over again. Morgan was only thirty-three years old and still romantic, and he insisted on courting her, luring her, as if every October were their first. If she had just packed her suitcase and carried it down the hill and moved in he would have been disappointed, might even have tossed her out, and probably would have pouted all through the winter.

Every October he arrived at her door soon after the others had gone: a grinning, hairy, solid little man. "Dammit," he said, "you're a good-looking woman!" He came up behind and put his arms around her and ran his hands down her breasts and stomach and thighs. "Dammit, you've got it all over them other girls!" She slapped his hands and he went away for a while. But he came back again and again. He told her he was getting so randy for you-know-what that he was scared he'd go crazy and run screaming over the hills behind. He asked her how would she like to be raped. He brought gifts: chunks of smoked fish, handfuls of shells he'd found, magazines left behind in the cabins by tourists. It was usually about a week before Hallie recognized the signals that said it was all right for her to start giving in now. She stopped slapping his hands, stopped threatening to radio out for help, stopped keeping her distance. She packed her suitcase.

This year though, when the last boat had sailed out of sight down the strait, she didn't feel like going through all that drawn-out procedure, she just didn't have the energy. "Cut it out," she said. "I can't see any point in all this fooling around. Can't I just pack up and move down?"

But he insisted. "What do you want to be?" he said. "A whore?" His breath smelled of smoked fish.

"All right, I'll pretend then. I'll pretend I won't do it but we both know I will. How can it be any fun?"

He put his hands on her and told her what a good-looking woman she still was but she slapped the side of his head hard enough to knock him against the wall. "What the hell?" he said, his blue eyes hot with tears.

"You wanted me to pretend, well I'm pretending. Now leave me alone."

He grinned at her. "You don't want me to touch you because you've put on weight."

"Go to hell."

"You're afraid if I touch you I'll find out how fat you've got," he said, leering. "I saw you gorging yourself all summer on them apple pies. Putting on pound after pound."

"I'd like to know how you noticed what I was doing when you never once tore your little piggy eyes off that blonde bitch from Seattle."

"Shoving it in when you thought no one else was looking. Putting on layer after layer of fat. Turning into a big cow."

"I haven't put on a single pound, and," skirting his outstretched hand, "you'll just have to take my word for it."

Two days later they were just getting to the stage where he would threaten to rape her when the stranger arrived and interrupted the whole business.

It was the worst October she could remember. Black cloud moved in and sat on them like a heavy lid. Rain came down steadily through night and day. A wind had whipped the sea into such a turmoil and thrown the tide so high up the land that sometimes Hallie expected to wake up in the morning and find herself floating. It was always a small surprise to discover no walls had been ripped off, no windows bashed in, no pieces of roof lifted. She kept a fire roaring in the cast-iron stove and got up several times during the night to shake the grates and add more wood. If she didn't drown, she would probably burn to death.

She was on the boardwalk tossing garbage down for the few gulls that still clung to the coast when she saw the stranger's boat. At first she thought it was nothing but a driftwood log, dipping and leaping with the waves, and when it got closer there appeared to be something alive, a large bird perhaps, perched in the middle and riding. It wasn't until it had entered the bay and came rushing in towards shore that she saw it was a small aluminum boat with a man inside holding on for dear life and not even trying to steer with the handle on the useless little outboard motor. She ran down the boardwalk and across the beach in time to see it thrown ahead onto the gravel, sucked back, then thrown ahead again far enough for the man to leap out, fall to his knees, get up again, grab the rope, and drag the boat up high enough to tie it to a log. He turned two pale runny eyes on her and said, "Thank God I got to civilization."

"You didn't," she said. "There's only me and Morgan and all these empty shacks. Even our radio set-up went on the blink a couple days ago."

He wiped a hand over his wet face, shook himself like a dog, tipped forward to let water run off the back of his neck. "It'll have to do," he said, flicking an ear. "I'm not going back out into that."

Morgan came out of the boat house, walking—as he always did—as if his body besides being solid and heavy was also hot and he had to keep both hands and arms well away in order not to get burned. He looked the little man over like an interesting log the sea had washed in, then looked at Hallie as if to say, "Now what have you done?"

"We better get you somewhere and dry you off," Hallie said.

The little man bent down again and wrung out his straight blond hair, then flung it back with a snap that could have broken his neck, and turned to look out at the water. "I wouldn't want to've spent much longer on that," he said.

"You wouldn't've," Hallie said. "You'd've been in it before long, dead as a thrown-back dogfish. Come on, let's get you over to Morgan's place, warm you up."

Morgan stood in their way and scowled at Hallie. Then, suddenly, he smiled as if the scowl had been about something else altogether, and said, "Don't you think your place would be better?"

"Nothing wrong with yours," she said. "It's good and warm."

"Too warm," Morgan said. "And too small. I bet you've got a nice fire on up there in the café, maybe even a cup of coffee."

"Look," the man said, "I don't care where you put me, just so long as I can go somewhere to dry off. I may drown right here on shore if you keep arguing." And he started walking up the slope towards the café.

When they'd stripped him down to dry out his clothes there wasn't very much to him. In his undershorts he looked like a young boy—Hallie had seen bigger bones in a turkey—but his face was the face of a man in his forties. When he handed over his clothes for her to hang up above the stove, looking so small and drenched and lost, she wanted to tickle him under the chin and say, "Cheer up, little man, you haven't fallen off the end of the world!" But there was something about his face, a long narrow pointed face with sunken cheeks and pale fast-moving eyes, that told her if she so much as touched him, treated him like a child, he would snarl and growl and maybe knock her hand away with one of those frail arms.

"Here," she said. "You can put on my robe and we'll dry out your undershorts too."

18

Morgan eyed him as if he expected to see him turn into a rat and start gnawing the house down. Hallie could see resentment already settling in around his mouth.

"I'm a teacher," he told them when his white jockey shorts were hanging on the line over the stove and he was wrapped up in Hallie's red chenille bath robe. He found a cigar in one of his pockets but it was too wet to light and he threw it in the fire, spitting pieces of damp tobacco off his tongue. "I taught high school geography but I quit my job in June and started exploring up and down this coast."

"You should've tried elementary," Hallie said. "The kids wouldn't't've been so big and scary there."

The little man looked at Hallie as if she were the stupidest pupil he'd ever run across. Then he looked up at the bare rafters. "My name is Hamilton Grey," he said. "I have never been afraid of a person, big or small, in my life. Least of all a geography student. What scares me is not people but mankind." And he looked at her again, as if it were all her fault, as if she were the mother of the whole blessed lot. "The stupidity of mankind appals me."

Hallie looked at Morgan and Morgan rolled his eyes. "I don't know anything about smart or stupid," she said. "Nice is good enough for me. If a person's considerate of other people it don't matter how much brains he's got."

He looked up again and snorted. He and the rafters knew she'd just proved his point. "Nice people are spilling oil into the oceans," he said. "Nice people are busy inventing new biological warfare weapons."

He told them he had this theory. Whatever your instincts tell you is right is exactly wrong. He told them instincts were good enough for the individual's survival but all wrong for society. For example, he told them, everybody's instinct says pornography increases sex crimes but the opposite is true, look at Denmark. He told them everybody's instinct says if a kid is bad hit him but that is the surest way to make him worse. Look at wild land, he said, instinct says tame it, kill all the scary animals, log off the useless trees, turn it into something we can handle. And prisons too, he said. The whole idea of punishment is instinctive but does exactly the opposite to what is good for society.

"Mister Grey," she said. "Is there anything at all good about people in your opinion?"

He looked as if he'd never encountered that question before. He thought for a long time, stroking his pointed jaw. Finally, he said, "Yes, one thing. His potential. Man has one thing—mind— that makes everything possible."

"How long you plan on staying?" Morgan said.

"I didn't plan anything. My motor's conked out."

"I can fix that," Morgan said.

"And I'm not setting out again as long as this storm keeps up."

When Hallie went out into the kitchen Morgan followed her and said, "You let him have your bed and come on down to my place tonight."

She told him he'd better watch his tongue. "There's a spare bed in my back room," she said. "Besides, what would he think of us?"

"He already doesn't think much of us. It wouldn't make any difference."

"He's a school teacher," she said. "It wouldn't be right. I just couldn't do it."

Morgan sat down and tried to pull her onto his knee but she held back. "He doesn't care. It's none of his business."

"My son-in-law is a teacher," she said. "I won't do it."

"In that case," Morgan said, "we will have to get rid of him." It wasn't easy. All the next day he worked on the little man's outboard motor. He took it apart, washed every piece in gasoline, put in new spark plugs. He replaced a part in the water pump. By evening it was running as smooth as a new motor but the storm hadn't died down.

"Looks like it's settled in for a long haul," Mr. Grey said, looking out the front windows of the café. "I'm not heading out into that." He brought all his equipment in from the boat—his tent and sleeping bag and cooking utensils and food and books—and dropped them in the middle of Hallie's floor.

"Put them up on the stage out of the way," she said.

So he set up camp on the raised alcove beside the piano that Hallie played whenever there was a crowd that wanted to dance. There was a harvest moon painted on the back wall with SWING YOUR PARTNER printed across it. He set up the tent as if he could foresee rain coming through the roof, laid out his sleeping bag inside, and opened up his camp stove.

"I'll radio for a plane," Morgan said.

"No plane would fly in this," Hallie said. "And besides, the set is broke."

And while he spent the next day trying to get the radio set to work, Hallie tried to find out more about Hamilton Grey. Because it was a long time since she'd talked to any teacher except her son-in-law, a sharp-eyed man who made her nervous, she didn't know how to go about making conversation. She scrubbed floors and cleaned windows and stacked furniture in the dance room and he listened to her questions from behind a book, sitting on the edge of the stage.

"You got somebody somewhere worrying about you right now? Somebody scared you're drowned?"

A page turned. "Mmph."

"No wife? No children, no parents?"

He lowered the book and looked at her. "If I had all that lot hanging around my neck, would I be sailing up and down the strait taking my own sweet time? There isn't a soul to care if I end up at the bottom of the ocean."

"It may not look like it," Hallie said, "but I've got a family. A grown daughter."

There was no indication that he had heard her but she continued. "She's married to a teacher too, like you, only he teaches chemistry and is a lot taller. They live in the same house my husband and I lived in for all twelve years of our marriage, right on the damn highway, only the highway's been widened since then, and every time a car goes by you'd think it was coming right through the living room. I'm surprised they don't move out and build a house of their own, but I guess all the savings they have get used up just living through the summer. They've got two kids."

He turned a page, then turned back to reread the bottom line and turned again.

"I bet you never thought I was a grandmother," Hallie said.

He looked up to see if he'd missed anything, then looked down again.

Hallie shifted chairs around noisily. "If bad manners is something they're teaching at universities now you must've got top marks but I can't say that I'm impressed."

He closed the book but kept a finger between the pages. "What I'm wondering," he said, "is why you haven't gone back to stay with your daughter. How come you're all alone up here with that Tarzan the ape-man when you could be with your family?"

"Scared I guess," she said, quickly, because if she had paused to think about it she would have told him none of his business. "I'd be back on the bottle in a week if I went down there. I'd be so useless—don't know how to talk to kids, not even my own grandchildren, without feeling like a fool—and that long beak-nosed son-in-law watching me like a hawk to see what makes me tick— I'd be throwing back the rye just to get through the day."

After supper Morgan came into her kitchen and said he hadn't been able to get anything on the radio. He sat down at her table, spread out his elbows, and slurped up a cup of coffee. He swore after every mouthful.

"Morgan," she said. "Would you say I'm getting old looking?"

"Naw."

"Well, since he came you haven't said one nice thing to me. If I'm getting old and fat just tell me."

"Hell no," he said, and pulled her down onto his lap. He dug fingers into the flesh of her thigh. "You're still a good-looking woman."

"That Mr. Grey makes me feel old and stupid."

"Oh him," Morgan said, and threw a sneer at the wall that separated the kitchen from the café and dance room. He ran one hand up the inside of her skirt but she put her hand on top of it and held it still.

"You're not doing much to get rid of him," she said. "Maybe he'll be here all winter."

He looked down at the lump his own hand made under her skirt and scowled. "I'll get rid of the bastard," he said, and pushed her off him so he could stand up. "But first I guess I better go in and tell him about the radio."

After Morgan had gone back to his boat house Mr. Grey told her the ape-man had nearly attacked him. His hair was on end, as if he had been running his fingers through it backwards, and his quick pale eyes were darting everywhere. Hallie couldn't help feeling sorry for him; after all he was a teacher and probably not used to people like Morgan, mean and free, without school rules to hold him back.

But just when she was beginning to feel warm inside with the pity she felt, he started to laugh, confusing her. He took out a handkerchief and blew his nose, one hard snort on either side. "You know what he told me?" he said.

"Don't listen to him," she said. "Morgan's liable to make all sorts of threats he won't carry out. There's not much harm in him."

"He said, 'You know what you're buttin' in on?'"

"What?"

"He said I walked in on the middle of a mating ritual, that's what he told me."

23

"A mating dance of two horny people," Morgan had said. "You landed in here when we'd hardly got started. Hell, every year we go at it all over again like a couple of rutting mountain sheep, only we wait until after the season." He rolled his eyes as if to say, You know what I mean. "Right through the summer while the tourists are here we don't hardly talk to each other. She lives up here in her dance hall serving meals and I live down there in my boat house. A person wouldn't even think we knew each other."

"This is none of my business," Mr. Grey had said.

But Morgan had gone on. "Then every October we look around, see, and there's nobody left here. The tourists are all gone. The loggers, they're back but they're inland a ways. So pretty soon we're sniffing around each other, see, and then we're snarling and clawing each other. Finally we land in bed like a clap of thunder and that's where we spend most of the winter."

"Like a couple of animals!"

"You bet, mister," Morgan had said. "You ever see a mountain sheep going after it? If he wants to he can run sixty miles an hour on his back legs. Think about that coming together!"

Hallie didn't wait for Mr. Grey to tell her anything more that Morgan had said or how he had got around to almost attacking him. She left the room and shut the door behind her, gently so he wouldn't think she was upset. She stood stiffly for a long time in front of the little mirror that hung over the kitchen sink, her head throbbing like an inboard motor, her hand laid out stiff and white against the vibrations of her breast. She was a good-looking woman—the mirror told her that—and not even the dyed hair could make her look cheap. She was one of those women who kept their looks, who stayed smart and slim and attractive even into old age, but that was a different thing from what Morgan had made her sound like. It wasn't a mountain sheep he made her sound like; it was a mink.

She went out onto the boardwalk and sat on a bench that leaned against her front wall. The wind had died down a little and the rain had stopped falling but the surface of the water was still slate-black and heaving. There wasn't a gull to be seen, gone inland for safety. She sat facing all of it, wouldn't have moved even if an earth tremor had sent the whole building down crazily into the bay, and felt the hot flush of shame creeping up her face. The crashing of the waves against the pilings beneath her was no stronger in her than the beating of her own heart. She wanted a drink.

Hallie Crane had felt real shame only once before in her life. She wasn't a person who did things she later regretted. Most of her actions were deliberate, considered, and consistent. Memories were usually pleasant. But once, just once, she had fallen into something she was so ashamed of that even now, eighteen years later, its memory could send her to bed for a day or more. When the phone call came telling her that her husband had died in the Vancouver hospital, she was at a community dance, nearly drunk. Her daughter had taken the message.

That wasn't me! she wanted to scream at the memory of it. That wasn't the real me, that was someone else.

And now, too, she wanted to tell that little school teacher in there that he had been given the wrong impression. She wanted to set things straight in his mind. She went back into the kitchen, checked her face in the mirror, and walked into the café where he was helping himself to a handful of sugar cubes.

"You shouldn't listen to Morgan," she said. "He's given you the wrong impression about us. Probably wanted to shock you."

He threw a sugar cube into his mouth and crunched it between his teeth. "Is there some place around here where a person can go for a walk?"

When they both had their rain clothes on, she led him up the trail that climbed in a series of switch-backs up the slope of the hill behind the buildings. "Deer made this," she said, "and elk."

The wet leaves of salal and Oregon grape knocked against their legs and soaked the bottom half of their slacks. When Mr. Grey hung onto a small scrubby pine to help pull himself up a particularly steep part of the trail, its roots were so shallow in the rocky soil that he pulled it right out and fell backward a few feet and rolled over against a windfall fir.

At last they reached the top, however, and she stood aside for him to see that beyond it there was only a small swampy valley of burnt snags and another, higher hill. "From down there I thought this was the end," he said, and she told him no, that it was only the beginning. "Just the first small step. It goes up and up and finally you're above timber altogether and in year-round snow and then it drops straight down into the Pacific."

The fishing camp below was nearly obscured by the fine rain which had started and by the mist. The small handful of buildings looked as if they too, like Mr. Grey, had been washed in by the tide and left stranded between the sea and this hill. Smoke from the little café stood up in a thin white column, then spread out level and flat as if somewhere between the roof and the top of the hill there was an invisible ceiling.

Hallie sat down on a rock. No matter how hard she looked she could not see the mainland mountains through the dense grey wall of cloud. Below, the tiny figure of Morgan left one of the cabins and walked across to the boat house. "You shouldn't pay him any attention," she said. "He'll just give you the worst impression of things."

Mr. Grey sat down on the ground beside her. "It doesn't matter to me," he said. "I don't give a damn what you two do. When I get out of here I'll probably never think of either one of you again."

She could see him going through his life, wiping out the people he met as if they were only figures on a chalkboard. Or as if he were that wall of cloud, blocking out the whole world.

"There's nothing about you that's special. There's no way that

26

either one of you have touched me or entered me or altered my life. When I leave I'll be the same as when I arrived, my life won't be changed, and there won't be a thing about my stay here worth remembering."

Hallie gritted her teeth. He may be a smart school teacher who thought he knew everything but there was one thing she knew better than he did. "You can't touch someone else without it affecting your life in some way," she said.

"Ah, but here's the difference: you haven't touched me." He broke off a branch of salal and started chewing on its tip. "You circle around me, you and that hairy ape of yours, making faces and screeching noises at me, but it's as if I'm watching from inside a bubble of glass. You can't penetrate. You can't touch me. You never will. I'll go on watching your mating dance without being affected in any way."

Hallie shuddered. "Mating dance?" He sounded as crude as Morgan. "Is that what you really think, just because he said it? Do you really think I'm like that?"

But he didn't answer. He found the veins in a salal leaf more interesting than her. He probably thought she had never done anything educational in her whole life, never even read a book. Well listen, she had. She told him about this story she once read, an old-fashioned tale in some book somebody'd given to her when she was a little girl. This girl in the story, this Proser-something, was out running around in a place something like this, pulling a bush right out of the ground just like Mr. Grey had and up out of that hole came old Pluto, the king of the underworld, riding in a chariot, and hauled her off against her will down into his deep horrible black place.

"Proserpina," he said. "I know the story, yes." He got up and started following the trail back from the edge, towards the swamp. She hurried to catch up to him.

"Her old lady found her all right," she said, "but not before

27

she'd half broken a promise not to eat a thing down there. So for the rest of her life, if you can believe it, she had to spend six months with her mother and six months down in the underworld with him."

"With Pluto," he tossed over his shoulder. "I didn't think anyone remembered those tales any more." They were walking on logs now; the ground was soft and damp, with a musty swamp smell. Burnt snags stood around like silent black totems.

"Anyway, that's what I feel like. Only I don't get six and six. I get three months, four if I'm lucky, of normal living with people treating me like a human being. Then along comes October and he starts in dragging me down."

"Morgan?" Mr. Grey stood on the edge of the little lake, a hundred feet of green scum in front of him, a log laid out on it like a wharf. He turned and his pale eyes crinkled, as if he was ready to disbelieve whatever she was going to say next.

Hallie stopped walking. "Pulling me down into his hell with him. Clawing at me and slobbering and pulling me down, living in slime."

Mr. Grey walked out onto the log, straight out over that floor of scum. "If I remember the story right, the girl didn't mind it so much. She got so she kind of liked old Pluto."

Hallie felt as if she might explode. "Nobody likes living in hell," she cried.

At the other end of the log he turned and faced her. "The whole world loves it," he said. He looked slightly amused, as if she were a child run up against something every adult understood. "As soon as a human being chooses to pay attention to his five senses he's electing to live in hell." He let her chew on that for a while, then bounced a little on the log to watch it disturb the thick surface of the lake. "If he pays attention to the demands of the senses, if he uses them to make judgments, if he listens to their reports of pain and disease, he's living in hell. There's nothing so special about you."

Hallie walked by herself back to the edge of the slope and sat down. After a while he came up behind her and she said, "All right, mister, you know so much. Is there a way out?"

He chuckled. "Sure there is," he said. He started down the hill. "I guess you were hoping I'd say everybody is doomed to be miserable and so you're pretty normal after all. D'you think that just because I'm soured on humanity I don't see its possibilities? Well, lady, like it or not, there are some happy people in the world."

"Who?" she demanded.

He stopped on the trail and looked up at her. "It'd be a lot easier for all of us if we didn't look around once in a while and see people who can smile."

"Who are they?" she said, running down to catch up and nearly crashing right into him.

He pushed his face so close to hers she had to step back. He spoke as if he were chipping the words out one at a time, once and for all. "Those who refuse to ride in the chariot!"

Hallie felt as if his breath had turned all of her into some cold rigid material. She looked into his eyes, pale, murky, trembling from the force of his words. A thin, barely visible red line ran from the edge of one grey disc down into the corner by the tear duct, casual as a lost thread. He was human. He was human. She lifted one hand and brushed a finger against his cheek.

Mr. Grey leapt back from her touch and tripped over a rock. He rolled over and over down the hill, slid a few feet, then rolled again until he slammed up against a tree. By the time Hallie got down that far he was on his feet again, walking with a slight limp down the deer trail to the fishing camp.

She'd handled it all wrong, she knew. She hadn't even behaved the way Hallie Crane normally would. That night in bed she thought of all the people she had known back home, the friendly nosy country people who had been her neighbours for nearly twenty years, and she tried to see herself as they would. Hallie Crane?

You want to know how Hallie Crane would treat a little shit like that, spouting his nonsense? She'd throw back her head and laugh. You'd see her long white throat. You'd hear her deep harsh laugh. Hallie Crane has the sexiest laugh a man ever heard and that's exactly what she'd turn on that smart-alec school teacher. She'd laugh and ask him who the hell he thought he was.

But she hadn't done that. She didn't even have her old laugh any more. She'd kept her looks and her figure and her long slim legs, but somewhere along the way she'd lost her deep throaty laugh. Those people wouldn't recognize her without it. No wonder she's scared to come home, they'd say. Hallie Crane without her laugh isn't Hallie Crane.

And she knew that she would never go back. There was nothing strong enough to pull her back to that place; not friends, not daughter, not grandchildren. She didn't want to see her son-in-law again. She didn't want to see the house again, or the small farms that surrounded it. Some day, maybe, she would send down enough money for her daughter and the children to fly up and spend part of the summer with her. That would be nice. Her daughter could help out in the café, talk to the tourists, find out that the kind of life her old lady lived wasn't so bad after all. Maybe Morgan would take them fishing.

While Hallie was lying in bed planning her future she heard Mr. Grey get up and go outside. Just keep on walking, she thought, walk right on over the mountains and down-island until you find the road, then keep on walking still. You've stirred up here all that needs to be stirred. How nice it would be to wake up in the morning and find he had gone, that he had shoved out to sea in his boat and disappeared. She would worry perhaps, for a few minutes, that he was in danger or even drowned, but soon she would say it was his own choice and forget him.

Though Hallie believed a little in the power of thought, she never expected immediate results. The sound of lumber breaking, snapping like kindling, and a long scream right outside the café brought her up out of the bed and to her feet. Outside her front door she discovered a large section of the boardwalk railing had been broken away. There was no sound below but the slapping of the sea. "Mr. Grey?" she said, in case he was close by and watching her. But no answer came so she yelled his name into the dark. She felt for a moment as if she were alone, the only person left in the world, abandoned. She screamed for Morgan, who came up the slope eventually with a strong flashlight he aimed down into the water, splashing sloppily around the pilings, and it wasn't until morning that they found Mr. Grey's body, back under the boardwalk and nudging like a dead fish against the rock her house was built on.

"You son of a bitch," Hallie said to Morgan. "Did you do this?" Morgan came up close and looked hard at her. The rain was rolling off his flattened hair and down his face, dripping from the end of his nose. "Do you think that?" he said.

She looked into his eyes, steady as stone. "No," she said, and turned away. She went back into the café and waited until he had fished the body out and came to bang on her door.

"We'll have to bury him," he said.

She shuddered. "We're not that far from civilization. It doesn't seem right."

She turned away but he stepped in and walked around to face her and wrapped his arms so tight around her she couldn't move. She could smell the smoked fish on his breath, could see the black spikes of his week-old beard. She tried to push away but his grip was too tight, his arms too strong.

"What're you going to do?" he said.

"Going home."

"Hell you are. You're home now."

"I mean down-island, back to my family. I'll fly out as soon as the weather changes. I want to get away from this goddam hole."

"You'll never go back there again and you know it."

During the following week the storm continued. Waves hit the rocks and leapt up almost as high as the boardwalk railings. The wind, coming in from the strait like a giant flat hand, bent the seaside pines and firs down almost to the ground. Morgan walked up to the café every day and tried to talk her into moving down to the boat house but she didn't talk to him at all. She rolled up Hamilton Grey's sleeping bag and folded his tent and left them piled on the stage beside the piano for the day when the RCMP would be finally contacted and come to ask questions about his death.

At the end of the week Morgan came to the door and asked if she wanted to help bury the little school teacher. She nearly laughed and said "No, but thank you for thinking of me," but instead just shook her head and shut the door in his face. Through the window of a back room she watched him drag the body out of the shed and haul it, wrapped in one of her blankets and laid out flat on a piece of canvas, up the steep slope of the hill. She ran out into the rain with Mr. Grey's books, scrambled up the hill until she caught up with Morgan, and said, "Throw these in too." She tossed the books, whose titles she hadn't even noticed, onto the canvas beside the body and hurried back down the hill before he started digging the grave.

That evening the wind was quieter, the rain silent, but Morgan still hadn't fixed the radio set. Hallie sat for a long time at the window, looking out to sea, listening to the intense beating of her own heart. Then she packed her suitcase and walked down the boardwalk, slowly, casually as if she hoped for a ship to appear from behind the point of land and sail in to pick her up by the time she got down to the gravel beach. But no ship came and Hallie Crane walked past the beach, gravel crunching under her heels, walked past Mr. Grey's little aluminum boat still tied to a driftwood log, and knocked lightly on the boat-house door.

Inside, she put down her suitcase and took a good look around. "The first thing you can do," she told Morgan, "is go up and bring down my own bed. I'm just here for the company."

"Sure you are," he said, and shut the door.

"I can't stand being alone for long."

"Sit down," he said. "I was making some coffee."

She smiled. "Did you dig a deep enough grave?"

"Deep enough so the rain won't wash him out, shallow enough for people or relatives to dig up if they want to see the body."

"He had no relatives," she said, taking off her coat. "He said he had no one." She smiled. She would like to have laughed, like the old Hallie, but she turned instead to the window and looked out for a moment across the little bay. "He told me there was no one in the world who could touch him, not even us."

Four Days from Oregon

Madeleine Thien

I

ONCE, IN THE MIDDLE OF THE NIGHT, our mother Irene sat on our bed and listed off the ways she was unhappy. She looked out the window and stroked our hair and sometimes she lapsed into silence, as if even she didn't know the full extent of it, where to finish, when to hold back. And all the things that made her unhappy were mixed in with things that made her happy, too, like this house. It was full to the brim. Sometimes, she said, she sat in the bathroom because it was the smallest room with a door that locked. But even then she could hear us, me and my sisters Helen and Joanne, and our father, all of us creaking the floorboards and talking over the television and filling the quiet. Hearing us pulled her out every time. She would come out of the bathroom and track us down. She said she wanted to tuck us under her arm like a rolled-up paper and run away.

We were just kids then—Helen was nine, Joanne was seven, and I was six—but we thought of our mother as a young girl. She cried so much and had a temper. She joked about running off on her thirtieth birthday. "Almost there," she told us, joking. "Better pack your bags."

When our mother was unhappy, she broke things. She slammed the kitchen door over and over until its window crumpled and shattered to the floor. In our bare feet, we tiptoed around the pieces. Our father ignored it. He said, "Tell your crazy mother there's a phone call for her." He said *crazy* with a funny look in his eye, like he didn't really believe it. But we saw it ourselves, the plates flying from her hands, her face empty. Our father turned away and left the house. He walked slowly down the alley.

Only once did Irene leave us. We waited for her tirelessly. In the middle of the night, in our bed wider than a boat, we listened for her car on the road. We fought sleep, but she didn't come that night or the next. While she was gone, our father sat at the kitchen table like an old man. Already his hair had tufts of grey and his skin hung loose around his mouth and eyes. "Like a dog," he said, running his hands over his head. "Don't I look just like a dog?"

My sisters and I rode our bikes up and down the alley. When we were winded, we played in the garage, climbing up onto the roof of our father's brown Malibu. He poked his head in, said, "What's this, now?"

"Tea party," Helen told him, though we weren't really doing anything.

He nodded, "You like it better in the garage than in the house. It's your mother. There's something wrong in her head."

One day after school, she was back on the couch, her fingers ragged from worry. "I missed you," she said, pulling us in. My sisters and I sat on top of her body. We held her arms and legs down while she laughed, struggling to sit up.

Sometimes Irene was well and she put on the *Nutcracker Suite*, twirling us around the room. At times like this, she would embrace our father. She would kiss his face, his eyebrows and mouth.

They waltzed around the living room. She kept stepping on his feet. He shrugged. "It's not the end of the world," he said.

Our mother shook her head. "No," she told him, "it never is."

The first time Tom came by, he shook our hands. He said, "So you're the Terrible Threesome," winking at us. Irene told us he was someone she worked with in the department store. He worked in Sports and Leisure. The second time he came, he brought three badminton rackets and a container full of plastic birdies. He and Irene sat on the steps, drinking pink-tinted coolers. We batted the racquets through the air, knocking the birdies from one side of the lawn to the other. Joanne, always moody, aimed one through the tire swing. Another cleared the fence and landed in the neighbour's yard.

"Can't you hit straight?" Helen said, impatient.

Tom stood up on the balcony, waving his arms in the air. "I can bring some more tomorrow!"

Joanne turned her back on him and whipped one into the hedge.

Afterwards, Helen pocketed the last remaining birdie and we went down to the storage area beneath the porch. We planted the birdie in a cinder block, covered it with mud, then left it to bake in the afternoon sun. Through the floorboards we could hear Irene's voice, shy and laughing, and the long silences that came and went all afternoon, interrupted by the creaky sound of the screen door swinging shut. We watched Tom drive away, his hand stretching out of the car window, waving back to us.

Our father came home at six o'clock. Helen told him the screen door needed oiling again and he took us out back, oil on his hands. He rubbed the oil along the metal spoke so that when he threw the door open again it closed slow as ever, but without a sound on the wind, just the quiet click of the latch closing.

My sisters and I sat outside with him, our bare legs dangling between the porch steps. Our father pulled a photograph from his pocket. He'd come across it at the office, he explained, a picture of Main Street from a hundred years ago. In the photograph, there were no cars, just wide streets but no concrete, dirt piled down, women in long dresses, their hems bringing up the dust. I told my father I couldn't imagine streets without cars, trolleys and everything, horses idling on the corners. He said, "It's progress, you see, and it comes whether you welcome it or not."

Our father laid the photograph down. He said he could stand on the back steps and stare out until the yard fell away. He could see the house where he grew up, plain as day. It was in another country, and he remembered fields layered into the hillside. A person could grow anything there—tea, rice, coffee beans. I would always remember this because he had never talked about these things before. When he was young, he wanted to be a priest. But he came to Canada and fell in love with our mother.

We spent that summer sunning in the backyard. Helen would grab the tire swing and hurl it loose. Joanne and I lay flat on the grass, fighting the urge to blink, watching it swoop towards us. The tire raced above us, rubber-smell fleeting and then blue sky.

We were there the day Irene came running out in her bare feet. She was wearing a white flowered dress, and her hair, wet from the shower, had soaked the back. My sisters and I stood up uncertainly when we saw her coming. She grabbed our wrists and dragged us into the house and upstairs to her bedroom. Through the window we saw our father turn into the alley, then drive straight onto the back lawn. He climbed out, forgetting to slam the car door behind him. We heard him running up the stairs. "Irene!" he yelled. "Irene!"

She looked at us. "Tom will be here soon."

"Irene!" Our father pounded the door with his fist. "Open this goddamned door!"

She shook her head at us. "He wasn't supposed to find out until later," she said. We stood beside the bed, next to her luggage, three plastic-shell suitcases, pale green, lined up all in a row. I went over to Irene and pulled at her arms, trying to get her attention. She looked past me, then stepped up to the door, unlocked it, and our father burst inside, his arms swinging. He was still in work clothes, suit pants and a white dress shirt. He was raging at Irene, saying, "I know, I knew it all along! You think I *didn't* know?" My father drove his fist into the closet door and the wood splintered. Then he turned around and grabbed the curtains and pulled them off the rod and the fabric balled up on the ground. We heard tires on gravel, turned to look through the window and saw Tom's car pulling up against the curb. Our father sank down, crying. "Do you know what I've put up with? Everything you do. All your crazy talk. Is this what I deserve?"

Irene folded her arms across her chest and stared at her feet. I wanted to go to my father but I could barely recognize him. His face was red and puffy, streaked with tears. We heard the front door open, Tom coming up the stairs. All of us listened to him and waited and then he was there. He held his back straight, looked right at Irene, and came into the room.

I thought my father would stand up, come at him, splinter his face the way he'd splintered the closet. He would tell Irene that enough was enough. But my father got to his feet, his face slick with sweat, and walked towards us. He crouched down to touch us but I backed away from him. My sister Helen said, "Dad, what's happening?"

He looked at her, his face old, suddenly. "You're going with them," he answered, his voice barely audible. "That's what your mother wants." He turned away from us and said to Irene, "Go wherever the hell you want." He never even looked at Tom.

Irene went to the window and watched him stagger down the back steps, walk across the lawn to the car. She screamed down at him to get out. She went over to the desk, picked up a stack of papers, old bills, letters, and flung them out the window. They showered the lawn. She kept screaming for him to get out, get out, even while he was reversing the car. Helen looked out the window and said, "He's left." Irene didn't hear. She pulled his clothes from the closet, shirts and pants tangled together, and threw them after him. Tom came and put his arms around her but she pushed him away. My sister Joanne ran out of the room, down the stairs, and out onto the back lawn, in the direction of our father's car. But Helen and I just stood there, watching in shocked silence. Helen turned to our mother and said, "What have you done?" Irene sat down on the bed, unmoving.

That night, we climbed into Tom's car. I was sitting up in the front seat, between Tom and Irene. Tom turned out of the driveway and I looked back at the house, all the lights on.

Behind us, my sisters stared straight ahead, exhausted from the arguments and the yelling. They clutched their backpacks to their knees. "Mom?" Joanne said, when Tom pulled onto the highway and the city vanished behind a corridor of trees. "Mom?" Joanne said again.

"What is it?"

"Where are we going?"

Irene smiled, her face gentle. "Don't worry."

"I'm worried."

"Don't worry. We won't get there tonight."

"When?"

"Tomorrow night."

"How long are we going for?"

"Just a few days. I promise. Just a little while. I didn't think it would happen this way. But it's okay. I'm not angry."

Joanne leaned back rigidly in the seat. Beside her, Helen reached her arms out and held on to her.

Irene turned and watched them in the side mirror, her fingers tapping absently on the passenger-side window.

II

Irene was leaving our father because she was in love with Tom. In the car, she explained to us how she had married our father when she was nineteen. He was a good man, she said. He loved her very much and she had loved him. But now she was thirty, and he was thirty, and they had changed. She wanted to do what was best for us. "It's nobody's fault," she said, turning to look at me. "Everything will be okay." Tom drove straight ahead. On a winding road, he pulled over and Irene jammed her body out of the passenger door. She leaned over and threw up on the gravel.

My older sisters fidgeted in the back seats. Helen had a habit of biting her lips until they bled. She chewed her fingernails raw. She was forever picking at herself, pulling loose bits of skin from the corners of her mouth, her elbows and cuticles. Irene always said to let her be, she'd grow out of it one day. In the car, Helen nibbled angrily on her fingers. "Where are you *taking* us?" she said at one point, kicking the back of Irene's seat with her sneaker. Tom glanced at her in the mirror but no one answered. Joanne stared grimly out the window and I fell in and out of sleep, lying tipped over on top of Irene's legs. None of us spoke.

The clock on the dashboard read 1:00 by the time we got to Long Beach. Tom drove right up on the sand and parked the car. We couldn't see anything but the moon and the stars. Tom explained about the moon and gravity, how the tides were pulled in and out.

He turned to look at us. "Why the glum faces?" he asked. "You'll see. In the morning it will be beautiful." I had moved into the back seat by then, and my sisters and I were huddled together. Tom smiled. "Oh, I see," he said. "I can see what it's going to be like. You girls are a team, right? *Triple Trouble.*" He laughed out loud.

"Why don't you just shut up?" Helen said.

Irene stretched her arm out and touched him. "Not now. It's too late for jokes."

Tom lowered his chin. He got out of the car by himself, a gust of wind tearing through the open door, and began unloading the trunk. There was a big orange tent with metal poles that Tom assembled in the dark. Irene shone a flashlight out the car window, the beam tracing circles across the trees and the sky.

She spoke to the dashboard. "Don't tell anyone your names. Not for a little while yet, okay? Not until we sort things out."

Tom built a fire, tramping off into the night and returning with an armload of wood. We fell asleep in the car and Irene woke us, half dragging and half carrying us inside and tucking us into sleeping bags. We slept side-by-side all in a row: me between Irene and Tom, then Helen and Joanne. Tom had left the fire burning. Helen spoke up in the darkness. "That's a fire hazard. You better put it out."

"Enough," Irene said.

Tom turned over and faced the tent wall and all of us lay in silence.

We hated them so much it hurt. Helen kept a journal and she wrote: *Irene is not our real mother. Our real mother is living with our real father and we've been kidnapped by these hooligans. When the time is right, my sisters and I will run away.* We walked in single file along the beach, Joanne rushing ahead, Helen staying back to wait for me. Together, we poked at sand dollars and starfish, combed the sand for unbroken shells. Helen said to me, "Do you understand what's happening?"

I nodded.

"We're moving. Do you know why?"

"Yes." I knew all too well.

"Don't worry," Helen told me, shaking her head. "We'll stick

41

together. I'm going to take care of us." In front of us, Joanne ran in circles then collapsed into an angry ball. We sat beside her, watching the tide move in.

That first night on the beach, Tom shook his head at us, said, "What have you been up to all day? I was going to take you swimming." He showed us how to crouch down on our hands and knees and blow the fire so smoke rose thick from the wood. After dinner, Irene washed our hair under the cold-water tap, her fingers rubbing circles. She told us to go and dry by the fire and we stumbled away. Tom poked at the embers with a tree branch.

"How long will we stay here?" Helen asked.

Tom shrugged, "Who knows?"

"You shouldn't have brought us, then."

Irene stood behind us with her hands on her hips. "No," she said. "But it was either that or leave you altogether." Tom looked at her and Irene looked away, embarrassed.

Our mother slipped off her sandals and sat cross-legged on the ground beside us. She held out her arms for us but we just stood there, watching. She took hold of us and crowded us into her lap. We resisted at first but the smell of her seeped into our noses and her hair swung around and wrapped us in a dark cave. We held on to her too, our six hands grasping her wrists, her arms, anything we could reach. "It's only temporary," she said, kissing our hair. "Just to see. We'll wait a few days and then go home."

Tom said. "Wait a second, Irene—"

"They're my kids," she snapped. "They're mine, okay? I just want to wait and see."

Tom leaned towards us and touched her face with his thumbs. Irene shook her head and held us tightly. I wanted to run at him, stop thinking and push him down, fill his mouth with sand, push it up his nose until he stopped breathing. My whole body could be angry, mad as when Irene pushed the television over and the screen cracked and broke.

Tom unzipped the tent and crawled inside, Irene staring after him. The wind blew smoke from the fire all around us. "Wait for me here," she said, gently removing our hands. She crawled after Tom into the tent.

We watched smoke from the fire drift above our campsite, no sounds from either them or us. Every so often Joanne scratched at the dirt with her feet to say that we were still there. By the time Irene came out again, the trees were indistinguishable from the night. She poked at the fire with a branch, sending a gust of embers into the air.

We paced the beach. With the tide out, it seemed possible to walk forever. Other kids played with plastic shovels, dumped out bucket after bucket, ran ocean water through the moats of their castles. We wandered circles around them, taking stock of their clothes and their toys. I wanted to go home even if it meant more of the same, Irene picking up the dishes one by one and throwing them out onto the back porch. Our father read the paper at the kitchen table. Sometimes when Irene screamed and screamed, he looked at her with complete incomprehension, not knowing why her face changed like that, why she scratched welts on her arms and then slid down against the wall like she was falling. Coming home from school, one of our friends cried when she saw the spoons and knives all over the floor, the bottles and the cracked dishes.

My sister Helen was the most pragmatic of us three. She said, "When we're sixteen, we can go home again."

Joanne stared morosely at her feet. That afternoon, she lay down in her shorts and T-shirt and we slowly buried her in sand.

During the days, my sisters and I avoided swimming in the ocean. Years ago, our father had taught us to swim. In a green lake, we floated on our backs, our bodies losing buoyancy. Our mother stood knee-deep keeping watch, pointing out to our father which one of us was going under, and he would pop us up as if we were weightless, keep us floating on the surface.

On our second night at the beach, we heard strange animal noises. Helen said it was a bear, pawing at our tent with his paws. Joanne tried to wake Irene but she just rolled over and sighed in her sleep. I dreamed Tom was sitting in the bathtub and I pushed the electric radio into the water. His body slapped against the bathtub. I watched in disbelieving silence until he died, his chest grey and shiny, sliding slowly underwater.

The next day, Irene forced us to go on a picnic. They took us to an outcrop of giant, black rocks where the tide came up in towering breakers. Tom said, "That's a whale," and pointed to where none of us could see. We sat at a nearby picnic table, chewing cold chicken and looking off into the distance.

Tom said, "Shall we go out a little farther?" Hand in hand, he and Irene walked up to the rocks, then climbed out on their hands and knees. At rest, they looked like seagulls, perched and waiting.

"Jerks," Helen said, her eyebrows tensed.

Behind us, Joanne walked silently through our picnic site. She was gathering things one by one—the glass bowl of potato salad, the two-litre bottle of orange pop, Irene's sunglasses.

"Are you making a run for it?" Helen asked.

Joanne ignored her. She climbed up onto the rocks above a shallow pool. Turning her back to us, she held the glass bowl out. Irene had just bought it, along with our groceries. It shimmered in the air. Joanne turned to look at us and her hands opened. The bowl tumbled down, cracking hard on a rock. She let go of the pop bottle. It fell upright, bouncing as it went. Then Irene's sunglasses.

I turned and saw Tom running towards the picnic site.

Joanne waved her empty hands. "Goodbye," she said. "Goodbye."

Tom was standing there, his mouth open. "What has gotten into you? For Christ's sake," he said, shaking his head. "For Christ's fucking sake." He picked up what was left and pushed past us to the gravel parking lot.

"For *Christ's fucking sake,*" Joanne said.

Irene just stood and watched us, her expression calm. There were drops of water on her skin and the sun caught on them and made them glitter. She started to move closer but we stared her down. She stopped walking, brushed her foot in the dirt and drew a line. Her voice was low. "You don't believe me now, but it's better like this. I know you think it couldn't be. You think nothing is worse than this. But believe me, there are worse things."

She put her arms around our shoulders and took us with her, back to the car.

Off the rocks and onto the gravel, I tried not to hear anything, not Tom or Irene or my sister's shoes on the rocks or the wind on the ocean or the rain starting to fall. We got into the car and Tom pulled roughly away from the parking lot.

After the car hit the highway, we were going fast and smooth. Tom said, "This is what I think. I think we should leave tomorrow. You don't think he'll follow us, right? You said so yourself, he doesn't give a damn. Four days is long enough. If he doesn't care, let's just go."

Our bodies fell together as if the car were tipping, one body slumped to the next. Irene's voice was barely audible. "Yes," she said, nodding. "Let's leave tomorrow."

Joanne was crying in the back seat. "How do you know?" she said. "How do you know he doesn't care?"

Helen put her hand on Joanne's head and stroked it back and forth. "Mom left a note. I saw it. He could come if he wanted to."

Tom looked sideways at Irene then back at the road.

"You have to tell us where we're going," Helen said. "It isn't fair to keep us in the dark."

45

"To stay with my sister," Tom said. "She has a cottage, right beside the ocean, just like here."

Irene's voice was barely audible. "Tom and I will take care of everything. When it's warm you can swim in the ocean. I'm going to get a job. In a store maybe. You'll meet all new kids."

"We already have friends," Helen said.

"New kids," Irene said, smiling stubbornly. "You'll make new friends."

Joanne shook her head. "We don't want new friends or a new school. You said we'd go back. You promised. You said we'd stay here a few days and then go home."

Tom cut in, "Look, it isn't easy for any of us."

"I don't know," Irene said.

"How come you can't keep your promises?"

"Don't talk to me that way."

"You *lied* to us. You said we'd go home."

"I didn't say that. I said maybe. Maybe isn't the same thing. And anyway it's too late to go back now."

"Why is it too late?"

"Because I've decided, okay?"

"You never asked us," Joanne said. "Maybe we would have stayed with him. Maybe we wouldn't have missed you. Do you understand? I miss him, maybe we wouldn't have missed you."

Irene didn't move. "I'm sorry," she said. "This wasn't the way it was supposed to happen."

She leaned towards Tom and then she half turned and her face was against his sleeve. We were waiting for her to lash out, to bang her fist against the window or throw something, smash the cassette tapes on the floor. But she stayed where she was and Tom patted her shoulder steadily. My sisters and I held still, as if we could change things by refusing to move.

The car hit eighty, ninety, one-twenty, and Tom looked side-ways at Irene. He was nothing like our father. Tom's face was handsome and strong, and his hair, light blond, curled in tufts. Our father's face was dark and sad. Our father combed his hair with Brylcreem until it shone. He smelled of eucalyptus and cooking and warmth. But he and Tom looked at Irene with the same expression, mixed-up sadness and love and strange devotion.

Our last night on the beach, we listened to them breathing, the heaviness of it like their bodies were emptying out. We listened for animals, for a bear to come crashing through the trees. It could hear that breathing, we thought, and it would be drawn to us.

They said words aloud, mumbled liked they were whispering secrets. She said, "Tom," and he started awake, put his arm around her.

Joanne complained that her stomach hurt. She pressed it with her fingers, wondered aloud if she had cancer, or if she were dying, slowly, in the middle of the woods and no one around. We heard other campers walking by, saw the finger-probe of their flashlights sliding across the tent, heard the trudge-trudge of their feet on gravel. I lay with my forehead pressed against Helen's neck. Every so often she would loop one arm across my shoulders, as if to reassure me.

Still Irene and Tom slept. Even when the ocean sounded so loud it seemed like it was coming right at us, all the land pushed under like a broken bowl, they slept, breathing heavily. We fell in and out of dreams, finally waking hours after they had risen. Tom slid the metal poles smoothly through the loops and the tent came down, the orange fabric floating like a parachute towards us.

III

On the fourth night, we arrived in North Bend. One by one, we climbed out of Tom's car. I remember Irene standing in the motel

47

parking lot looking over us. Tom had gone into the office alone to sign for the keys. The wind fanned Irene's hair out around her face and she looked at us, then down at her shoes, then back at us again. Standing under the motel lights, I thought none of this was real. Even then, I thought Irene would change her mind, she would take us home again and all of this would end.

They were standing in the motel room, their coats still on, when Irene broke down. Tom was walking from room to room, testing the light switches. "What will I do?" she said suddenly, raising her voice in desperation. "What have I done?"

Tom's voice was muffled in the background. Irene screamed that he had tricked her, he had made her come with him.

"Irene," he said. "Irene."

My sisters and I crept out the motel door, into the concrete parking lot. We stood beside Tom's car. Truthfully, I can't say that we were angry with her. Only that everything she was no longer surprised us. From where we stood we could see the ocean. If we looked down, we could see where it met the sky in a thin white line. The air smelled salty and cold. Finally, our mother came outside. "We'll go home," she was saying. "Tomorrow morning. We'll pack everything up and go home." She was looking past us, as if directing her words to the lights across the courtyard, to other people in other motel rooms. We didn't even bother answering. Helen reached over and held our mother around the waist. The top of her head was level with Irene's elbow. Joanne and I kicked at the gravel with our sneakers, sending the little rocks pinging off the cars. We heard the far-away whistle of a kettle going off and when we looked back, we saw Tom standing there, an outdoor lamp lighting his face, drawing fireflies to the air above him.

In the morning we woke up and found Tom and Irene sprawled together on the motel couch, their arms and legs tangled, Irene's hair spread out against Tom's hands.

This is my most vivid memory of my father: he was leaning over the veranda, his white shirt brilliant in the sun. Something about seeing him standing there, the neighbourhood quiet in the background made me want to confide in him. My father reached his hand down to rest on my shoulder. I held up the badminton birdie we had buried in mud. "Guess who gave this to me," I said.

My father raised his eyebrows.

"I got it from Tom."

"Tom who?" He took his handkerchief out and folded it once, then again.

"Tom from Sports and Leisure," I said. I explained that Tom came to visit all the time. And he brought us presents. Badminton racquets and bouncy balls. He and Irene sat up here in the afternoons, drinking and doing nothing. But I was sure that she liked him. The way she laughed all afternoon.

"Is that right?" my father said, after a moment. "And what do you think of Tom?"

I shrugged. "He's nice."

We stood quietly then, admiring the backyard. My father said he had always disliked the fence. It was made of cinder blocks stacked up one by one but he would much prefer a wooden gate. Then he turned and walked into the house. I stood looking at the yard. My sisters were playing on the tire swing, sitting spider, face-to-face, their arms and legs entwined. They swung back and forth and finally they looked up at me as if they knew what I had said, but they just kept swinging, the yellow rope extending out, my sisters hugging each other. I stood by myself, scared suddenly by what I had done.

When my father came home the next afternoon, and Irene forced us upstairs, I should have said then that I'd made a mistake, but I didn't. Irene started packing. She took the hot dogs from the freezer and threw them in with our T-shirts and sweaters. Tom had to do everything all over again. My sisters and I just sat and watched, nodding silently or shaking our heads, rejecting the extra sweater, accepting the crayons. Staring dumbly at Tom while he combed our hair and gave us grilled cheese sandwiches. I thought my father would return and everything would reverse itself. When Tom pushed the suitcase closed I started to cry. "I didn't mean it," I told Tom, hitting his chest with my fists. "I said I'm sorry. I didn't mean it." He picked me up and I kicked at him but it did no good. Irene kept bringing things out to the car, one box after another. Tom held on to me, though I was awkward, my arms and legs shooting out. I cried so hard his shirt was soaked. He whispered into my ear so that no one would hear, "I'm sorry. I'm sorry, too. I'm sorry," until I was finally quiet.

In the car, Tom took me with him into the front seat. When the car stopped at the intersections, he would look over at me without speaking. He would rest his hand on my knee, a moment of consolation, until the car began moving once more.

Eventually, it was Tom my sisters went to, instead of Irene. They told him about their boyfriends, the girls in school, the nights they crept out of the house and slept on the beach. They saw his sympathy I think. When Irene had her breakdowns, they saw how he comforted her and didn't let go until she was well again.

My father had never been so patient with her, but even so, I yearned for him. I would try to get Irene to talk about him but she would shake her head, say, "Why do you ask me these things?" Once she asked me if I was trying, really trying to make her crazy, and another time, if I still had not forgiven her.

"This is the way things worked out," she said. "It does no good trying to imagine it differently."

From the time I was seven, I wrote to my father. His letters, though few and far between, were caring though restrained. After years of writing to him, I found it difficult to get past the first few sentences. *Dear Dad,* I'd write. *I hope you are keeping well.* I'd write about North Bend, or respond to the questions he asked about school. *Dear Dad,* I wrote once. *I am very sorry for everything that has happened,* but I never sent this letter. It was like writing a confession to someone from a dream. My father, himself, gave only the most general details of his life, and never asked for more from me. I can't blame him really. He probably still imagined me as a six-year-old child; he did not know me otherwise.

Not long ago, I said to Irene, "Did you ever know that I was the one who told? I was the one who gave everything away."

"If it wasn't you, it would have been one of the others." She shrugged. "It's over, in any case, and I'm not sorry."

I should have asked Irene why everyone else could pick up and go on when that was the thing I found most difficult. Who left who, I often wondered. In the end, who walked away with the least resistance.

Over time, it was easy to love North Bend. That first year, we spent countless afternoons on the boulevard, watching the tourists. They moved in great, wide groups, clutching ice-cream cones and cameras. At the tourist office, they posed beside the World's Largest Frying Pan—the town's main attraction. The frying pan is sixty feet high and stands upright, wooden handle pointing to the sky. Tom told us it was given to the town in 1919, as a tribute to the women who stayed behind during the First World War.

Irene laughed and nodded her head. "It's big," she said, peering up along the carved wood handle. "A great big pan."

Come winter, the tourists disappeared and half the shops boarded up for the off-season. One afternoon, Tom ushered my sisters and me up to the frying pan and sat us down on the lip. The chill wind blew our hair all messy and Tom snapped a picture, the three of us hugging each other, laughing into the cold. Then we all started off along the waterfront, Tom closing his eyes and walking blindly across the sand. He let a gust of wind push him forward, his feet stumbling through the foam and water. We laughed, holding our arms out too, tossing about like dizzy birds, the wind tripping us up. Tom pretended to lose his balance, falling sideways on the ground, the freezing tide pouring over him. He sat up, laughing and spitting while we stood over his body, pretending to stomp him.

"No, no," Irene said. "You'll catch your death of cold."

We pretended to kick Tom in the stomach. "Enough!" he roared, leaping up, shaking foam and water from his head. My sisters and I scattered along the beach while he ran after us, Irene's voice barely audible in the background. "No! Stop it! Jesus Christ, be careful!"

That afternoon, he snapped close-ups of us, the lens of his camera inches from our faces, our hair tangling in front. Days later, he put a picture of Irene and the three of us up on the wall, my sisters and I transformed into bold sea creatures, the clouds and the sky brimming behind us. "What about you?" Helen asked, when we stood admiring the photograph. "Why didn't you put up one of you?"

"Me?" he said, laughing. "I'm just the photographer, nothing more."

Irene stared hard at the picture, her expression sad all of a sudden. She looked from Tom to us, as if from a great distance, then she turned and left the room. Tom did what my father had never done—he followed her, down the front steps, into the street. From inside, we could see the two of them standing together, heads touching, a moment of stillness, before they started back into the house.

One night, when Joanne was seventeen, she came home drunk and sick. She and Tom sat on the front steps all night. Her boyfriend, she wept, was sleeping with someone named Elsa, and had been for months. Joanne stomped up and down the stairs in frustration, then collapsed on the bottom step. "I don't even like him anyway," she sobbed, "so why does it hurt so much?"

Irene and I sat at the kitchen table, eavesdropping. There was no response from Tom.

Joanne told him she was sick of North Bend, sick of living by the water, the floods in winter. Listening to her, I thought of the groups of old men leaning their fishing lines out the back of their pickups, reeling fish in from the highway, how Joanne and I used to drive by and watch them. She told Tom she didn't know what to do next, thought alternately of running away, of drowning herself. There was no way she was going back to school.

"Why don't you run away, then?"

She started crying again. "Why do you want me to leave?"

Tom's voice was tired. "It's not a lack of love. I don't want you drowning. That's all." He gave her five hundred dollars right there. Irene didn't interfere. She sat at the kitchen table, letting Tom do what he thought was right. In the morning Joanne packed her things and left, caught a bus straight out of Oregon and headed north. My sister Helen moved out not long after. She'd met a bio-technologist from Vancouver and married him. We threw a big party for her at the house, then they drove away to Canada.

These days, our town is visited by many tourists. They come from far and wide. On a Saturday during the busy season, the cars hail from every state, from Alaska to New Jersey, and from all across Canada.

I am in charge of the walking tours, the 9:30, 12:15, and 3:00 groups. We start at the town hall and head east along the boulevard, past Flotsam & Jetsam, the Whale's Tail, and Circus World, with its natural and unnatural artifacts—fish dishes, glass buoys, bone fossils. Circus World boasts the skeleton of a half-goat, half-human boy, mounted in a glass case. For one dollar, you can buy a snapshot of him and send it, postage paid, anywhere in the country. The tour ends at the big frying pan.

It's the *why* of it that nobody understands. I tell my father's version of the story, the frying pan as war memorial, erected as a tribute to the women who stayed behind. Then I tell my mother's version, the frying pan for the sake of the frying pan, one monumental gesture. North Bend's Eiffel Tower, the wooden handle visible for miles.

The Japanese tourists giggle, cupping their hands to their mouths. But the big East Coast men with Hawaiian shirts and baseball caps tell me, "You can never have a thing too big. We've got the skyscrapers, you know. *Skyscrapers.* Unbelievable." They tilt their heads back then, and focus on the air above.

Tom and Irene own a sporting-goods store in North Bend, selling things like scuba gear, flippers and surfboards. In the mornings, Tom takes a walk inland, just for the pleasure of turning around again and walking downhill to the ocean. Irene stands on the front steps looking out for him. She has a longing for him. I could be standing right beside her and she wouldn't even know me.

I am thirty years old and I don't know if I will ever leave this town. I should, of course, just to see the world. But I would want to come back here. Some changes happen so slowly, you can't know until it's done—my parents aging, the beach washing back from the water. Maybe when I am sixty, the town itself will have receded. All of us who stay here will creep backwards too, watching and watching for change, then being surprised when it strikes us, out of the blue. No reason but the fact that it is all different. In our house uphill from the ocean, Irene and Tom and I sit in the kitchen reading books and magazines. From morning until night we can hear the water and the wind and the two mixing together. At night I can hear their voices through the walls, and the past finally seems right in its place. Not everything, not large, but still present.

Measuring Death in Column Inches

(a nine-week manual for girl rim pigs)

Zsuzsi Gartner

THERE ARE NO SACRED COWS at 3:00 A.M. when you're measuring death in column inches. Remember, there are many rules, but only one that really counts: Rim pigs don't cry.

Week One: Even though you work with the alphabet in the dull of the night, try not to neglect your appearance. Wear inappropriate fabrics and colours to keep the element of surprise alive. Three-tone bowling shoes with mauve satin cowgirl shirt and worsted tweed trousers. Polo shirt, silk boxer shorts festooned with lyrics from The Poppy Family's greatest hits and orange espadrilles. And, for a special treat, wear your bra on the outside of your T-shirt.

Say: Oops.

Say: Kidding!

Say (as if implying *you* have a life): I was just at the Grant Lee Buffalo gig at the Starfish Room and boy am I tired.

Anyway you put it, your fellow rim pigs—two successfully suburban fathers and two failed fathers—will not know what you're talking about. Realize that if camaraderie is to be achieved, you've got to try a different tack.

If truth be told, none of the graveyard shift copy editors are prime physical specimens. Dave, the slotman, sports a kind of nightly uniform, sweat pants with a Super Mario print all over them. The kind of sweats they make for oversized men that you see the steroid-enhanced guys from Gold's Gym wearing because normal clothes just won't fit. Dave's sweats ride low, giving him plumber's butt, dark hair tufting out from between his wedge. You imagine being one of his kids and living in terror of having him bend down to tie your shoelaces when he picks you up at school. Then there's Gustav, a.k.a. The Montrealer, slightly soiled and desperate. He always has a button missing off his shirt. On better nights he fastens the spot with a safety pin. On worse nights the shirt gapes open when he leans forward, exposing untended flesh.

Even the late night reporters are pale and furtive. Little Anny on the parks board-slash-police beat only has her springy, aerobicized calves going for her. Her skin looks as if it's been left underwater too long, and her hair looks crunchy, like you could grab a fistful and just snap it off. You will soon discover that it's all that sleeping—or trying to sleep—during the day, with the aluminum foil crackling against the window panes. Like constant artillery fire. Ear plugs give you headaches, and although they cut out some noises, they amplify others—the gurgle of a drain upstairs can sound like it comes from inside your very own chest. The thinnest wafer of light cuts through REM sleep like a hot laser. And the dreams, in your sealed up room, in the hot summer air, can be fetid.

Week Two: Learn quickly that you aren't allowed to cherry pick. The slotman puts copy to be edited and headlined, and photos that need cutlines into a little two-tiered wire basket. You're supposed

56

to take the first thing that happens to be on top and then call it up on screen.

You and your confrères are the last line of defence between the newsmakers and the public. Often your concoctions—the headlines, decks and cutlines—are all anyone will read. Pride yourself on your tallies of death and destruction, your puns, your ability to always find a verb that fits. Your Peanut Buster Parfaits of disaster, both man-made and natural.

There is something about working in the dead of night, with the fluorescent lights singing unevenly in their tubes overhead, that arouses in you a primitive and playful spirit. Fish a CP wire story on unemployment rates out of the basket without leaving your seat, smartly spearing the corner with your pen of choice, a red Uni-ball. Feel a vague sense of communion with bears who can swat trout out of a mountain stream just like that. Feel clever, even though no one has noticed. Feel a twinge in your neck because you contorted it at an unruly angle in order to nab the story without having to scurry all around the rim to Dave's desk.

The ink bleeds through the hole.

A feeling of continual exhaustion will descend like a musty furniture blanket in the second week. You will be tempted to fight back.

There used to be an empty lot behind your apartment building, a lovely wreck of a lot littered with exploded chunks of concrete laced with twisted rebar, big-headed purple thistles waving in the wind, the candy wrappers caught in their prickly leaves fluttering like hideous moths, discarded syringes poised like scorpions. The kind of place you would most certainly act out your post-apocalyptic fantasies if you were still a kid. It's a reminder of how the world, your world, would look if we all just stopped being so damn careful. Now someone has decided to build a house there and the activity makes mincemeat of your sleep. It sounds as if a small army is stapling the house together, instead of using proper, old-fashioned tools like hammers. Dull thuds you might be able to take, but this feels like Gene Kelly and his cartoon mice practicing on the ceiling of your frontal lobes.

Storm over to check it out, but not before first scrubbing the stalagmites of sleep off your bottom lashes and flattening your bangs with the moistened heel of your hand so you don't look as deranged as you feel. "Why yes, ma'am," one of the guys says, "Yes, we are stapling it together." And the workmen all hold their staple guns out towards you, as if they're a firing squad and you've been convicted of stealing bread in a country with zero tolerance for bad behaviour.

Ask (in what you think is a queenly manner): "But how long will it last?"

"Oh, a good thirty years, give or take. These aren't your ordinary staples," one of the guys says.

You, of course, meant the noise.

Week Three: Accept that mistakes are made. Usually harmless ones. Say the guy is called Jack Greene in the story and Jeff Green in the cutline under the photo. Readers will pounce on this. "Lookit this," they'll say, poking at your cutline with their forks, egg dribbling down the page, congealing in a pearly strand, "Whatta buncha idiots." Well, yes, that's right, you may think, we are idiots. Idiots who know the difference between concrete and cement, between careening and careering, and CARE!

Tell your friends: "You have to have an idiot gene of some sort to do a job like this." Wait for them to disagree vehemently. Stir your coffee thoughtfully even though the cup is empty. Keep waiting. Ask for a refill. Change the topic.

The late night reporters ignore you—cut a wide swath as they walk by, sneer. It's a caste system and you're one of the untouchables. But instead of collecting garbage and burning it, you're elevating it. There's an element of fear, too, for sure. There, but for the grace of God and goodwill of the managing editor, go I. Maybe rim-pigitis is a contagious disease. Remember grade five when all the boys scribbled "Julia fleas" on the backs of their hands with coloured pens. Think about how Julia must have felt. Wonder if it screwed up her adulthood. Wonder if it's the kind of thing you'd tell your children. "I was the biggest nerd of my elementary school class. I got caught lining the inside of my desk with little balls of snot and didn't have any friends." Decide not. Most definitely not.

Anny, the dishevelled little go-getter with the Ron Zalko-cized calves bounces through your part of the newsroom, coolly averting her eyes. You shake your bag of Skittles at her, even though you hate to share the treats that help you make it through the night. "Hey, Anny, have a candy." She barely breaks stride, flapping her dead fish hand in your direction. "Thanks. I'm on deadline." Sisterhood is no match for the latest hijinks of the Vancouver Parks Board. All that self-satisfied wrangling over whether some dumpy parkette is better served by mounting yet another statue of a WWII soldier or a metal cube representing the victims of a more contemporary ill. *Lest We Forget.*

Decide *you* are a statue. Sit there frozen in position, hands poised like crabs above the keyboard, vowing to not move until someone touches you and breaks the spell. Be prepared to wait an awfully long time.

On your only night off, go to a party with your new boyfriend where you don't know a soul. Everyone there seems to be associated with films. Not movies, films. And not just any old films, but something called visual essays, which you later learn are actually just documentaries that don't make a lot of sense unless you have a doctorate in post-colonial post-feminist post-gender studies.

If someone asks you what you do, tell them you're a carpenter. Talk knowledgeably about revolutionary new advances in house construction, namely, the use of staplers. Talk about how the kickback action really builds muscles, namely, pectorals.

Tell your incredulous audience that they can go ahead and feel your pecs. Your boyfriend comes over with an achingly cool Japanese beer just as you're striking a which-way-to-the-beach? pose and asks, "Rodin's *Thinker* with menstrual cramps?"

Decide you dislike him for his inability to comprehend your shame and fatigue.

Decide you like him for his ability to mock menstrual cramps in a post-colonial post-feminist post-gendered crowd.

Later, after many Sapporos, corner the guy who made a visual essay about Bertrand Russell and ask him to tell you what the difference is between concrete and cement. Decide that his inability to differentiate means he's not as smart as he thinks he is.

He says: "You should know. You're in construction."

Phone your mother long-distance and tell her you hate your job. "But you have a good job," she says.

Say: I sleep with aluminum foil in the windows. I feel like a turkey basting in my bed.

Say: I eat open-faced chili burgers for lunch at 4:00 A.M.

Ask (petulantly): Is this why I got a poli-sci degree?

She tells you to be thankful you have a bed and be thankful you have lunch. She reserves judgement on the poli-sci degree, because, well, let's just say she warned you. You hang up before she starts telling you about how the only time she and her sisters got oranges was when they left their shoes (with the cardboard soles) out on the porch on the eve of Saint Nicholas Day.

Across the alley, the staple gun men are singing a cappella— "Up on the Roof," of all things. You wonder if someone has slipped Xanax into their Cheerios, or Ativan into their thermoses. You wish a talent scout would come by and spirit them away in a long, tacky white limo with a soft drink logo on the side. They're young, agile. They're Canadian boys and probably already know how to skate, so they could join the Ice Capades doing some sort of Village People redux act. And why not? Just why the heck not? Stamp your little foot for effect. Dust bunnies rise from the parquet floor in a fury—rabid, grey, feral, gathering courage and growing in number through your neglect. They trust in Nietzsche: Those who do not destroy us, make us stronger.

Although, if you were to be perfectly honest, all the Nietzsche you know could be gleaned from the opening credits of *Conan the Barbarian*.

Week Four: Make an effort to get to know your fellow rim pigs, after all, they're the only ones who'll talk to you instead of at you besides the donut cart woman. Decide Dave the slotman's not so bad. He's tacked magazine photos of Susan Sarandon all over the pillar beside his desk along with a crayon drawing by his daughter Kristal of what looks like a Sikh temple, but could be a bird cage. It lends him a certain complexity, this attraction to an actress of a certain age. After all, it could have been Pamela Anderson Lee. You find something reassuring about Dave—his comfortable slovenliness, the way he whistles theme songs from kiddie cartoons as he dummies up the pages, the way his wife makes sure that at least his socks match.

Gustav the Montrealer, on the other hand, has the look of an unloved man. It's not just the missing button, it's his needy air. He used to work as a reporter at *Le Devoir*, or so he tells you, and he never lets a night go by without reminding everyone that he's a *real* journalist and this rim pig thing is only a temporary gig. He confides in you one night, thinking you can relate. To sensitive men. Because you're a gal. He tells you he left a son behind out east after his wife kicked him out. He spends a good part of his time sending e-mail messages to his son, who's only five but can evidently read at grade six level—in English *and* French. He tells you he wants to pitch a column to the features editor on contemporary men's issues.

He says (*sotto voce*): "There's a whole segment of the population that's not being served in the popular press. You know, the father thing. The pain thing. The anger thing."

Say (in French): "You mean huffing and puffing and drumming and stuff, reclaiming the maligned little beast—sorry, little *boy*—within?"

He looks quizzical and then laughs a fake jolly-hearted laugh and touches your forearm with the tips of two fingers, showing he knows his Dale Carnegie, indicating he thinks you've said something terribly funny. You don't know which is worse. That you've mocked him, or that you've discovered—*confirmed*—that he doesn't understand French, or that his fingers, you've just noticed, have been chewed until they've bled, the hangnails peeled off, leaving thin scabby strips. They're the fingers of the nervous little boy you and your friends shoved into the older girl's bathroom during one recess at Sacred Heart, alone with the Kotex machine, while you piled your squealing bodies up against the door so he couldn't get out even though he pushed and pushed until his small heart was bursting. The boy, Eugene, ended up crawling out the window and had to be rescued from the fire escape by one of the nuns. When Sister Scholastica reached the bottom rung, she sat down and slung him across her knee and started to spank him. The crackle of plastic was shocking, even to you. But that didn't stop you, eyes wide, from excitedly whispering, "Eugene still wears diapers." There was no need, of course, to whisper: *Pass it on.*

The Montrealer, as if he can see into your rusted-out carbody of a Catholic soul, avoids talking directly to you from this point on. Out of the corner of your eye, you'll be aware that his hands, on occasion, tremble.

You fare better with The Matador. The Matador has a trait you must admit you envy. He has this incredible posture. In this nocturnal universe of slouching men, he stands out, ramrod straight even under duress, like George C. Scott playing Patton. He has settled into the numbing delirium of the job with a Zen-like aplomb. Nothing seems to phase him, or move him. He is the perfect rim pig, smartly robotic, emotionless as a Vulcan, except for the deep pleasure he gets from hearing about stupid deaths. You only have to

Say: Hungarian woman falls in barrel of cabbage juice and drowns,

Say: Kansas man punctures brain by accidentally ramming car antenna up left nostril,

Say: Toronto Blue Jay kills seagull with homer,

and a deep, indecorous chortle will rise from his belly and burble up his throat and out of his mouth, masking the thin, prissy whine of the fluorescent lights for a few seconds. His laughter is steam—it scalds and leaves something sulfurous in its wake.

Just don't ask him about his daughter who lives a few miles away in Coquitlam and who he's not allowed to see. And she's only three, so e-mail is not an option.

The Pumpkin usually sits to the left of you and is what they call a lifer. He's been here for longer than anyone can remember and perhaps thinks that if he just keeps really quiet, he can stay forever. The Pumpkin has seven children and a wife to feed. He has beautiful, long eyelashes—as do all his children—and for some reason those eyelashes break your heart.

The Pumpkin is kind. The Pumpkin is inoffensive. The Pumpkin, you realize, might as well wear a sign reading: Kick Me.

Pick a day, any day. "Hey Murray," Dave says, "Do you think they should let the U.S. extradite those two pricks from the Island who killed the one guy's parents and retarded sister in

63

Bellingham?" The Pumpkin stops, his fingers raised above his keyboard, looking uncertain. "Sure, Dave. I guess they deserve it."

The Matador scoops the puck. "But Murray, you know they'll probably fry. Don't you Catholics have some opinions about that?" This is where The Pumpkin starts to sweat and looks around for moral support. You try to flash him a look of concern, smiling wryly and winking, but he just thinks you're flirting and turns even redder. "You're right, maybe we should keep them here."

Dave says, "Right, Murray. Make them do fifty push-ups or ten Hail Marys or something." Now the Pumpkin smiles a watery smile, thinking he's said something witty, and then sees the smirk on Dave's face and the disdain on the Matador's. He hurries to the bathroom while everyone, including you, snickers. The Pumpkin spends a lot of time in the can summoning the strength to do his job.

Start to say: You guys—

Then remember: Nietzsche.

Decide he's in there turning into superman and that he might just come out and bash in everyone's head. Wish that your look of empathy had been less wishy-washy, more distinct. Vow to practice blinding glances of compassion in front of the bathroom mirror on your break, if you're not too tired.

What does it take to push a man over the edge? Nine out of ten disgruntled U.S. postal workers agree: Not a whole heck of a lot.

Consider circumstances under which you might kill. Imagine you have a daughter—seven? strawberry blonde but has begged for highlights? My Little Ponies™ are strewn all over the hallway and you tripped on one earlier that day and twisted your ankle and whaled on her. And during a party a man—a friend's friend's friend? uninvited? jovial uncle? choirmaster? blonde monster in nice khakis and Florsheim shoes? high school dropout beaten by stepfather and driven mad by the Scott Joplin tune that spews incessantly from the speakers of the ice-cream truck he drives due to reduced opportunities (he really wanted to be a vet, loves animals, it truly broke his heart)?—enters her bedroom. Seconds later you stand in the doorway and see him burrowing under the covers behind her. You return, limping because of the ankle, with a meat cleaver—still flecked with minced cilantro from the guacamole you made for the party?—and chop off his head, surprised at your own strength. Surprised it was so easy. Thinking about it now, grit your teeth so hard your jaw just about cracks. Wonder what would be a worse trauma for this unknown daughter: the rape itself, or the head—the neck a bloodied stump—rolling to the centre of the bed and her mother standing above, wild-eyed, a Chinese meat cleaver in her hand?

To know you would readily kill—to have considered the possibilities—brings a grim relief.

At least you don't call guys like that *Mister* here like they do in the *Globe and Mail*. *Mr.* Olsen. *Mr.* Bernardo. *Mr.* Lepine. *Mr.* Karadzic. And *Miss* or *Ms.* Homolka, is that one lump or two? You don't know what you'd do if you had to do that, probably want to quit. Probably wouldn't, though. Just like your compadres there in Toronto don't quit over it. But don't think it doesn't bother them. Rim pigs dream in Technicolor.

Week Five: Learn to look death in the face and laugh. Remember: Rim pigs don't cry.

The formula for what you do here is simple. You could call it the slide rule of tragedy. Take the number of dead and divide it by the number of miles the site of the disaster/murderous rampage/political upheaval lies from the epicentre—which in your case is Vancouver. Then multiply the figure by the importance of that place or the dead to your readers on a scale of zero to ten (this last part is subjective, of course). For example, a plane crash in South

America would have to involve at least fifty dead to make it into the paper with three column inches at best. A plane crash up north may get three column inches on page A6 even with only two dead. A plane crash at the Abbotsford Airshow, one dead, makes fourteen column inches on the front page. Two dead in Azerbaijan due to rock slide, well, that wouldn't even make the wire, if they're Azerbaijanis. A Burnaby couple killed in Azerbaijan due to rock slide? Now you're cookin' with gas!

You do get bonus points for ironic circumstances. For example: Fitness guru dies of heart attack. Eighty-eight killed in Punjabi village by flooding dam during feast day celebrating opening of said dam.

You could say that you do body counts in inches here, and that's all you do.

Strangely, you wake up most afternoons to find your pillow covered with big, wet blotches. Decide you were drooling. Try to remember your dreams. Even if you can't remember the specifics, you're aware they're always filled with a weird chiaroscuro effect. That's the essential difference between those who dream in their sleep during the day and those who sleep and dream at night, this razzle-dazzle mix of light and shade to create an illusion of depth. All that, *and* Technicolor, especially when it comes to blood and auras.

Bodies plummeting through water in chiaroscuro light, feet encased in cement—or is that concrete?—blocks. Bodies piled by the shed like cordwood in chiaroscuro darkness, still too green to burn. And you, you're the one with the measuring tape and the maniacal laugh.

Week Six: See Week Five

Week Seven: Take in a photo to make your desk area more homey.

But remember, it's not really *your* desk, so don't forget to put it away in your mail slot at the end of your shift. It's tough to decide whose photo to bring. A picture of your boyfriend will just remind you of what you're missing and how this job is ruining your life. You have no nieces or nephews. Your brother's never caught a big, huge fish. You have no dog. You decide on Pamela Anderson Lee. This will remind you that things could be worse. You could be a perky, super-natural blonde bombshell who no one in their right mind would make the subject of a visual essay. This way, at least, you stand a slim chance.

The Matador raises his eyebrows. Decide he's kind of attractive at a certain angle in a wan, androgynous way.

Say: I like her, okay?

Say: It's just so you don't confuse us. Ha ha.

Say: Kidding!

Your bra, on the inside of your T-shirt, feels saggy.

The explosion comes in the middle of the week at about 3:00 A.M. There's a dull boom that you barely notice because it comes from so far away. Later you'll remember thinking that it sounded like the nine o'clock gun, but, of course, it couldn't be since it was nowhere near nine o'clock.

It's the sirens everyone reacts to and soon all the phones in the newsroom are jangling. Martin, the young guy from the *Delta Mirror* they brought in to replace the ambitious Anny who's now on courts, is going nuts. He doesn't know which phone to pick up. He runs to the windows to look outside, which is stupid, you think, since the only view is of the back parking lot.

Pick up the nearest phone. Take notes. Realize that you, too, can be a reporter. Anyone can. Just take down the facts, Jack. And don't forget to ask if there were any fatalities. But this is harder than it sounds. You just can't form the word 'dead' in your mouth. But there's always hurt—hurt is easier.

Say: I've got the scoop. It's at Broadway and Cambie.

Say: A pizza parlour blew up.

Say: There's glass everywhere.

When Dave asks who you were talking to, force yourself to be honest.

Say (quickly): I don't know.

The Matador's laugh rises up sharp, hot, sulfuric.

Riding the Broadway bus home at 7:30 A.M., you find that the street has already been largely cleared. Workers are putting new plate-glass windows up at the Royal Bank, while small business owners are busy measuring, taping, sweeping, up and down the block. Enormous piles of glass are heaped on the sidewalks and sparkling mounds line the gutters like some dangerous new drug.

Decide to ring the bell and get off the bus even though it's not your stop and your brain is zinging with fatigue, the skin pulled tight across your temples. All that glass is mesmerizing. It looks positively Arctic. Forget the summer heat for a moment and stroll along as if you're on a polar expedition. Stand on a large slab of cracked blue glass and imagine you're an Inuit grandmother sent off to die on her very own ice floe. Decide the idea sounds peaceful. Think about how quiet it would be, lulled to sleep by the waves sluicing across your hands and feet, the ice cracking imperceptibly beneath you as you drift off to sea. All those other worn-out grannies floating on the water.

Try not to be embarrassed when the woman from the Label Clippers store shakes you awake and flags you a cab. Brush slivers of glass nonchalantly from your jeans with a crumpled chocolate bar wrapper.

Back at work, several miles away, the windows are intact. The glass on the picture of Pamela, tucked away in your mail slot, has a hairline fracture, invisible to the human eye.

Week Eight: Resist the temptation towards melancholy. This will be difficult, but not impossible. Very difficult, but not quite impossible. Okay, formidable. But you're a big girl with lots of outer defences. A regular rhino skin. Ex-Catholic, ex-virgin, ex-dreamer, ex-editor of a student newspaper, ex-fighter pilot. All these exes make for great epidermis.

You have grown somewhat preoccupied by death in these waning days of summer. Your childhood best friend's mother dies of a disease she shouldn't have had. Lung cancer. A woman who's never smoked a cigarette in her life. Must have been from all those chemicals she was breathing in all those years of cleaning other people's toilets, your mother tells you. You never knew. She lived in a beautiful big house in a leafy sub-development with her husband and two children. A Fisher-Price life. An immigrant's dream. She could afford to have someone come and scrub her own toilet, stick their head in her Jenn-Air. You find yourself in a parking lot outside the Arts Club Lounge on Granville Island howling at the cloud-shrouded moon.

Your soon-to-be-ex boyfriend says: "Get up. You're drunk." Which is somewhat true.

Tell him: "This is true grief. I'm howling at the moon to mourn, okay?"

These are full-blown werewolfian howls. Your throat aches and you fully expect thick hairs to sprout from the backs of your hands. You later wonder how you got those little bits of gravel embedded in your knees.

Your eyes glow green when you cry this much and the next day you walk the streets with alien orbs, chewing over the mutability of human life, wondering why the rocks that spin out from under the rear wheels of cabs accelerating too quickly at intersections don't puncture veins in fragile necks, the fragile necks of those you love and your own fragile neck in particular, forgetting that rim pigs don't cry. You pass the Sweet Marie Variety and through the window you see the owner's little girl—the one with the deadly straight bangs—sitting on the counter by the cash register trying to balance a spoon on her nose. You want to tell her to keep practicing because life is the ultimate balancing act.

Mouth advice at her through the glass: Don't eat yellow snow. Don't take any wooden nickels. Don't clean other people's toilets. And don't mess around with Jim. Somehow this makes you feel better.

During the night, at work, things are easier. But during the day, death lurks in every corner of your dreams. A friend comes out of the shadows at twilight in a green Austin Mini to pick lilacs from your garden for her eighty-five-year-old father—to bring him back from confused anger to gentle lucidity. She doesn't tell you this. You just know. He rages in your closet, garbled animal noises. You can't make out what he's saying, but you know he wants to die. You clip the lilacs like big clumps of grapes and your friend leaves with an armful, their smell sweetly sickening. You wake up to the crackle of foil and the whoop of a car alarm from up the street somewhere.

Phone your mother long-distance every day, twice a day sometimes—just to say hi—until she asks, "What are you, nuts?"

Across the alley, the staple-gun guys are oddly silent. No show tunes, no rat-a-tat-tat. And it's 2:00 P.M., past their lunchtime and well into the most cacophonous part of the day. You wonder if the house is done, ready to receive its owners, bright young things with lots of money who will sleep peacefully under exquisite percale sheets—240 threads per inch—on the former post-apocalyptic playground. Look out your kitchen window just in time to witness a terrifying sight. One of the men, the youngest—honestly he couldn't be more than sixteen—is standing on the newly-finished chimney, arms extended. You can't see his face, but you can see the sharp little shoulder blades sticking out of his sweaty back like the beginnings of wings. He sways a little. One man carefully straddles the roof, holding his right arm out to the boy, saying something soothing that you can't quite hear, while the rest wait on the ground. You notice that the sky behind them drips like molten lead, clouds churn, fingertips touch in chiaroscuro light, thunder claps—applause from on high for a moment brought to you by Michelangelo.

Say: Whew, it's just a dream.

Say (trying not to sound clichéd): But it seemed so real.

Say—

Just then the man trying to save the boy slips, sending cedar shakes into the air, and a man on the ground, who looks like he could be his brother, screams, "Tony!" in a way that is anything but dreamlike.

Week Nine: Realize that this is more careening than careering.

The photograph, of a skinny man in a cheap cardigan, is the kind of thing you've been trying to avoid. You've been doing the un-thinkable—cherry-picking—and you haven't been caught yet. You've been deft, but you've mostly been lucky. A sleepy item on Senate reform; a quirky tidbit on virtual spelunking (Caving for Claustrophobics!); a gushy feature on the reunion of twin sisters separated for forty-five years who find each other through a recipe club specializing in marshmallow dishes—a testament to the re-silience of the human spirit, brought to you by Kraft. Those are the kinds of things you can handle. But here it is, the first thing you grab, a face, the face of Matias Zupan, grieving Slovenian father, a face that speaks for the wounded. Matias Zupan, a bony fellow of indeterminate age in a cheap cardigan, a garment so un-like a decent sweater that you have to wonder where it came from.

Perhaps it was sent by a harried relation—a guilt-ridden second cousin? younger brother?—who's now in Hamilton. He saw the writing on the wall and left the day after Tito died and now is successful enough with his dry cleaning business? janitorial service? pizza joint? to be able to send pillowcases full of clothes from Honest Ed's to those he left behind. But trying to make a story of it, making light, doesn't change anything. Matias Zupan, in a carefully knotted tie, contorts his face in anguish. He is held up by two other men at a graveside, his toes, in old Adidas, barely skimming the ground. You slip it under the newspaper on your desk, this obscene portrait of grief, but not before touching the tip of your pinkie finger to the man's lips. Overhead, the fluorescent lights sing. One tube flickers, then pops.

There's a telephone call for you way across the room, at the entertainment desk for some reason. It can't be your soon-to-be-ex since he knows which number to call. Your heart tumbles around like a crazed acrobat as you cross the newsroom in slow motion wondering why the worst phone calls come in the middle of the night.

It's your mother. You ask what's happened, your nerves jangling.

She says: "I'm just calling to say hi."

You don't respond.

She laughs: "Hi, hi, hi!"

She says: "It's about your father"

But your father, and this is a fact, has been dead for seventeen years.

Back at your desk which is not really *your* desk, someone's moved the newspaper and the photograph of the skinny man at his son's graveside lies exposed at your elbow. His pants are so sharply ironed that you can see the fine crease even in this poor wire copy. Did his wife cry as she ironed them? Are the tears pressed into the slacks? Did she iron to erase the ache in her heart? You know that under the same circumstances you couldn't iron. You couldn't plug it in. You couldn't get the crease just so. You can't even iron under the best circumstances. The tears charge forward, undammed, damned, unstoppable. They shoot from your fingertips and pour from your ears.

As the ground drops away, you crawl into Matias Zupan's mouth, so wide and welcoming in its grief. All of you fits easily inside the cavity of his body. Here in the dark it feels good to lie quietly for long minutes, listening to his breath and yours, trying to get your breathing in sync with his, but you're always a little off. As if his is the real thing and yours just the echo. Light a candle and look around. His ribcage gleams in the flamelight. It's stunningly fragile and beautiful, like forbidden ivory. You're the ship in the ship in the bottle. Run your tongue over his ribs. They taste like tar.

After that, just sit and watch the wax drip onto your hand and listen to the fluorescent lights out there, somewhere overhead, faintly sizzle and hiss.

Troller

Kevin Roberts

THE SEA BURST AGAINST THE BOW where Bill lay on the starboard bunk, and the boat timbers shivered and trembled the full thirty-six-foot length of the *Pacific Maid.* Mel, the skipper, had been sick for three days now and so had his son, Bert, and the fishboat was barely under control. Bill lay there in his floater jacket, the rubber tailpiece drawn up between his thighs and hooked to the front. Bert had made a number of cracks about that, but as soon as the wind hit the boat, when they passed the moaning fog horn of Tofino harbour, Bill'd put the jacket on and left it on. This was his first trip as a deckhand on the outside and the sheer size of the Pacific disturbed him deeply. Two bad seasons on the inside coast, no sockeye run, no pinks worth a damn, and his small fishboat had been claimed by the Royal Bank. He'd had no choice but to find a job, start again at the bottom, as a deckhand on a large Pacific troller. And he was lucky to get on with Mel, he knew. But he didn't want to be here.

He had been stunned on that first day out when Mel had confessed that he was always seasick for the first couple of days, and sometimes for longer in bad weather. It seemed crazy, even dangerous, to put yourself into a job where you suffered so much, where control over your body was in such jeopardy. But, Mel had added, seasickness was a lot more common than most fishermen admitted. Greed and pride kept them at it; that, and the strange attraction the sea had for some men. That was the hardest to believe.

Above him, outside in the dark, the wind thrummed on the wires of the poles like a mad guitarist. Beside him on the other bunk, Bert moaned, and above and behind him, Mel lay suffering in the wheelhouse bunk. The gale rose and fell in wild bursts and he was glad he could not see the swells, topped with flying white lace, that rolled ominously and endlessly from the heart of the dark Pacific.

Four days ago, they'd smashed and rolled their way fifty miles out from Tofino, the weather channel voice predicting failing winds and sea. They'd fished that first morning, their thighs braced hard against the sides of the fish-well in the stern, slapping the gurdies in on only half the lines because the yawing, pitching boat could not be held straight, even on the Wagner autopilot. It was a monstrously unstable world, where the sky swung like a mad chandelier, and at the bottom of a swell, the boat seemed totally enveloped in the seething grey sea. He had not realized how totally enveloped in the pitching bowl of the Pacific they were, until they encountered another fish boat, the *Ocean Rambler,* about the same size, and its toy-like struggle to lift up from the weight of the sea, smashing endlessly on its bow, caused him to fear that this other frail cockle of wood, a quarter of a mile away, could not, would not rise this time, or the next, out of the green mass that rolled again and again and again, pushing the whole boat down and down, until, when both boats were on the bottom of the swell, the *Ocean Rambler* would disappear completely from sight. It was then, too, that he realized that the *Pacific Maid,* his own boat, must also look a frail shell waiting for one great wave to take it under.

They had caught fish that first day, coho and a few medium springs, but the big fish broke the lines or ran amok with ease about the barely controllable boat. He had brought one big spring alongside, thirty pounds, maybe more, and swung the gaff down and into its head, but, instantly, the boat yawed and the gaff and fish pulled beyond his strength and he let go before he too was tipped into the maelstrom. The skipper's curses were torn from his lips by the wind as he came aft in a running crouch. He shouldered Bill aside, and with huge hands, crisscrossed with the white scars from nylon fish-line, manhandled the flapping spring with the gaff still in its head into the checkers, and expertly killed it with a single blow behind the head.

Though he could not hear Bert's jibes from the other side of the boat, he was embarrassed, but not for long. The skipper, with a sudden lurch, pushed by him again, green-faced, and with a sudden lurch, vomited into the spume. Bert soon followed his father and both of them leaned over the side and vomited time and time again.

It was then that he'd taken charge, scuttled to the wheelhouse to adjust the Wagner, crouched and run back to run the lines, pulled the salmon, ran out the lines again, cleaned the fish and stocked them in the checkers. But the wind and sea grew and the main line and the deep line on the starboard side crossed and tangled and for half an hour he struggled to bring both of them in and clear the gear. The skipper watched, red-eyed, and finally told him to pull all the lines in and lash them down.

Incredibly, though the skipper stopped regularly to retch overboard, Mel worked with him until all the gear was on board and the lines and lead cannonballs lashed down with cutty hunk. Together they pulled the prostrate Bert into the wheelhouse and down into the bunk. Bill went out again to the stern, staggered back with armful after armful of salmon, crawled deep down into the hold of the boat, stuffed handfuls of ice into the cleaned bellies of the fish and stacked them into the waiting ice.

"Sea-anchor, Bill," mumbled Mel pointing to the bow. "I'll run the boat up, you drop it." Bill looked through the window. The weighted parachute with the red Scotsman buoy was lashed to the foredeck. It had to be eased overboard so it sank and opened deep beneath the sea. A long rope, coiled now on the bow, then ran from the capstan on the bow down to the chute flowering under the sea. With this down the boat rode easily, moving with the tide a mile or so in and out, on the ballooned tension of the underwater anchor. But it was dangerous to put out in a high wind. If the chute snapped open in the gale the rope would whip out like a snake striking. If the boat was not held tight against the smashing swell, the rope jerked about and the feet and body of the man, already threatened by the great wash of water pounding against it, could be washed overboard instantly. The very idea of walking out there, out to where the grey sea bounded onto the bow, was almost too much for him, except for the haggard look of the skipper, white-faced and red-eyed. He knew then that he had to do it, not just for them on the boat, but for himself, because the sea was building relentlessly and it was doubtful if they could turn and run safely before it back to Tofino. The danger of broaching, or of the stern going under in the massive rolling seas was such that he looked an instant at Mel, and saw in his watering eyes that there was only one choice.

And he had shuffled grimly out along the deck, gripping the handrail tightly with both hands, past the wheelhouse and out onto the bow. There, the first burst of swell knocked him soaking and breathless to his knees. Worse, the suck of the sea off the deck rushed about him and loosened his footing. In the second or two before the next wave burst upon him, he worked with one hand on the lashed parachute. He timed his work so that in the brief dip of the bow, before the next swell deluged him, the parachute and its chain and rope were freed. He hooked one foot about a stanchion, braced the other, and in the same two-second dip, let the parachute and rope slip through his left hand over the side. Despite his efforts the rope kicked and jumped and burnt his wrist and hand.

It was not classic seamanship. There were many men of the West Coast fishing fleet for whom this act was daily bread, but for him, the final "tung" of the rope tight against the capstan, the red Scotsman floating before the boat now easing back, was a gong of triumph. He sat, hanging onto the rail, his knees braced against the stanchion, totally exhausted, wet through, and not at all jubilant. His hands were scored and torn by the rope. He thought of the poached salmon steaks he'd seen once for an exorbitant price, served in silver chafers in a restaurant on Sloane Square in London and the enormity of the callous economics of it made him burst out with laughter. Eventually, he crawled back on his knees, gripping the rail, and got into the wheelhouse.

He told himself through clenched teeth that this was it, that never again would he risk the plunge and certain death in that cold and bitter sea. It was over. He'd get a shore job, pumping gas, unloading fish, anything to avoid this pulse and roll and madness of the sea.

The skipper sat with his head down on the wheel, and Bill crawled past him and down into the bunk next to Bert. The boat now rode more easily, tossing like a massive child whose fever has broken and, even though the sea still smashed and burst against the hull, he fell quickly asleep. He dreamed he was in a strange moving bed with a beautiful green woman who undulated under and away from him every time he tried to possess her.

A rumbling sound growing nearer brought him to wakefulness. He got up unsteadily, his limbs rigid with cold, and stepped up into the wheelhouse. Mel lay asleep on the wheelhouse couch, his white face garish every second or two from the flash of the strobe light on the mast top. The sea was unabated. Green frills ran constantly up and down the wheelhouse window, obscuring the bow light. On the port bow half a mile and closing, at the tops of the massive swells, he could see a row of lights in the whirling darkness. He fervently hoped the radar operator on the freighter out there was awake and that the many blips of the fishing fleet tossing at anchor were clear in the stormy night. The freighter passed quickly, unperturbed it seemed by the muscular walls of water in which it moved. He wished then, as many fishermen have, for a boat so big the sea could not threaten it. He thought, too, of the wreaths rotting on the Anglican Church wharf at Bamfield, and the inscription, "O Lord your sea is so strong, and our boat is so frail."

He looked about him at the unutterable darkness, the wild wind and crashing sea, and felt a great loneliness, until, in the distance, the quick flash of a tiny strobe appeared, another fishboat, anchored too in this hissing vortex, and another flash, and another, and suddenly all about, at the top of the swells, the flick, flick, sometimes miles away, sometimes closer, magical in the storm. Bill felt strangely and utterly comforted by the pattern their lights made, flickering, miles away from home and warmth and safety. Again he looked at his hands, throbbing now with the red lines of the chafe marks. He knew it was a mark, along with the lights, of a community; the boats of the West Coast fishing fleet, held by the flowers of their sea anchors, a pattern of faith one with the other in this arduous endeavour upon the encircling sea.

A Garden of Her Own

Shani Mootoo

A NORTH-FACING BALCONY meant that no sunlight would enter there. A deep-in-the-heart-of-the-forest green pine tree, over-fertilized opulence extending its midriff, filled the view from the balcony.

There was no window, only a glass sliding door which might have let fresh air in and released second- or third-hand air and the kinds of odours that build phantoms in stuffy apartments. But it remained shut. Not locked, but stuck shut from decades of other renters' black, oily grit and grime which had collected in the grooves of the sliding door's frame.

Vijai knew that it would not budge up, down or sideways. For the amount of rent the husband paid for this bachelor apartment, the landlord could not be bothered. She opened the hallway door to let the cooking lamb fat and garlic smells drift out into the hallway. She did not want them to burrow into the bed sheets, into towels and clothes crammed into the dented cream-coloured metal space-saver cupboard that she had to share with the husband. It was what all the other renters did too; everyone's years of oil—sticky burnt, over-used, rancid oil—and of garlic, onions and spices formed themselves into an impenetrable nose-singeing, skin-stinging presence that lurked menacingly in the hall. Instead of releasing the lamb from the husband's apartment, opening the door allowed this larger phantom to barge its way in.

Vijai, engulfed, slammed the door shut. She tilted her head to face the ceiling and breathed in hard, searching for air that had no smell, no weight. The husband was already an hour late for dinner. She paced the twelve strides, back and forth, from the balcony door to the hall door, glancing occasionally at the two table settings, stopping to straighten his knife, his fork, the napkin, the flowers, his knife, his fork, the napkin, the flowers. Her arms and legs tingled weakly and her intestines filled up with beads of acid formed out of unease and fear. Seeing a smear of her fingerprint on the husband's knife, she picked it up and polished it on her T-shirt until it gleamed brilliantly, and she saw in it her mother's eyes looking back at her.

*

Sunlight. I miss the sunlight—yellow light and a sky ceiling miles high. Here the sky sits on my head, heavy grey with snow and freezing rain. I miss being able to have doors and windows opened wide, never shut except sometimes in the rainy season. Rain, rain, pinging on, winging off the galvanized tin roof. But always warm rain. No matter how much it rained, it was always warm.

And what about the birds? Flying in through the windows how often? Two, three times a week? Sometimes even twice in a single day. In the shimmering heat you could see them flying slowly, their mouths wide open as if crying out soundlessly. They would actually be flicking their tongues at the still air, gulping and panting, looking for a window to enter and a curtain rod to land on to cool off. But once they had cooled off and were ready to fly off again, they could never seem to focus on the window to fly through and they would bang themselves against the walls and the light shade until they fell, panicked and stunned. I was the one who would get the broom and push it gently up toward one of these birds after it looked like it had cooled off and prod, prod, prod until it hopped onto the broom and then I would lower it and reach from behind and cup the trembling in my hand. I can, right now, feel the life, the heat in the palm of my hand from the little body, and the fright in its tremble. I would want to hold on to it, even think of placing it in a cage and looking after it, but something always held me back. I would put my mouth close to its ears and whisper calming shh shh shhhhs, and then take it, pressed to my chest, out the back door and open my hand and wait for it to take its time fluffing out right there in my open hand before flying away.

But here? There are hardly any birds here, only that raucous, aggressive old crow that behaves as if it owns the scraggly pine tree it sits in across the street. This street is so noisy! Every day, all day and all night long, even on Sundays, cars whiz by, ambulances and fire trucks pass screaming, and I think to myself thank goodness it couldn't be going for anyone I know. I don't know anyone nearby.

Too much quiet here, too shut off. Not even the sound of children playing in the street, or the sound of neighbours talking to each other over fences, conversations floating in through open windows, open bricks. Here even when doors are open people walk down hallways with their noses straight ahead, making a point of not glancing to even nod hello.

Oh! This brings all kinds of images to my mind: the coconut tree outside my bedroom brushing, scraping, swishing against the wall. Green-blue iridescent lizards clinging, upside down, to the ceiling above my bed.

And dinner time. Mama's voice would find me wherever I was.

"Vijai, go and tell Cheryl to put food on the table, yuh father comin home just now." Standing in one place, at the top of her meagre voice she would call us one by one: "Bindra, is dinner time. Bindra, why you so harden, boy? Dinner gettin cold. Turn off that TV right now! Shanti, come girl, leave what you doin and come and eat. Vashti, go and tell Papa dinner ready, and then you come and sit down." Sitting down, eating together. Talking together. Conversations with no boundaries, no false politeness, no need to impress Mama or Papa.

But that's not how it was always. Sometimes Papa didn't come home till long after suppertime. Mama would make us eat but she would wait for him. Sometimes he wouldn't come for days, and she would wait for him then too.

But there were always flowers from the garden on the table. Pink and yellow gerberas, ferns, ginger lilies. That was your happiness, eh Mama? the garden, eh? And when there were blossoms you and I would go outside together. You showed me how to angle the garden scissors so that the plant wouldn't hurt for too long. We would bring in the bundle of flowers and greenery with their fresh-cut garden smell and little flying bugs and spiders, and you would show me how to arrange them for a centre-piece or a corner table or a floor piece. The place would look so pretty! Thanks for showing that to me, Mama.

Mama, he's never brought me any flowers. Not even a dandelion.

I don't want him to ask how much these cost. Don't ask me who sent them. No one sent them; I bought them myself. With my own money. My own money.

He's never given me anything. Only money for groceries.

Late. Again.

I jabbed this lamb with a trillion little gashes and stuffed a clove of garlic in each one with your tongue, your taste buds in mind. I spent half the day cooking this meal and you will come late and eat it after the juices have hardened to a candle-wax finish, as if it were nothing but a microwave dinner.

I want a microwave oven.

Mama, why did you wait to eat? If I were to eat now would you, Papa, he think I am a bad wife? Why did you show me this, Mama?

I must not nag.

*

Vijai remained sleeping until the fan in the bathroom woke her. It sputtered raucously, like an airplane engine starting up, escalating in time to fine whizzing, lifting off into the distance.

Five-thirty Saturday morning.

She had fretted through most of the night, twisting, arching her body, drawing her legs up to her chest, to the husband's chest, rolling, and nudging him, hoping that he would awaken to pull her body into his and hold her there. She wanted to feel the heat of his body along the length of hers, his arms pressing her to him. Or his palm placed flat on her lower belly, massaging, touching her. He responded to her fidgeting once and she moved closer to him to encourage him, but he turned his naked back to her and continued his guttural exhaling, inhaling, sounding exactly like her father.

Eventually Vijai's eyes, burning from salty tears that had spilled and dampened the pillow under her cheek, fluttered shut and she slept, deep and dreamless, until the fan awakened her.

When the sound of the shower water snapping at the enamel tub was muffled against his body, she pulled herself over to lie in and smell his indentation in the tired foam mattress. She inhaled, instead, the history of the mattress: unwashed hair, dying skin, old and rancid sweat—not the smell she wanted to nestle in. Neither would the indentation cradle her; she could feel the protruding shape of the box-spring beneath the foam.

84

She debated whether to get up and thanklessly make his toast and tea, or pretend not to have awakened, the potential for blame nagging at her. She slid back to her side of his bed, the other side of the line that he had drawn down the middle with the cutting edge of his outstretched hand. Vijai pulled her knees to her chest and hugged them. When the shower stopped she hastily straightened herself out and put her face inside the crack between the bed and the rough wall. Cold from the wall transferred itself onto her cheek, and layers upon layers of human smells trapped behind cream-coloured paint pierced her nostrils.

Vijai was aware of the husband's every move as she lay in his bed. Water from the kitchen tap pounded the sink basin, then attacked the metal floor of the kettle, gradually becoming muffled and high-pitched as the kettle filled up. He always filled it much more than was necessary for one cup of tea, which he seldom drank. The blow dryer. First on the highest setting, then dropped two notches to the lowest, and off. The electric razor. Whizzing up and down his cheek, circling his chin, the other cheek, grazing his neck. Snip, snip and little dark half-moon hairs from his nostrils and his sideburns cling to the rim of the white sink basin. Wiping up, scrubbing, making spotless these areas, and others, before he returns, are her evidence that she is diligent, that she is, indeed, her mother's daughter.

At this point in the routine she always expects a handsome aftershave cologne to fill the little bachelor apartment, to bring a moment of frivolity and romance into the room. In one favourite version of her memories, this is what normally happened in her parents' bedroom at precisely this point. But the husband would only pat on his face a stinging watery liquid with the faintest smell of lime, a smell that evaporated into nothingness the instant it touched his skin.

She held herself tensely, still in the crack between the bed and wall, as he made his way into the dark corner that he called the bedroom. The folding doors of the closet squeaked open. A shirt slid off a hanger, leaving it dangling and tinkling against the metal rod. Vijai heard the shirt that she had ironed (stretched mercilessly tight across the ironing board, the tip of the iron with staccato spurts of steam sniffing out the crevice of every seam, mimicking the importance with which her mother had treated this task) being pulled against his body and his hands sliding down the stiff front as he buttoned it.

Then there was a space empty of his sounds. The silence made the walls of her stomach contract like a closed-up accordion. Her body remained rigid. Her heart sounded as if it had moved right up into her ears, thundering methodically, and that was all that she could hear. She struggled with herself to be calm so that she could know where he was and what he was doing. Not knowing made her scalp want to unpeel itself. Then, the bed sagged as he kneeled on it, leaned across and brushed his mouth on the back of her head. His full voice had no regard for her sleep or the time of morning. He said, "Happy Birthday. I left twenty dollars on the table for you. Buy yourself a present."

The thundering subsided and her heart rolled and slid, rolled and slid, down, low down, and came to rest between her thighs. She turned over with lethargic elegance, as if she were just waking up, stretching out her back like a cat, but the apartment door was already being shut and locked from the outside.

*

The streets here are so wide! I hold my breath as I walk across them, six lanes wide. What if the light changes before I get to the other side? You have to walk so briskly, not only when you're crossing a wide street but even on the sidewalk. Otherwise people pass you and then turn back and stare at you, shaking their heads.

And yet I remember Mama telling us that fast walking, hurrying, was very unladylike.

I yearn for friends. My own friends, not his, but I'm afraid to smile at strangers. So often we huddled up in Mama's big bed and read the newspapers about things that happened to women up here—we read about women who suddenly disappeared and months later their corpses would be found, having been raped and dumped. And we also read about serial murders. The victims were almost always women who had been abducted from the street by strangers in some big North American city. Mama and Papa warned me, when I was leaving to come up here, not to make eye contact with strangers because I wouldn't know whose eyes I might be looking into or what I was encouraging, unknowingly. It's not like home, they said, where everybody knows everybody.

No bird sounds—there are not quite so many different kinds of birds here. Yes, Papa, yes, I can just hear you saying to stop this nonsense, all this thinking about home, that I must think of here as my home now, but I haven't yet left you and Mama. I know now that I will never fully leave, nor will I ever truly be here. You felt so close, Papa, when you phoned this morning and asked like you have every past year, how was the birthday girl. You said that in your office you often look at the calendar pictures of autumn fields of bales of hay, lazy rivers meandering near brick-red farmhouses, and country roads with quaint white wooden churches with red steeples, and you think that that's what my eyes have already enjoyed.

"It's all so beautiful, Papa," I said, and knowing you, you probably heard what I wasn't saying. Thanks for not pushing further. I couldn't tell you that he is working night and day to "make it," to "get ahead," to live like the other men he works with. That he is always thinking about this, and everything else is frivolous right now, so we haven't yet been for that drive in the country to see the pictures in the calendars pinned on the wall above your desk. He doesn't have time for dreaming, but I must dream or else I find it difficult to breathe.

At home the fence around our house and the garden was the furthest point that I ever went to on my own. From the house, winding in and out of the dracaenas and the philodendrons that I planted with Mama many Julys ago, feeling the full, firm limbs of the poui, going as far as the hibiscus and jasmine fence, and back into the house again. Any further away from the house than that and the chauffeur would be driving us! And now? Just look at me! I am out in a big city on my own. I wish you all could see me. I wish we could be doing this together.

Papa, you remember, don't you, when you used to bring home magazines from your office and I would flip through them quickly looking for full-page pictures of dense black-green tropical mountains, or snow-covered bluish-white ones? Ever since those first pictures I have dreamt of mountains, of touching them with the palms of my hands, of bicycling in them, and of hiking. Even though I never canoed on a river or a big lake with no shores, I know what it must feel like! I can feel what it is to ride rapids like they do in *National Geographic* magazines. Cold river spray and drenchings, sliding, tossing, crashing! I still dream of bicycling across a huge continent. I used to think, if only I lived in North America! But here I am, in this place where these things are supposed to happen, in the midst of so much possibility, and for some reason my dreams seem even further away, just out of reach. It's just not quite as simple as being here.

This land stretches on in front of me, behind me and forever. My back feels exposed, naked, so much land behind, and no fence ahead.

Except that I must cook dinner tonight.

What if I just kept walking and never returned! I could walk far away, to another province, change my name, cut my hair. After a while I would see my face on a poster in a grocery store, along with all the other missing persons. The problem is that then I wouldn't even be able to phone home and speak with Mama or Papa or Bindra and Vashti without being tracked and caught, and then who knows what.

Well, this is the first birthday I've ever spent alone. But next time we speak on the phone I will be able to tell you that I went for a very long walk. Alone.

I think I will do this every day—well, maybe every other day, and each time I will go a new route and a little further. I will know this place in order to own it, but still I will never really leave you.

Mama, Papa, Vashti, Bindra, Shanti,

Mama, Papa, Vashti, Bindra, Shanti.

Mama. Papa. Vashti. Bindra. Shanti.

*

Twenty-four years of Sundays, of eating three delightfully noisy, lengthy meals together, going to the beach or for long drives with big pots of rice, chicken and peas, and chocolate cake, singing "Michael Row Your Boat Ashore," and "You Are My Sunshine," doing everything in tandem with her brother and sisters and Mama and Papa. This particular characteristic of Sundays was etched deeply in her veins. (Not all Sundays were happy ones but recently she seems to have forgotten that.)

It would be her twenty-fourth Sunday here, the twenty-fourth week of marriage.

The only Sunday since the marriage that the husband had taken off and spent in his apartment was six weeks ago, and since he needed to spend that day alone Vijai agreed to go to the library for at least three hours. Before she left the house she thought she would use the opportunity to take down recipes for desserts, but once she began walking down the street she found herself thinking about

89

rivers and mountains. She bypassed the shelves with all the cook-ing books and home-making magazines and found herself racing toward valleys, glaciers, canoeing, rapids and the like. She picked up a magazine about hiking and mountaineering, looked at the equipment advertisements, read incomprehensible jargon about techniques for climbing.

After about forty minutes, not seeing herself in any of the maga-zines, she became less enthusiastic, and eventually frustrated and bored. She looked at her watch every fifteen minutes or so and then she started watching the second hand go around and count-ing each and every second in her head. When three hours had passed she remembered that she had said at least three hours, and she walked home slowly, stopping to window-shop and checking her watch until an extra twenty minutes had passed.

The strength of her determination that they not spend this Sun-day apart warded off even a hint of such a suggestion from the husband. What she really wanted to do was to go for the long drive up to a glacier in the nearby mountains. That way she would have him to herself for at least five hours. But he had worked several twelve-hour shifts that week and needed to rest in his apartment.

She went to the grocery store, to the gardening section, and bought half a dozen packages of flower seeds, half a dozen pack-ages of vegetable seeds, bags of soil, fertilizer, a fork and spade, a purple plastic watering can, and a score of nursery trays. She brought it all home in a taxi. Enough to keep her busy and in his apartment for an entire Sunday. She was becoming adept at find-ing ways to get what she wanted.

He never asked and Vijai did not tell that from her allowance she had paid a man from the hardware store to come over and fix the balcony sliding door. She stooped on the balcony floor scoop-ing earth into nursery trays. He sat reading the newspaper, facing the balcony in his big sagging gold armchair that he had bought next-door at a church basement sale for five dollars. She was aware that he was stealing glances at her as she bent over her garden-in-the-making.

*

I wore this shirt, no bra, am stooping, bending over here to reveal my breasts to you. *Look at them! Feel something!*

I might as well be sharing this apartment with a brother, or a roommate.

*

She feels his hands on her waist, leading her from behind to the edge of his bed. Her body is crushed under his as he slams himself against her, from behind, grunting. She holds her breath, taut against his weight and the pain, but she will not disturb his moment. She hopes that the next moment will be hers. She waits with the bed sheet pulled up to her chin. The toilet flushes and, shortly after, she hears newspaper pages being turned in the sagging five-dollar gold armchair.

Later, deep-sleep breathing and low snoring from the bedroom fills the apartment, dictating her movements. She sits on the green-and-yellow shag carpet, leaning against the foot of the husband's armchair, in front of the snowy black-and-white television watching a French station turned down low enough not to awaken him. Something about listening to a language that she does not understand comforts her, gives her companionship in a place where she feels like a foreigner. She is beginning to be able to repeat advertisements in French.

Yellow with Black Horns

Terence Young

EVELINA IS DRAWING HEARTS of all sizes. Her stick carves a fine channel, pushing lumps of wet sand to either side. When the stick breaks in her hand, she crosses her arms and shakes her head, turns to a Chinese family digging clams about twenty yards away. *I have to leave you for a minute,* she says. *My chalk has broken.* The Chinese family continues to dig.

Evelina walks toward the driftwood that sits just above the high tide line, her arms swinging soldier-like. From a pile of bleached slivers of cedar and fir, she chooses a replacement and returns. She finishes the largest heart and stands inside it. The wind coming in off the water lifts her hair off her shoulders and across her face.

Yes, she is saying. *That's very good.* She draws a lady with long hair. *What else can we put in our hearts?* She points her stick at a hotel in the distance. She draws a man with a hat and a moustache. *Today I will draw my brother, too, because next week is his birthday.* She draws a boy, and beside the boy she draws a cat, but by the time she has finished, the ocean is tugging at her heels.

Evelina does not understand the tides. She thinks the water is trying to trick her. Her father explained to her once about the moon, but there is no moon in the sky today. Evelina hates the way, piece by piece, the sea eats her hearts. She gathers up her socks and shoes and moves away from the water.

Her whole family is at the beach today, but not for the party. That's not until next week in the backyard. She draws another heart and steps inside. She draws the apple tree and then the piñata.

"Evelina! Time to go!"

Across the flat grey stretch of sand, Evelina can see her mother picking up the blanket and shaking it. She lifts the tartan square so that it floats on the wind and when it begins to fall, she gives it a good snap. Once, twice, three times. Each time she does it, the sound of the blanket's snapping reaches Evelina like an echo. Her father has left the beach ahead of everybody else. He is already walking toward the path, through the swordgrass and spindly young alders, to the parking lot. Evelina's brother Peter is tugging at his father's arm and crying. He would stay all day if his parents let him. Evelina extends her left arm behind her, imagining the weight of her brother pulling, digging his feet into the sand. She watches her father's steady steps. When her brother trips over a piece of wood, her father keeps moving, dragging Peter until he finds his feet again. She runs across the sand toward her mother who has just finished closing the lid on the picnic basket. On her way, Evelina detours through some of the shallow, sun-warmed pools. Each time her feet enter the tepid water, she wants to sit down and cover her legs, cold now from the wind, but she can see her mother's hands struggling with the leather straps on the basket, so she keeps on running.

"How is it there's always more to take home than we brought?" her mother asks as Evelina comes up the beach toward her.

Evelina smiles, but her mother doesn't look at her. Her face is turned toward the path and the hole in the line of trees where Peter and his father are disappearing from view. Evelina sits down on a log and brushes the sand from her feet before she puts on her runners. When she finishes, she picks up the folded blanket and follows her mother to the car. Evelina drops her stick in order to carry the blanket properly. As she lets it fall, something pulls at it. *Maybe it's the moon,* she thinks.

By the time they reach the parking lot, Peter is no longer crying. He is making faces at them through the rear window of the blue Pontiac. Evelina's father already has the engine running. His window is rolled down, and he is tapping his fingers on the rim of the steering wheel, keeping time to the radio. The watery tune drifts out into the air along with the smoke from his cigarette. Evelina's mother lifts the trunk lid and puts in the picnic basket and the blanket. As she is opening the door of the car to join her brother, Evelina feels her mother's hands on her shoulders and the gentle pressure of her face as she buries her nose in Evelina's hair. "You smell good," she says.

On the way home, Evelina thinks about the party. *I am six,* she reminds herself. *Peter is excited, because he will be four. I am older. I can wait.* She thinks about the apple tree in their backyard and her brother's friends. Tomorrow she and her mother are going to make the piñata while her father takes Peter out to their grandmother's. Nobody speaks as they drive home. Nobody except Peter, who is talking to the shells he clutches in either hand.

"Shut up, you," one shell says.

"I'll getcha," says the other.

They fight.

Sometimes late at night, after the family has been out visiting or to a movie, Evelina will see her mother slide across the front seat of the car to lean her head on her father's shoulder. And then her father will lift his arm and pull her in tight beside him. Evelina loves his arm, his big arm. She likes to fall asleep watching their shapes blur in the glow of passing headlights.

But today her mother sits with one hand on the armrest, her eyes fixed on the forest beside the highway. Maybe she is looking for deer, or raccoons. For a few minutes, Evelina watches for deer with her mother, but soon gives up and starts to draw hearts on the mohair seat covers.

The next morning, Evelina doesn't bother her mother about the piñata. The phone rings at breakfast, but when her father answers it nobody is there. After he sits down at the table, it rings again, but still there is nobody on the other end. Her father says hello a few times. "What's the matter?" he says into the receiver. "Cat got your tongue?"

"Cat got your tongue, monkey got your bum," yells Peter. He yells it again and again from his seat at the "special table." Peter is not big enough to sit in a normal chair like everybody else, but he refuses to use a booster seat.

"Pervert," Evelina's father says calmly into the phone, hanging it up with a firm clunk. He picks up a piece of toast from his plate and eats it standing up. He stuffs the final corner into his mouth and plucks Peter from his chair.

"Peter," he says. "Oh, Peter, Peter, nothing sweeter." He twirls Peter above his head like an airplane and plunks him back down. "Will *somebody* get this child ready so I can get to work on time? Not everyone gets the summer off, you know."

"Just call me 'somebody,'" Evelina's mother says.

"What did I say?" Evelina's father asks, grinning broadly. "Did I say something, Evelina?"

Evelina doesn't know what to answer. She looks at her mother, but her mother only shakes her head and takes a cloth to Peter's mucky face. Evelina goes back to her room to play with her dolls. From here she can listen through the heat vent to her family in the kitchen below. She can tell when it's not a good time to go downstairs. Peter hasn't learned this yet, not to be a nuisance. Evelina can hear him as he follows his father around the house asking him where they are going. She can hear her mother rummaging through the shoe drawer and the worn brass hinges as her father struggles with the back door. "Fine, then," he says after a few minutes. "Off with you, Peter."

Evelina can pick out her brother's small feet on the back porch. She recognizes the heavy footsteps of her father following him. Her father forgets to close the door behind him, but today her mother doesn't say a thing. As far as Evelina knows, Peter doesn't even have his shoes or coat on, but they go out anyway. Evelina waits a minute and then comes downstairs to find her mother in the livingroom watching the car back out of the driveway. When her mother turns around, she is biting her lip and her eyes are looking far away like the time she let the doctor take Peter to stitch up a nasty cut in his thumb. For a moment, Evelina thinks she should say something, but then the look on her mother's face changes. "Oh, you," she says. "Would you like to make the piñata now?" Evelina is glad she didn't have to ask.

In the kitchen, her mother pulls out a pile of newspapers from under the sink and shows Evelina how to tear them into strips. The two of them sit on the kitchen floor tearing newspaper and placing the strips into a pile. Evelina's mother mixes flour and water together in the bucket they use for washing the car and when the paste looks like pancake batter she picks up the bucket and tells Evelina to follow her down into the basement.

The basement is dark, lit only by two bulbs with pull chains. Evelina doesn't like to go down there, even during the day. The lights can't be turned on from upstairs. Every time her mother asks her to get a jar of pears from the preserve closet, Evelina wishes she could use the flashlight her father keeps in his top drawer. At night she loses her way and circles the floor, groping in the black air above her head for the chain. Today, in the dull light of the basement's only window, her mother finds the pull chain quickly.

Evelina's mother sets down the bucket of paste and goes to a large standing cupboard beside the washing machine. From the very back of the top shelf, she pulls something out. At first Evelina doesn't know what it is, but when her mother spins it around on the string tied to its middle, she sees it is a bull, shaped from the rusty chicken wire they had used one year to keep cats out of the garden. Nothing very much ever grew in their garden so her father had turned the small black square of dirt into more lawn. He rolled up the chicken wire and shoved it behind the tool shed. What surprises Evelina is her mother. When did she go out to the shed and retrieve the wire? How could she have made such a thing without anyone knowing?

The bull isn't large, but it has horns like a real one. Her mother sets it down on the cement floor and shows Evelina the hole in the top where they will hide the prizes they bought last week in Chinatown and how the stomach of the bull is hinged so it will break open and let them fall out.

Evelina's mother starts dipping the strips of newspapers into the bucket of paste. When they're covered, she takes them one at a time and wraps them around a part of the wire frame. She covers the legs first, showing Evelina how to overlap the strips. "This way it will be strong," her mother says. "The boys will have to work hard to get their prizes."

She tells Evelina again of the time when she, too, was a little girl and broke her arm after a fall from the maple tree outside her window. Evelina likes to think of her mother running and climbing trees and bossing her sisters around. Evelina listens again to how the neighbour drove her mother and her grandmother to the hospital and how the doctor fixed her arm by placing it in a cast. "Today, you and I are the doctors," she says. "We're making this bull strong the way Dr. Whitely made my arm strong."

Evelina imagines one of her own arms sheathed in layers of cloth soaked in plaster, cool, soothing, covering her wrist, her forearm and elbow inch by inch and freezing them into a hard white L. She looks at the bull taking shape in front of her, its wire skeleton and paper skin. She thinks of the bull finished, the prizes tucked safely inside the dark cavity of the bull's stomach. The paste drips from their hands onto the floor. Evelina wipes her forehead and leaves a wide streak of white in her hair.

"What was I thinking?" says her mother. "Take off your blouse and skirt. Socks and shoes, too."

Evelina strips off her clothes, and after hanging the bull from a wooden beam above the big laundry tubs, her mother strips down as well. They climb up and sit facing each other on the outer rims of the twin tubs, the bucket of paste balanced between them and their thighs pressing into the smooth cement edges of the old basins.

"Now we can make as much mess as we want," her mother says, starting in on the bull's shoulders and neck. Sun filters through the dusty curtains of the window above them. The bull hangs half-made on the string while Evelina's mother smoothes the dirty white skin that seems to grow out of her fingers.

In Chinatown the week before, Evelina and her mother had looked in store after store for toys and candy to fill the piñata. They walked past groceries that spilled out onto the sidewalk with boxes of vegetables and fruit. Roast ducks turned on spits in windows and swirling neon letters lit up ceilings and restaurant arches. Men in dark suits stood in clumps, smoking and talking loudly. In one of the stores, rooms opened into more rooms and everywhere tables were piled high with brightly painted trinkets. Evelina walked around, losing her mother and then finding her again. When they had seen everything, they left through a back door and ended up in a long, thin alley with open doorways that revealed steep staircases disappearing into the darkness. They stopped for lunch at a café with polished wooden booths and shared a plate of fried rice.

Evelina drank pop; her mother drank Chinese tea. Evelina hoped that the waiter thought she and her mother looked like the sort of people who belonged in Chinatown, that he was treating them the same way he would a Chinese person.

"I'm sorry you don't have a sister," her mother had said as they were leaving the café. "Sisters are so much fun. We could pretend, if you want. Would you like that? Would you like it if I pretended I was your sister?"

"No," Evelina had said.

"Why not?" her mother asked. "I think we'd be wonderful sisters. We could live in an apartment together and have tea parties for our friends."

"What about Peter," Evelina asked, "and Dad?"

"They could have an apartment too," her mother said. "We'd let them come and visit us."

"No," said Evelina. She didn't like this game. Her mother was playing it too seriously, as if Evelina's answers really mattered. As though they could really do such a thing, if only Evelina would say yes.

"Oh, Evelina," her mother said. "Don't you think it would be fun?

"Yes," Evelina said," but who would be our mother?"

Evelina doesn't know they are finished until her mother says they are. Instead of taking a bath, Evelina stays in the deep cement tub while her mother fills it with warm water. She is still small enough that if she crouches the water will come right up to her shoulders. The cold cement sides are an inch thick, but they get warm quickly as the water pours in. When Evelina closes her eyes, she feels as though she is sitting on the rough bottom of the wading pool at the park. She can almost hear the children splashing around her and see the other mothers stretched out on towels, talking and smoking. Evelina blinks and sees her mother, and then the bull, still wet above her, drying quickly in the muted sunlight.

The phone rings while they are dressing and Evelina's mother runs upstairs to answer it. Evelina listens and in a second she hears her mother talking. This time it's not a pervert. Her mother's voice is quiet and soft. It drifts down the basement stairwell and makes Evelina think of walking on the lawn. She towels herself dry and dresses quickly, but her mother has already hung up by the time Evelina joins her in the kitchen. "Who was that?" Evelina asks.

Her mother opens the fridge. "Are you hungry?" she asks. "Should we have some lunch now?"

The phone rings again and Evelina's mother turns from the refrigerator. "What a bother," she says. "Let's not answer it. Let's pretend we're not home. I'll make us some sandwiches and we'll have a picnic in the back yard." The phone continues to ring as her mother pulls a new jar of mayonnaise from the cupboard, a tomato and some lettuce from the crisper. "You find a blanket and spread it on the grass," she says. Evelina runs to the linen closet. With each insistent ring, she searches more frantically for a blanket. The ringing follows her out the back door and down the steps. When it refuses to stop, Evelina is almost ready to cry. She wants her mother to do something, to pick the phone up and scream at the person. Evelina is angry enough to do it herself. In another minute, she'll go into the house and tell that person to stop it, just to stop it, but then the sound is gone. A few minutes later, Evelina's mother steps out onto the back porch with a tray of sandwiches and a pitcher of Kool-Aid.

The air is warm in the backyard and when they have finished eating Evelina's mother brings the piñata out into the sun. It's Evelina's job to choose the paints. Evelina has never seen a bull, apart from the one in the stars her father showed her. *Each star a sun,* he had told her, *just like ours.* "Yellow," she tells her mother, "with black horns."

When they've finished, Evelina paints a bright red heart on the bull's chest, and then the two of them carry the piñata into the basement, where they hang it from a wooden beam in the darkness of the coal bin.

In the evening, Peter and his father return from their visit to grandma's. Peter carries a peach pie their grandmother has sent along. He places it proudly on the kitchen counter. "Tea party tonight," he says.

Peter is too young to care about Evelina's day, to wonder what Evelina was doing while he was at their grandmother's. Nevertheless, when he asks Evelina to help him build a fort under his bed, she is so relieved not to have to lie that she plays with him much longer than usual. There are still several days to go, but Evelina can see her brother doesn't suspect a thing.

Before bed, the whole family gathers for tea and pie in the livingroom. Evelina's father cuts four big pieces and passes them around. "Where did you go today?" he asks her mother.

"Nowhere," her mother says. "Evelina and I had a picnic in the backyard."

"Because I phoned a couple of times and there was no answer, that's all," he says.

"We didn't want to answer it because we thought it might be that pervert calling again. He called this morning after you left, you know."

"What did he say?" her father asks.

"Nothing," her mother says. "Not a thing."

Evelina visits the bull many times before the weekend. She doesn't even mind hunting for the pull chain. She doesn't take the piñata down, just stands outside the coal bin looking up into its black reaches, where she can barely make out the form of the bull turning on its string in the breeze she's brought with her. She tries to picture her brother seeing the piñata for the first time. *Will he really be surprised?* she wonders. *Will he think it's magic?* One day she pretends she doesn't know the bull is there, that she has come

101

upon it while looking for something else. In the livingroom above her head, her mother is lecturing Peter. "Don't stick your lip out at me," she is saying. Evelina, frightened, jumps back from the entrance to the coal bin. She thinks the bull has spoken to her.

On Saturday morning, Evelina wakes to the sound of the car backing out the driveway below her window. Her father's head craning to look behind him and the chrome of the Pontiac's grill are all she sees. In the kitchen, she finds her mother wiping up a spill on the floor. She's pulled her night-gown up past her knees and cinched it into a knot at her waist. Evelina watches from behind as her mother pushes a cloth back and forth over the bright red squares of linoleum tile, sopping up a pool of black coffee and squeezing it out into a dirty saucepan. A quarter to eight and Peter isn't even awake yet. His birthday isn't really until Monday, but Evelina still can't imagine how he can sleep so late. She moves to the table and sits down, waiting for her mother to notice her. In the top of the garbage bucket, she sees some shards of pottery, the crescent curve of a cup handle.

"Which one broke?" she asks.

"Oh, precious," her mother says, pulling herself around. "The Donald and Mickey." She hugs her knees and looks at Evelina. "I'm so sorry."

Why would anyone use that mug when they knew it was mine? Evelina thinks.

Her mother gets up and pours Evelina a glass of juice and fixes her some toast. "Evelina," she says, "I need you to be a big girl, today." Evelina waits. "I won't have the car like I thought I would, so now someone will have to stay home with Peter while I walk to the store. Can you do that for me?"

Evelina isn't surprised by the request. When she hears the words come from her mother's mouth, she almost expects them. What startles Evelina, though, are the deep valleys of bloodless skin

102

that have appeared between her mother's knuckles, the lines of taut muscle running down her neck.

Her mother unknots the night-gown bunched at her side and moves toward the hall. "If I leave now, I'll be back before the kids get here. Give Peter some cereal when he gets up. Don't fiddle with the toaster, okay?" More instructions trail down the stairs and over the banister. In the time it takes Evelina to finish her breakfast, her mother dresses, puts on some mascara and a little lipstick, checks the elements on the gas stove twice and leaves, locking the door behind her. Evelina hears her mother descend the front steps, the slap of her shoes on the cement walk. She listens until the footsteps fade completely and she is alone. She gets up and walks over to the garbage bucket to look at the pieces of her broken cup. She puts her fingers through the handle, removes them, then folds the top edges of the garbage bag over so the pieces are hidden. A lawn mower ignites the air somewhere down the street. Two cats screech at one another. Upstairs, Peter leaps from his bed onto the floor and yells for Evelina's mother to bring him his favourite shirt. At the same time, the phone rings, but Evelina ignores it and runs upstairs.

The birthday party is to start at 1:00 p.m. and Evelina's mother returns home at 11:30. She comes in through the back door, followed by a man carrying four large bags of groceries. He places them on the kitchen table and leaves, accepting the change Evelina's mother offers as he goes. Evelina watches quietly as her mother sits down to pull off her shoes and light a cigarette. Peter is in the livingroom with his bag of green army men. He has boxed together a cave from all the cushions on the sofa and the muffled sounds of his war games filter through to the kitchen.

Evelina's mother holds out an arm. "Come here, beauty," she says.

Evelina allows herself to fold into her mother's lap, her head tucked under her mother's chin. The smell of cigarette smoke on her mother's clothes is not unfamiliar, but it is rare, something reserved for late evenings and guests.

"We have lots of time," her mother says. "Lots of time."

The sun is high and the sky cloudless. Evelina and Peter trail coloured streamers around the backyard and unfold lawn chairs while their mother prepares party favours and ices a store-bought white cake. With her icing kit, she writes *Happy Birthday Peter* in red across the top and places four candles strategically around the letters.

A neatly-dressed boy from two streets over rings the doorbell at precisely one o'clock, gift in hand. His parents wave from the sidewalk as he enters. "Four-thirty?" they ask as Evelina's mother waves back.

"Four-thirty," she says.

Other boys are already coming up the walk. Peter takes each boy's present and runs through to the dining room where he places it beside other presents on the table. Outside, several boys have already attacked the swing set. One boy is in the apple tree yelling down at the others to come after him. Evelina tries to show another how to use a badminton racquet. She throws the bird to the boy, and after it lands on the ground the boy swings.

Evelina's mother appears on the porch and claps three times. "Line up for games," she says, and the boys scramble to be first, as Evelina knew they would.

There are enough boys for a good game of pig-in-the-middle, and not quite enough for an egg-and-spoon race. Evelina is "it" in hide-and-seek, but Geoffrey, whose own birthday party is next weekend, gets scared and starts crying when Evelina jumps out at them. Her mother balances a penny on the top of a pile of flour and gives all the boys a teaspoon. Each boy removes a spoonful of flour and the one who makes the penny fall has to run around the house.

Just before they stop for hotdogs, Evelina sits the boys on the grass under the apple tree and makes them close their eyes. She gives each boy a piece of paper, a pencil and a book to use as a drawing table. "Draw a cat," she says, "and no peeking." Evelina learned this game from her grade one teacher and often plays it on her own. The boys draw carefully with pencils tightly clenched between their fingers and tongues pinched between their lips. When Evelina tells them to stop and open their eyes, they look upon their work in silence. Cross-legged and confused, they stare up at Evelina. A trick has been played on them, but they are not sure what it is.

Hot dogs are brought out in a pot of boiling water and served with mustard and ketchup on white buns. Peter tells his mother he is going to eat four. "Save room for cake," she tells him.

Evelina knows it is time for the piñata, but doesn't want to start without her father. He will want to watch Peter try to get the prizes. She has already asked her mother once when he will arrive. Reluctantly, Evelina disappears into the basement. From the beam in the coal bin, she unhooks the piñata and carries it out into the bright sunlight. All the boys turn in her direction as she appears, their mouths still full of wiener and bread.

"Surprise!" Evelina shouts. She explains to Peter and the others what her mother has told her, that in Mexico the children have birthday parties too but that at their parties they have a piñata full of prizes for everybody.

"You will have to work hard," she tells them, and describes how they are to get the prizes out of the bull. The boys rush to line up and because it's Peter's birthday he gets to go first. Evelina ties a blindfold around his head and hands him a heavy wooden stick. Then she spins him in a circle and sends him off in the direction of the piñata. "You can have three tries," she tells him.

Peter's first swing sends him off balance and he falls to the ground. Evelina helps him up. His next two swings miss widely. Evelina is disappointed for him, but she also worries about what will happen to the thin plaster shell of the bull's body when one of the boys actually hits it. A boy called Stephen takes his turn next, but he, too, strikes only the air. Others follow, even farther from the mark. Evelina decides to stop spinning them before she sends them off and allows them four tries instead of three. One boy nicks the leg of the bull and sends it careening from side to side.

"Can I have a hit?" Evelina's father comes through the gate into the backyard. He walks up to the line of boys and stands waiting. His jacket is unbuttoned and a tie hangs out of the left pocket where it has been stuffed in haste.

"It's the piñata," Evelina says. "For Peter's birthday."

"I'm a boy," her father says. "I want to play, too."

Evelina is silent.

"Come on, sweetheart," her father says. "Cover my eyes." He kneels down on the grass and closes them.

Evelina's mother is sitting in a white metal chair under the clematis that hangs from the porch. She is holding a cup of coffee and smiling thinly at Evelina. Evelina takes the handkerchief and covers her father's eyes, tying it in a loose knot at the back of his head. His hair is stiff with grease. She hands him the stick.

"Spin me, Evelina," her father says, standing.

Evelina places her hands on her father's waist and turns. She might as well be trying to twist a fir tree. Her father's body passes beneath her hands as he completes a circle and stops.

"Okay," her father says. He strides toward the apple tree and raises the stick. The back of the bull is broken from the force of her father's blow, crushed inwards to reveal the web of rusty chicken wire that holds the bull together.

Evelina turns to her mother sitting in the white chair, her cup of coffee lying empty on the grass. She is pointing at Evelina's blindfolded father, trying to say something, but short bursts of laughter like hiccups keep interrupting her words. "A little late for that," she says. "Aren't you just a little too late?"

106

Evelina turns back in time to see her father taking up the stick again for a second blow. He stands as though he is at bat in a baseball game, his arms drawn back ready to swing. This time he hits the bull full in the stomach. The wire hinges break and a yawning gap appears in the underbelly, spilling popguns, Chinese yo-yo's and magic rings onto the grass below.

Peter and the others move in to scoop up the treasure, grabbing as many prizes as they can hold.

Evelina's father pulls off the blindfold and leans on the stick. "There you go, boys," he says. "That's how it's done."

Evelina had imagined the piñata would crack slowly, like the shell of an egg when a chick is born. She certainly didn't think her father would want to join in the game or that her mother would find it so funny when he did. *It's all wrong*, she thinks. *Everything is wrong*. She starts pulling the boys back from the pile of prizes. She rips the candies and cheap toys out of their pockets and slaps their hands to make them drop what they are holding. Peter runs by her, dodging, keeping himself low to the ground, responding quickly to this new development in the game. He is going back for more, but Evelina catches him by the scruff of his neck and hits him hard across the side of his face. She hits him again and then again until he cries. "Hey!" she hears her mother say. "Hey, now!"

Ucluelet

Maria Hindmarch

DON'T GET LOST, SAYS LEFTY as I step up onto the gang-plank to get off at Ucluelet. I won't, I say. Are you sure, he says, we don't want you getting picked up by a fisherman. Sure, I'm sure, I say and keep going. Jan, bring us a back a couple of cold ones will you? says Beebo as I step off the gangplank. I'm not going to the pub, I answer. Make that one for me too, eh? shouts Ken, yummy-bodied Ken, who is standing, one jean ripped at the knee, just a few feet down the dock. You have to pass it, says Beebo, if you're going to go anywhere.

As Beebo talks, a load is swinging down from above and Hal is steering the empty towmotor over. I step out of the way of both. Hal jerks the machine, fast. It halts right next to me. For a second I'm startled but come to quickly, laughing slightly, and Hal catches my look, smiles; we're together a moment, and then I watch Ken and Beebo stretching up to touch the underside of the loaded flats. I can see all of Ken at first, his eyes dazed almost (like sometimes in bed) there but not there, his long chest and shoulder muscles pressing out from under a many-coloured T-shirt. He and Beebo grab the boards and slowly Ken's outstretched arms and face disappear behind the load, then his shoulders, his chest, a four-inch strip of tanned skin between his shirt bottom and belt, his hips; boxes of canned pears, sacks of potatoes, bales of wire come between us, and then suddenly, on top, I see his overgrown crewcut and blue eyes.

How about it? shouts Ken over the load. I don't feel like it, I answer as Hal shifts gears then centers the prongs and jerks them in, under, through the flats. C'mon Jan, says Beebo. I glance into his curliness, turn up to Hal who half-smiles. He backs the towmotor, fast, turns it, heads towards the edge of the wooden shed which is part of the dock and the green Ford truck there. Everyone will be too busy to notice, says Beebo as Ken wanders over to me. Why not? Ken asks. I'm afraid. Of what? he says, getting caught by the skipper? I don't look at him, feel my face tighten, look over to Beebo. Forget it, Beebo says, we were only teasing.

I walk towards the ramp feeling their eyes follow me, not just Ken's and Beebo's, but Hal's also, and the Second Mate's, Chuckles, and the three men's from town who are loading the Ford. I try to ignore it, notice my work shoes, feel the boards of the dock almost slap my feet 'cause they don't move like the *Nootka* does. Only a few yards more, but getting there, like walking through a corridor in high school, takes so long. And even if they're not looking, I feel the weight particularly of Hal's eyes, so centered, so certain, and Ken's, lighter, but knowing me in a way I don't like to be known. Because he has made love with me, he can make me feel awkward, not consciously, but he does it without thinking and in some ways that's worse, damn him.

I kick the damp dirt that covers the long, wooden ramp and glance up at the shining village: a curved slope which slants down; the crest, all covered in bush, is almost directly up from where I am; the buildings, their tops, some of the sides standing out through

109

the green, are either over and down to the left or over and slightly down to the right; and the wet street, its blackness, runs at an angle from the ramp. I feel like I'd like to slide up over it, to fly through the cut it makes, to touch the fir tips, the unpainted fence, even the shaggy poles as I pass. Just as I start to run, a guy behind me on the dock shouts: watch out for the bears! The what? I say as I turn to the men beside the truck. The bears, says the Nordic one in an open green shirt, the woods are full of them. Okay, I shout back, I was going to stick to the road anyway.

I turn and again start to walk up the ramp. Bears, he's gotta be kidding, that's the type of thing my Uncle Andy used to say, only it was cougars. The village seems more distant now and, on a clearing high up to the right, the last of the sun makes a side window of a tin-roofed shack shine gold; but since it won't be dark for another half-hour or so, I've nothing to worry about, and besides that I've never been afraid of the dark or woods anyway.

I stop and lean on the railing for a moment, pick off a wet splinter, stick it in my mouth. I glance up at the gold window again and wonder about the people who live there, then turn to the water, the fishboats, a bobbing Coke tin. The boats, a few yards down the bank, are mostly white on top. Their poles form almost a forest as they sway, well over a hundred, above their bodies, the ships, the floats. The forest of white seems almost suspended there, the reflection, the extension of it, nonexistent because the land forest and the hill cuts off the light, creates a water/earth/tree darkness of its own. I pull the splinter out from between two back teeth but part of it sticks so I poke it with a piece of fingernail as I watch two men fixing an engine in one of the boats. Then, I make out five guys drinking/yakking/listening to a radio. One of them whistles up and they all look or shout or say something, but I can't hear what because of the distance and the *Nootka's* noise, so I smile and start going again.

Ahead on the right, there's a general store and old vine-covered house; then there's a curve in the land and everything else is the woods as far as I can see. I take a deep breath of salt-fish-boat-motor air and start to run. The first thing I notice when I step off the ramp onto the paved road or main street is how hard it seems; it feels as though the blacktop comes up to smack my feet rather than feet going down to meet it. I take four steps just to feel the hard surface then move off onto the dirt shoulder, past the library, which is new, just like any plaster building in Vancouver, but it has orange and yellow flowers growing haphazardly in its garden, and the grass hasn't been cut recently so in that way it's better even though the windows are aluminium framed and not nearly as attractive as the high criss-cross ones of the general store on my right. The store needs paint, but the light on what used to be is perfect; the store has a slow not-too-many-people-go-to-it-anymore look, but obviously, at one time, it was the main building in town. Maybe that's why the library garden looks okay—they didn't take it up and redo it all in rows—they must have just taken down a house and built the library on the land.

I pull out a piece of couch grass, suck the yellow-green tip, wonder what it was Hal said about rows. I guess he didn't, I just thought he did when he was talking about the guys not being able to keep a shore job, and I saw the city then all in straight lines and rectangles, the people moving evenly on the surface of its streets, no ragged indents, like here. Ahead, a little monument of some sort stands on my right, covered in salal and alder, and on my left, just ahead, the government liquor store, recessed back, not in line. It's closed, of course; it's past six. I step up onto the cement sidewalk, the Ucluelet Lodge, a two-storeyed ochre-coloured building, is flush against it.

French fries and coffee come into my nose as I pass the beauty parlour at the bottom end. White sheets cover the chairs. And next, the café, licensed; several men (the only woman in it is the waitress) are eating and drinking and two teenage boys, more dressed up than the others, are leaning on the juke box smoking cigarettes. They're not really dressed up; they both have on tight jeans, their shirts are ironed carefully, tucked in just so, and their hair has been combed towards the center with parts on both sides . . . like it didn't take just a minute to do it and definitely there was a mirror. I scurry past the windows of the empty lobby to the corner where the men's entrance to the pub is, look up at the hill, want to get out somehow, up there—the tips's only a block and a bushy half away—but don't for some reason. I turn, look down the angled road. I can't see the dock, just the edge of the ramp and the lights. I find myself going left, walking rapidly, not thinking about the men or the beer or Ken or anything at all.

Between the gravel there's a piece of coloured glass. I stoop, pick it up, roll the blueness in my palm. After a moment or so, I come out of the stoop and am right in front of a half-wooden, half-glass door. I step up to it, look through the thick-filmed glass; a big-bellied man is leaning over, doing something to someone who's sitting there; walls which aren't walls, I can't figure it out. I turn the brass knob. Open it slowly. Walk in. The men don't look up. The two of them, one a barber and the other an Indian, seem to hang there in a cubicle near the front on the right, while in the back, far to the left, pool balls bump each other. There's a closed Coke machine a few feet in front of me and stacks of empty pop cases and beer cartons form almost a wall to my immediate right. I watch the big-bellied barber, who I guess collects the empties to sell them later, slowly shave the old Indian with one of those long straight razors.

I step towards the pop cooler while looking at the two of them, and neither notices me. The barber dips his razor in an oval enamel bowl; he wipes it with a cloth, then holds the old man's head as he shaves. I glance to the counter on the left; behind it is a wall with one shelf covered in stuff: dice, cards, O'Henrys, Jersey Milks, Player's Tobacco, and three bags of stale popcorn stapled to a card which originally held twenty or more. To the sound of the balls, I open the pop machine and no one says anything—the barber keeps shaving and the men in the back move. Rather than see any of them, I look down into the metally water: Ginger Beer, 7-Up, Mandalay Punch, Coca-Cola, Ginger Ale, Orange Crush. I can't decide. Maybe I'm not supposed to be in here at all.

I look up at the beam in front of me. On a poster for a dance last month, there's a girl I recognize from high school who looks tougher now. I look down again, can't get over it, here, her, and one of the guys I used to play in a dance band with. I pick up the Ginger Ale—he must be no more than twenty-one and it's his band now—not Canada Dry but Nanaimo Bottling Works, much browner, the taste more full, I used to love it, but I hesitate, see that no one's watching, put it back, pick up the Orange, maybe this place *is* for men only, not Orange Crush but Mission, better than Crush; I place it on the metal opener but just before I open it, I stop, hold it, the cold wetness, don't know what the rule is if there is one about pool halls, see the Lime-Rickey, not the green stuff but the ouzo white which came out first. My god, they got every choice here, three I really want.

I look up at the barber. Maybe I'm taking too long. I assume he's the owner. He hasn't got on a white frock but a blue shirt with little red hairs coming through the splits where the buttons just hold over his belly. He's shaven the right side of the wrinkly brown face and is just beginning the left; probably doesn't even know I'm here yet, or, if he does, he's in no hurry. Well, the whole place is in no rush for that matter, kinda nice, so unlike the city. I can almost see the whole front section of the poolroom; after a man hits the ball, he picks up another stick, chalks it, and the other men (one Japanese, two white, one Indian) stand around while he takes another shot. I start to open the orange again but don't, put it back, pull out the Lime-Rickey and open it. No one, not one person, has said one word.

I begin to go towards the barber but don't. Instead, I swallow sharp lemony-lime and delicate other tastes. I wander to the counter to the sound of bumping billiards and stand there, looking: Chuck-Wagon Stew, just two cans; handkerchiefs in dusty cellophane, rabbits' feet, four left on a faded card, a light brown. I drink my pop, look at the green metal light shade over the billiard table. The Indian kid is now shooting, is that what they call it, I don't know, anyway he has the stick and after he hits the balls with one ball the other men stand away while he gets ready for another shot. A skinny-legged spider skitters over nailclippers to one of the wooden crib-boards that lean upright from the shelf to the wall. I finish drinking and put the bottle down on the counter, wander over to the window, look at the dead flies on the sill, try to see out, there's nothing, turn slowly, and the barber smiles, comes over to me, belly jiggling, and I place silver in his wet hand which has a dab of foam on the index finger. He takes the money, puts it in this big-flied-pant pocket, and I say thank you and leave. The old man is still in the chair and still has not moved one bit. Mine were the only words spoken during this entire time.

I close the door softly and run in the darkness, where to, I don't know, along a dirt road, down a dirt lane. Bushes, grass, trees on the side. The *Nootka's* engine and winch throb and whine louder and louder; wherever I am, I am getting closer to her, can hear her. The branches and leaves are shaking/trembling. Funny I feel no breeze, only the motion past my body, and ahead, through the darkness, there's a gulley, a clearing, maybe water moving. I come out of the bush the lane must have led to and there *is* a small opening; that is, the trees stop and there's a trail ahead where they start again. I'm too far to the right, that's it, over there up the dip must be the library, but if I just keep going, surely this will lead me to it, the water, at least a moment ago I thought I saw it, and once I get there I can always get out, follow the shoreline that is. So I take the trail through the trees which again leads down, fast, it's sharp, I hold onto the salal, drop, catch my balance, lead more carefully this time with my right foot, get the feel of the rock first, then come down to it by clutching the wet roots and letting go once my foot knows where it is.

My left foot feels out through the dark wetness and again my hand clutches salal. I slide, land, and here I am surrounded by bush, and the ship's racket is loud, very close, but no light in this dense foliage. I grope out with my hands, touch wet prickly branches which drip on my skin, stoop, feel for an opening. And there is one, a thin slit, which I crawl through, not far, but scratchy. Stairs, there are stairs. I stand at the top of them for a moment just breathing as my hands do my long hair up. Then I start to walk down, to go towards the engine throb. No railings and my leg my skirt are caught in thorns, a blackberry branch. I try to lift it to disentangle, step closer. As my right hands hold the thick branch, my left pulls the skirt out thorn by thorn. I slowly move it with both hands, pass it, take two steps, let it fall back and suddenly, below me, I hear other branches and water.

The branches are getting louder. For a moment, I just stand there. The best thing to do, my dad always said, is stay put, don't move at all. I do, try to, my blood swoops to my center, and I try not to make noise as I gasp, gulp the air.

In a moment, I realize it is *someone* not *something* on the steps: thank god. Whoever it is, is coming up. I try to say, hi there. But I can't because nothing comes out. In a moment, there he is, a cowboy-belted young man just three steps away. Whatya doin' here? he asks. I just look down at him and he stops, waits for my answer: I, I, I'm trying to get over there. I point. Wanta have a drink? he says, I'll show ya. No, I say, can you, can you tell me how to get to the dock? I won't try anything, he says, I promise. I, I got lost, I say as I turn around then start to lift the blackberry vine again. Let me do that, he says as he brushes against my bum and back. I step down and he gets the branch while I still feel his touch and the motion through me. We don't have to be alone, he says as

115

I come up to him, I'll get my buddies so we're not alone, you don't have to worry about that. No, I say as he lets me pass, you don't understand, it's nothing to do with you at all. I look at the step. I, I just have to get back. You sure got in the wrong place, he says as he lets the branch go. It makes a heavy crashing sound with light whips as the leaves cut through the air.

I know that, I think as I step off the last stair. Just go that way, he says as he comes up from behind me, it'll take you there. Uuh, thank you, I say as I turn and sorta smile but not really 'cause I'm scared and gotta get. Thank you, I say again and just leave him there standing on the stair as I head back. Sure you don't want me to come with you, he says. No, I say, I'm all right, I know where I am now, but thanks, I say as I step over a log, thanks a lot, I say to his outline, the face non-distinct, the body masked. And I turn/run along the narrow path, tall couch grass on its sides, no lights yet but the alder's getting thinner. The library, ahead I can see the library. I don't think (a light, a clouded light through the trees) I'd want to (it's at the end of the ramp) do that again. Suddenly the trees stop and above the shed there's the *Nootka*'s light. I pause on the widening path, the *Nootka,* her light, my ship.

The King of Siam

Murray Logan

WHEN I WAS SIXTEEN YEARS OLD my father decided, a few
months before he left for good, that we should spend some time
together. I didn't know and likely didn't care that he would be
leaving. I don't think that he knew himself, so you can't really
read anything into his sudden decision to get to know me.

We were eating dinner, the three of us, early because Dad was
going to the track and the first race was at 6:30. I think my mother
had long stopped worrying about what my father did or when he
did it. He was like some very small-scale natural disturbance, a
sudden hailstorm, a clogged drain in the sink, something you dealt
with and then completely forgot. Nothing personal, nothing to get
excited about.

The idea seemed to come to him in mid-chew. His fork hovered in front of his face, empty, waiting to scoop up more of whatever it was we were eating, and then he sat back and placed the
fork on his plate. He finished chewing and, looking at a spot precisely between me and my mother, said, "Maybe I'll take the boy

with me tonight." He turned his head to my mother, to me, and returned to his meal. "That OK with you, Gary?" he asked, his mouth full again.

My turn to look at my mother, who showed nothing. "Sure," I said, "I guess so."

"Good," my father said, "good." He wiped his plate with a piece of bread and pushed back from the table. "We'd better get going, then. We don't want to miss the first race, do we?"

"No," I said, "we don't want to miss the parade to post."

My father laughed. "'We don't want to miss the parade to post,'" he repeated, mimicking me. "What do you know, the boy's been paying attention to his old man. The kid's learned a thing or two from his old man."

We took the bus. The Silver Limo, my dad called it. He'd sold our old Ford a while before and now made a big to-do about the benefits of being a bus-rider. I'd heard it all before and was embarrassed to have him say it again, especially since we all knew why he'd sold the car. There was no stopping him.

"Pick a man up, drop him right off, no fuss and no muss, eh Gary? Like the King of Fucking Siam and his Number One Son. Can't be beat."

"Right," I said. "Number One," I said. The bus had started out mostly empty but now as it rattled along Hastings Street it began to fill. Men got on, sometimes two or three together, but more often one at a time. Chinese, White, mostly older but some looking almost as young as me—you could tell that we were all headed to the same place. Almost all squinted at folded newspapers, making little notes in the margins with stubby pencils and Bic pens all scarred up with tooth marks.

"Where's ours?" I asked, nodding my head at the racing forms.

My dad laughed. "Hold your horses, Ace. All in good time." He leaned in to me, whispering. "These yokels all think they're on to something. You stick with your old man, he'll show you what's what." He looked up and down the aisle, not bothering to hide his contempt. "Yokels," he said again, louder. No one looked up.

We poured off the bus when it pulled up across from the PNE grounds. I'd been to the PNE before, of course, but only in the daytime and back when I was a kid. Now, trooping across the fairgrounds with this crowd of men, joining streams that came from other directions, all headed towards the gates of Ex Park (as my father called it; I saw now, in concrete letters above the turnstiles, that we were entering Exhibition Park), I might have been in a totally different city.

A city where everyone moved just a little bit faster than you were used to. I'd noticed us picking up speed as we walked from the bus, the whole crowd surging forward like everyone in it knew he was just that much late for something. Now my Dad paid for us both to enter and we rushed with the rest of the men into the Ex.

Dad pulled up short in front of a little kiosk. "OK, *now* we buy the forms," he said. He laid a dollar bill down and the man in the kiosk handed him a racing form and another paper, this one printed on yellow newsprint. He also gave Dad a stubby little pencil, like the ones I'd seen on the bus. I didn't catch the price of the papers, but the pencil was three cents.

"Why not bring a pen from home?" I asked.

My father looked at the pencil, then at me as if I'd asked why the sky is blue and the dirt brown and not the other way around. "It has to be one of these," he said. "That's the way you do it. Come on."

We charged off again. We passed through a big room, the size of a barn. Nothing but bare concrete floor and walls, one wall made up of a row of little booths, the betting wickets, each with a short line of bettors already waiting. Men clustered around scribbling in their forms or looking up at the TVs that hung from concrete pillars. One set of TVs showed the names and numbers of

119

the horses that would run in the first race, while another showed the empty track. My dad didn't even slow down but kept us rushing right through this room.

We went through a big set of glass doors to the outside, where I saw the track for the first time. I didn't see much of it, and I didn't see any horses, because we immediately went through another set of glass doors and down a flight of concrete steps. Even before the smell of stale beer hit me I could tell we were in a bar.

My father led me to an empty table and we sat down. The table, one of about twenty in the room, was round with a white Arborite surface. The chairs were metal, looked like they were meant to be stacked, and uncomfortable.

"Um, Dad," I said, hunched over the table and not looking around. "You know I'm only sixteen, right?"

I don't think he heard. He was twisted in his chair, facing the bar at the other end of the room. A couple of men my father's age or older leaned against it, talking. Each wore an open red vest over his white shirt and big belly. Neither of them looked at us.

"Yo!" my father called, holding an arm in the air. He waved his hand with its thumb tucked in, four fingers spread, and called again. "Yo, how about some service here?"

The men didn't appear to hear or see us, but one of them went behind the bar and started pouring beer. When he'd covered a tray with full glasses he came out from behind the bar, picked up the tray, and began going from table to table, setting glasses down whenever someone jerked a finger or nodded a head at him.

We were his last stop. He set two glasses down in front of my father and then waited, not really looking at me but not not looking either. His face and neck with its rolls of fat were shiny with sweat.

"It's OK," my father said, "he's with me."

This seemed to have no effect on the man, either good or bad. He stood there.

120

"He's my boy," my father said. "Old enough to have a couple with his old man, don't you think?"

The man stood impassive for a few more seconds, then shrugged and placed two glasses in front of me. My father handed him a two dollar bill and held his hand out, palm up, waiting for his change. The man just grunted at him, then turned and headed back to the bar. "Asshole," my father muttered, quietly. Then he called out, "Keep the change!"

The man stopped in his tracks, turned, and for a moment, a sign flicking on and then quickly off again, he smiled. I had the idiotic realization that his teeth were better than you would expect, a really nice looking smile in fact, and then he turned again and returned to the bar and his fellow waiter, who hadn't moved.

"Cheers," my father said, and tilted a glass at me. I picked up one of my glasses and tilted it back at him. "Um, cheers," I said. I took a sip and put the glass back down. I'd had beer before, of course, and might have liked it. This was different, though. Practically flat and with a strong soapy taste, as if the glasses hadn't been rinsed well enough. My father didn't notice. He drank half of the glass down in one long swallow, his jaw moving as though he were chewing the beer. He stopped, winked at me over the glass, and then finished it off. "Now that hits the spot," he said. He poured the dregs from the empty glass into his second beer and set the empty down near the edge of the table. I saw that the glasses had white lines painted on them, about a finger's width below the rim. That evening, as I watched my father drink beer after beer and always pour the last of the old into the new, the beer would rise above that white line but never overflow the rim. He did it with an ease and what I'd now have to call grace. It was the only time I saw my father be really good at something. "Drink up," he said, holding his fresh glass. "Drink up."

With two fresh beers in front of my father and me still trying to sip at my soapy first one, we opened the racing forms. My father

121

showed me how each race was handicapped on its own page, with all the information for all the horses laid out there. Columns and columns of tiny numbers that gave the horse's racing history, how old it was, how much weight it carried, whether it ran better on a firm or muddy course. All of this and more, much more, laid out in tiny print for us to use in forecasting the race.

Though I soon saw that my father had a simple system. He'd scan the page of intricate detail, mumbling to himself, making scratches with his red pencil. Then, when he'd gone through the ritual, he'd see what the experts had recommended. The gold paper had their picks, along with comments like: "First start . . . bred for speed . . . merits close look" or "Long odds in season debut, was wide into first turn, recovered to beat half the field . . . rates upset chance." Which sounded a lot like the horoscopes my mother swore by and my father scorned. But the horse horoscope also had someone named "Old Sam" and someone named "Mister Gold" who picked the three winners for each race. My father's system was to see where these two agreed and then bet that horse. Even as a sixteen year-old I could see that as a system it wasn't much.

I went with my father to bet the first race. You couldn't make the bets from where we were drinking the beer, you couldn't even see the track. We climbed up the stairs and went through the two sets of doors back into the big concrete room. My father lined up to bet two dollars on the number five horse, Billy Boy, to win. We collected the slip of paper with the bet recorded on it, then returned to our seats in the bar. We watched the race on a black and white TV that hung from the ceiling. My father didn't seem to feel one way or the other when Billy Boy came in fifth or sixth.

"I'm going to walk around," I told my father. "Go look at the horses."

"Sure, sure. Check out the talent for me, that's the secret." The waiter set two more beer in front of my father. When he reached out to pick a dollar bill off the table, my father's hand darted out and grabbed him by the wrist. "Hey, I pay for a full glass of beer." The beer in one of the glasses didn't quite come up to the white line, and my father let go of the waiter and tapped at it with his index finger. The waiter, the one with the surprising smile, grunted and poured a splash of beer from the last glass on his tray. "That's more like it," my father said. The waiter just blinked at my father and drank off the rest of the glass in one huge gulp. He scooped up my father's dollar and headed back to the bar. I left.

I walked down through the clots of people to the rail at the edge of the track. The ground the horses ran on was dirt, loose dirt like potting soil, and you could see the marks from all the hooves. One horse and its jockey were standing all alone at a little podium near the finish line. A man walked up, flashed a picture, and walked away. The jockey jumped down from the horse and he too walked away while someone else led the horse off to wherever it was supposed to go. The jockey was even smaller than you'd expect, smaller than any adult I'd ever seen. The only thing I really noticed about him were his boots. I guess they were supposed to look good at a distance, across the track on the back of a horse. Up close they looked like doll's boots, cheap ones with broken-down ankles, made of shiny black vinyl. Something that only looks good from far away.

I hung around until the next race, about twenty-five minutes. First I just sort of wandered around, looking at people, trying to hear what they were talking about. Mostly it was just like on the bus coming here, as if bus after bus exactly like ours had filled the place up. I half expected to see two or three sets of me and my dad wandering round.

Finally the horses came out, each one walking beside some kind of trainer horse, maybe a friend if horses have friends. So these pairs of horses walked around the track, giving everyone a look at them. Then the real racehorses all lined up, down at the start, loaded into a big green metal gate of some kind. A bell rang and all the horses came charging along, rounded the corner and mostly disappeared, almost out of sight. You could still see them, but it was hard to tell which was which and they were so far away that almost no one cared, anyway. But then they came charging around the far corner, down by where they'd started from, and people started to get interested again. The horses thundered down the straightaway and that was that, the race was over. Then I got to see the winning horse and jockey have their picture taken, and the jockey walk away in his little doll's boots, the same as before. I went back to the bar.

My dad had more beer in front of him, of course. He also had his arm around a woman who was now sitting at our table. I shouldn't have been too surprised at that but I was. Even with all the things that had happened in our lives, this wasn't something I thought I'd see my father do. I didn't show it though, just walked over and sat down.

My father leaned close and winked at me. "Gary, I want you to meet a friend of mine. This is Shirley." He winked again.

"Pleased," Shirley said and held out her hand. She was my mother's age, or close enough, with badly permed hair and too much make-up. She was smoking a cigarette and when she left it in the ashtray to shake my hand I could see the thick grease smudge from her lipstick on its butt, red on white. I stared at her. I think I was hoping she was some kind of blonde bombshell, this woman with my father's arm around her, some stunner against whom my father had no chance. But she wasn't, she wasn't at all. I suppose some kind of loyalty to my mother tinted my view but, as I watched my father nuzzle at her ear, which she either ignored or somehow failed to notice, I could not imagine what he was thinking.

"Pleased," she said again. I shook her hand and she smiled at me. She had a smear of lipstick on one of her front teeth and I could see that she was already very drunk. She was drinking beer out of a wine glass. I watched as she finished the small glass and then, with the same practised grace I'd seen in my father, refilled it from one of the regular glasses. She sipped from the wine glass and caught me staring at her. "It's more ladylike," she said, holding the glass by its stem in front of her face. The smear of lipstick was still there.

"Uh huh," I said, not sure what she wanted from me.

"Some people think it's stupid. Some people don't think it's ladylike, they think it's . . . stupid." She took a tiny, elegant drink and waited.

For once in my life I knew what to do. "You can't worry about what people think," I said. She nodded, still waiting. "The hell with them," I said, "I don't think it's stupid. I think it's . . . nice." And it might have been a lie as I said it, but it became the truth the moment it left my lips.

She smiled and put down the glass. "You'll do," she said. She leaned over and kissed me on the cheek. "You'll do."

More beer arrived. I managed to finish my first glass and pour its dregs into my second. Neither my father nor Shirley noticed. Shirley had started calling my father, whose name was William, Wayne. That was the only notice she seemed to take of him, except to occasionally pull his fingers away from groping at her breast. So the three of us sat there, me sipping at my beer, Shirley holding her wine glass and seeming to notice nothing, and my father, hunched over almost sideways, pawing at Shirley's breast. I watched him stick his tongue out and poke it in her ear, not just nibble at the lobe the way he had been, but stick his tongue into the hole of her ear. I felt sick.

"Dad," I said. "Dad, do you remember when I was a kid and we'd go on picnics, you, me, and Mom? Dad?" He took no notice of me. His hand was fully under Shirley's blouse now, cupped over her breast. His fingers didn't move, or not much, but just lay there, clamped to her breast. At least he was no longer at her ear but was once again sipping a beer, staring off into space. I looked up at the TV that was showing a section of the empty track.

"We'd pack up a blanket and dishes and plates and pack them all into a box." I could see the box now, making it wood, an old mandarin orange crate. Was that big enough? I made it big enough, if you knew how to pack everything just right, the way we did. I imagined a river. "And we'd drive out into the country, along an old side road, and stop by a little stream? We'd always go to the same spot, our spot by the river?" I still stared up at the TV, watching the empty track. "And it was just the three of us, you and Mom and me? Going to our secret place on the river? Do you remember that, Dad? Do you remember that?" Because I almost could. I could almost see it, see this happy family with their picnic and their little stream flowing by. More than anything I needed that little stream to be real, to be a happy memory.

"Sure," my dad said, though he couldn't have really heard all the crap I was making up, "sure, by the river."

"I'll be outside," I said. I went out and walked through the bleachers and right down to the edge of the track. I leaned against the railing and watched the horses come out and line up and all the rest of it. I was right by the finish line and this time I noticed the jockeys whipping the horses as they thundered down to the finish. Slashing at their backs and sides with little whips, as if the horses weren't already running just as fast as they possibly could. I didn't know what to watch after that, or where to go. When the winning jockey walked away after having his picture taken, I wanted to run after him and push him down. I wanted to grab his whip and hit him with it, ask him how he felt, how he liked it now. But I didn't. I let him walk away because I knew there was nothing I could do to help the horses. And I think I was afraid that what I was feeling was stupid, little kid worries, and that by even having those feelings I was failing at something larger, some test of adulthood. After quite a while standing there, watching a race go by, then looking out on the empty track, then watching another race, I went back to the bar.

My dad was sitting by himself, slumped in on himself in his chair. As I sat down the waiter came by and picked up the two beer, one full and one half gone, that were in front of my dad. He picked them up in one hand, a finger inside each glass pinning it to his thumb. He didn't seem to care that his fingers went into the beer, or that he spilled beer across our table. "He's cut off," the waiter said to me. "Time to take Daddy home." He laughed at that, pleased with himself. "Time to take Daddy home." He turned and walked back to the bar. I watched him pour the beer out and place the empty glasses upside down in the glass washer.

I shook my father, grabbing him by his shoulder and rattling him hard. "Come on, Dad, we have to go." You hear people talking to drunks and they always use this particular voice. It's a voice I hate, the same voice you hear when you're a little kid and being told something completely obvious by an adult. But it's a voice that works and I used it now. "Come on, Dad, we're going." I stood up and tried to heave him to his feet, grabbing under his arms and pulling.

"Where's Shirley?" he said, half rising before sinking back into his chair. "Where Shirley?" His voice was that mixture of belligerent and contrite, a drunk's voice, a voice of his I knew well. Only this time, rather than playing against my mother's quiet insistence it was playing against mine.

"She's gone, Dad. I don't know. She's gone. Come *on*, Dad, we have to go." I got right behind him and really put my back into it. He finally realized what was happening and, together, we got him to his feet.

"Shirley's gone?" he asked me, looking around as if he might find her hiding in one of the corners.

"Yes, Dad, Shirley's gone. Jesus."

He nodded several times as if working it all out in his mind. Then he took one of those detours that maybe you need twenty beer to follow. "I'm no good, Gary. I'm no damn good at all. You and your mother, you and your mother—"

127

Jesus, he's going to start crying, I thought. "Come on, Dad, let's go." I put my arm around his shoulder and half carried, half dragged him out of the bar. Once up the stairs and through the doors he seemed to come around a little bit and we made it through the betting room and back outside without a problem. Back under the concrete letters that welcomed us to Ex Park. He was moving fine, head down and walking quickly, when he stopped suddenly in the middle of the parking lot.

"Wait," he said. "You wait." He lurched off between two parked cars, half disappearing into the shadows. I turned away, looking to see if anyone else was in the deserted parking lot, waiting for the familiar noises to begin. After a couple of false starts, like the moans of someone in deep pain, my father was violently and noisily sick. I heard a wave of his vomit splash against the pavement, him gasp raggedly for breath, then another wave. He half retched a third time, a deep writhing sound from down low, but nothing came. I heard him spit, hawk up phlegm and God knows what from the back of his throat, and spit again. Still I didn't turn around, just kept staring out at all the cars all neatly lined up in their rows.

"OK," my father said, "let's go." He put his arm around my shoulder and half leaning on me led us off to the bus-stop.

The bus shelter on Hastings was empty, since the races were still on. My father hadn't even lasted until the last race. I sat him down on the bench and, in the light from the street, saw that his shoes and pantlegs were splashed with vomit. He sat with his elbows on his knees, head hanging down, spitting dryly between his feet. The King of Siam. I searched my pockets and found change enough for both of us to get home, then went and leaned against a post, looking down the street for the bus.

We waited almost forty minutes, me against my post, my dad either spitting between his shoes or rocked back, eyes closed, half asleep against the back of the shelter. Only one person came by the whole time, an older woman with a heavy shopping bag, and she made one of those "tchkk" noises with her teeth when she saw my dad. She was careful to give him lots of room as she passed, moving right over to the edge of the sidewalk. She shook her head at me as if to say, "Isn't it a shame," and I rolled my eyes at her in agreement. Like it was the two of us who were family and this guy, this drunk on the bench, was some pathetic stranger. Then she was gone and I had something else to feel lousy about.

By the time the bus came my father was out cold, his head resting on his chest. I yelled at the driver to hold on and shook the hell out of my dad. He opened his eyes, looked square at me and said, deadly serious and completely incomprehensible as only a stone drunk can be, "One monkey doesn't make a circus, Gary. You remember that." He closed his eyes.

"Jesus, Dad, wake up." I was almost hysterical with frustration. I grabbed his arm and as violently as I could yanked him to his feet. Once up he stayed up, rocking back and forth, and I put his arm around my shoulder and with him leaning on me walked him to the bus.

The bus driver was watching all this through the windows of the closed door. I got Dad to the curb but the driver didn't open the door right away. He stared at us for a few more seconds and then something must have made up his mind for him because, finally, the door wheezed open. I wrestled my dad up the stairs into the empty bus.

The driver said nothing as I half dragged, half carried my father in. Once I had him stuffed into a seat, face smeared against the window, eyes closed, I returned to the driver. I counted out the change, dropping coins from my right hand into the palm of my left, eyes down, hoping that if I could just move ahead from minute to minute, eventually the night would be over.

I dropped the coins in the chute. I really looked at the driver for the first time. He was a big guy, his chest and arms tight in the blue driver's jacket. He probably thought himself tough, or near-tough, because he had one of those biker's moustaches that dropped down almost to his chin. He sat leaning forward, forearms resting on the big flat steering wheel, head turned to look at me. His eyes flicked over my father and back at me.

"Tough night," he said, a little smile on his face.

I think now he meant it to be friendly. I think probably he looked at this sixteen-year-old kid and at his father stinking of puke and stale beer and he tried to make the kid's night maybe one percent better. Looking back I like to think that was what he was doing.

But I lost my mind. My dad, me, my mom, the crappy little picnic river that never existed, the jockeys in their crummy little boots whipping the horses, everything seemed to explode out of me at the same time.

"Fuck you!" I screamed at the bus driver. "Fuck you, you don't know anything. You don't know anything about us!" My voice was a high screech in my ears, the voice of a child, and I didn't care. I tried to say something more to the driver, something important, something adult, but nothing could get past my shuddering sobs. Tears and snot ran down my face and I wiped them with my sleeve. I took a long jerky breath, then another. I was shaking so hard I thought I might fall down. And the driver watched all of this without doing or saying a thing, maybe afraid to interrupt me, maybe something else. I was still crying, but now I'd pulled myself back into some kind of self-control. I rubbed at my eyes again, staring hard. "That's my dad," I said. "That's my dad."

The driver shrugged, then turned and put the bus in motion. I went and sat next to my father who woke up enough to lean against me and then fall back asleep, his head on my shoulder. We stayed like that all the way home.

That's my last real memory of my father. It's something I cling to, for whatever reason.

After Hours, After Years

Liza Potvin

IT IS NOW MANY YEARS since I have seen him. Twenty, to be
precise, for this summer marks the anniversary of our encounter
in France. Only tonight when this West Coast evening dampness
twists my unclothed flesh like an unwelcome blanket, when my
tongue is thick and parched with memory, does his image return
to haunt me. A trick of the moonlight spilling through the venetians
and patterning the corridor, stark contrasts, ribbed shapes of blindness and light.

Not that I desire to be with him again, except in the abstract:
the idealized lover who inspires my daily life, defines by com-
parison the piquancy of the remembered past, reminds me I am
still one unto myself, unpossessed. No, I am happy, content, married to a man whose steady gaze keeps me peacefully anchored,
whose rhythms blend harmoniously with mine.

And yet. His name slips out of me unbidden, murmured in half-
sleep. Aziz. The syllables resonate with the nostalgia of a sensual
summer, the soft hum of cicadas along the back streets of Nice,

the city of escape. A Mediterranean summer, the Marché aux Fleurs overflowing with jonquils, violets, and the ripe birds of paradise, obscene in their naked beauty. It is as if I am still lured by Aziz down unknown alleyways, clasping his warm hand. In the old city, Aziz and I are enticed by the rich scents of onion pizzas sold by street vendors, alerted by the multicoloured laundry flapping in the sea breeze. Wandering along the Promenade des Anglais in the late afternoon, we marvel at the living carpet of oil-slicked bodies, sun-worshippers who pass the day "on the rocks." (How little I knew then of politics, Aziz. To think that each of those flagstone steps along the promenade was constructed by exhausted French peasants, at the bidding of the rich English residents who were annoyed at the failure of their orange crops that season. Idle Victorian aristocrats, grown bitter without the luxury of citrus, determined to make everyone else equally acrimonious.) The four-mile long boulevard interrupted by islands of palms and carnations that obstruct our passage and bring us to breathtaking halts in speech. One day we visit the wealthy villa that we sight from the quai, now the Musée Masséna, where we laugh for an hour at the ridiculous representation of Napoleon as a Roman Caesar. From here, the eastern part of the boulevard becomes the Quai des États-Unis, where the best restaurants jut their culinary chins out at us.

Tonight in the Cowichan Valley, I can hear cicadas again, in the deep of summer. Tonight I am spiraled backwards into our time together, the solemn wandering of backstreet pensions where matronly faces emerge from obscure windows and leer at the two of us, but deign to address only me: "Mais lui, il n'est pas français." The implication in those narrow-set eyes, nostrils flaring in condescension, that I am a whore of the lowest sort. Answered by angry sparks in the eyes of Aziz, his silence more ominous than any reproach, as yet one more door is closed to us. Even when we decide to gamble our precious funds and offer a tip, a bribe, the reply comes back the same: "Pas de chambres. C'est la saison touristique." And finally, we repose on a park bench, where rich women walk their manicured poodles, and it becomes clear that I shall have to rent a room on my own, sneak him in after dark. The thief of my dreams. Hours of waiting for him to appear, sadness and liquor on his breath, to finally wrap his warm skin around mine, to whisper between the sheets. Conspirators, giggling like children in the dark. Afterwards, I creep down the hallway to the bathroom, a towel draped sarong-like around my hips, his shirt flung loosely over my goosefleshed arms, sleeves flapping like stunted wings. The warmth of my satisfied skin, the chill of the bare tiles. And the Mistral, far off in the night, the sâcré vent that the French love to blame for all their ills, howling beyond the massive slab stone walls which shield us by dark. Thinking, I am tasting the sands of Africa, as the grit scrapes my teeth in the morning.

At first they said it was because of his name. Un étranger. The wicked ironies of names: mine French, but Canadian, diluted over two centuries. I am from far away, alienated. His is Algerian, from a country worthy of French occupation but never French recognition. Three generations his family has laboured for them here in France, three generations of sweat, the same sweat I taste on his skin each night as the cobalt sky closes over the red and pink wounds of the sun. Un étranger: even to me, never having comprehended until too late the depth of his passion. Or maybe pride.

To each other we are strangers in the flesh only briefly. I begin my journey across the ocean towards his body in complete innocence. As a scholarship student in Toulon, I am fleeing the predictable grid of Canadian summer roads in favour of the paths I weave through the words of Rimbaud and Baudelaire. Aziz is a doctoral student in economics at the same university. Later, after we have touched one another finally, made indelible marks upon each other's skin, he discusses his theories and predictions with me as we lie on the beach, drinking a litre of dark Alsatian beer which has gone flat, and passing a cigarette back and forth between our fingers, then between our lips. He takes deeper drags from the cigarette than I do, so the cigarette is always overheated by the time he returns it to me. It is for pleasure that he studies, Aziz assures me (this is the summer we vow never to do anything but for the pleasure of it), since no one in France will ever hire, let alone take seriously, the predictions of an Arab economist. He turns away slowly as he says this, shielding his eyes, which narrow into oblong slits at the periphery, to encompass the line where horizon and sea meet. The depth of his brown eyes straining to absorb all that blue.

But at the beginning of this particular summer, before the colour blue threatened to engulf us entirely, he works as a cashier in the cafeteria where I take my morning meal, and we make small talk as I pay for my croissant and café au lait. This is how we meet. Hushed exchanges over the aromatic steam of coffee and freshly baked breads. I must have made my decision then. Watching him eat his breakfast, slowly and meticulously, with long and elegant fingers, obviously enjoying his food. A man totally absorbed in the present. (When did I invent that rule for myself? The one that allows me to determine whether or not to sleep with a man only after observing the way he eats. Men who consume in five minutes meals I have taken hours to prepare I dismiss easily. Men who wolf down and do not really taste their food, who are methodical or indiscriminate or indifferent in their appetites will never be good lovers. The ones who are overindulgent will also think too much of their own pleasures in bed. But watch out for the ones who offer to share morsels from their plate with you, or who feed you with their fingers, whose lips smack in appreciation! My litmus test: bedroom manners follow table manners; it has not failed me yet.)

Besides his work in the cafeteria, Aziz has other work that allows him to cross my path and occupy my thoughts. Having associated Aziz with melting butter and warm kitchen smells, this startles me initially. I note that he also drives the bus that has been hired by my professor to escort our class to a small local museum. He is engaged for other menial tasks. Later he explains to me that he has been unable to find full-time work over the summer, and combines several part-time jobs in order to save for his studies in the autumn. One day when I return from the beach where I have been suntanning and reading, Aziz is sitting languidly on the stoop outside the cafeteria following his afternoon shift. Words come easily to both of us at first, and then there is a long pause where we can only stare at one another awkwardly, then cast our eyes to the ground. Nervously, I excuse myself, saying I must shower off the salt from my skin and change for dinner. He says he is also heading for the showers, and sighs deeply. "Why don't we shower together?" I ask. (Where do these spontaneous outbursts originate?) He glances up from the steps quickly, as if to make sure I am not making fun of him. I am not sure myself if I am joking or not, until I read his eyes. Then suddenly we cannot leave there soon enough: Aziz towards the workers' residence and I towards the women's. We have agreed to meet in the shower in my complex. I cannot remove my clothes quickly enough, fumbling with buttons, shaking sand from my sandals and bathing suit. When we clasp each other under the shower, it is as if we have always known each other, as if soaping each other's flesh were a cherished act of familiarity. His hands cup me under the base of my spine as he swings me towards him and presses me against the wall, and suddenly we are children discovering a new rhythm, riding a teeter-totter, his weight and strength lifting me high into the air with a breathtaking suddenness before I am lowered back into clouds of steam. By sheer dint of will, my thighs pushing down, I tip my pelvis back and encounter his resistance with a thud that sends me back up, the lovely sensation of being propelled through air, suspended above the floor. When the ride is over, the ground seems too close, too slippery, and there is an explosion of stars below.

Other flashes: white suds on his brown skin. And after, in my room, his dark lashes tinged with what look at first glance to be tears, but I realize later are only water droplets. The laugh of his strong white teeth emerging from his full lips. It is the texture, the fullness of those lips, all that was never uttered, that haunts me now. The heat of summer, slick on our bellies. If cicadas could speak . . .

For weeks after this first encounter, I smuggle Aziz into my room after hours and we lie together on my cramped iron cot. My studies are deteriorating. In bed we read my books of poetry together, and my real French improves under his gentle instruction; he laughs at my mispronunciations of various slang words, and teaches me expressions that would make my professor blush. Afterwards we sleep on my balcony, where it is slightly cooler, a sheet soaked in the water from my basin draped over our bodies, or lie there smoking cigarettes and drinking cheap red wine when the heat is too overwhelming. One night, as I lie wilted and drifting into sleep, he looks at me and says in rapid-fire French, "So, what is this for you? Am I some kind of trophy for you? Tell me, do Arabs fuck the same as Canadians?" I am stunned by his anger, summoned from my sleep by the sharpness of such unjust accusations. And while I am still trying to formulate the words to calm him, he pulls me on top of him, burying his rage inside me. Slowly this fades until we make love with an undefined sadness. After we cease mouthing to dispel the melancholy, silence descends upon us, and by the morning all trace of his outburst has disappeared. Nothing is mentioned about it ever again, and after several days, I pretend to have forgotten it happened at all.

What thrills me most about being with Aziz is his indefinable sense of mystery, and his devotion to discretion. He refuses to touch me in public, will not even hold my hand. In fact, he barely acknowledges any relationship to me. Arab custom, he explains. Only vulgar people make crass displays in public. (Aziz, Aziz, why did you have to defer to custom, you who pride yourself on being a renegade? Why could you not have told me the real motives, your fears, how you wanted to feign invisibility, the way your body recoiled, immobile, under the scrutiny of the French? The same amber-toned body I know as warm and supple beneath the sheets.) I leave him my key under the pillow in the mornings as I slip out for classes, so that he can lock the door behind him. At the cafeteria for lunch, as I push my tray towards his cash register, he slides the key under my serviette so deftly that his movement is imperceptible to anyone but me. Returning my change, he presses the coins into my palm, and his fingers brush mine momentarily; in spite of the electricity that this sends through our skin, he manages to avoid eye contact. At first I feel hurt by what I perceive to be his coldness, or change of heart. Later I learn to delight in the contrast between his public nonchalance and his private fervor.

The summer proceeds deliciously, and I yawn in my classes from lack of sleep. I am blissfully unconscious of the rest of the world. My thighs and my neck bear small bruises, and my legs barely transport me from the classroom back to my evenings with him. After hours. The only hours of the day that matter to me anymore. Although I am afraid to admit it, I am falling in love. When I reveal my feelings to Aziz, he confesses that he feels the same. These declarations propel us onto a new level of passion, more unbearable than the first, and I am weak in the knees as I float back to the classroom after two hours of sleep, my belly alive and humming with his song. It does not seem possible that such love can end.

Five months prior to my arrival in France, I had planned a trip to Italy with my girlfriend Suzanne, and tomorrow she will be here to collect me. I think I will not be able to endure this interruption, as much as I want to spend time with Suzanne. When she arrives, I meet her at a café opposite the train station, and over coffee tell her I have fallen in love. At first she is delighted, asks

137

eagerly for details, but can barely mask her disgust when she sees a man with coffee skin saunter over to our table. Once she had told me that she saw nothing wrong with interracial relationships, but her face, seeing my joyful acknowledgment of Aziz, tells me otherwise. She greets him in a restrained manner and the evening proceeds awkwardly. Finally the three of us decide that Aziz will take the train to Nice to meet us the following week, and all three of us will have two weeks together, if he leaves his job early. That is when my hopes flare. That is when the trouble begins.

After a strained week in Toulon, Suzanne leaves on her own for Italy. I will not go there now.

Aziz arrives at the train station in Nice, stepping out into the humidity and looking almost like a bewildered boy until he sights my face in the crowd. Small thunderclouds gather slowly in the sky above him. A premonition of fear haunts me, but it is dispelled as soon as I feel his cheek against mine. It is true that we spend many happy hours in the Chagall museum in the hills of Cimiez above the city. And that we are gifted with an incomparable view of the Bay of Angels from the exquisite little gardens in the Franciscan museum where we visit the grave of Matisse. We feel rich because entrance to museums in Nice is free and our pocketbooks are growing thin. But we remain trapped inside our tiny room until midmorning, the heat already soaring. By then we will be certain that the corridor will be clear of the proprietor, who might detect the presence of Aziz. As we linger late into the night in the darkness of cheap bars, thick with smoke or the fumes from the marc imbibed by old men, some oppression steals in upon our joy. What seems at first to be a lighthearted affair becomes cumbersome with doubt and suspicion as the summer wears thinner on us.

One evening Aziz announces that we are going to visit some of his Arab friends in the outskirts of the city, insisting that he will go alone when I protest I am too tired after our day at the beach. In a darkened bistro, I am introduced to several men, then ignored for the remainder of the evening, as the passionate cadence of Arab voices surrounds me. No one looks at me directly; I feel invisible. When Aziz finally indicates his readiness to depart, he flings his arms around me and pulls me toward the exit in what at first I believe is a sudden outburst of effusiveness. I am startled at this unusual display. After emotional farewells to all his copains (why then the customary refusal to be publicly demonstrative with me?), Aziz is sullen and uncommunicative. I feel as if I am being carted home, booty from a conquered town. Whereas, I realize with shame, I think of him as my prize, the exotic treasure I smuggle into my room by night. When I confront him with my anger at being treated like a toy, he flares, clenches his fists by his side, and says nothing. But back in our bed, we are transported by the same waves repeating themselves, tides rolling across our flesh, ocean rhythms memorized by our senses from our daily pilgrimages to the sea. In spite of myself, I open to him like a sea lily, petal by petal. I marvel at the contrast between his dark limbs and my light skin as our bodies lie sleepily entwined.

In my dreams that night, I am falling, falling, yet I can neither reach the bottom nor swim up through endless layers of space to grasp the white net at the surface. When I break through the resisting net, I can still see nothing but darkness overhead. Struggling across vast distances, I cry out as I awaken, turn to Aziz for comfort. But his back is turned toward me, as sharply defined and unyielding in the moonlight as granite.

Tonight again the moonlight defines the meandering creek that borders the property my husband and I have purchased. There are diamonds sparkling sinuously in the dark creek water that conjure up my memory of Aziz, of how many times we used to sit by the water's edge at night. How we said good-bye no longer matters, for it was woven into our beginnings. I do remember how dignified he appeared as he turned to go, his strong face in profile, how he never hesitated nor looked back once, how swollen my flesh felt for weeks after we parted, how my thighs ached at the thought of him. It astounds me now that I have such clear memory pictures of that hazy summer, focused in spite of the obscuring heat, the cruelly brilliant glare of the sun. Neatly encased and labeled behind plastic in my photo album, the few photographs I have yield no mystery. The mental picture which I summon now, on this sultry summer evening, is unforgiving in its clarity and harshness: Aziz crouched over the glistening porcelain bidet, a parody of Rodin's Thinker, imitation bronze thighs and sinuous limbs, only the high, round moons of his buttocks caught white in the light spilling in from streetlamps. The degradation, the humiliation of that posture. He does not want to risk using the shared toilet in the hotel corridor, lest he be discovered. Aziz does not know that I am awake, nor that I observe him, and I take care that my body betrays no movement. I know that his feigned contemplation, his cautious silence, designed not to wake me, arises from his pride and another kind of beauty, one seldom praised in classical sculpture.

Now I can no longer look at Rodin without feeling my heart contract, without trembling with rage and love and a sadness so intense that it escapes articulation, gathering mutely at the back of my throat. Twenty years. Two full decades to reach this clarity. (My ignorance, my love.)

The air shimmers. It is scorchingly hot again tonight. Sleep is but one of the many unkept promises I made to myself earlier in the evening. I wander to the edge of our property, which slopes down toward a creek bed, and opens further out onto a pond. My feet make slurping noises as I glide across the grass; a low mist shrouds the pond like cotton wool. The water is prolific with insects that leap across its surface, leaving web-like patterns too dizzying to trace. My eyes close heavily, and I force them open. In the distance, cicadas sing a pulsating song so forlorn that I shiver and have to close my eyes again.

Dirty Shade of Blue

Jenny Fjellgaard

MAD DOG TRIED TO RUB THE SLEEP out of his eyes, succeeded only in making them feel like sixty-grit sandpaper. He sat up, swung his legs over the side of his single mattress, scratched what itched, and gave a head-to-heel bear shake. Then he reached into his duffel bag for a clean pair of shorts, found none, leaned down, grabbed his used ones off the floor, and turned them inside out. Damn it, he would have to do laundry tonight before he could hit the sack. Just what he needed after his fourteenth fifteen-hour day.

He could tell by the air in the cardboard bunkhouse that she was a cold bitch out there this morning. The red straps alone wouldn't cut it. Mad Dog glanced across the room at his woollies, hung out to dry on a hook in the corner. They looked like he felt. In one generation they'd become the bad guys. He'd heard stories about the Vietnam Vets who expected to come back war heroes, then found out everyone hated them for doing their job. Humans or trees. No goddamned difference to some.

Even his wife would say, "The world is changing, Danny. You

can't keep operating in the past." He didn't need Jamie giving him the gears too. His dad, his uncles, his grandpa, everyone Danny knew had worked, or were working as loggers. He would be the final member of the Shepherd family though. Last time in from camp he'd ordered a computer for Tyler's birthday. He wasn't about to let his kids use their bodies for bushwhacking. They would have choices. Not that life in the bush was so bad. At least he wasn't sitting in some high-rise in Vancouver, or south of the border, making bad decisions about places he'd never even seen.

Danny 'Mad Dog' Shepherd rolled his shoulders and gave his neck a stretch from side to side. His shoulder joints were seizing up on him, and his elbows weren't doing much better. Too many years spent monkey wrenching and not enough cardio. Jamie told him he was entering heart attack territory, but he couldn't imagine paying money to go to a gym and exercise like she did. Just throw a few of those pipe wrenches around, try to put the track back on the loader with a crow bar, or knock out a rusty U-joint with a twenty pound sledge hammer, then see what you want to do after work, he told her.

He reached up, yanked his long johns off the hook and climbed into them, slipped the red straps on over top, and grabbed his cleanest gear-dope-stained T-shirt. Everything Mad Dog owned was covered in that thick, black grease. Even his hands. His hands never came clean, at least, what was left of them. He could read his life story in his mangled fingers. Lost most of one after his wedding ring got caught on a metal pin when he jumped out of the juicer. He hung by it until it broke off. The finger and the ring. Had the end of another one pinched off when he was working on the hydraulic cylinder. Needed a skin graft to close that sucker up. By his hands you'd think he was eighty, not forty-three.

Mad Dog splashed some cold water on his face, in a hopeless attempt to rejuvenate his tired body. He looked at his haggard reflection. Two weeks since his last shave. No point around these goons. Could use a haircut too, but whenever he got to town, he didn't seem to find the time to do anything, but take care of all the shit he didn't do because he was stuck out in the Earl's Creek boonies.

He could hear Mother Tucker's thunder snores echo through the walls from his room at the other end of the bunkhouse.

"Hey, Mother. Crummy leaves in twenty minutes," Mad Dog yelled down the hall.

"Eat shit."

"That's why they pay us the big bucks. If you don't want to eat shit, get out of the outhouse." Mad Dog looked back at the mirror with tired brown eyes. He pulled his Stanfield over his head, ignored his screaming shoulder joints, and left for the cookhouse. He barely had time to tie on the feed bag and fill his thermos before the crummy would take them out to Camp 24.

"Hey, Cookie. Where's the bacon this morning?" Mad Dog asked.

"You see bacon? If you see bacon, there's bacon. If you don't, there ain't."

"Move along, Dog. Never mess with the most important person in camp, or we're all screwed," Skinner said. Skinner was the straw boss. Figured that gave him the right to be head of the weekly poetry recital. Every Friday night there would be fifteen or twenty loggers sprawled around the bunkhouse, taking turns reading whatever they had written that week. Sometimes they'd improvise, most often at the expense of whoever made the biggest screw-up of the week. They didn't mind bustin' their asses at work. Kept them too busy to be lonely, but they needed the laughter in the evenings to keep from getting camp fever.

"Mad Dog, snap out of it. Crummy's warmed up and waiting," Skinner said.

"Where the hell's my rain gear?" Mother cut in.

"Whatcha need rain gear for? Looks more like snow," Skinner said.

"Where the hell you been? It's pissing down rain."

"The road's gonna be gumbo. Hope the trucks can make it up the grade, or I'll be out there all day in the soup, winching them up the adverse with the cat."

Skinner headed out to the shop truck. Mad Dog and the crew piled in the crummy. The fallers had left half an hour earlier in their own rig, then headed down the Skookumchuck Narrows in the Silver Side for a forty-five minute boat ride, and another fifteen minute crummy ride up the switchbacks.

Mad Dog had great respect for the fallers. His dad had been a faller, now they called him the Six Million Dollar Man, what with all the metal plates and screws that held his legs together. Even a metal plate in his head where one tree he fell barber-chaired and drove him into the salal. He couldn't hear much either, because saws never used to have mufflers, and he had white hands disease. There isn't an old faller alive who couldn't show you what years of vibrating chainsaws can do to a man's circulation, but then they were the lucky ones. Mad Dog couldn't even remember the number of loggers he'd seen airlifted, or carried out on a stretcher, more often than not in a body bag.

When the men got to the claim they piled out of the crummy and headed off to their machines. All morning it had hovered around freezing. The rain threatened to turn to snow. If the machinery wasn't warmed up for long enough metal would crack, and the oil would be thicker than tar. A mistake like that could cost a guy his machine. With metal fatigue the only thing it would be good for was melting down for scrap iron.

Mad Dog ran the hydraulic loader. He was the key man at the sort. Part of the bush hierarchy. Fallers were at the top of the heap, because their bodies took the biggest beating, and they had the greatest chance of being killed at work. At the sorting ground work stopped and started around Mad Dog. The tugboat operator followed his instructions to the letter. The trucks got loaded when he chose, and in the order he decided.

Mad Dog eyeballed the juicer and circled slowly, checked the oil, made sure the hydraulic levels were up, stuck a finger in the rad hole to feel for water, hoisted himself up into the old girl, turned the night switch on, and hit the key. He watched Tugboat Teddy walk down the dock and jump in the sidewinder. Teddy had her screaming like an alley cat in no time, then he untied the tug, and was off to tow in the first boom before the juicer even idled down.

Mad Dog checked a few hoses while the loader warmed up. All he needed was the Ministry of Environment breathing down his neck over an oil leak. They'd be stuck to him like shit to a blanket if one of his hoses blew this close to the water. Wasn't like in the old days when you could clear-cut a whole setting, and no one gave a damn if you replanted a single seedling. In some ways he missed the old days. Mostly just the money. He quit school after grade ten, and by the time he was sixteen he was pulling in more than he could spend. Not much incentive to go back to school after he earned enough money to buy a car and a motorcycle over one summer vacation spent bucking for his old man. Why sit still in a classroom to learn stuff you knew you'd never use, when you could stay outside, breathe clean air, and get paid for it? He refused to spend his days anywhere else, but in the woods with the bears, and eagles, where he could watch the salmon run upstream, or the newborn Bambies try out their legs for the first time. Who else gets to see the sun rise over the top of a snow-covered mountain peak?

After he pulled himself back into the loader, Mad Dog took off his hard hat, and wiped away the sweat that was already beading up on his hat band. He picked up the mike for his two-way radio. Most of the conversations he had were filled with static hum. Even when he phoned home to Jamie he had to use the two-way. No cellular service out here. It was like living in an isolation tank. Each man to his own machine or cut block. Couldn't interrupt when the other person talked. First guy to press the button on his mike got his say. The rest had to wait their turn. Aside from the music of the forest, the static-filled conversations on the radio and the roar of machinery were the only noises they heard. Jimmies were the worst. They were the meanest, loudest motors on the god-forsaken planet.

"Hey, Flare Butt. You're first truck. Get that wood buggy up here, pronto," Mad Dog said into his two-way.

"Can't you hear that Jimmy screaming behind you? He has a flat sack. He's out of the truck. Better take Mother first," Skinner said.

"Well, I got two loads already decked. Whenever you're ready, Mother," Mad Dog said.

It took Mad Dog twenty-five minutes to load each truck. He was good at his job. Smooth as a well-greased nipple. When he first started Skinner used to complain that he couldn't load his plate with mash potatoes. Now he could operate the grapple like it was an extension of his arm. He'd even pick dead salmon out of the salt chuck, and throw them into the tugboat, or at the truck drivers when they tried to cinch up their wrappers. Once he caught Flare Butt right across the ass with a coho, but then it was pretty hard to miss a target two ax handles wide. Flare was as round as he was tall. Mad Dog was looking forward to watching him try and pull the wheel off his truck. Wouldn't be able to tell which was the tire and which was the nut behind the wheel.

"Hey, Dog. You still on the radio?" Mother said.

"Go ahead."

"Wasn't that you painting that old tin can loader of yours blue yesterday?"

"Yah."

"Didn't know you had one of the three bears for a helper. Take a look over by the ridge. Bear's got a blue face."

"Little fucker only has three legs."

"Three legs and a blue face? You shittin' me?" Tugboat cut in.

"What else is he working on there?" Mother said.

"My damn oil can. He's chewing it to rat shit," Mad Dog said. "He'll be shitting blue all day."

"Those white-collared bastards don't know what they're missing. Not every day you get to see a shitty blue bear." Mother let out a loud roar into the mike, more amused with his joke than the rest of the crew. He was like a bear himself, about six foot four with the biggest mitts you could ever imagine. You'd swear they were bear paws, not hands.

Whenever Mother finished a cold brew, he would crush the life out of the can, like it was made of tin foil, then tell one of his stupid jokes, and bust-a-gut until tears rolled down his cheeks. He never got anyone else's humour though. Even Skinner's poetry didn't sink in, and you don't have to be a rocket scientist to understand his logger rhythms. You just have to clear your head, lean back, and enjoy the story. Trouble was, Mother never figured out the story. He would always interrupt with questions, then Skinner would forget the words and start swearing at him. Next thing you knew Skinner would fire Mother, and Mother would quit, but by morning the war would be forgotten. They learned to mend their fences fast as a matter of survival. Never knew when you'd need someone to watch your back.

It was easy to tell a new guy on the claim. He would be Bill, or Ralph, or Jason, something like that. That was before the christening. Sometimes it came about because of the job he did, like the Hooker, or what he did in his spare time, like Banjo. Flare Butt was the obvious one. His backside was like the flared butt of a fallen tree. The best ones, though, were the names people got when they did something that let you know they were green. Those names stuck for life. Like Omar the Sheik, who made the mistake of talking sweet to the bullcook, who happened to be the only woman in camp. If you can call something that hard-looking a woman. The next day someone had nailed a bright red sign half-way up a cedar that said, "For a good time call Omar. 1-800-two-hump."

By the time Mad Dog finished loading the last truck, the first ones were back to the sort for their next trip. The threat of snow had passed, but the West Coast rain continued to fall like only it can. The roads were slicker than snot on a doorhandle. Skinner said the donkey trail was getting so greasy they might have to call it a day.

They were always losing time because of the weather. Could be shut down for too much snow, or not enough snow, too much rain, or fire season. When they worked on side-hills the wind would bring them to a standstill, to say nothing of contract years, when the weather would finally cooperate, but they'd be out walking the picket line.

"Hey, Mother. Forgot to call in your miles," Mad Dog said. He lifted his finger off the receiver's button, but the only reply was static. "What's up with Mother? Hasn't called in his miles. Flare Butt, you heard from Mother?"

"Holy shit!"

"What is it, Flare?"

"It's Mother. Over the bank at four mile."

"What happened?"

"The fuckin' gumbo," Flare's voice came over the radio in a strangled cry.

"Can you see him?" Mad Dog said.

"Musta jackknifed."

"Can you see him?"

"I'm leavin' the truck. Call for help. There's no way . . . "

"Flare . . . Flare . . . Shit. Skinner, you on the radio?"

148

"On my way," Skinner said.

"I'm going down in the shop truck."

"I'll get the crew. Be right behind you."

Mad Dog didn't even bother to shut down the juicer. He ran for the shop truck and headed down to mile four. Damn it, Mother. Hang in there.

The next thing Mad Dog remembered was doing a sliding run down the mud bank to Mother's logging truck. The truck had flipped on its side, and the load had shifted forward, folding the bullboard over like a slab of bread with the cab as filling. He knew without even prying open the door that Mother didn't have a hope in hell of surviving. Mad Dog and Flare could only stand beside the truck and wait for the equipment they would need to cut open the metal coffin. This wasn't the first body he'd had to haul out of the bush. He didn't know how they managed to get the job done without coming apart.

Instead they shut-down, like the machinery they worked in, the machinery that hacked off fingers, arms, legs, and lives.

It was nightfall by the time they'd airlifted Mother's body out. The investigators would fill the camp tomorrow, conduct some interviews, then the crew would leave for home, to try and say good-bye to another friend.

"I'm phoning my wife on the radio. Anybody want me to give her a message to pass along to their family?" Mad Dog asked. No one answered.

"Jamie, it's me."

"Dan. Danny, is that you? There's a lot of static on this end. Finally remembered Tyler's birthday, did you?"

"When was Tyler's birthday?"

"The same day every year, November 21st."

"How old is he?"

"Danny Shepherd! He's thirteen, and Sandy is nine, and Evan is eight. You remember Evan don't you? Dark brown hair, puppy

149

dog eyes, just like his daddy. Speaking of puppies, we got Tyler a brindle boxer for his birthday. He's got the biggest feet and... Why are you phoning, Danny?"

"Mother's dead."

"When?"

"This morning."

"What happened?"

"Missed the corner."

"Sorry . . . I'm sorry."

"Yah. See you tomorrow."

Mad Dog watched the shuffling feet and shifting bodies from behind his sunglasses. By the look of the ragtag crew none of them owned suits, but they cleaned up real nice. A new shirt lying on the bed this morning. Right size. Dark blue, his favorite colour. Jamie knew him so well. Just in case, she said when she popped a wad of tissue in his chest pocket. The hard part was sitting still for the service. They weren't any good at immobility, especially indoors. It was like being back in kindergarten, except for the suspenders and shaven faces.

After the church service they headed to the cemetery. Mad Dog was glad for the room to stretch his legs, and he was sure the other guys were as well. They were more comfortable outdoors with nature playing accompaniment instead of the church organ. Mad Dog was the first to break the silence.

"I didn't remember that Mother's name was Arthur."

"I never knew it was Arthur. I only knew him as Mother."

"How many funerals this year?"

"Four or five, I think."

"The Gavin brothers died in February. Remember the one shot himself after he backed over his brother with the 980?"

"Then there was Carpenter, Reefer, and now Tucker."

"Did you say Perp? What about Perp?"

150

"No, Perp just lost a leg. Runaway log came right through the cab of his truck."

"At least he can still walk. Stormin' Norman's in a fuckin' chair."

"What happened to him?"

"Fallin' out near Gold River. Widow-maker. Saw wasn't even idling when the bloody snag broke loose. Caught him across the shoulder. Sent shock waves down his spinal cord."

"My cousin's in a chair too. Cessna crash-landed on a frozen lake around Prince George. He was on his way home from a camp up near Fort St. John. If it wasn't for the six foot snow cushion, they'd have all been toast."

"What was the name of that guy that disappeared up near Fort Nelson two weeks before his retirement? Thought maybe a grizzly or a black bear got him."

"Charlie something. Can't remember for sure. Hey, Skinner, when do we head back to camp?" Mad Dog asked.

"Beaver's gonna fly us in to Earl's Creek tomorrow morning. Be on the dock by four," Skinner said. "You ready to go back?"

"What the hell else am I gonna do?"

The Man With Clam Eyes

Audrey Thomas

I CAME TO THE SEA BECAUSE my heart was broken. I rented a cabin from an old professor who stammered when he talked. He wanted to go far away and look at something. In the cabin there is a table, a chair, a bed, a woodstove, an aladdin lamp. Outside there is a well, a privy, rocks, trees and the sea.

(The lapping of waves, the scream of gulls.)

I came to this house because my heart was broken. I brought wine in green bottles and meaty soup bones. I set an iron pot on the back of the stove to simmer. I lit the lamp. It was no longer summer and the wind grieved around the door. Spiders and mice disapproved of my arrival. I could hear them clucking their tongues in corners.

(The sound of the waves and the wind.)

This house is spotless, shipshape. Except for the spiders. Except for the mice in corners, behind the walls. There are no clues. I have brought with me wine in green bottles, an eiderdown quilt, my brand-new *Bartlett's Familiar Quotations.* On the inside of the front jacket it says, "Who said: 1. In wildness is the preservation of the world. 2. All hell broke loose. 3. You are the sunshine of my life."

I want to add another. I want to add two more. Who said, "There is no nice way of saying this?" Who said, "Let's not go over it again?"   The wind grieves around the door. I stuff the cracks with rags torn from the bottom of my skirt. I am sad. Shall I leave here then? Shall I go and lie outside his door calling whoo—whoo—whoo like the wind?

(The sound of the waves and the wind.)

I drink all of the wine in one green bottle. I am like a glove. Not so much shapeless as empty, waiting to be filled up. I set my lamp in the window, I sleep to the sound of the wind's grieving.

(Quiet breathing, the wind still there, but soft, then gradually fading out. The passage of time, then seagulls, and then waves.)

How can I have slept when my heart is broken? I dreamt of a banquet table under green trees. I was a child and ate ripe figs with my fingers. Now I open the door—

(West-coast birds, the towhee with its strange cry, and the waves.)

The sea below is rumpled and wrinkled and the sun is shining. I can see islands and then more islands, as though my island had spawned islands in the night. The sun is shining. I have never felt so lonely in my life. I go back in. I want to write a message and throw it out to sea. I rinse my wine bottle from last night and set it above the stove to dry. I sit at the small table thinking. My message must be clear and yet compelling, like a lamp lit in a window on a dark night. There is a blue bowl on the table and a rough spoon carved from some sweet-smelling wood. I eat porridge with raisins while I think. The soup simmers on the back of the stove. The seagulls outside are riding the wind and crying ME ME ME. If this were a fairy tale, there would be someone here to help me, give me a ring, a cloak, a magic word. I bang on the table in my frustration. A small drawer pops open.

(Sound of the wind the waves lapping.)

Portents and signs mean something, point to something, otherwise—too cruel. The only thing in the drawer is part of a manuscript, perhaps some secret hobby of the far-off professor. It is a story about a man on a train from Genoa to Rome. He has a gun in his pocket and is going to Rome to kill his wife. After the conductor comes through, he goes along to the lavatory, locks the door, takes out the gun, then stares at himself in the mirror. He is pleased to note that his eyes are clear and clam.   *Clam?* Pleased to note that his eyes are clear and clam?   I am not quick this morning. It takes me a while before I see what has happened. And then I laugh. How can I laugh when my heart is cracked like a dropped plate? But I laugh at the man on the train to Rome, staring at himself in the mirror—the man with clam eyes. I push aside the porridge and open my *Bartlett's Familiar Quotations.* I imagine Matthew Arnold—"The sea is clam tonight . . ." or Wordsworth—"It is a beauteous evening, clam and free . . ." I know what to say in my message . . .

The bottle is dry. I take the piece of paper and push it in. Then the cork, which I seal with wax from a yellow candle. I will wait just before dark.

(The waves, the lapping sea. The gulls, loud and then gradually fading out. Time passes.)

Men came by in a boat with a pirate flag. They were diving for sea urchins and when they saw me sitting on the rocks they gave me one. They tell me to crack it open and eat the inside, here, they will show me how. I cry No and No, I want to watch it for a while. They shrug and swim away.   All afternoon I watched it in pleasant idleness. I had corrected the typo of course—I am that sort of person—but the image of the man with clam eyes wouldn't leave me and I went down on the rocks to think. That's when I saw the divers with their pirate flag; that's when I was given the gift of the beautiful maroon sea urchin. The rocks were as grey and wrinkled as elephants, but warm, with enormous pores and pools licked out by the wind and the sea. The sea urchin is a dark maroon, like the lips of certain black men I have known. It moves constantly back/forth, back/forth with all its spines turning. I take it up to the cabin. I let it skate slowly back and forth across the table. I keep it wet with water from my bucket. The soup smells good. This morning I add carrots, onions, potatoes, bay leaves and thyme. How can I be hungry when my heart is broken? I cut bread with a long, sharp knife, holding the loaf against my breast. Before supper I put the urchin back into the sea.

(Sound of the wind and the waves.)

My bottle is ready and there is a moon. I have eaten soup and drunk wine and nibbled at my bread. I have read a lot of unfamiliar quotations. I have trimmed the wick and lit the lamp and set it in the window. The sea is still tonight and the moon has left a long trail of silver stretching almost to the rocks.

> (Night sounds. A screech owl. No wind, but the waves lapping.)

I go down to the sea as far as I can go. I hold the corked bottle in my right hand and fling it towards the stars. For a moment I think that a hand has reached up and caught it as it fell back towards the sea. I stand there. The moon and the stars light up my loneliness. How will I fall asleep when my heart is broken?

> (Waves, then fading out. The sound of the wild birds calling.)

I awoke with the first bird. I lay under my eiderdown and watched my breath in the cold room. I wondered if the birds could understand one another, if a chickadee could talk with a junco, for example. I wondered whether, given the change in seasons and birds, there was always the same first bird. I got up and lit the fire and put a kettle on for washing.

> (The iron stove is opened and wood lit. It catches, snaps and crackles. Water is poured into a large kettle.)

When I went outside to fling away the water, he was there, down on the rocks below me, half-man, half-fish. His green scales glittered like sequins in the winter sunlight. He raised his arm and beckoned to me.

> (Sound of the distant gulls.)

We have been swimming. The water is cold, cold, cold. Now I

sit on the rocks, combing out my hair. He tells me stories. My heart darts here and there like a frightened fish. The tracks of his fingers run silver along my leg. He told me that he is a drowned sailor, that he went overboard in a storm at sea. He speaks with a strong Spanish accent.

He has been with the traders who bought for a pittance the sea-otters' pelts which trimmed the robes of Chinese mandarins. A dozen glass beads would be bartered with the Indians for six of the finest skins.

With Cook he observed the transit of Venus in the cloudless skies of Tahiti.

With Drake he had sailed on "The Golden Hind" for the Pacific Coast. They landed in a bay off California. His fingers leave silver tracks on my bare legs. I like to hear him say it—Cal-ee fórn-ya. The Indians there were friendly. The men were naked but the women wore petticoats of bulrushes.

Oh how I like it when he does that.

He was blown around the Cape of Good Hope with Diaz. Only they called it the Cape of Storms. The King did not like the name and altered it.   Oh.   His cool tongue laps me. My breasts bloom in the moonlight. We dive—and rise out of the sea, gleaming. He decorates my hair with clamshells and stars, my body with sea-lettuce. I do not feel the cold. I laugh. He gives me a rope of giant kelp and I skip for him in the moonlight. He breaks open the shells of mussels and pulls out their sweet flesh with his long fingers. We tip the liquid into our throats; it tastes like tears.   He touches me with his explorer's hands.

(Waves, the sea—loud—louder. Fading out.)

I ask him to come with me, up to the professor's cabin. "It is impóss-ee-ble," he says. He asks me to go with him. "It is impóss-ee-ble," I say. "Not at all."

157

I cannot breathe in the water. I will drown. I have no helpful sisters. I do not know a witch.

(Sea, waves, grow louder, fade,
fading but not gone.)

He lifts me like a wave and carries me towards the water. I can feel the roll of the world. My legs dissolve at his touch and flow together. He shines like a green fish in the moonlight. "Is easy," he says, as my mouth fills up with tears. "Is nothing." The last portions of myself begin to shift and change.

I dive beneath the waves! He clasps me to him. We are going to swim to the edges of the world, he says, and I believe him.

I take one glance backwards and wave to the woman in the window. She has lit the lamp. She is eating soup and drinking wine. Her heart is broken. She is thinking about a man on a train who is going to kill his wife. The lamp lights up her loneliness. I wish her well.

Revisionism and Lesser Sorrows

D. M. Fraser

IN HIS NEW SOLITUDE, Dumbo Nelson has changed or perhaps, as I suspect, merely changed *back*. If he's no longer the man
we knew, or imagined we did, it may only be that he's become
once again, at last, the man he must have been before we knew
him. Who was it, anyway, who used to live behind that untrou-
bled, wide-open face that smiles so innocently in his family por-
traits and boyhood snapshots? I tell our friends that the new Dumbo
shouldn't be regarded or treated as a stranger just because he happens to be one at the moment; it's not as though for no apparent
reason he'd suddenly taken up surfing, or sadism, or Science of
Mind. After all, I remind the doubters, the old boy still drinks
beer, smokes the same brand of cigarettes, mangles the mother
tongue as fluently as ever. If now he chooses to spend all day
staring at picture books of Portuguese Baroque architecture,
scrutinizing glossy brochures for hotels he'll never stay in,
cruises he'll never sail on, so be it. It's *his* affair. He doesn't
seem unhappy. The imagination has its own ineluctable needs,

its own strategies to fulfill them. It would be premature to worry about Dumbo yet.

We amble aimlessly along the beach, this lovely afternoon, carefully not looking at the cheap postcard scenery all around us. The sand is thick with people doing what they've always been told people ought to do on such a day, in such a radiant city, in this age of displeasure. *So here we are in Paradise,* Dumbo says with manifest distaste. Brattish children are trying to fly kites, throwing pebbles at one another and at us, squatting in the muddy waves that loll like bored hookers against the shore. The sun is fierce, the air steamy, but Dumbo is wearing his invariable all-weather outfit: heavy cords tucked into rubber boots, plaid woollen shirt, ancient Harris Tweed jacket from the Sally Ann. His neo-Cowboy hat advertises a famously right-wing brewery in Colorado. I've remembered to bring along a flask of decent whiskey, and at frequent intervals we pause to partake of it; I observe that he's no more morose than he ever was, only a little quieter, somehow more concentrated— as if, after some transient paralysis, he were teaching himself to walk.

Meanwhile there's a quality to our silence that I haven't noticed before: an almost palpable wanting to speak that is also, simultaneously, a fear of speaking, of uttering something unutterable that could, if misinterpreted, estrange us forever. Of course that possibility has always hovered over our encounters like a helicopter in trouble, but today I hear no coughing of engines, no dying whir of rotors, just an absence of noise more alarming than any sound in itself. I can't help thinking of Louise, whom Dumbo and I both loved, and faithfully shared without distress, and honorably lost to the rhetoric of the times. I think of Louise in Hawaii, whither she has fled, as she bravely told us, to put herself together. I conceive of this as a labour of sublime futility, the building of a skyscraper out of scattered matchsticks; and I wonder, too, if Dumbo himself is thinking about Louise. But evidently he isn't. *We don't see enough of each other,* he says finally, and straight to me. And again, somewhat later: *Do you realize that we've never done this before? That in all these years, living here, we've never once until now gone for a goddamn walk on the goddamn beach?* Dumbo's voice is full of wonder, without a trace of regret. It's as though he'd discovered an unfamiliar flavour of ice cream, and was trying to decide whether he liked it.

At Charlotte's party, everyone feigns astonishment when I bring Dumbo. My God, Charlotte says to him, winking salaciously at me, I thought you were dead. And: *Hey old buddy you're looking great,* Charlotte's protégé says, passing him a beer. Dumbo clutches the bottle fervently, self-consciously, in both hands, lest it get away from him and crash to the floor. But the fact is that he does look great, sort of—weathered, wise, shaggy and inscrutable, a mountain man out of context. All he has to do is stand there, glowering mysteriously, nursing his thoughts like his beer; nobody really expects him to mingle, to make small talk, to dance, to seduce or be seduced. *I'm out of context here,* he whispers to me as we're standing at the buffet, and I answer absentmindedly, *You would be, anywhere.* He grins and squeezes my elbow, slopping my Tequila Sunrise. Some of the nastier guests are watching us eagerly, presuming an intimacy which may not exist. So *that's* what Nelson's been up to, I overhear, and I'm annoyed with myself for smiling, for that's precisely what Nelson has not been up to. We fill ourselves with plenty of Charlotte's smoked salmon, potato salad, chili and chicken livers; I switch to gin after the tequila runs dry; Dumbo finds himself in a game of strip Crazy Eights with Charlotte, her protégé, and a distinguished gay poet whose complaisant wife strokes my hand mechanically as we watch. Actually, she watches; I close my eyes and pretend to be absorbed in the music, which is *Das Lied von der Erde* rescored for synthesizer, electric jew's-harp and a scrambled tape of the Mormon

Tabernacle Choir, with a solo part for castrato. The beat is disco. Sometime toward birdsong, Dumbo rescues his costume and we leave the party, arm in arm, not in the manner of lovers or even drinking buddies, but like near-senile bachelor brothers each of whom believes that the other will fall down and die without the support of the other's frail grasp.

In the Chevy, Dumbo lets down the convertible top and we drive heedlessly through the rain, past block after block of faceless pink and beige stucco apartment complexes until we reach the one in which he has lately taken up residence. At the wheel of my car, he seems uncharacteristically shrunken, and the illusion is sustained when we're outside in the orange-lamplit parking lot, leaning against the fenders: for the first time in memory, we appear to be of equal height and weight. I don't know why this hallucination is important to me. He says, as one would address an ethical conundrum to a night-school Philosophy seminar, *You've never made love to me, have you? Would you like to come upstairs and try?* I'm not as startled as I probably should pretend to be. I've heard the same semantics applied to a great many desired and impossible things: cocaine, lottery tickets, video games, a job picking prickly pears in Penticton. I glance at him in a parody of acquiescence, saying inwardly, *Yup, I'll go upstairs and try anything, for the likes of you.* But he's out of the lot and lost in the lobby before I can open my heartless mouth.

In a secondhand store in my neighbourhood, Dumbo buys a hundred damaged back issues of *Road and Track*. He buys a purportedly Victorian pocket watch from which the hands are missing. He buys yet another Harris Tweed jacket even rattier than the first; it's too tight on him, too vast for me, but he wants it for patches. He buys, to appease me, a dogeared copy of *The Meaning of Birth and Death Revealed Through the Karma of Jesus,* by Reuben Esterhazy, or somebody, D.D. Afterwards, in the greasy spoon next door he says, whether to me or the waitress I can't determine, *We can't go on not meeting like this.* He orders the Salisbury steak, I the Denver omelette, though neither of us is remotely hungry. When the food arrives, he studies it scientifically for evidence of mushrooms, clams, and herpes, all of which he knows derive from the same spores, unleashed on a overly trusting public by word of mouth. The platters of applied grease grow cold in the interim. *Denver and Salisbury,* he says sadly, *how far apart can you get?*

A punk-like band is playing a free benefit concert in Memorial Park, competing with the Dreadnought League softball game and the soup-kitchen lineup at Mercy Mission. On the horizon there's a full moon crawling skyward, bland as a round of imported cheese. Dumbo is restless. *I need an anchor,* he mutters, not necessarily to me. *I need a rudder, a compass, a spinnacle and binnaker, bloody hell I need a sextant if nothing else.* What *I* need is a pair of ears in working order. It's the first time he's referred to Louise since she left us, or we left her, whichever happened in which blinking of an errant eyelash. Ah, you'll find something, I squeak to console him, meaning of course *someone,* that rich and all-accommodating mindless flesh, and furtively his embarrassed smirk meets mine and holds it; then he says, *No, no I won't, and that's all there is to it.* The band is lighting matches under a song which has to do with, among other triumphs of the will, vivisection, kiddie porn, nuclear waste and the sorrows of unplanned parenthood. Nobody is paying attention to the softball game. The chorus line in front of the Mission is shuffling inexorably toward a social planner's vision of supper. The sky shivers and darkens; that growl from the waterfront may be thunder or an industrial accident, the death of a friend or the birth of chemical warfare, hell on wheels or heaven in the small intestine.

Puppylike, I drag Dumbo the shortest route back to my shelter, where he's never stayed longer than the time it takes to rout me out of it. He doesn't say, *How can you live like this?* but when we close and bolt the door he has the answer, anyway. He stands at the window, presumably looking out, silently, blocking the pink light that wafts in from the industrial zone: a black oblong, featureless, unknowable. Things to say occur to me, float into mind and out of it like drugged fish. Platitudes, sentimentalities, bad lines from old movies half-watched on television, very late at night, after too much cheap whiskey, too many purposeless quarrels with indifferent people.... I'm not ready to say goodbye to Dumbo yet, but in this silence now there's a sour foretaste of goodbyes to come, cabbage simmering on a smoky stove.

Later we'll drink again, argue without conviction about anything at all, reconcile without forgiveness. Toward morning, if at least one of us is lucky, we'll fall asleep, curled up together on the floor, just as if we'd been doing it all our lives.

Certain of our friends undertake to rehabilitate him, having long ago given up on me. What Dumbo lacks, they announce, is a mission in life, a Goal, so to speak. They dream up all manner of busy things to occupy him: reading to the blind, for instance, grocery stealing for shutins, passing out incendiary leaflets in the street. He leaps into these activities, at first, with unbecoming alacrity. Is it possible that this is what he'd wanted all along, a meaningful life for chrissake? But the fit doesn't last. The blind ask him to read the right-wing tabloids, paperback romances, the Book of Numbers. The shutins send him out to score heroin and demerol or—worse—granola and quack vitamins at health food stores all the way across town. After an hour of earnest leafleting, he shows up at my door with a bloody nose, two black eyes and a cracked rib. To console him we drink my landlord's bourbon, listen to Golden Oldies on kiddie radio, ignore the magenta sun dying behind the cruise ships and idle freighters in the bay. Dumbo will not be rehabbed. That is self-evident.

After he goes, I realize that we haven't said goodbye.

Then it dawns on me, fleetingly, that Dumbo is still very dear to me, or newly dear, in a way I hadn't expected, hadn't thought about. I want to freeze all our incidents, all our instants, for future consumption, to have him on ice against the day I'm lonesome, or mad at the world, or simply re-disillusioned. I want the whole of life to consist of exactly our kind of occasion, unintended, un-repeatable, perfectly inexplicable to anyone but us. Absurdly I'd put my arms around Dumbo Nelson if he were here, and perhaps in a world of winter—he'd be glad enough to accept the token without resisting, without surprise or protest, holding his tongue until I let him go. *It won't work,* he'd say at last, matter-of-factly, and I'd have to swallow that, for the matter of fact it's always been. It never could have worked.

Meanwhile in the gathering night, I am free to remake history as I see fit.

Shiners

Caroline Adderson

LAURENCE IS WADING STIFF-LEGGED into the lake, plastic bucket in one hand, the other reassuring the top of his head. Their grandmother has got him to put on a little sailor cap. Blue trunks, Thad's of two years before, sag at the crotch. On his chest are raw pink marks, a tender mottling where scabs were peeled off too soon.

Sun-warmed shallows show minnows. Like the blades of small new knives, they are painfully silver, alluring. A cluster hovers over grey-green pebbles. The water is knee-deep to Thad, thigh-deep to Laurence.

Thad says, 'Give me the bucket.' Poised, he bends low, careful that his shadow does not cross the fishes and disperse them or, blocking light, unsilver them so they disappear. He is feeling for the best moment to strike. Then Laurence, sucking in his breath, causes Thad to start. His movement disturbs the water, sends out ripples that counter the waves and make a tiny liquid jarring. The minnows flick across the rocks, the yellow sand bottom of the lake, and away.

'Little shit,' Thad hisses.

'I didn't do anything!' says Laurence.

'You breathed!'

Laurence pulls the sailor cap over his eyes. He groans. Throwing down the pail, Thad leaves the water to lie on the sand. Laurence comes and stands over him. 'I didn't do anything. Tha-ad? Or are you just mad again because you failed?'

This question is without malice, Thad knows, but it's of little consolation. He opens one terrible eye and Laurence cowers. Even before Thad moves, Laurence begins running down the beach, arms flailing. This is why he runs so slowly, Thad thinks. Not because he has a plastic thing in his heart, but because his arms move faster than his legs and through so much air, so inefficiently. Thad lets him go a distance, then leaps, sprints, catches Laurence by the swimming trunks, yanks him to the ground, pushes his face in the sand, grinds it there. Laurence sits up spitting sand out of his mouth. There is a circle of red around one nostril.

'You big shit.' He tilts back his head and pinches his nose. He never cries.

Thad says nothing. He begins, though, chewing on his bottom lip, the way he does when he is sorry. When he has been unkind. He has failed at school, failed grade six because he watches too much television someone said. Probably the teacher. What he misses most are the Saturday morning cartoons.

Their grandmother calls from the cabin. Thad helps Laurence to his feet, replaces the cap and walks with his arm around his brother.

She is watching the boys, the little one scurrying like a distressed insect, Thad so big and hale. She doesn't much like children, yet these grandchildren keep coming around. Thad is okay; she has a soft spot for the bad ones who can never get it right. Laurence, sick in the heart from birth, is treated too much like a holy thing and she can't believe it hasn't gone to his head. The girls, though, are the worst with their plastic radios, flip-flop sandals and flowery beach towels, always hysterical over spiders.

She was never interested in children, yet her whole life has been kissing bloodied knees, reciting idiot rhymes, giving care. It's perfunctory second nature now. At thirteen she was plucked from school to mother her sisters. She remembers herself in bare feet and a hand-me-down cardigan, they were that poor. The three little girls playing with a feather boa that came off a relief train. At seventeen she was working as a domestic for an engineer and his wife. She used to bring their children around to Nathan's flat and leave them with a Ukrainian downstairs who could play the accordion. While she and Nathan made love on his sofa they heard through the floorboards the wheezing of Old World melodies and the accordion became for them, half in jest, the most erotic of instruments. She didn't worry about the children finking because one was retarded and the other she could pinch and slap into submission and, anyway, the engineer was in love and wouldn't say boo to her.

Then looking after her own child, living with her mother and sister, suffering their self-righteousness. Nathan was in the army stationed abroad, so she wore her mother's wedding ring. Dependence, constant petty bickering, it was the worst time for her and as a consequence she could never love her first child. Undernourished and colicky, he repelled her. Now almost fifty, he wrote her a letter telling of breakdowns and divorces, saying he is unable to feel loved in his relationships, asking once and for all what she had against him. She felt sorry for him and wrote back that he was her precious treasure, when in reality he is the personification of all her woes and frustrations. She had five more children by Nathan and now has eight grandchildren.

The cabin is just beyond the beach and a narrow spread of wild grass, sitting in the shadow of pines. Crossing the grass, both boys are watchful for snakes. They are hopeful snake-catchers. Sometimes Thad turns over the stones on the path for this purpose, exasperating their grandmother because he never replaces them. They talk of pythons and boa constrictors, anacondas, but will gladly settle for less.

Carlyle, their Labrador gone blind, lies in the doorway. Thad gives one of the ears, worn and tatty as an old flag, a sharp tug. Grunting, the dog swings its head frantically, staring out of silvering eyes.

'Are you teasing again?' She stands on the other side of the screen door, a thick-middled figure in a cotton dress, white braid hanging over her shoulder. There is a cragginess in her voice that could be anger, but is really age and fatigue.

'You saw me, didn't you!'

'Shhh.' She makes the sound of dry leaves on concrete, of light rain, to let him know she was not accusing. He is so touchy. She smiles. She still has her own teeth, scary teeth Laurence says, one broken off diagonally. Shaking her head, she opens the door, handing them their T-shirts as they file past.

Although the summer days draw out, long as a skein of bargain twine, light until eleven o'clock, the cabin, in the enclave of tall pines, the circle of continual scent and shadow, is always dark. There are electric lights but because they attract insects—great clumsy bat-winged moths, mosquitoes—their grandmother rarely uses them. Instead they have oil lamps; the boys like these better anyway.

Laurence and Thad sit opposite one another at the table. She sets before each of them an enamel dish of beans, a wiener sliced across the top. There is a story about these metal dishes, that they were given to their grandmother after their grandfather's stroke when she hurled her every piece of china against the side of the cabin. It is a story Laurence does not believe; Thad fancies she threw them at their grandfather and that is why he had a stroke.

Thad grimaces at the food. She laughs and feels Laurence's forehead, asks, 'Good day?'

'Good day!' says Laurence, full of beans.

When she goes for the lamp, Thad bends back his spoon and catapults a piece of wiener at his brother.

'We're going to get the eggs after supper,' she says, setting the lamp on the table. She touches a match to the wick. The flame springs and shadows slip into the room, flattening themselves around the walls.

'Do I have to go?' asks Thad. There is a girl Thad's age at the farm where they buy eggs. She wears her hair cropped and a halter top through which he can detect two soft cones of flesh. Last week she called him a lunkhead. 'I won't go.'

After supper they step behind the Chinese screen that separates their sleeping area from the kitchen and pull jeans over their now-dry swimming trunks. Their grandmother is in the bedroom setting up the tray for their grandfather. This visit the boys have seldom looked in on their grandfather. Not a pretty sight like he used to be, their grandmother says. The boys go out and sit on the beach and wait for her.

'What are you thinking about?' asks Laurence.

'Rocky and Bullwinkle.' He traces a snaky mark in the sand with his foot, then points over the water. 'Look. Do you see it?'

'What?'

'There. A canoe.'

Laurence stands and, shading his eyes, studies the imaginary line where water wets sky.

'Are you blind?' says Thad.

'There isn't any canoe!' Laurence cries.

She feeds him less than gently, spoon scraping across naked gums. When she met him he was lathing broom handles in a factory and his forearms and wrists were so large he could not close the cuffs on his shirt. That was 1935 and no other man has interested her since. Such a beautiful skull and hair she could grab in both hands

170

and still not catch half of. Even in old age, before his stroke, she never lost physical desire for him.

When his job closed and he went on relief she would give him her liquor rations and bring fruit and chocolate from the engineer's house. Then the war broke out and they were separated for two terrible years while she, knowing he would not be faithful, prayed that at least he would not marry overseas. He did return, but because he had run away from the army, they came up north just like fugitives and nearly starved the first winter, she pregnant again. Nathan began running fishing expeditions on the lake and they built two cabins. One day he had a vacationing police constable as a client.

The years Nathan spent in prison, she worked in a garment factory to support their three children. When he was released in 1950, they were finally able to marry. They spent their honeymoon night back in their cabin quarrelling through the tense climax of realized dreams. He hit her in the face, breaking her tooth. It did not dim her happiness; such struggle was part of love. She was always proud of his strong body and his force, his good looks.

She wipes the flaccid face with the bib, then feels around under the quilt, checking padded pants for moisture.

In the station wagon, Thad climbs over the seat to the very back and lies beside the spare tire among the clutter of egg trays and flower pots and old newspapers. Laurence sits in front with their grandmother.

'We're going to have a storm,' she says. 'Look at that sky.'

Thad presses his face against the glass and sees the thickening grey. The tree stands they pass are completely still. He almost expects to hear Laurence suck in his breath from the tension. When they pull into the farm, it appears deserted, the animals gone away to wait out the rain.

Their grandmother takes an egg tray from the back as the brothers clamber out of the car, slamming doors. She gives it to Thad and he and Laurence go to fetch the eggs while she rings at the house.

The egg shed is for washing and storing. It stinks of chicken dirt and mouldy feed. They enter, Laurence plugging his nose, and the girl is standing with her back to them, bending over the sink. She wears denim cut-offs and that halter-top, the frayed ties double-knotted against boys. Her sneakers and bare legs are muddied.

'Heggs please,' says Laurence, still plugging his nose.

She turns and looks at Laurence, her expression softly curious, and Thad realizes she knows something about them. She sees him.

'Lunkhead.'

He reddens, but cannot think of a suitable reply.

'If you want heggs, you can wash them yourself,' she tells Laurence, feigning contempt and holding out the brush. He grins. Last week she let him wash too.

Laurence talks to the girl as he cleans the eggs under the dribble of tap water. Thad stands behind with the tray and she loads.

'We almost caught these shiners today.' He hesitates. 'Thad almost caught them.'

'What's a shiner?'

'A small fish. A—'

'Punch in the eye,' says Thad.

She glances at him. She has blue eyes and in the left one, under the pupil, a spot of yellow. Seeing it, he immediately lowers his gaze to the bib of her halter top.

'Then I sneezed or something. Anyway, we didn't catch them after all.'

'Too bad.'

'Yeah. Thad got mad.'

'Lunkhead,' she says.

Thad reddens again. Then it occurs to him she just might know he has failed a grade. He drops the tray and shouts at Laurence.

'Why don't you shut up? Why don't you go straight to hell?' There is a long silence. He has never said go to hell in his life. It is something he heard on television.

The girl will not look at him. She pats Laurence on the head. 'It's okay. You two clean that up and I'll wash the eggs.'

At Thad's feet, the yolks are the same colour as that spot in her eye.

In no time they are walking silently up to the house, Thad biting hard into his lip. She puts the tray on the hood of the car and they go to sit on the steps. Their grandmother is standing in the parlour with the woman who owns the farm. She is a widow and the mother of the girl, Thad remembers. He can hear them now through the screen door, talking about Laurence.

'Born that way,' their grandmother says. 'This year he had an operation.'

'And now?'

'He's fine, thanks be to God. They put a rubber ball or garden hose or some such thing in his heart. Be right as rain soon. Now it's the elder boy we worry about. Thad was shaken up bad.'

'Because of his brother being sick?'

'You know how children blame themselves. Anyway, he had trouble at school and whatnot. Bad imaginings.'

The other woman clicks her tongue softly. 'He thought he was going to lose his brother.'

'Oh, the temper! I see it like this,' says their grandmother. 'Love on account of fear is a difficult thing to manage. It wells up and gets kind of desperate. Don't we know about that? Watching husbands go?'

On the step, Laurence promises a snake. 'But don't blame me!'

'For what?'

'If it steals an egg and swallows it whole!'

Driving back, all of them in the front seat, it begins to rain. Only one windshield wiper works so the brothers watch the road through blear and smear. Presently the horizon lights up in sheets, then fades, lights again, this time cut through by brilliant jags.

The worst thing about a storm is that they must stay inside. Laurence, used to long hours of solitude, hunches over the table reading a *Scamp* comic. Their grandmother washes dishes. Thad does not usually read, so he paces. Every time he passes Carlyle lying behind the telephone stand, the dog growls.

'Old shit,' says Thad and he slips into the bedroom and stands staring at his grandfather.

The old man sits in a wing-backed armchair beside the bed. A patchwork quilt is tucked around his legs, his obvious knees like the bulbs of those glass telephone wire insulators on the shelf above the sink. Though the body is aged, the face, perhaps from swelling, seems young and unlined. His eyes are a clear grey, milky hair a fringe around his glowing head. His mouth hangs slack and a line of spittle crosses his chin, darkens his breast. Laurence is there now standing next to Thad.

On the table by their grandfather is a bowl of mints, clear like ice. Thad crosses the room and takes a candy, unwraps and pops it in his mouth, sits on the bed. He throws one to Laurence who misses and must feel around for it under the bureau.

Thad cocks his ear toward their grandfather. 'What? Speak up! You want one too, Grandpa?' He grins at Laurence.

Laurence comes and takes a candy, stands there holding it, staring at the floor. Thad giggles.

'What?' asks Laurence, smiling. 'What's so funny?'

Soon they are both on the bed, holding their bellies, directing their laughter into the bedspread. Neither can identify the source of this mirth; it is just one of those moments between brothers. Then Laurence sits up and puts the wrapped candy in their grandfather's mouth. Immediately he begins sucking, an innocent look of surprise on his face like an infant not expecting the nipple. The tail of cellophane between his lips turns around and around.

174

'Do it again!' says Thad.

It is too funny, the way the old man puckers his lips like a fish, how he tongues a second candy, gentle greed. Even when he coughs, the wrappers tickling, the brothers are stifling each other's laughter with their clowning hands.

They hear the telephone ring and tear out of the room.

'Yes, they're fine,' says their grandmother. 'Here they are now. Here's Laurie.'

He grabs the receiver and begins babbling. 'Shiners! Don't you know what shiners are? Mom! They're minnows! You really didn't know?'

Thad takes the phone and she asks him how he is doing without a television. He says he has not even noticed.

After they hang up, their grandmother herds them into the kitchen for washing, then lets them pee from the door stoop. There is a bathroom but that is not as much fun. She takes an oil lamp and sets it on the table behind the Chinese screen so the boys can chat before going to sleep. She lays her hand across Laurence's forehead, then kisses them both. Coming through the wall so faintly is the sound of their grandfather coughing. They strip off their jeans and T-shirts and pile onto the bed, still in trunks.

'I want that side,' says Laurence, meaning the side next to the table so he'll be the one to put out the lamp.

'No way,' says Thad.

'Big shit,' says Laurence feebly.

Thad cuffs him on the head. 'Little shit.'

In the bedroom their grandfather coughs raggedly, persistently. They hear their grandmother's voice too, softly first, then rising to alarm.

Suddenly the overhead light is on. The boys have not seen electric light for almost two weeks and it pains and startles. She is standing over them, her hair loose and her dress half-unbuttoned.

175

They have never known her angry and this is fury. She shakes a clotted scrap of cellophane in Thad's face.

'He was choking!'

'Laurie did it!' Thad blurts, then takes his bottom lip between his teeth.

Laurence stares animal-faced.

'Did you?'

'Yes.'

Leaning over Thad, she grabs Laurence by the arm. She shakes him out wildly, as if his badness is dust.

'My man, big man,' she sighs, drawing his limp arm out of the sleeve, running her hands over the angles of his bones. She is naked herself, gnarly bare toes on the cold wood floor, breasts sloping to rest on the shelf of her belly. She leans into him, ear-to-ear, slides her hands under his buttocks and this way can lift him from chair to bed. The plastic undersheet crackles like fire as she lays him out long. He is staring loose-mouthed at the ceiling. She climbs into bed and lowers herself carefully on top of him, spreads her big thighs around the bracket of his jutting hips, rests her elbows by his shoulders and bends to kiss his face, his unresisting mouth. 'Big man.' There is no tuneful respiration of an accordion, just the rain outside rushing against the roof in wind-sent waves and the chimes that hang in the pine boughs clanging like cymbals.

The boys lie in shocked silence staring at the ceiling beams, the hillscape shadow of their profiles on the cabin wall. Somehow a moth has made its haphazard way into the cabin and it drives itself stupidly against the lamp. Thudding, thudding. In the bedroom, their grandmother is murmuring.

Laurence sits up and, clutching fearfully at his own legs, begins to cry. Not aloud, that is not his way, though neither is crying. He just sits there staring, his face twisted, tears and mucus flowing.

'I did a mean thing!'

'Shut up,' whispers Thad. He gnaws his lip.

'I did such a mean thing to Grandpa!'

'Shut up, please!'

Laurence, face in hands, falls into the pillows. Spasming grief, he clenches and unclenches his body. It seems like hours Thad must suffer Laurence's quivering, hear his cloggy, gasping breath until it finally rises to a snore twice the size of him. Then Thad is alone in the discordant night—wind chimes clashing, their grandmother murmuring, the moth's monotonous self-battering. He touches his finger to his lip and stares at it. He is bleeding.

Being Audited

George Bowering

"OH CHRIST, I'M BEING AUDITED!"

Yes, I heard that one more and more often. Then also

"Did you hear that Barrie's being audited?"

"They went after fishermen last year and painters the year before. This is the year for writers."

For years and years I just ignored or envied the stories of writers, many of them just hobbyists, as far as I was concerned, who were filing with the income tax people as Authors, and clapping on their berets to loll on beaches and in bistros on the Balearics on the proceeds.

"You should file as an Author."

To hell with that. I am serious. I am interested in writing, not a career, not a bank account. I dont know how to roll over a term deposit or how to get the butter on a croissant, anyway.

"You should get an accountant. Look at Dave; he bought his Volkswagen on his tax rebate."

For years I had thought the hell with it, I am a young writer, and some day I will be rich and famous. And I still wont wear a beret. Then the years went by. Some day I will be famous. You are already famous, said my friend the really famous writer. Then the years went by and I said the hell with it; some day I will be inescapable in the anthologies.

Sometime in those years I started filing my taxes on the long form, claiming a few hundred dollars for paper and stamps and so on, and there were no questions asked. You can claim a room for your writing office, someone said, or maybe I read it in a magazine I wasnt discounting as an expense. I was living in a small house, so I claimed a deduction of one-fifth of my rent.

Outside my room I could see the rain falling on the yellow leaves tamped into the gutters alongside the sidewalk. Some birds that didnt give a dropping for the south were competing with the filthy pigeons in the parking lot of the hamburger drive-in across the street. My daughter was born, and I really did like changing diapers, though I dont think I admitted this to my wife.

"You should talk to Garry," said my wife.

"Who," I asked with my usual wariness, "is Garry?"

"The tax consultant. I have told you this for three years in a row. You should talk to Garry. He saved thousands of dollars for Miriam. You should at least talk to him."

"Yeah, maybe," I said, bending my head over the second chapter of a novel I would later be afraid to offer to a publisher.

"You stupid bugger," added my wife.

We moved into a bigger house, and though there were a lot more than five rooms I kept claiming a fifth of the mortgage for a reduction, feeling all the while that I was bringing my country and its citizens to ruination because of it. I didnt know that all this while a friend of mine was discounting the costumes he did public poetry readings in. I just sat over my IBM Selectric, piling up the chapters of a novel I would never offer to a publisher because I could not stay interested enough to find out what was going to happen in the last chapters.

But writers ten years younger than I were going to see Garry and telling stories of the wonderment they felt as their rebates arrived in those windowed envelopes. You stupid bugger, said my wife every morning while I pushed some spoon-sized shredded grain into my mouth.

"All right," I said. "Next year for sure."

About three years later I made my way to Garry's townhouse just the other side of Chinatown. It was a funny street, tarpaper roofs for a while, then rows of alternative architecture. I mean something they call post-modernism here in Vancouver, and row-housing along the streets three blocks from the beach in Malaysia. Short birds were pecking at a dead body in the vacant lot across the street. Well, they were pecking at something hidden by the tall grass and old furniture parts. I was a little disappointed in myself, getting older and accepting the world in which personal rewards were as important as the desire to reshape the world's imagination. I also felt daunted, as I always have, whether I have to speak to a president or a waitress.

Garry was jolly, too big for his suit, and a chain-smoker. He smoked like a busy American, pushing the long butts into a niche in the huge ashtray, grabbing another cigarette out of the open package on the desk. He talked and talked and laughed, and set me totally at ease. His eyes went round and his brows shot up as he told me we could rewrite my tax returns for the past three or was it four years, and scoop up a rubble of dollars, all legally.

"Have you been writing off your library?" he asked, 4H pencil poised.

"I should save all my receipts for books?"

"Do you subscribe to magazines?"

"I subscribe to about forty magazines, from Australian critical journals to American baseball periodicals."

Baseball periodicals, I thought. Now I am conspiring. The pencil did its business.

"How big is your personal library?" asked Garry, jabbing a cigarette into its niche with energetic anticipation.

"About the same size as the library at McGill," I said, "but I have a better collection of contemporary poetry."

"Have you been claiming depreciation on your impressive library?"

"What? My books are getting more valuable as time goes by," I boasted.

"Ho ho. You have a lot to learn, my boy."

"I dont want to learn," I said.

"Quite right, sir. We are going to make you a tidy bundle. To comfort you on those nights when the muse has abandoned you for fairer but more fleeting climes."

He told me to bring all my records, my old tax returns, the measurement of my house and garage, and my wife the next time I came.

"You stupid bugger," said my wife, when the check arrived. "You should have done this years ago." She went right to the bank and started a term deposit.

So began my new life as a receipt-keeper. I began to understand why certain people, after we had all pitched in ten bucks to pay for our share of the meal, would pocket the cash and take care of the bill with their credit cards. Now I would sheepishly ask for a receipt from any fly-by-night paperback store, mumbling that my tax-man insisted on it. It became my habit to stuff receipts for anything into my fat wallet. I had to start carrying an Italian shoulderbag to relieve the weight on my ass pocket. I cant remember whether I wrote it off.

But all the while I told myself, I reminded myself, that I was doing all this to please my wife. I was still the pure youth who went into the writing game because my country needed it, because the young writers in the books I had read before I was a young writer, were sensitive people, romantic figures precisely because they were willing to forego the usual pleasures of the up-and-coming, to sit alone late on Saturday night, destroying their hopes for a long life with crushed cigarette packages and instant coffee rings on every exposed sheet of paper.

Meanwhile, year by year my wife studied all the financial sections of the newspapers, and the business magazines, and every brochure she could find in the racks at the banks and trust companies and credit unions that jostle one another for space along 41st Avenue. She started to invest her salary and mine in baffling plans with banky sounding names and baffling initials. Conniving with Garry, she tried to persuade me that it was fiscally clever to borrow even more money rather than paying off the debts you already had. The government was passing more and more rules as fast as they could, to cover up loopholes, but they were also pressed to keep the rules that favour investment in Canadian corporations; and banks and trust companies and credit unions are Canadian corporations.

My wife routinely took money from one account in one bank and deposited it in another account in the bank across the street, a few minutes before the banks closed for the weekend, shaving a little interest off both of them, she explained to me.

"What do I care about all that?" I said. "My only concern is to make a paragraph that will cause someone to gasp or sigh."

"You'll have to find time to do that later on the weekend," she replied. "Right now you have to come to Vancouver Savings and sign some papers."

I hardly have any time to write as it is, what with teaching and marking papers, and cooking, and weeding, and driving the kids to all those places kids have to go to keep up with their late twentieth century. And you cannot write off the orthodontist or piano teacher anyway.

But every spring I made my trudge to Garry's tropical bungalow, where he would show me photos from his place in Ireland, and hand him the envelopes filled with receipts. And sometime later I might hear the figure attached to the rebate I theoretically received from Ottawa. I have never actually seen or touched any of the money. My wife always has some kind of iron-clad reason why it has to be applied to some open wound in the latest term deposit or RRSP or demand loan or daily interest scam.

But all the while the big house around my tax write-off writing room was growing bigger and newer and less convenient. Architects and engineers, carpenters and plumbers and tilers stomped their boots through the rooms and whined their machines outside my nervous and delicate chamber of the lyric dream. I could never look through a casement window without noting that that casement window had not been there a week before. I wondered how the hell my muse was going to recognize the place when she made her next visit from the mount where she and her sisters never had to make renovations.

"Jeeze, I nearly flew right on by. When did you get the new paint job on the fence?"

"I think it's a new fence. This year's tax return."

"You needed a new fence? I've been wearing this same diaphanous gown since I helped Percy Shelley write *Prometheus Unbound*."

"Dont ask me about fences. Right now I am having trouble with a poem called *Allophanes*."

"Your usual hassle with structure?"

"Dont talk to me about structure."

"How much do you have invested in this new poem with the suspiciously Greek name?"

"Dont talk to me about investment."

"All right. I'll come and visit you in the wee hours. I have some rounds to make in Kitsilano anyway."

"Thanks."

"But do something about that casement window. John Keats at least took the glazier's name label off his. And as I remember, he wasnt anywhere near as healthy as you are."

When I was a young writer, and even when I was a fairly young writer, I used to be happy about the fact that I moved from apartment to apartment every year, and never stayed in the same city for longer than three years. That way I always knew what year it was. When I think back to the death of John F. Kennedy, I remember that I was living in Calgary, so I know that it happened between 1963 and 1966. I had my first McDonald's hamburger while I was living in Montreal, so I know that it was between 1968 and 1971. But I have been living in the same house, or rather at the same address for twelve years! So when someone asks me when some event occurred, I can only say that it might have been 1974 and it might have been 1980.

So I dont remember exactly what year it was that I heard that my byzantine tax returns were going to be audited. I can only tell you this: that it was the year they went after writers. And this: it was the year they took the walls off my house.

Let me explain—though I think that I should warn you: this will be a story involving the federal government's concern for human comfort, the international threat of soaring Arab oil prices, and the alacrity with which so-called private enterprise will jump in and make dollars out of joy or distress.

Sometime, a few years ago, while we were living in this house, or a facsimile of it, big ads began to appear in all the Canadian newspapers, urging patriotic Canadians to stuff their house walls with more insulation, to reduce our national dependency on the punitive and capricious pricing policies of OPEC. We would all pull together to make us snug, and cut our fuel bills. In temperate Vancouver we started to see those centrist billboards again. We have got used to seeing big ads for snow tires chugging through deep snow, as we zip by in our Japanese cars over rain-slick pavement. Pictures of a real "Canadian winter." Those of us who are writers and scholars or literature professors are familiar with the notion, as we are told by Ontario-Quebec litcrit that the Canadian sensibility is expressed in poems and novels about impending human defeat at the hands of frightful winter nature. Now we were exposed to thousands of portrayals of happy Canadians making garrisons of the homes against the hideous spirits of some northern Ontario arboreal deep-freeze.

So sincere was Ottawa's (read Toronto's) care for her parka-garbed children that the government was prepared to make semi-forgiveable loans to house-owners who would shove guck between their exterior walls and their interior ones, and under their roofs. Their favourite recommended substance was a fast-hardening foam called urea formaldehyde.

"I dont know," I said. "That sounds awful. It sounds poisonous. At least it sounds like a combination of piss and that stuff they kill and preserve laboratory animals with."

"Are you a famous scientist?" enquired my wife the financial wizard.

"You know very well that I am an insufficiently famous writer," I rejoined.

"Well, I am a locally famous investment analyst. And I have all the information at hand. UFFI is the most efficient and easiest-to-install insulation in the world. The government has access to the best of scientific research and advice. Oil prices will go up and up. The foam will be a most sensible investment."

Whenever I hear of some purchase being an "investment" I strain my neck, looking around for a snake-oil drummer.

"We live in Vancouver," I said. "This is where people from the prairies move to get away from Northrop Frye winters. The climate hasnt changed much in the past sixty-five years since the house was built, or even in the six or twelve years since we bought it. We dont have any insulation. We dont even use our fireplaces."

"Come on," said the federal government [this is a rough translation], "if you do not get in on this limited-time offer you will be a bad Canadian, a profligate wastrel and a fool among your peers."

"All right," said my wife.

"Just give me fifteen minutes some time," I beseeched no one in particular. "I think I can write three wonderful sentences on this story I've had in my notebook for seven or is it four years."

Minutes were hard to come by for a while. Men in masks were tromping through the house, men outside were drilling holes in the stucco and through the cedar shakes under the stucco, a huge machine in the street was shooting gooey white stuff through a hose and into the holes. Traffic was screeching to a stop to watch these Martians pump security into a citizen's "major investment." The world of Canadian fiction had to wait even longer for my sentences.

All the birds in the neighbourhood deserted their leafy home.

When it was all done, when the five hundred holes in the wall were patched with something three shades away from the original colour, when our Pacific Rim Japanese Current winter finally came, we sat patriotically in our various rooms and tried to imagine how warm we felt. The loan we took out to pay for our share of the job was just another debt. At least we didnt have to shell out a couple of hundred dollars for snow tires.

Astute, college-educated readers will have come to the opinion by now that the use of the house is symbolic, either of the house of fiction, in Jamesian terms, or as the psyche's image of self in the Freudian sense. Could be, but that is no lasting comfort to the writer, who has to live somewhere.

A few years went by; maybe as many years as I used to spend in one city. In the United States of America newspaper and magazine articles began to appear, telling American and otherwise captured citizens that people who lived in UFFI houses were being poisoned by the walls and roofs. We had noticed that since getting the urea formaldehyde envelope we were no longer bothered by insects indoors.

"That formaldehyde really does its job," I said, having given up writing for the afternoon. The story was really getting old now.

"Not funny," said my wife.

"Maybe insects just dont like a place that's so warm in the winter," I offered by way of compromise.

"It's not funny if our daughter's health is being threatened by this stuff," she said.

After a year or so the Canadian government admitted that there might be something wrong with the stuff. The ads started appearing in the newspapers again. The companies that had formed a few years earlier to pump in the foam were now proclaiming themselves experts in removing it. The government said it would, after a lot of hectoring, kick in with a couple thousand dollars to help patriotic you-know-whats to rip out the guck.

"How much?" I shrilled.

"Well, twenty-seven thousand dollars. We live in a big house," she admitted. "But it will be an investment in our health, and especially our daughter's health."

"Invest! Invest!" I advised.

So the Venusians laid seige where the Martians had scored their fleeting victory. This crew wore even more fearsome masks. Not content to drill circular holes in our unfortunate house, they carried implacable weapons of destruction and attacked the very structure of one's identity.

"The Walls Do Not Fall," I tried to shout over the sounds of battle.

"What?"

"Literary allusion," I said.

"You want to move over a bit?"

The walls fell. The Venusians raked all our possessions into piles in the middle of each of the overly-numerous rooms, and covered them with enormous sheets of thick plastic, securing the latter to the floors.

It was time to retreat.

We moved out of the house, or what was left of it, and went our various ways. My wife domiciled herself in a hotel suite in Richmond so that she could be close to her college. My daughter and I slept at a succession of friends' houses, on couches, in basement rooms, in a solarium. It went on for weeks that stretched inevitably into months. It meant driving all over the Lower Mainland every day, to my university, to my daughter's school, piano lessons, skating lessons, and so on, to restaurants for breakfast, to the dentist as usual, to distraction in our spare time. My job was getting harder to do. My story was lying somewhere between the paprika and the electric iron under a sheet of plastic which itself was under a drift of sawdust and poisonous foam particles. It was examination and final paper time, and Christmas was coming. I spent my birthday in bed for the following reason:

It was then that for the first time in my life I caught pneumonia. That made it a little more difficult to do all that crosstown driving and teaching.

That's when Miss Chan from the tax department called.

"We want all your receipts and other records from the tax years 1977 to 1981 [let's say]. Have them at this office in three days."

"My house has been torn down. It is full of poisonous dust. The records will be hard to find because they are nailed down in a pile of god knows what under plastic, and there are huge machines and many extra-terrestials all over the place. I have to mark a hundred and twenty papers in three days. And I am in bed with pneumonia for the weekend."

"Well, we have our problems too," said Miss Chan.

"What is your favourite Canadian book, Miss Chan?"

But she had hung up.

It was a tremendously cold weekend in Vancouver. In my back yard the cherry leaves were frozen in packs to the dead lawn, and there were great chunks of broken wood and stucco on the cherry leaves. Semi-feral cats hunkered in the back lane. The sky looked like soiled washcloths frozen solid. Even the voices on the car radio had slowed down. Maybe we were getting a Canadian winter after all. But then where was the snow? Dont ask, you fool, came the expiration from the corner of my one ragged lung.

I picked my chilly way through a hole where a wall had been in my middle age, and crawled under the first in a succession of brittle plastic covers. Thin blood dripped from my nose onto the sad bundles of socks and teeshirts. Damn, I thought, I havent seen that wide tie with the logo of Expo 67 on it for years.

Under the sixth plastic sheet, on the fourth day, I found some old receipts in a box along with my 1954 Baseball Digests. On the sixth day I coughed for an hour, my chest feeling like the subject of a poem by Pat Lane, and my almost-useless fingers closed around some more documents. I gave up looking any more, and drove down to Garry's retreat. It was warm in there.

"Can I just sit here till it's time to pick up my kid?" I asked.

Chuckle chuckle.

He was used to my bravado and hi-jinks. I was serious. I think I fell asleep for a while, in my sheepskin jacket in his easy chair.

"Can I write off the medication and mileage?" I enquired.

Chuckle chuckle.

As it turned out, Garry managed to save me more than I had hoped for. I lost about seven hundred dollars because I couldnt find the receipt for one plane trip. Oh, and I probably lost about ten years off the end of my life. I could still feel my lungs when I bent over at third base the next summer.

189

"Next year they'll go after actors and dancers," said one knowledgeable friend and outfielder.

"Once you've been audited and they dont turn you up as a fake, they'll leave you alone," said the catcher. "It might turn out to be to your advantage. Now you can get away with lots of stuff you never dared try before."

"I just want my lungs back," I said, wincing as I swung unsuccessfully at a low outside curve. "I just wish this hadnt started. It wound up costing a hundred and fifty thousand dollars."

"I thought the UFFI-removal was twenty-seven thou."

"My wife figured that since the walls were down for the UFFI anyway, she might as well get a few renovations done."

"Your place will always look like Saigon Alley," said the nonplaying husband of the first baseperson.

A few more years passed, probably two, and never more than two days went by in succession that heavy-booted workmen did not tromp the floors, which themselves kept changing, or stumble around the heaps of building materials in the yard, where my wife was supervising artisans and working stiffs whose task it was to rebuild the gardens of Ninevah.

"If Albert arrives, tell him I have just gone to dump my Canada Savings bonds from the Royal into the term deposit at the credit union," she would say.

"Who is Albert?" I would ask.

"I told you. He's the architect who is bringing me the plans for the pergolas."

"What is a pergolas?"

"Plural. Pergolas. Cant stop to explain again. Have to go fix the term deposit."

"What's a term deposit?"

"That's what you signed the papers for last Friday, you stupid bugger."

"What should I make for supper?"

"I dont know what's in the fridge. Surprise me."

It is hard to hammer out a novel while some guy in a plastic baseball hat is hammering out your porch wall. But unless you write stuff and get money for writing it, you arent a tax-deductible writer.

"Are you writing for money?" enquired a tired-looking muse one night in the early autumn.

"Why? Is it against the rules?" I asked, a little testily.

"Well, I dont remember John Keats living in a palace," she said, and I detected for the first time a little—not exactly a sneer, but an expression that suggested that she was thinking she might be wise to put a little distance between us.

"Hey, I had pneumonia last winter. Serious stuff. I can still feel it when I have two cigarettes in a row."

"John Keats didnt get consumption from remodelling his house. When he said 'forlorn,' he wasnt talking about the prime interest rate."

She had me there, and I knew it.

"I throw myself on the mercy of the court," I said.

That got a very small smile from her.

"All right," she said, carefully measured resentment in her feathery voice. "I'll give you one rather nice final chapter."

And she did. When I woke and read it, it was as if I had never written it. It was as if I had wakened and found myself in my grandmother's little house in Penticton, 1948.

The fall proceeded nostalgically, as it did every year in Vancouver. I had first come to Vancouver in the fall, many years before, to take up the adventure of big-city university attendance. They always called it university attendance in those days, as if one was making a decision in one's life that would make not only oneself but one's society as well grateful in the long years to come. In the fall in Vancouver in those days there was a never to be equalled beauty in 3.00 A.M. streetlamp glisten on fallen leaves (we didnt have many deciduous ornamental trees at home), and there was always a smell of woodsmoke in the air. For several Septembers in a row I returned to Vancouver, to find after some anxiety a basement room in Point Grey, and to set up my portable typewriter against a concrete wall under a window that looked out on the ankles of passing coeds and duffers.

Fall was pretty nice this year. The smell of woodsmoke is not around any more, because the city is even bigger, and people are forbidden to burn summer cuttings and other rubbish out back of the house. But there was still a feel of that old magic. It is different now that one has a tax-writeoff computer and can set it up above-ground. But the leaves are still there, with gleaming chestnuts among them. The American League team won the World Series for the second year in a row, but even that couldnt ruin everything.

But then my wife gave me the news about Miss Chan.

Miss Chan had gone on to better things, probably marriage and a joint bank account. Probably a two-car garage and pay-TV. She had been replaced by a Mr. Wong, who had taken it into his head to familiarize himself with his new position by going over my account.

This was (and probably still is) Mr. Wong's position: George Bowering is not a "serious writer." I have not heard Mr. Wong's definition of the term, because so far I have corresponded with him only through his department's labyrinthine forms and through my consultations with Garry. I do not know what Mr. Wong's favourite Canadian book is. Perhaps by "serious writer" he means someone he has heard of, someone who gets mentioned in *People* magazine, or who sells movie rights for a million razbuckniks.

Anyway, Mr. Wong is not satisfied with Miss Chan's leniency. He says that what I do is a hobby. He says that a writer really has no use for a computer—computers are business machines. I think I know what Mr. Wong took at university. The thought enters now:

maybe I failed Mr. Wong in first year English! He thinks that I have been pulling a big scam, writing off my writing room. I wonder what he is going to say when I present him with the receipt for my second computer.

Garry told me that Mr. Wong picked the wrong year and the wrong target. Garry rubbed his pencil-filled hands together and chuckled, and said I have nothing to worry about. But I havent been able to contact Garry lately. He is in Ireland. But I have nothing to worry about. I am going to write off the microdisc I am recording this kvetch on.

I used to worry that the income tax department might stumble across some of the material the other government departments have on me. Now I hope they do. This was the year that the Department of External Affairs sent me to represent the country's culture in Australia, Italy, Berlin, Switzerland and Holland. The Department of External Affairs thinks that I am a serious writer. So does the Canada Council. So do I.

I kind of miss Miss Chan. I sent her a copy of my book, *Kerrisdale Elegies*. I wanted to find out how she thought it stacked up alongside Rilke. But she must be reading it still; I havent heard from her. I guess I will send a copy to Mr. Wong. I wonder whether he thinks that Rilke is a serious writer.

I kind of miss my muse, too. She hasnt been to visit me since I came back from Europe. I thought I saw her one night on the *Kurfürstendam* in West Berlin, but I was hurrying to catch the last subway home to my apartment in Dahlem, so I will never be sure. When I got home from Europe, though, I hardly recognized my house. So I will understand if it takes her a while to find it, too.

The reader will wonder whether there might not have been a more satisfying ending to this story. All right.

Mr. Wong tried to rise from his chair, but he was exhausted. He fell forward across his desk, his glasses flying off his face at the impact, flipping twice in the air and sliding across the polished linoleum floor.

"You are more serious than anything I could have imagined," he managed to say. "I cant fight Ottawa and you both. Go, go, please dont look at me like this."

My wife and I and Garry walked arm in arm out into the light drizzle of February in White Rock. Gulls called derisively from the long sandy stretches of low tide. We paid them no mind.

"You were wonderful," she said. "I have not seen you like this since our early days at the Writer's Club."

"I could not have done it without you, you and your financial expertise," I admitted.

She nudged me with the elbow I held to my side.

"Oh, and Garry," I added.

Garry chuckled.

He stood back, chuckling, as my wife and I embraced there in the parking lot next to the beach, the grey sky and the grey water taking on a light tinge of silver.

"I'll pay for the parking," I said.

"This time dont forget to get a receipt, you stupid bugger," she said.

Traplines

Eden Robinson

DAD TAKES THE WHITE MARTEN from the trap.

"Look at that, Will," he says.

It is limp in his hands. It hasn't been dead that long.

We tramp through the snow to the end of our trapline. Dad whistles. The goner marten is over his shoulder. From here, it looks like Dad is wearing it. There is nothing else in the other traps. We head back to the truck. The snow crunches. This is the best time for trapping, Dad told me a while ago. This is when the animals are hungry.

Our truck rests by the roadside at an angle. Dad rolls the white marten in a gray canvas cover separate from the others. The marten is flawless, which is rare in these parts. I put my animals beside his and cover them. We get in the truck. Dad turns the radio on and country twang fills the cab. We smell like sweat and oil and pine. Dad hums. I stare out the window. Mrs. Smythe would say the trees here are like the ones on Christmas postcards, tall and heavy with snow. They crowd close to the road. When the wind blows strong enough, the older trees snap and fall on the power lines.

"Well, there's our Christmas money," Dad says, snatching a peek at the rearview mirror.

I look back. The wind ruffles the canvases that cover the martens. Dad is smiling. He sits back, steering with one hand. He doesn't even mind when we are passed by three cars. The lines in his face are loose now. He sings along with a woman who left her husband—even that doesn't make him mad. We have our Christmas money. At least for now, there'll be no shouting in the house. It will take Mom and Dad a few days to find something else to fight about.

The drive home is a long one. Dad changes the radio station twice. I search my brain for something to say but my headache is spreading and I don't feel like talking. He watches the road, though he keeps stealing looks at the back of the truck. I watch the trees and the cars passing us.

One of the cars has two women in it. The woman that isn't driving waves her hands around as she talks. She reminds me of Mrs. Smythe. They are beside us, then ahead of us, then gone.

Tucca is still as we drive into it. The snow drugs it, makes it lazy. Houses puff cedar smoke and the sweet, sharp smell gets in everyone's clothes. At school in town, I can close my eyes and tell who's from the village and who isn't just by smelling them.

When we get home, we go straight to the basement. Dad gives me the ratty martens and keeps the good ones. He made me start on squirrels when I was in grade five. He put the knife in my hand, saying, "For Christ's sake, it's just a squirrel. It's dead, you stupid knucklehead. It can't feel anything."

He made the first cut for me. I swallowed, closed my eyes, and lifted the knife.

"Jesus," Dad muttered. "Are you a sissy? I got a sissy for a son.

Look. It's just like cutting up a chicken. See? Pretend you're skinning a chicken."

Dad showed me, then put another squirrel in front of me, and we didn't leave the basement until I got it right.

Now Dad is skinning the flawless white marten, using his best knife. His tongue is sticking out the corner of his mouth. He straightens up and shakes his skinning hand. I quickly start on the next marten. It's perfect except for a scar across its back. It was probably in a fight. We won't get much for the skin. Dad goes back to work. I stop, clench, unclench my hands. They are stiff.

"Goddamn," Dad says quietly. I look up, tensing, but Dad starts to smile. He's finished the marten. It's ready to be dried and sold. I've finished mine too. I look at my hands. They know what to do now without my having to tell them. Dad sings as we go up the creaking stairs. When we get into the hallway I breathe in, smelling fresh baked bread.

Mom is sprawled in front of the TV. Her apron is smudged with flour and she is licking her fingers. When she sees us, she stops and puts her hands in her apron pockets.

"Well?" she says.

Dad grabs her at the waist and whirls her around the living room.

"Greg! Stop it!" she says, laughing.

Flour gets on Dad and cedar chips get on Mom. They talk and I leave, sneaking into the kitchen. I swallow three aspirins for my headache, snatch two buns, and go to my room. I stop in the doorway. Eric is there, plugged into his electric guitar. He looks at the buns and pulls out an earphone.

"Give me one," he says.

I throw him the smaller bun, and he finishes it in three bites.

"The other one," he says.

I give him the finger and sit on my bed. I see him thinking about tackling me, but he shrugs and plugs himself back in. I chew on the bun, roll bits of it around in my mouth. It's still warm, and I wish I had some honey for it or some blueberry jam.

Eric leaves and comes back with six buns. He wolfs them down, cramming them into his mouth. I stick my fingers in my ears and glare at him. He can't hear himself eat. He notices me and grins. Opens his mouth so I can see. I pull out a mag and turn the pages.

Dad comes in. Eric's jaw clenches. I go into the kitchen, grabbing another bun. Mom smacks my hand. We hear Eric and Dad starting to yell. Mom rolls her eyes and puts three more loaves in the oven.

"Back later," I say.

She nods, frowning at her hands.

I walk. Think about going to Billy's house. He is seeing Elaine, though, and is getting weird. He wrote her a poem yesterday. He couldn't find anything nice to rhyme with "Elaine" so he didn't finish it.

"Pain," Craig said. "Elaine, you pain."

"Plain Elaine," Tony said.

Billy smacked Tony and they went at it in the snow. Billy gave him a face wash. That ended it, and we let Billy sit on the steps and write in peace.

"Elaine in the rain," I say. "Elaine, a flame. Cranes. Danes. Trains. My main Elaine." I kick at the slush on the ground. Billy is on his own.

I let my feet take me down the street. It starts to snow, tiny ladybug flakes. It is only four but already getting dark. Streetlights flicker on. No one but me is out walking. Snot in my nose freezes. The air is starting to burn my throat. I turn and head home. Eric and Dad should be tired by now.

Another postcard picture. The houses lining the street look snug. I hunch into my jacket. In a few weeks, Christmas lights will go up all over the village. Dad will put ours up two weeks before

Christmas. We use the same set every year. We'll get a tree a week later. Mom'll decorate it. On Christmas Eve, she'll put our presents under it. Some of the presents will be wrapped in aluminum because she never buys enough wrapping paper. We'll eat turkey. Mom and Dad will go to a lot of parties and get really drunk. Eric will go to a lot of parties and get really stoned. Maybe this year I will too. Anything would be better than sitting around with Tony and Craig, listening to them gripe.

I stamp the snow off my sneakers and jeans. I open the door quietly. The TV is on loud. I can tell that it's a hockey game by the announcer's voice. I take off my shoes and jacket. The house feels really hot to me after being outside. My face starts to tingle as the skin thaws. I go into the kitchen and take another aspirin.

The kitchen could use some plants. It gets good light in the winter. Mrs. Smythe has filled her kitchen with plants, hanging the ferns by the window where the cats can't eat them. The Smythes have pictures all over their walls of places they have been—Europe, Africa, Australia. They've been everywhere. They can afford it, she says, because they don't have kids. They had one, a while ago. On the TV there's a wallet-sized picture of a dark-haired boy with his front teeth missing. He was their kid but he disappeared. Mrs. Smythe fiddles with the picture a lot.

Eric tries to sneak up behind me. His socks make a slithering sound on the floor. I duck just in time and hit him in the stomach.

He doubles over. He has a towel stretched between his hands. His choking game. He punches at me, but I hop out of the way. His fist hits the hot stove. Yelling, he jerks his hand back. I race out of the kitchen and down to the basement. Eric follows me, screaming my name. "Come out, you chicken," he says. "Come on out and fight."

I keep still behind a stack of plywood. Eric has the towel ready. After a while, he goes back upstairs and locks the door behind him.

I stand. I can't hear Mom and Dad. They must have gone out to celebrate the big catch. They'll probably find a party and go on a bender until Monday, when Dad has to go back to work. I'm alone with Eric, but he'll leave the house around ten. I can stay out of his way until then.

The basement door bursts open. I scramble under Dad's tool table. Eric must be stoned. He's probably been toking up since Mom and Dad left. Pot always makes him mean.

He laughs. "You baby. You fucking baby." He doesn't look for me that hard. He thumps loudly up the stairs, slams the door shut, then tiptoes back down and waits. He must think I'm really stupid.

We stay like this for a long time. Eric lights up. In a few minutes, the whole basement smells like pot. Dad will be pissed off if the smoke ruins the white marten. I smile, hoping it does. Eric will really get it then.

"Fuck," he says and disappears upstairs, not locking the door. I crawl out. My legs are stiff. The pot is making me dizzy.

The woodstove is cooling. I don't open it because the hinges squeal. It'll be freezing down here soon. Breathing fast, I climb the stairs. I crack the door open. There are no lights on except in our bedroom. I pull on my jacket and sneakers. I grab some bread and stuff it in my jacket, then run for the door but Eric is blocking it, leering.

"Thought you were sneaky, hey," he says.

I back into the kitchen. He follows. I wait until he is near before I bend over and ram him. He's slow because of the pot and slips to the floor. He grabs my ankle, but I kick him in the head and am out the door before he can catch me. I take the steps two at a time. Eric stands on the porch and laughs. I can't wait until I'm bigger. I'd like to smear him against a wall. Let him see what it feels like. I'd like to smear him so bad.

I munch on some bread as I head for the exit to the highway. Now the snow is coming down in thick, large flakes that melt when they touch my skin. I stand at the exit and wait.

I hear One Eye's beat-up Ford long before I see it. It clunks down the road and stalls when One Eye stops for me.

"You again. What you doing out here?" he yells at me.

"Waiting for Princess fucking Di," I say.

"Smart mouth. You keep it up and you can stay out there."

The back door opens anyway. Snooker and Jim are there. One Eye and Don Wilson are in the front. They all have silver lunch buckets at their feet.

We get into town and I say, "Could you drop me off here?"

One Eye looks back, surprised. He has forgotten about me. He frowns. "Where you going this time of night?"

"Disneyland," I say.

"Smart mouth," he says. "Don't be like your brother. You stay out of trouble."

I laugh. One Eye slows the car and pulls over. It chokes and sputters. I get out and thank him for the ride. One Eye grunts. He pulls away and I walk to Mrs. Smythe's.

The first time I saw her house was last spring, when she invited the English class there for a barbecue. The lawn was neat and green and I only saw one dandelion. There were rose bushes in the front and raspberry bushes in the back. I went with Tony and Craig, who got high on the way there. Mrs. Smythe noticed right away. She took them aside and talked to them. They stayed in the poolroom downstairs until the high wore off.

There weren't any other kids from the village there. Only townies. Kids that Dad says will never dirty their pink hands. They were split into little groups. They talked and ate and laughed and I wandered around alone, feeling like a dork. I was going to go downstairs to Tony and Craig when Mrs. Smythe came up to me, carrying a hot dog. I never noticed her smile until then. Her blue sundress swayed as she walked.

"You weren't in class yesterday," she said.

"Stomachache."

"I was going to tell you how much I liked your essay. You must have done a lot of work on it."

"Yeah." I tried to remember what I had written.

"Which part was the hardest?" she said.

I cleared my throat. "Starting it."

"I walked right into that one," she said, laughing. I smiled.

A tall man came up and hugged her. She kissed him. "Sam," she said. "This is the student I was telling you about."

"Well, hello," Mr. Smythe said. "Great paper."

"Thanks," I said.

"Is it William or Will?" Mr. Smythe said.

"Will," I said. He held out his hand and shook mine.

"That big, huh?" he said.

Oh no, I thought, remembering what I'd written. Dad, Eric, Grandpa, and I had gone out halibut fishing once and caught a huge one. It took forever to get it in the boat and we all took turns clubbing it. But it wouldn't die, so Dad shot it. In the essay I said it was seven hundred pounds, but Mrs. Smythe had pointed out to the whole class that halibut didn't get much bigger than five hundred. Tony and Craig bugged me about that.

"Karen tells me you've written a lot about fishing," Mr. Smythe said, sounding really cheerful.

"Excuse me," Mrs. Smythe said. "That's my cue to leave. If you're smart, you'll do the same. Once you get Sam going with his stupid fish stories you can't get a word—"

Mr. Smythe goosed her. She poked him with her hot dog and left quickly. Mr. Smythe put his arm around my shoulder, shaking his head. We sat out on the patio and he told me about the time he caught a marlin and about scuba diving on the Great Barrier Reef. He went down in a shark cage once to try to film a great white eating. I told him about Uncle Bernie's gillnetter. He wanted to know if Uncle Bernie would take him out, and what gear he was going to need. We ended up in the kitchen, me using a flounder to show him how to clean a halibut.

I finally looked at the clock around eleven. Dad had said he would pick me and Tony and Craig up around eight. I didn't even know where Tony and Craig were anymore. I couldn't believe it had gotten so late without my noticing. Mrs. Smythe had gone to bed. Mr. Smythe said he would drive me home. I said that was okay, I'd hitch.

He snorted. "Karen would kill me. No, I'll drive you. Let's phone your parents and tell them you're coming home."

No one answered the phone. I said they were probably asleep. He dialed again. Still no answer.

"Looks like you've got the spare bedroom tonight," he said.

"Let me try," I said, picking up the phone. There was no answer, but after six rings I pretended Dad was on the other end. I didn't want to spend the night at my English teacher's house. Tony and Craig would never shut up about it.

"Hi, Dad," I said. "How come? I see. Car trouble. No problem. Mr. Smythe is going to drive me home. What? Sure, I—"

"Let me talk to him," Mr. Smythe said, snatching the phone. "Hello! Mr. Tate! How are you? My, my, my. Your son is a lousy liar, isn't he?" He hung up. "It's amazing how much your father sounds like a dial tone."

I picked up the phone again. "They're sleeping, that's all." Mr. Smythe watched me as I dialed. There wasn't any answer.

"Why'd you lie?" he said quietly.

We were alone in the kitchen. I swallowed. He was a lot bigger than me. When he reached over, I put my hands up and covered my face. He stopped, then took the phone out of my hands.

"It's okay," he said. "I won't hurt you. It's okay."

I put my hands down. He looked sad. That annoyed me. I shrugged, backing away. "I'll hitch," I said.

Mr. Smythe shook his head. "No, really, Karen would kill me, then she'd go after you. Come on. We'll be safer if you sleep in the spare room."

In the morning Mr. Smythe was up before I could sneak out. He was making bacon and pancakes. He asked if I'd ever done any freshwater fishing. I said no. He started talking about fishing in the Black Sea and I listened to him. He's a good cook.

Mrs. Smythe came into the kitchen dressed in some sweats and a T-shirt. She ate without saying anything and didn't look awake until she finished her coffee. Mr. Smythe phoned my house but no one answered. He asked if I wanted to go up to Old Timer's Lake with them. He had a new Sona reel he wanted to try out. I didn't have anything better to do.

The Smythes have a twenty-foot speedboat. They let me drive it around the lake a few times while Mrs. Smythe baked in the sun and Mr. Smythe put the rod together. We lazed around the beach in the afternoon, watching the people go by. Sipping their beers, the Smythes argued about who was going to drive back. We rode around the lake some more and roasted hot dogs for dinner.

Their porch light is on. I go up the walk and ring the bell. Mrs. Smythe said just come in, don't bother knocking, but I can't do that. It doesn't feel right. She opens the door, smiling when she sees me. She is wearing a fluffy pink sweater. "Hi, Will. Sam was hoping you'd drop by. He says he's looking forward to beating you."

"Dream on," I say.

She laughs. "Go right in." She heads down the hall to the washroom.

I go into the living room. Mr. Smythe isn't there. The TV is on, some documentary about whales.

He's in the kitchen, scrunched over a game of solitaire. His new glasses are sliding off his nose and he looks more like a teacher than Mrs. Smythe. He scratches the beard he's trying to grow.

"Come on in," he says, patting the chair beside him.

I take a seat and watch him finish the game. He pushes his glasses up. "What's your pleasure?" he says.

"Pool," I say.

"Feeling lucky, huh?" We go down to the poolroom. "How about a little extra this week?" he says, not looking at me.

I shrug. "Sure. Dishes?"

He shakes his head. "Bigger."

"I'm not shoveling the walk," I say.

He shakes his head again. "Bigger."

"Money?"

"Bigger."

"What?"

He racks up the balls. Sets the cue ball. Wipes his hands on his jeans.

"What?" I say again.

Mr. Smythe takes out a quarter. "Heads or tails?" he says, tossing it.

"Heads," I say.

He slaps the quarter on the back of his hand. "I break."

"Where? Let me see that," I say, laughing. He holds it up. The quarter is tails.

He breaks. "How'd you like to stay with us?" he says, very quietly.

"Sure," I say. "But I got to go back on Tuesday. We got to check the traplines again."

He is quiet. The balls make thunking sounds as they bounce around the table. "Do you like it here?"

"Sure," I say.

"Enough to live here?"

I'm not sure I heard him right. Maybe he's asking a different question from the one I think he's asking. I open my mouth. I don't know what to say. I say nothing.

205

"Those are the stakes, then," he says. "I win, you stay. You win, you stay."

He's joking. I laugh. He doesn't laugh. "You serious?" I ask.

He stands up straight. "I don't think I've ever been more serious."

The room is suddenly very small.

"Your turn," he says. "Stripes."

I scratch, missing the ball by a mile. He takes his turn.

"We don't want to push you," he says. He leans over the table, squints at a ball. "We just think that you'd be safer here. Hell, you practically live with us already." I watch my sneakers. He keeps playing. "We aren't rich. We aren't perfect. We. . ." He looks at me. "We thought maybe you'd like to try it for a couple of weeks first."

"I can't."

"You don't have to decide right now," he says. "Think about it. Take a few days."

It's my turn again but I don't feel like playing anymore. Mr. Smythe is waiting, though. I pick a ball. Aim, shoot, miss.

The game goes on in silence. Mr. Smythe wins easily. He smiles. "Well, I win. You stay."

If I wanted to get out of the room, there is only one door and Mr. Smythe is blocking it. He watches me. "Let's go upstairs," he says.

Mrs. Smythe has shut off the TV. She stands up when we come into the living room. "Will—"

"I asked him already," Mr. Smythe says.

Her head snaps around. "You what?"

"I asked him."

Her hands clench at her sides. "We were supposed to do it together, Sam." Her voice is flat. She turns to me. "You said no."

I can't look at her. I look at the walls, at the floor, at her slippers. I shouldn't have come tonight. I should have waited for Eric to leave. She turns to me. "You said no."

She stands in front of me, trying to smile. Her hands are warm on my face. "Look at me," she says. "Will? Look at me." She is trying to smile. "Hungry?" she says.

I nod. She makes a motion with her head for Mr. Smythe to follow her into the kitchen. When they're gone I sit down. It should be easy. It should be easy. I watch TV without seeing it. I wonder what they're saying about me in the kitchen.

It's now almost seven and my ribs hurt. Mostly, I can ignore it, but Eric hit me pretty hard and they're bruised. Eric got hit pretty hard by Dad, so we're even, I guess. I'm counting the days until Eric moves out. The rate he's going, he'll be busted soon anyway. Tony says the police are starting to ask questions.

It's a strange night. We all pretend that nothing has happened and Mrs. Smythe fixes some nachos. Mr. Smythe gets out a pack of Uno cards and we play a few rounds and watch the Discovery Channel. We go to bed.

I lie awake. My room. This could be my room. I already have most of my books here. It's hard to study with Eric around. I still have a headache. I couldn't get away from them long enough to sneak into the kitchen for an aspirin. I pull my T-shirt up and take a look. There's a long bruise under my ribs and five smaller ones above it. I think Eric was trying to hit my stomach but he was so wasted he kept missing. It isn't too bad. Tony's dad broke three of his ribs once. Billy got a concussion a couple of weeks ago. My dad is pretty easy. It's only Eric who really bothers me.

The Smythes keep the aspirin by the spices. I grab six, three for now and three for the morning. I'm swallowing the last one when Mr. Smythe grabs my hand. I didn't even hear him come in. I must be sleepy.

"Where'd they hit you this time?" he says.

"I got a headache," I say. "A bad one."

He pries open the hand with the aspirins in it. "How many do you plan on taking?"

"These are for later."

He sighs. I get ready for a lecture. "Go back to bed" is all he says. "It'll be okay." He sounds very tired.

"Sure," I say.

I get up around five. I leave a note saying I have things to do at home. I catch a ride with some guys coming off the graveyard shift.

No one is home. Eric had a party last night. I'm glad I wasn't around. They've wrecked the coffee table and the rug smells like stale beer and cigarettes. Our bedroom is even worse. Someone puked all over Eric's bed and there are two used condoms on mine. At least none of the windows were broken this time. I start to clean my side of the room, then stop. I sit on my bed.

Mr. Smythe will be getting up soon. It's Sunday, so there'll be waffles or french toast. He'll fix a plate of bacon and eat it before Mrs. Smythe comes downstairs. He thinks she doesn't know that he does this. She'll get up around ten or eleven and won't talk to anyone until she's had about three coffees. She starts to wake up around one or two. They'll argue about something. Whose turn to take out the garbage or do the laundry. They'll read the paper.

I crawl into bed. The aspirin isn't working. I try to sleep but it really reeks in here. I have a biology test tomorrow. I forgot to bring the book back from their place. I lie there awake until our truck pulls into the driveway. Mom and Dad are fighting. They sound plastered. Mom is bitching about something. Dad is not saying anything. Doors slam.

Mom comes in first and goes straight to bed. She doesn't seem to notice the house is a mess. Dad comes in a lot slower. "What the—Eric!" he yells. "Eric!"

I pretend to sleep. The door bangs open.

"Eric, you little bastard," Dad says, looking around. He shakes me. "Where the fuck is Eric?"

His breath is lethal. You can tell he likes his rye straight.

"How should I know?"

He rips Eric's amplifiers off the walls. He throws them down and gives them a good kick. He tips Eric's bed over. Eric is smart. He won't come home for a while. Dad will have cooled off by then and Eric can give him some money without Dad's getting pissed off. I don't move. I wait until he's out of the room before I put on a sweater. I can hear him down in the basement chopping wood. It should be around eight by now. The RinkyDink will be open in an hour.

When I go into the kitchen, Mom is there. She sees me and makes a shushing motion with her hands. She pulls out a bottle from behind the stove and sits down at the kitchen table.

"You're a good boy," she says, giggling. "You're a good boy. Help your old mother back to bed, hey."

"Sure," I say, putting an arm around her. She stands, holding onto the bottle with one hand and me with the other. "This way, my lady."

"You making fun of me?" she says, her eyes going small. "You laughing at me?" Then she laughs and we go to their room. She flops onto the bed. She takes a long drink. "You're fucking laughing at me, aren't you?"

"Mom, you're paranoid. I was making a joke."

"Yeah, you're really funny. A laugh a minute," she says, giggling again. "Real comedian."

"Yeah, that's me."

She throws the bottle at me. I duck. She rolls over and starts to cry. I cover her with the blanket and leave. The floor is sticky. Dad's still chopping wood. They wouldn't notice if I wasn't here. Maybe people would talk for a week or two, but after a while they wouldn't notice. The only people who would miss me are Tony and Craig and Billy and maybe Eric, when he got toked up and didn't have anything for target practice.

Billy is playing Mortal Kombat at the RinkyDink. He's chain-smoking. As I walk up to him, he turns around quickly.

"Oh, it's you," he says, going back to the game.

"Hi to you too," I say.

"You seen Elaine?" he says.

"Nope."

He crushes out his cigarette in the ashtray beside him. He plays for a while, loses a life, then shakes another cigarette out one-handed. He sticks it in his mouth, loses another man, then lights up. He sucks deep. "Relax," I say. "Her majesty's limo is probably stuck in traffic. She'll come."

He glares at me. "Shut up."

I go play pool with Craig, who's decided that he's James Dean. He's wearing a white T-shirt, jeans, and a black leather jacket that looks like his brother's. His hair is blow-dried and a cigarette dangles from the corner of his mouth.

"What a loser," he says.

"Who you calling a loser?"

"Billy. What a loser." He struts to the other side of the pool table.

"He's okay."

"That babe," he says. "What's-her-face. Ellen? Irma?"

"Elaine."

"Yeah, her. She's going out with him 'cause she's got a bet."

"What?"

"She's got to go out with him a month, and her friend will give her some coke."

"Billy's already giving her coke."

"Yeah. He's a loser."

I look over at Billy. He's lighting another cigarette.

"Can you imagine a townie wanting anything to do with him?" Craig says. "She's just doing it as a joke. She's going to dump him in a week. She's going to put all his stupid poems in the paper."

I see it now. There's a space around Billy. No one is going near him. He doesn't notice. Same with me. I catch some guys I used to hang out with grinning at me. When they see me looking at them, they look away.

Craig wins the game. I'm losing a lot this week.

Elaine gets to the RinkyDink after lunch. She's got some townie girlfriends with her who are tiptoeing around like they're going to get jumped. Elaine leads them right up to Billy. Everyone's watching. Billy gives her his latest poem. I wonder what he found to rhyme with "Elaine."

The girls leave. Billy holds the door open for Elaine. Her friends start to giggle. The guys standing around start to howl. They're laughing so hard they're crying. I feel sick. I think about telling Billy but I know he won't listen.

I leave the RinkyDink and go for a walk. I walk and walk and end up back in front of the RinkyDink. There's nowhere else to go. I hang out with Craig, who hasn't left the pool table.

I spend the night on his floor. Craig's parents are Jehovah's Witnesses and preach at me before I go to bed. I sit and listen because I need a place to sleep. I'm not going home until tomorrow, when Mom and Dad are sober. Craig's mom gets us up two hours before the bus that takes the village kids to school comes. They pray before we eat. Craig looks at me and rolls his eyes. People are always making fun of Craig because his parents stand on the corner downtown every Friday and hold up the *Watchtower* mags. When his parents start to bug him, he says he'll take up devil worship or astrology if they don't lay off. I think I'll ask him if he wants to hang out with me on Christmas. His parents don't believe in it.

Between classes I pass Mrs. Smythe in the hall. Craig nudges me. "Go on," he says, making sucking noises. "Go get your A."

"Fuck off," I say, pushing him.

She's talking to some girl and doesn't see me. I think about skipping English but know that she'll call home and ask where I am.

At lunch no one talks to me. I can't find Craig or Tony or Billy. The village guys who hang out by the science wing snicker as I go past. I don't stop until I get to the gym doors, where the headbangers have taken over. I don't have any money and I didn't bring a lunch, so I bum a cigarette off this girl with really tight jeans. To get my mind off my stomach I try to get her to go out with me. She looks at me like I'm crazy. When she walks away, the fringe on her leather jacket swings.

I flunk my biology test. It's multiple choice. I stare at the paper and kick myself. I know I could have passed if I'd read the chapter. Mr. Kellerman reads out the scores from lowest to highest. My name is called out third.

"Mr. Tate," he says. "Three out of thirty."

"All riiight," Craig says, slapping my back.

"Mr. Davis," Mr. Kellerman says to Craig, "three and a half."

Craig stands up and bows. The guys in the back clap. The kids in the front laugh. Mr. Kellerman reads out the rest of the scores. Craig turns to me. "Looks like I beat the Brain," he says.

"Yeah," I say. "Pretty soon you're going to be getting the Nobel Prize."

The bell rings for English. I go to my locker and take out my jacket. If she calls home no one's going to answer anyway.

I walk downtown. The snow is starting to slack off and it's even sunning a bit. My stomach growls. I haven't eaten anything since breakfast. I wish I'd gone to English. Mrs. Smythe would have given me something to eat. She always has something left over from lunch. I hunch down into my jacket.

Downtown, I go to the Paradise Arcade. All the heads hang out there. Maybe Eric'll give me some money. More like a belt, but it's worth a try. I don't see him anywhere, though. In fact, no one much is there. Just some burnouts by the pinball machines. I see Mitch and go over to him, but he's soaring, laughing at the ball going around the machine. I walk away, head for the highway, and hitch home. Mom will have passed out by now, and Dad'll be at work.

Sure enough, Mom is on the living room floor. I get her a blanket. The stove has gone out and it's freezing in here. I go into the kitchen and look through the fridge. There's one jar of pickles, some really pathetic-looking celery, and some milk that's so old it smells like cheese. There's no bread left over from Saturday. I find some Rice-A-Roni and cook it. Mom comes to and asks for some water. I bring her a glass and give her a little Rice-A-Roni. She makes a face but slowly eats it.

At six Dad comes home with Eric. They've made up. Eric has bought Dad a six-pack and they watch the hockey game together. I stay in my room. Eric has cleaned his bed by dumping his mattress outside and stealing mine. I haul my mattress back onto my bed frame. I pull out my English book. We have a grammar test this Friday. I know Mrs. Smythe will be unhappy if she has to fail me. I read the chapter on nouns and get through most of the one on verbs before Eric comes in and kicks me off the bed.

He tries to take the mattress but I punch him in the side. Eric turns and grabs my hair. "This is my bed," he says. "Understand?"

"Fuck you," I say. "You had the party. Your fucked-up friends trashed the room. You sleep on the floor."

Dad comes in and sees Eric push me against the wall and smack my face. He yells at Eric, who turns around, his fist frozen in the air. Dad rolls his sleeves up.

"You always take his side!" Eric yells. "You never take mine!"

"Pick on someone your own size," Dad says. "Unless you want to deal with me."

Eric gives me a look that says he'll settle with me later. I pick up my English book and get out. I walk around the village, staying away from the RinkyDink. It's the first place Eric will look.

I'm at the village exit. The sky is clear and the stars are popping out. Mr. Smythe will be at his telescope trying to map the Pleiades. Mrs. Smythe will be marking papers while she watches TV.

"Need a ride?" this guy says. There's a blue pickup stopped in front of me. The driver is wearing a hunting cap.

I take my hand out of my mouth. I've been chewing my knuckle like a baby. I shake my head. "I'm waiting for someone," I say.

He shrugs and takes off. I stand there and watch his headlights disappear.

They didn't really mean it. They'd get bored of me quick when they found out what I'm like. I should have just said yes. I could have stayed until they got fed up and then come home when Eric had cooled off.

Two cars pass me as I walk back to the village. I can hide at Tony's until Eric goes out with his friends and forgets this afternoon. My feet are frozen by the time I get to the RinkyDink. Tony is there.

"So. I heard Craig beat you in biology," he says.

I laugh. "Didn't it just impress you?"

"A whole half a point. Way to go," he says. "For a while there we thought you were getting townie."

"Yeah, right," I say. "Listen, I pissed Eric off—"

"Surprise, surprise."

"—and I need a place to crash. Can I sleep over?"

"Sure," he says. Mitch wanders into the RinkyDink, and a crowd of kids slowly drifts over to him. He looks around, eyeing everybody. Then he starts giving something out. Me and Tony go over.

"Wow," Tony says, after Mitch gives him something too.

"What?"

We leave and go behind the RinkyDink, where other kids are gathered. "Fucking all right," I hear Craig say, even though I can't see him.

"What?" I say. Tony opens his hand. He's holding a little vial with white crystals in it.

"Crack," he says. "Man, is he stupid. He could have made a fortune and he's just giving it away."

We don't have a pipe, and Tony wants to do this right the first time. He decides to save it for tomorrow, after he buys the right equipment. I'm hungry again. I'm about to tell him that I'm going to Billy's when I see Eric.

"Shit," I say and hide behind him.

Tony looks up. "Someone's in trou-ble," he sings.

Eric's looking for me. I hunch down behind Tony, who tries to look innocent. Eric spots him and starts to come over. "Better run," Tony whispers.

I sneak behind some other people but Eric sees me and I have to run for it anyway. Tony starts to cheer and the kids behind the RinkyDink join in. Some of the guys follow us so they'll see what happens when Eric catches up with me. I don't want to find out so I pump as hard as I can.

Eric used to be fast. I'm glad he's a dopehead now because he can't really run anymore. I'm panting and my legs are cramping but the house is in sight. I run up the stairs. The door is locked.

I stand there, hand on the knob. Eric rounds the corner to our block. There's no one behind him. I bang on the door but now I see that our truck is gone. I run around to the back but the base-ment door is locked too. Even the windows are locked.

Eric pops his head around the corner of the house. He grins when he sees me, then disappears. I grit my teeth and start run-ning across our backyard. Head for Billy's. "You shithead," Eric yells. He has a friend with him, maybe Brent. I duck be-hind our neighbor's house. There's snow in my sneakers and all the way up my leg, but I'm sweating. I stop. I can't hear Eric. I hope I've lost him, but Eric is really pissed off and when he's pissed off he doesn't let go. I look down. My footprints are clear in the snow. I start to run again, but I hit a thick spot and have to wade through thigh-high snow. I look back. Eric is nowhere. I keep slogging. I make it to the road again and run down to the exit.

I've lost him. I'm shaking because it's cold. I can feel the sweat cooling on my skin. My breath goes back to normal. I wait for a car to come by. I've missed the night shift and the graveyard crew won't be by until midnight. It's too cold to wait that long.

A car, a red car. A little Toyota. Brent's car. I run off the road and head for a clump of trees. The Toyota pulls over and Eric gets out, yelling. I reach the trees and rest. They're waiting by the roadside. Eric is peering into the trees, trying to see me. Brent is smoking in the car. Eric crosses his arms over his chest and blows into his hands. My legs are frozen.

After a long time, a cop car cruises to a stop beside the Toyota. I wade out and wave at the two policemen. They look startled. One of them turns to Eric and Brent and asks them something. I see Eric shrug. It takes me a while to get over to where they're standing because my legs are slow.

The cop is watching me. I swear I'll never call them pigs again. I swear it. He leans over to Brent, who digs around in the glove compartment. The cop says something to his partner. I scramble down the embankment.

Eric has no marks on his face. Dad probably hit him on the back and stomach. Dad has been careful since the social worker came to our house. Eric suddenly smiles at me and holds out his hand. I move behind the police car.

"Is there a problem here?" the policeman says.

"No," Eric says. "No probulum. Li'l misunnerstanin'."

Oh, shit. He's as high as a kite. The policeman looks hard at Eric. I look at the car. Brent is staring at me, glassy-eyed. He's high too.

Eric tries again to reach out to me. I put the police car between us. The policeman grabs Eric by the arm and his partner goes and gets Brent. The policeman says something about driving under the influence but none of us are listening. Eric's eyes are on me.

I'm going to pay for this. Brent is swearing. He wants a lawyer. He stumbles out of the Toyota and slips on the road. Brent and Eric are put in the backseat of the police car. The policeman comes up to me and says, "Can you make it home?"

I nod.

"Good. Go," he says.

They drive away. When I get home, I walk around the house, trying to figure out a way to break in. I find a stick and jimmy the basement door open. Just in case Eric gets out tonight, I make a bed under the tool table and go to sleep.

No one is home when I wake up. I scramble an egg and get ready for school. I sit beside Tony on the bus.

"I was expecting to see you with black eyes," he says.

My legs are still raw from last night. I have something due today but I can't remember what. If Eric is in the drunk tank, they'll let him out later.

The village guys are talking to me again. I skip gym. I skip history. I hang out with Craig and Tony in the Paradise Arcade. I'm not sure if I want to be friends with them after they joined in the chase last night, but it's better to have them on my side than not. They get a two-for-one pizza special for lunch and I'm glad I stuck with them because I'm starved. They also got some five-finger specials from Safeway. Tony is proud because he swiped a couple of bags of chips and two Pepsis and no one even noticed.

Mitch comes over to me in the bathroom.

"That was a really cheap thing to do," he says.

"What?" I haven't done anything to him.

"What? What? Getting your brother thrown in jail. Pretty crummy."

"He got himself thrown in jail. He got caught when he was high."

"That's not what he says." Mitch frowns. "He says you set him up."

"Fuck." I try to sound calm. "When'd he tell you that?"

"This morning," he says. "He's waiting for you at school."

"I didn't set him up. How could I?"

Mitch nods. He hands me some crack and says, "Hey, I'm sorry," and leaves. I look at it. I'll give it to Tony and maybe he'll let me stay with him tonight.

Billy comes into the Paradise with Elaine and her friends. He's getting some glances but he doesn't notice. He holds the chair out for Elaine, who sits down without looking at him. I don't want to be around for this. I go over to Tony.

"I'm leaving," I say.

Tony shushes me. "Watch," he says.

Elaine orders a beer. Frankie shakes his head and points to the sign that says WE DO NOT SERVE MINORS. Elaine frowns. She says something to Billy. He shrugs. She orders a Coke. Billy pays. When their Cokes come, Elaine dumps hers over Billy's head. Billy stares at her, more puzzled than anything else. Her friends start to laugh, and I get up and walk out.

I lean against the wall of the Paradise. Billy comes out a few minutes later. His face is still and pale. Elaine and her friends follow him, reciting lines from the poems he wrote her. Tony and the rest spill out too, laughing. I go back inside and trade the crack for some quarters for the video games. I keep losing. Tony wants to go now and we hitch back to the village. We raid his fridge and have chocolate ice cream coconut sundaes. Angela comes in with Di and says that Eric is looking for me. I look at Tony and he looks at me.

"Boy, are you in for it," Tony says. "You'd better stay here tonight."

When everyone is asleep, Tony pulls out a weird-looking pipe and does the crack. His face goes very dreamy and far away. A few minutes later he says, "Christ, that's great. I wonder how much Mitch has?"

I turn over and go to sleep.

The next morning Billy is alone on the bus. No one wants to sit with him so there are empty seats all around him. He looks like he hasn't slept. Tony goes up to him and punches him in the arm.

"So how's Shakespeare this morning?" Tony says.

I hope Eric isn't at the school. I don't know where else I can hide.

Mrs. Smythe is waiting at the school bus stop. I sneak out the back door of the bus, with Tony and the guys pretending to fight to cover me.

We head back to the Paradise. I'm starting to smell bad. I haven't had a shower in days. I wish I had some clean clothes. I wish I had some money to buy a toothbrush. I hate the scummy feeling on my teeth. I wish I had enough for a taco or a hamburger.

Dad is at the Paradise, looking for me.

"Let's go to the Dairy Queen," he says.

He orders a coffee, a chocolate milk shake, and a cheeseburger. We take the coffee and milk shake to a back table, and I pocket the order slip. We sit there. Dad folds and unfolds a napkin.

"One of your teachers called," he says.

"Mrs. Smythe?"

"Yeah." He looks up. "Says she'd like you to stay there."

I try to read his face. His eyes are bloodshot and red-rimmed. He must have a big hangover.

The cashier calls out our number. I go up and get the cheese-burger and we split it. Dad always eats slow to make it last longer.

"Did you tell her you wanted to?"

"No," I say. "They asked me, but I said I couldn't."

Dad nods. "Did you tell them anything?"

"Like what?"

"Don't get smart," he says, sounding beat.

"I didn't say anything."

He stops chewing. "Then why'd they ask you?"

"Don't know."

"You must have told them something."

"Nope. They just asked."

"Did Eric tell them?"

I snort. "Eric? No way. They would . . . He wouldn't go anywhere near them. They're okay, Dad. They won't tell anybody."

"So you did tell them."

"I didn't. I swear I didn't. Look, Eric got me on the face a couple of times and they just figured it out."

"You're lying."

I finished my half of the cheeseburger. "I'm not lying. I didn't say anything and they won't either."

"I never touched you."

"Yeah, Eric took care of that," I say. "You seen him?"

"I kicked him out."

"You what?"

"Party. Ruined the basement," Dad says grimly. "He's old enough. Had to leave sooner or later."

He chews his last mouthful of cheeseburger. Eric will really be out of his mind now.

We drive out to check the trapline. The first trap has been tripped with a stick. Dad curses, blaming the other trappers who have lines near ours. "I'll skunk them," he says. But the last three traps have got some more martens. We even get a little lynx. Dad is happy. We go home. The basement is totally ripped apart.

Next day at school, I spend most of the time ducking from Eric and Mrs. Smythe before I finally get sick of the whole lot and go down to the Paradise. Tony is there with Billy, who asks me if I want to go to Vancouver with him until Eric cools off.

"Now?"

"No better time," he says.

I think about it. "When you leaving?"

"Tonight."

"I don't know. I don't have any money."

"Me neither," he says.

"Shit," I say. "How we going to get there? It's a zillion miles from here."

"Hitch to town, hitch to Smithers, then down to Prince George."

"Yeah, yeah, but what are we going to eat?"

He wiggles his hand. Five-finger special. I laugh.

"You change your mind," he says, "I'll be behind the RinkyDink around seven. Get some thick boots."

We're about to hitch home when I see Mrs. Smythe peer into the Paradise. It's too late to hide because she sees me. Her face stiffens. She walks over to us and the guys start to laugh. Mrs. Smythe looks at them, then at me.

"Will?" she says. "Can I talk to you outside?"

She glances around like the guys are going to jump her. I try to see what she's nervous about. Tony is grabbing his crotch. Billy is cleaning his nails. The other guys are snickering. I suddenly see them the way she does. They all have long, greasy hair, combed straight back. We're all wearing jeans, T-shirts, and sneakers. We don't look nice.

She's got on her school uniform, as she calls it. Dark skirt, white shirt, low black heels, glasses. She's watching me like she hasn't seen me before. I hope she never sees my house.

"Later?" I say. "I'm kind of busy."

She blushes, the guys laugh hard. I wish I could take the words back. "Are you sure?" she says.

Tony nudges my arm. "Why don't you introduce us to your girlfriend," he says. "Maybe she'd like—"

"Shut up," I say. Mrs. Smythe has no expression now.

"I'll talk to you later, then," she says, and turns around and walks out without looking back. If I could, I'd follow her.

Billy claps me on the shoulder. "Stay away from them," he says. "It's not worth it."

It doesn't matter. She practically said she didn't want to see me again. I don't blame her. I wouldn't want to see me again either.

She'll get into her car now and go home. She'll honk when she pulls into the driveway so Mr. Smythe will come out and help her with the groceries. She always gets groceries today. The basics and sardines. Peanut butter. I lick my lips. Diamante frozen pizzas. Oodles of Noodles. Waffles. Blueberry Mueslix.

Mr. Smythe will come out of the house, wave, come down the driveway. They'll take the groceries into the house after they kiss. They'll kick the snow off their shoes and throw something in the microwave. Watch *Cheers* reruns on Channel 8. Mr. Smythe will tell her what happened in his day. Maybe she will say what happened in hers.

We catch a ride home. Billy yabbers about Christmas in Vancouver, and how great it's going to be, the two of us, no one to boss us around, no one to bother us, going anywhere we want. I turn away from him. Watch the trees blur past. I guess anything'll be better than sitting around, listening to Tony and Craig gripe.

Marine Life

Linda Svendsen

In July I visit my mother and we drive directly from the bus station to a car wash, even though her Dodge shines. She likes the slow tracks engaging the wheels, the car in neutral, the thought of hot carnauba wax. An attendant collapses the aerial and tells her to keep her foot off the brake.

"It's like driving under the ocean," Mum says. "I knew the fins on this old Dodge were meant for something."

Mops swathe the car in suds and giant bristles hum above us, then drag across the hood, roof, and sides. Her hands droop over the steering column and she stares straight ahead, although she can't possibly see through the lathered glass. "Come here once a day sometimes," she confides.

"Why so often?"

"It's kind of fun." She winks at me. "It's dark."

An overhead vacuum dries the car after the rinse. We watch the drops of water creep unnaturally up the slope of the windshield and disappear. She tells me this vacuum will often draw a migraine out through her temples, and I mention the trick my husband knows, how Bill can gently press the circle of his mouth to my forehead and take away pain. We laugh about that.

In daylight again, she turns the ignition and we start towards home. "I wish they lasted longer," she says.

We sit on the patio and watch the sprinkler waver back and forth, into sun, into shade. I grew up on this patio. I flooded it in winter and practiced for Rink Cadettes, skating into dizziness. We sip ginger ale while waiting for supper to cook.

"Remember when you used to run through the sprinkler in your birthday suit?"

"Yup."

"Remember when you used to run through the sprinkler in Robert's galoshes?"

That was before they could afford a wading pool. Now my mother and stepfather, rich on credit, discuss installing a real pool in their backyard, even though summers are brief and mythical in Vancouver. The grandchildren might enjoy it.

"How do you feel, Adele?" She means my pregnancy.

"With my hands." I look over, but she doesn't get it. "Fine. I just want pizza all the time."

"Thought of names?"

"Not yet."

I'm visiting my mother because she wants me to learn mothering. She wants her intuition and skill to rub off on me somehow, as softly and easily as scented oil. And I ask her about delivery—should I be localized, should I keep a piece of the umbilical cord, take a bite of umbilical cord, should there be music?

"Every birth is different," she begins, happy in authority. "You'll know when the time comes."

Mum's spine is shrinking and tightens like a wet braid. Our heights don't match anymore—I lean over slightly to see the haphazard part in her hair. Earlier when we husked corn in the kitchen, she asked, "Adele, did you feel the floor tilt?" And I said no, but the fault line *did* extend as far north as Canada and we were overdue. "I lose my balance once in a while," she admitted, ripping a green sleeve. "It's the planet moving, I'm sure."

She is sixty-five, my stepfather fifty-three, and this difference pinches her sleep, her face. Each night before bed, her hands slippery with cold lanolin, she coaxes suppleness back into her skin. "I keep busy," she says proudly.

We listen to the lawn mowers. They sound like a small war in the distance.

Mum introduces me to her ceramics instructor. "This is my daughter Adele, who's going to be a mother, too," speaking as if conception is our family's unique personal achievement.

She shows me what she has made: two white antelope for the mantelpiece, mugs with the family's names—June, Robert, my sisters Irene and Joyee, my brother Ray—and Bill's and mine still to be sanded; a flowerpot in the shape of a hippopotamus, glazed shakers wobbly on chicken legs, a stork for Q-tips.

"Mum, have you ever tried to shape anything on a potter's wheel? Or throw clay?"

"No."

"Maybe you should try."

"I paint everything myself," she stresses. "That damn hippo took three days."

A group of schoolchildren trot over to the kiln. They've made an octopus family, plaques for the bathroom, and they want to test the bubbles that will be suspended above them. I turn around and notice my mother bending happily with the seven-year-olds, checking.

After supper one night I ask if she will play the piano. Mum plays without sheet music, from memory, songs with notes that sit far off upon the ledger lines. I always ask myself how her brain knows where every finger should pause. How she carried on a conversation about where my mittens might be when her hands were reaching for something else, some black key.

When I was younger she played for fashion shows, nurses' graduations, cocktail hours, cabarets. She gave out a card with a golden treble clef: *June Will Be Pleased to Play Your Request.* She dressed thematically and wore muumuus and thongs for tropical shows, a chocolate suit for funerals, and a tiny rhinestone tiara on New Year's Eve.

She signed contracts with Tiki Tai, Town and Country, Coconut Grove, and the Elks' Club. I knew these were not the Hollywood clubs written up in magazines, but I believed they were the hotspots of the Lower Mainland, branches of a continental chain. It wasn't until I was older and could drive that I noticed these cabarets were out on the highways, parked on suburban edges. The Tiki Tai is now the O. K. Corral, the Town and Country topless, and the other two lost to fire.

After a certain age, I never knew aunts and uncles. I knew waitresses, chefs, managers, and sub drummers (my mother's steady drummer had recurrent heart attacks). She and Robert held dinner parties and invited staff, not other musicians or relatives. My brother, Ray, dated a coat-check girl my mother knew. She also introduced him to dancers in the Polynesian floor show, and it wasn't uncommon to see paper leis dangling from the knob of his closed door.

I went to drive-in movies with my stepfather while Mum played and played. We saw *The Manchurian Candidate, The L-Shaped Room*, and much of the *Flubber* series. We also played a word game on our way to pick her up, using the billboards and neon signs as the clues. Robert would say, for instance, What's a frisky pig? And I would scan the print in sight for the next two blocks and find Buckingham Cigarettes illuminated in bold letters above me and shout. Since we always drove the same route, the game eventually became predictable and we listened to call-in talk shows on the radio instead. The announcer said, "Hi, doll," to the women callers and listened to them complain about Gerda Munsinger, German spy, sleeping with Cabinet ministers. Robert started calling my mother Doll.

In 1965 her contract at the Simon Fraser Dining Room was not renewed. This gig was elegant, downtown, and Mum wept on her piano bench at home. An Oriental woman, Sue Kim or Kim Lu, had been hired and she was classical. Twenty-two.

"Let me be the man in the family," Robert said. "You don't have to work anymore."

"They think I'm old," she said.

He made phone calls to the Musicians' Union and a rival dining room. Ray and I drove to the grocery in his convertible and bought smokes and doughnuts. He told me she cried for Robert's attention.

When we returned, Mum was practicing scales—majors, minors, chromatics—sliding up and down ivory, and she did this the whole afternoon.

Tonight she says, "You might have heard these before," and plays music to inspire labour: "I Can't Give You Anything But Love, Baby," "Yes Sir, That's My Baby," "Baby Face." She still has that touch.

"You're a tourist now,'" Mum declares, even though I was born and raised here. "You live up north."

"I don't live 'up north.' I live only one day away."

"Osoyoos is up north," she says, and decides to show off Vancouver. She won't let me drive, claims I'm not used to automatic, and I won't fit behind the steering wheel anyway.

We stop at the Planetarium and she selects a postcard for Bill, now working at the sky-watch site in Manitoba. She's found the Crab Nebula, a magnified photograph of space. "Send this to your stargazer," she suggests. We both write messages, each picking up the other's last word and carrying it a few phrases further.

"Why don't we go up the mountain and look at the view, Mum?" I say. "There's no fog."

She chooses the scenic route and we skirt the ocean—the nudists at my old haunt, Wreck Beach, and families at Locarno and Jericho. When we reach the north shore she can't locate the exact turn and makes lefts, a few rights, guessing randomly, even follows the sign with an arrow pointing straight up. "I thought I could drive here in my sleep," she says. "Are we even climbing uphill?"

"Yes." And we are. The car has geared down, the air is crisper, and I glimpse the snow on Grouse above us, but she is still lost. She won't accept my help.

My mother opts for a tall hill, closer to home and accessible. The view is less spectacular than broad, and she claims she can distinguish the Gulf Islands twenty miles distant. I can't see that far.

One evening Robert thumbs through my prenatal manual and finds it pretty funny. He puts mats on the grass and we try exercises together—Mum, him, and me sprawling on our backs and hugging knees close to our foreheads. We inhale in unison and relax by isolating different areas of the body—wrists, thighs, shoulders—tightening and releasing. This exercise takes ten minutes done thoroughly and Robert ends up drowsing with his mouth open.

Mum and I go into the house and she hands me two needles caught in a fistful of soft wool. "He's knitting a bootie for you," she explains.

"For me?"

"For the baboo. And I'm doing its twin."

228

I can't believe it, can't picture his longshoring hands clicking needles. "Since when does he knit?"

"Since lately," she says. "Sometimes he's not tired when I conk out, so he decided there's not much difference between counting stitches or sheep." She adds, "I chose the pattern."

I get upstairs to bed before they do and hear them evaluating a new Toyota while doing dishes. Robert wipes and estimates their trade-in worth. Folding my hands on my stomach, I speak slowly to my baby, "Where you had little buds, you have arms and legs, my little tidal wave. And now you have eyelashes, and now you have toenails." I'm certain it can hear, only three months from birth, and my mother says it's sensitive to light; she's read babies can tell night and day before they see it.

I hear Mum turning on the news and then I worry about my tactless nerves carrying sensations, uncensored, to the amniotic fluid: a sadness while stroking my mother's roses; the shock when the phone rings because I hope it's Bill and that he's all right. I wonder what my baby might already know.

Mum wakes me. "It's a bad dream." Her hand shakes my shoulder. "Adele, it's all right."

I sit up and look at her, groggy and nightgowned, on the edge of the bed. I'm in my old room, unfamiliar without my trappings: a collection of starfish, books on shamanism; totem poles. It's the spare room now, bare except for ivy cuttings. "I'm not having a bad dream."

"I heard you," she says. "You were yelling in your sleep."

"Damn it, Mum. You woke me up." I settle back down.

"*You* woke me."

"It was probably a train whistle."

"It was you.'"

I'm certain it wasn't. I vaguely recall dreaming about Bill and me driving through Wyoming and think she's woken me on purpose.

"Come have a cup of tea," she offers. "You'll feel better."

We hobble downstairs in our slippers and prepare tea and cinnamon toast. She remembers when I used to fight with people in my sleep. How she and Robert would be turning off the lights, or tucking our dog into his basket with a biscuit, and I'd scream, "Shut up," or "Go to hell, you dumb cluck," and make Groucho bark.

"Who were you so mad at?"

I don't know. I'm tired and want to go back to bed, but she's awake and ready to chat—about Ray's common-law love, about a branch she's booked to play for Job's Daughters, how she must rehearse.

About 2 a. m. she fetches a small china box and places it before me. She opens it and spreads tiny molars and bicuspids and incisors on the table, beside our saucers, and tells me it's my first set of teeth.

"You're kidding," I say.

"No," she whispers. "I'll always keep your teeth."

The next morning Mum asks if I'll go to her swimming class. It's held at the same complex as her ceramics workshop. The recreation centre runs several programs for seniors and she takes square dancing as well. "Do-si-do," she calls to me, coming out of the bathroom, and back to back, we switch places.

Tomorrow I catch the bus to my home in the Interior. I realize I haven't called my sister Irene yet, Ray, my hermit father, and have spent all my time with her and Robert. I say, "Yes, I'll come to your lesson."

When my mother stopped playing seriously, I was in junior high school. Only time on my hands, she said, and volunteered for the Christmas concert, embarrassing me with the amount of hair spray she used. She appeared for the oil refinery field trip, an unwanted chaperone, and pouted when I didn't sit with her. "Someday you'll wish you could ride on a bus with your mother," she said to me as she squeezed by. Once, she offered to pick me up after school and go for a shake. I saw her car approaching and ducked behind a hedge, and waved her airily on when she slowed, anxious.

She shopped and brought home blouses with big perky bows or hats that would sell big in Antarctica, furry things I refused to wear, socks with toes, and then apologized. "I know my taste is all in my mouth," she said. Even last birthday, when she mailed Snoopy sheets, she wrote, "If you and Bill want to return them, I have the receipt."

She packs for her swimming class: a fluffy towel, hairdryer, shampoo and conditioner, bathing cap, a suit with her Floaters crest prominent on the abdomen, and unnecessary goggles. She hasn't yet learned how to put her head under water and keep her eyes open.

At the pool she entered the changing room with other older ladies. "Hello, June," they say. "Hot today." They enjoy this ritual of totebags and lockers and a teacher telling them what to do.

I watch Mum change. Her stomach is loose and her legs are scarred from vein stripping, thigh to heel. She struggles with her suit and I clasp it for her at the back.

"Adele, why don't you take a dip?"

The other ladies seem to agree it would be refreshing. "Don't exert yourself, though, honey." Mum asks the instructor about my shorts and tank top and she says they'll be okay. The water will be soothing.

The class won't pay attention at first. They bob up and down in the pool, comparing gardens and bantering about the odd-even sprinkling rules. Mum playfully flicks water in my direction.

The instructor has them do widths using a paddleboard. My mother kicks with the rest of them, slowly, and crosses the pool. Then they practice their frog kick. These older women, uneasy amphibians, are more of land than water. They roll in the small current they create, and some surrender to the swell and kick solely from the knee, forgetting the glide. Their bones are brittle. Break a leg when you're sixty and it may never mend. And so a few just turn over on their back and float.

They are supposed to learn the basics of the modified breast-stroke today. Mum has mentioned it—how difficult it will be to coordinate arms, legs, and lungs. "As you glide, your chin lifts," the instructor explains, "and you inhale. Then, as you stroke, ex-hale."

I see my mother crossing the pool, going away from me; her breathing is erratic and rapid. The paddleboard supports her chest, but only her legs lend motion, as her arms reach out awkwardly. I'm nervous now: I realize we are all in the same water. I sense my baby drifting inside, and look at my mother, flailing towards the other side, and I am in between, some kind of lifeguard in the shallows.

Joe in the Afterlife

Annabel Lyon

JOE HAS BEEN KICKING his daughter out of the house since she was three. He can't help it, she's annoying. He shouts, but she whips books and cups at his head. Now, twenty years on, she's retreated to the bathroom as usual—violent, shaking, trying to get back inside herself. He likes it when Gaby loses control of her body like this, when she's angry.

Ellie, Joe's wife, has asked him to stop evicting the child. 'I'm leaving anyway!' shouts the brat in the bathroom. This is not news. Gaby lives half packed, waiting for the planets to align and the bluebirds to sweep her to a bachelor with hardwood and cable for four-fifty a month, in a gingerbread house with a chocolate landlord, on a major bus route through the enchanted wood. 'I'm serious,' Joe tells Ellie.

Still, they have this fiction, or he does, that she is leaving tomorrow or the next day.

The days have been coming up hot. Six a.m. generally finds Joe in the back garden with tea and *New Yorkers,* in the tiny cool-

233

ing slivered between night and day. He sleeps poorly, melancholic that he is, but enjoys the weightlessness of dawn. He floats up on it, and spends the rest of the day falling.

This morning Gaby appeared, eyes poached from sleep, airy-fairy in her little-girl nightie, with its ribbons and stitching. Had he woken her, nabbed her magazine, scored her mug?

'I dreamt a man was having his arms chainsawed off,' she said.

'Oh, please,' Joe said.

He knows what she needs. Her progress was arrested, he reckons, back in the creature stage, when she was supposed to learn to socialize with the other little crawlers at play school. But she got to books early and became a person while other people's offspring were still engaging little geckos. Now she won't leave the house. The stuff she collects for her apartment might as well furnish a tomb for the afterlife. Nothing gets used.

'You don't like anyone,' he said once.

'I like Sam Cooke and the Hollies,' she said. 'I like Gandhi.'

It's 1999. She needs a little push.

*

Later that morning, Joe steps out to taste the air. Gaby has her futon frame on chairs in the garage. She's stirring a pot of urethane with a foam brush. The milky liquid looks too thin to have a purpose. 'Don't come stand over me, Daddy,' she says.

'Mum thinks you might like our bread knife for the new place. Is this true?'

Gaby wants to start painting, doesn't want to be looked at. Joe knows. 'Oh, it's no secret I covet that knife,' she says.

'What is that stuff, milk?' Joe asks, turning back to the house.

'That's right,' she says.

Reaching for the doorknob, a pain in his arm stops him like a question. Are you sure? it asks. He's on his knees before he knows it, on his face. He or Gaby is laughing. Both, he thinks afterwards. Both, please?

*

Live on television, tethered astronauts are aloft, soundlessly patching their craft. The film lurches—intimate, faintly obscene—like film of insects.

Gaby sits beside him, absorbing images from the set. He's in her room, in her bed. He never allowed her to move her bed from her ground floor room to the attic loft and now he's in it, so.

An English nurse, bright and worthy as a new penny, comes and goes like a toy. She reminds him of the ambulance. That was a sunny day. A black flower had bloomed in his brain.

But will you look at this, Joe thinks, picking at an old, ongoing argument in his head. His daughter is an ascetic and a cold, cool woman. The walls and curtains are blue, the bookshelves are another blue. The girl herself slumps in a wicker armchair, puffed with cushions styled from a blue silk sari—*Ellie's* craft and thrift. Blue shadows puddle the corners. Otherwise the room is picked clean of personality, like a hotel room between guests.

And here sits Gaby, in her sandals and army surplus pants and the inevitable white T-shirt, no makeup, no jewellery, no graces at all, hugging her legs to her, mouth mashed to a knee, eyes on the set. He finds her easier to love in the summertime—small, impatient, muscled like a boy, strung up and down with blue veins. But she has an RRSP, which he finds ghoulish in a young girl with good skin.

He's so sick, he realizes.

The pennyworth nurse wears a cardigan, pink or green. After she leaves Gaby makes fun of her. She takes Joe's pulse. 'Bloody marvellous!' she says. 'Now touch your pain.' He can't much move, can't smile, although she's doing it for him. 'Brilliant!' she says.

Ellie brings food for each of them on a tray. She and Gaby eat spaghetti with chicken and olives. Joe sips the spoonfuls of gelatine she slips between his teeth. There is a machine in the corner between the bed and the wall, heavy and square, set down like a piece of luggage. No one pays it heed except Joe, who would like to know if he is attached to it.

Days have been flipping past, like cards; and their black backs.

The sickroom curtains are drawn; the TV is alive. His wife and daughter wear lovely flickering masks. He wonders where the astronauts are going. When he makes a sound to ask they slowly turn, they look at him in wonder.

*

The speech therapist wears a smart, creamy little summer suit with a daft sleeveless polka-dot blouse. When she removes her jacket he sees her arms are richly tanned, all the way up to the shoulders. He approves. She is after his heart with her careless skin—not like his own pair, with their fears of sun and estrogen and God knows. Although, to be fair, both he and his wife come from cancerous families. Barring the unforeseen, Gaby can expect to go that way, as Joe himself had expected, until now.

The speech therapist sits beside him on the bed and makes a business with flash cards and tape recorder, propping items on his leg. He feels placid and coddled, unfocused by her lovely skin. He senses her growing urgency—his hand squeezed, names repeated. His eyes swim in the dots on her blouse. Her throat too is nutty, her jaw, ears. Silver knots peg the lobes. What a lovely, babbling brook of a stupid woman. All right, he thinks. Just a minute.

He watches her mouth form shapes and his tongue butts tooth, trying to wet his dry lips. She disappears behind his head. *It's too soon*, or *It's no use*. The astronauts, stiff as big gingerbread men, don't speak clearly either. Their efforts emerge as radio cracklings in Houston. 'Roger that,' says Houston.

236

Gaby never turns the set off. She seems to need CNN like morphine. Is this what she does, long hours alone of a Saturday night?

I don't care, I think she's a lesbian, Joe told Ellie last month. It's fine with me. Safer in every direction when you think about it. All I'm saying is, at her age, she should be getting *out*. The astronauts give way to the death of a rock star, shot once accurately by the husband of a deranged fan. The fan had abandoned her family to stalk the singer, although at one time the whole family had been fans.

His daughter seems to hunger for this stuff. It lights her up, makes her laugh. When they play the rock star's famous song she hums along, snapping her fingers to the beat. 'This is for my dad,' she says, and sings the chorus into the microphone of her thumb. When the shot cuts back to the astronauts, she pounces towards the set, pointing. 'The empyrean!' she cries.

Ellie looks in. 'Gaby,' she says.

At first, Ellie is there at night, eating raisins and reading *Anna Karenina* and books about paint. The phone rings, giving her a start. 'Curses,' she says, picking raisins off the carpet. The phone rings too many times—won't she answer? The TV stays off at night and he misses it—imagines the pulse behind its bland black eye. *Stay,* he thinks often, of no one particular. Shapes in his mouth, sweet and pepper—*stay*. Nights are as usual the worst, a despair of small sounds. It's summertime, again or still, the progress of summertime, and the insects—their fine Swiss mechanisms—bother his reason. Gaby emblazons them to the walls with a slipper, not often enough. Saltwater sleep—he tries to get back under. But a mosquito has found his name and is repeating it, in its tiny tight language, over and over.

*

Gaby has started a diet, a thing he has never permitted. His mind's eye follows her to the kitchen—ripping up lettuces, drinking water as an appetite suppressant. Thinner than *what?*, he thinks, fretting.

The astronauts are down. There have been brochures, lately. Lately she has been showing him pictures, too close to his nose. 'It's a dorm, Dad,' she says, shaking her head. 'There's gonna be ivy.'

Now she upends a sack from the drugstore onto his knees. Small, shaped items click against each other, coloured sticks and circles. She opens a compact and shows him a neat flat square of, apparently, hot chocolate mix. 'Eleven ninety-five for dust,' she says. She powders her nose, then his. She pops a lid and squirrels up a tube of lipstick. In a minute she looks like a small child who's been eating fruit. 'All right?' she says. She wipes it off and tries again.

And then it's liquor store boxes, boxes, boxes. She and Ellie have spent the day on the floor taking kettles in and out of paper, it seems like, telling each other to put the books in small boxes and where is the list and thank you, thank you, you're sure I can take it?

'No one drinks coffee here any more anyway,' Ellie says.

I can buy a better one, Joe tells himself. I'm sick and I'm rich. I can have anything I want.

*

Time flows and overflows. 'Goofs wear make-up,' says the brat at the mirror, expertly now at the mirror, pinking in her lips. He looks at the loot from her jeans pockets, the precious piles—pennies, nickels, starfish of keys. She puts it all on and takes it all off, with tissues and puffs and costly waters, until her face is pure again. She sorts her boxes. The TV is alive.

*

'What did the doctor say?'

He hates his own voice, such as it is now—the animal speaking-sound he makes, all sonorous wadded tongue.

'I'm anaemic, for one thing,' she says. 'He says it's like I gave blood, but every day. He says I have to take supplements and eat, basically, more.'

'*Uh,*' says Joe.

'There's nothing like a soiled urinal to get you thinking about the future,' Gaby says. 'Personal hygiene is a long and winding road.'

Ads. She rises to a protest of bones, body static, and lopes, stretching, to the bathroom.

On the television, beautiful women are selling creams with their beauty and naughtiness. They wink and lightly finger their faces. Their decadence is ancient and irresistible. Even Gaby is a sucker for their balms. He once hated her—*hated* her—for buying a little cake of complexion soap for thirty dollars when she was fifteen and her skin was poor. Imagining *what?* But he thinks now of the old woman's body she carries about within her gradually revealing itself. Take care of her! She's here now! Eyes, voice, baby pudge, eaten by aliens! Skin tortured, voice transposed down, hands buckled and sheathed with arthritis, sure as Christmas. He wants her to get out there, get married, now, soon. What's your problem? he thinks to his child. Marry a man, marry a woman, what are you waiting for?

He seems to recall his own wedding, but with a deluxe, five-star wealth of detail that falsifies the memory. Ellie in her wedding dress, spitting in the garden. Guests flinging palmfuls of pins. Ellie in her wedding dress, in the hotel room, talking on the phone, nibbling her bouquet. Gaby already known, there in her little spaceship, inside Ellie. A single black seed, like a kiwi seed, lodged in his brain, behind his left ear.

Either he's getting better or he's getting worse. That, he realizes, is the answer.

Kiss. Doors slam. Gaby leaves.

After she's gone, Ellie decides to stencil the walls around him, to keep him company. She has low-odour paint. On the second day she abandons the template and goes freehand. *She's drawing on the walls,* flowers and such, twining lines up near the ceiling. She stands on his bed to reach her pencil into the corner, tracking and trailing graphite down the blue walls, her foot nudging his hip. On day five, frowning like an artist, she abandons her paints for a single colour, gold.

*

A speech therapist comes to the house, a West Indian woman in a white suit with a giddy tropical blouse. They make sounds at each other, smiling, and she leaves him with exercises. She will come each week until he is better.

Ellie no longer sits with him at night. It's cool and dark and dry in this painted room, with the whirr of jewelled insects exploring his daughter's woks and socks. Tonight they watched a program about space exploration. The narrator was lucid and seemed to peel back the mysteries of distance and light; Joe hoped children everywhere were watching. When it was over he felt like a steady ship. But then he asked, 'How long have I been down?'

Ellie looked at him. 'Three weeks,' she said. 'Including today.' What was she waiting for?

A door opened in his mind. 'Where does Gaby sleep?'

'At the dorm.'

Now, alone in the dark, this answer he finds familiar, although he knows it to be false. She is in the next room, of course, or the next; he can hear her fidgeting at night, like the princess bedded down with her golden pea. Her tiny sounds, tiny rages and incoherencies. Presently she will come and watch TV with him, as she has always done, cool in her skin, his little alien. He has her now.

Comforted, he floats on down summer's river, royalty inspecting the desert.

Righteous Speedboat

Mark Anthony Jarman

For no animal admires another animal.
  —Blaise Pascal (1623-1662)

EVEN NOW THE VIBRATING SCREEN maims the very molecules of my eyes but I have to gaze. How many bent berserkers, how many peckerwood imposters will they call to the silver microphone before they call to me, here with my nigh-on ruined vision? No finish at the net and hands of stone but I can read a play, backcheck like a madman and I move malevolently inside a snarling wind. Pins go down. That ought to be worth *something*, a few paydays, a winning smile from the bankteller. Tampa could take me down there with their palmetto bugs. Need be I'll go to the moon, I'll skate on Mars.

Maybe a scrounging team will grab me in a late round. Scrounging is okay, late round is okay. I could help a club in the Colonial League, work my way up. Just give me a contract. Or else I'm toast. I'm over-age, I can't go back to my junior team. I burnt a few bridges there, pissed off the scunt-eyed coach. I caught an elbow in the nose and saw visions of gasping lightning while the guy with said elbow slid away like a pulse to score the winning goal, to bury it topshelf. All season who had the best plus-minus on the club? *Moi.* I repeat: I had the best plus-minus on the team. Yet in front of everyone the coach really reamed me out. Up and down, went to town. He had no need to do that, to humiliate me.

Elbowed nose still throbbing, I moved in close to the coach, paused to get him wondering, feinted, then I gave his nose a shot: I clocked the coach. Nothing really. They want you to hit everyone else: *Him,* they say in Spokane, and you know what they mean. Bing bang bong. Do it to *them,* though, touch *them* and it's the end of the fucking world. They tell the reporters you're "difficult," you're a cancer on the team. Control freak wimps. Blue-legged fops. Pukely ticket-punchers. I say this much is obvious: the "difficult" players are the real action, living it, lean as whippets; they throb, eat at the air like engines.

I call my agent long-distance and he allows, *This is he.*

Doesn't look good, he says. Our noisy years are moments, he says.

I call my mother and she sighs, You had so much potential.

I'd call my friend from Salmon Arm but Ryan's lost his head. The bloody trail across the gravel road I still dream of, and the green radiator water burning my hair. Ryan's head rolling.

Once upon a time this was a happening bar but now it's a loser bar. The bar has no view at all, a pocked pallid concrete bunker, which is good. Night for day, no trees and no sky. You pay extra for trees and sky, the darkening harbour. You need no view. You need to hear your name echoing in that distant subsidized convention centre; those two sweet words in that room of tasteful blurred suits. Your name.

I like loser bars. They're quiet and I can think.

I think there is always some injustice. We depend on tales of injustice. At the small curved bar an intense young man is telling

243

a dark-eyed woman his specific story of injustice. He's well-dressed: black custom-cut pants and a beautiful shirt that is white and tapered. Gel gleams evenly in his hair. I decide his name is Laszlo. Someone looks after Laszlo's cuticles. Laszlo smokes. He collects things: plenitude, kudos, ivory elephants. The young woman is listening yet she is clearly fidgety, restless. Her dark eyes move in a sad poised face. I watch her dark eyes shiver. Her lipstick is almost black. She shows her teeth in a sad brief smile and it is everything. You learn everything. I can't stand the idea that it's all random.

Here's a guy, Laszlo says, leaning right at her, real good guy, he says.

Here's a guy, I don't know, so-called best friend.

Laszlo lowers his voice but I can still hear him. He's too close to her. This is a guy that. Feed him breakfast. Pick him up, take him to work. Give him a job and uh, *float* him. And uh, my mom has his cheque, some deductions of course, he looks at it, something's wrong, he says.

The young woman asks Laszlo a question.

Yeah, my mom, she had it. And he stole! He stole from us! Laszlo cuts the air with flat hand. I went by the next day. This is not the agreed . . . What is this—this, this holding company? None of your business. Well, I said. I was ready to kill—

The dark-eyed woman breaks into his story.

Sorry, she says, I *really* have to run. Give me a call, she says. Gotta go!

Oh, he says. A-O-KAY! he says brightly. Laszlo tries to get funnier after the serious story. He needs a fast transition. He picks up her key ring, a tiny flashlight hooked on it, and he sings into the tiny flashlight as if it's a microphone: I DID IT MY WAY! he belts out.

My Funny Valentine, he croons softly, eyebrows up like Elvis Costello.

They both try to laugh but still she takes her keys back, plunging them deep within her Peruvian satchel.

The young woman leaves briskly, outside to oaks up like oars in a spooky sky, and Laszlo glances around, ill at ease now, alone, no longer singing. Now he has to adjust himself, recast the last moments, her exit. His status has changed here. He peers around at the subterranean concrete tomb as if for the first time, at the monotonous hockey draft unscrolling on the monster TV screen. It's a crap shoot. Some of us are wanted in the first or second round. Some players wait all day and no one calls. I'm not flying down east for nothing, for crocodile tears in the arena seats and maybe your parents phoning your hotel room, telling you there's next year, or you could play in Italy or Blackpool. Everyone will lie to you at some point. They decide they know best. Some are allowed dignity; others scramble. I will scramble if necessary. I'm not 6'5" but I'll run my cranium into the Zamboni if that's what they desire. They can croon my name, tap me on the shoulder, and I'll get it done. Only connect. Call my name. I'm shallow. I want to hear my muddled name run through a silver microphone, to shake hands with a million people I don't know.

Laszlo shows the red-haired bartender something from his wallet. A sunlit photo, waterfront property, a speedboat docked. The speedboat has a blue canopy and a blue racing stripe.

Looksee, he says. Is that a nice place or is that a nice place? Just up island. Hey, tell you what. You want to go there, let me know. I'm driving up there practically every week. All the goddamn time.

He carries a photo of property in his wallet. Now: would I be any different? I'd probably carry a photo too.

Laszlo scribbles a note left-handed, passes it over. The bartender does not read the note. I order a Greyhound, bite from the small onion I always carry in my coat. I'd like some chowder or chili, some good cornbread or sweet potato. Carbohydrate loading just in case I get picked.

Laszlo points with his sterling silver pen at the bartender's red hair.

You must be Irish, eh?

No, says the red-haired bartender, looking irritated.

Our place up island: we've got ten acres, two hundred grand. Bay goes in like this—we own from this peak to here. Goes back, big trees. Ten acres. Laszlo keeps smoking. He opens his wallet again. He likes to open his wallet. The ferry system, this is how. . . . The schedule. Thursday. No, hold that. Tuesday. Right. You know why Tuesday?

He lights another smoke. Dull Clapton plays: post-heroin Clapton, post-lobotomy Clapton. I'm truly sorry his little kid fell out of the high-rise but I don't like the tape. I like Art Bergman's new single: *create a monster, something something, we got a contract, contract, who's using who?* Art Bergman, the crown prince of detox. The hockey draft is still on the screen. My draft. I'm so close to a contract, to treasure. Mr. Eric Clapton sells a billion boring records and no one wants me. The bartender doesn't ask why Tuesday.

On TV men in suits argue and wave clean hands enroute to the silver microphone; they must speak their pick, announce who will skate, who will consider a million seven, who will buy a sleek growling speedboat. Something is wrong though; men in suits argue like they're chewing a mouthful of bees. They act as if they don't know their pick. I'm available! I shoot out mental telepathy messages from this edge of the country. Me! I have a head on my shoulders.

The erudite GM bends over; he seeks the ear of the frowning coach. The GM straightens, walks to talk with the worried head scout, then puts glasses on the end of his nose, peers over some papers. A weird delay of some kind, a plot complication at the meat market. Just past the media tables I can see the cackling old owner who was jailed for fraud and mob connections, for taking the Fifth, for taking the assets, for chortling. Well, no one figured he was a choirboy.

They'll take a d-man, says one customer.

No, they need a centre. Definitely a centre, says another.

The GM at the mike finally mouths the name of the anointed, the chosen. A goalie! Takes a goalie! They have goalies in the system. They have goalies coming out the yin yang. Trade bait, but who? Trade the young guy? The backup goalie? Trade the older goalie the former cokehead?

They screwed up, someone in the bar says. They screwed up. He says this four times in a row.

They've been tricked. They traded up to get the franchise bruiser they wanted; they made a deal, and all parties agreed to square dance, to give and take. They agreed what bodies would be available when they got to the microphone but at the last second another team, a team without scruples, traded draft choices and future considerations, snatching the franchise bruiser out from under their red noses. Stole from them. Their *property*. We've been snookered, states the GM, we've been submarined. The GM's Byzantine manoeuvres and agreements are useless. I traded up for nothing, he thinks, all that trouble for another goalie. The troubled scout tears the bruiser's name off their jersey, his sweater waiting at their table. How sure they were. They don't have my name on a jersey. They have different tables for each team, like it's the United Nations, like it's the fate of the free world. Then there are prickly-pear and sea lions, sooty terns and albatrosses and California sea lions dripping in the sun on the colour TV. Another highly illogical car commercial that seems to be flogging some product other than cars. What exactly is it they are hawking? Vermillion and sienna sunsets? Oceanfront? Does it work? Do these ads actually move their lipstick-colour cars to the tire-kickers and lot lizards and lay downs and strokers?

Insects crash at the screen, hearkening tragically into their multi-hued harbour. They want to eat the TV light, the only game in town. I keep studying the draft but Laszlo studies two women who seat themselves at the bar. The first woman keeps her sunglasses on. She is taller than me. I see her and think *stature, presence*. Her friend is shorter, with lighter hair and the small peaceful face of a follower.

The woman in the dark glasses inhales hugely, exhales: Well, we broke up. Went pretty well considering.

Woman #2: No sobbing?

Woman #1: A little. (She pauses.) Him. Not me.

Woman #2: Let's go prowling!

Woman #1: No thanks.

Woman #2: Oh yeah. You're in THAT phase. Wait two weeks and you'll be crawling the walls.

Woman #1: No. I don't think so.

I realize she has someone lusty waiting, someone already drafted, but she hasn't told her friend. She broke it off with one guy to move to another. She possesses a five year plan.

Woman #2 complains, My roommates are doing it all the time and I have to sit and listen. I mean I can't help but hear it. I can't afford my own place. And he has to end up with *her*. I had such a crush on him. It was supposed to be *me*. I had hopes. Now I'm going nuts. Why do I have such bad luck with guys I like?

They sip their drink specials.

Woman #1 says, This older guy took me to an Icelandic film festival. The movies were like, what the fuck!?

AHA! I think. An older guy is chosen.

For me the charm of hockey was always its lack of charm. It wasn't hip. My agent says he'll call me back. He's busy with his "real" clients. I walk to the washroom and see a nickel gleaming at the bottom of the porcelain urinal. I do not pick it up. I look out at my nation. I have no nation. Okay—I have a wormwood nation.

Laszlo is talking to the two women: We'll take my Dad's speedboat across. If you don't have tackle we can get you some. Waterfront. On the water. Everyone said we paid too much. Local yokels laughing. Day later, $20,000 more. Who's laughing now? Very rare find. Very rare. Nice beach. Arbutus and oak. Beautiful property. We'll get some people. We'll go up there. Road trip! Road trip!

Well now, isn't waterfront always on the water? Woman #2 wonders.

What's the catch? I wonder. Why does Laszlo have to cajole people to go to this Shangri-La? Doesn't it come stocked with beautiful people? The way they stock a fish farm? A fat farm?

I realize Laszlo is talking to a different bartender. Bartender #2.

Bob Hope, Laszlo exclaims. Bob Hope's been there. We'd just fumigated so he wasn't too happy. Log cabin, some bugs. Ants I guess. Cedar. Wouldn't think so. Puzzling. That loser shirt, Laszlo says, laughing at the bartender.

Hey sport. Hey pal. This is my brother's shirt. My brother who died in an accident. A *fatal* accident.

Oh. Sorry.

Laszlo lights another smoke, looks around. On TV a GM slides right by a team's table, a team he used to coach. He jumped ship. He doesn't look and they don't look at him. He found the loophole he needed to break his contract, to dance with another party, a party other than the one that "brung" him.

Bob Hope's a card. Bob Hope says, Any chance of anything here? Something other than pinochle and Ovaltine? Nyuck. Know what I mean? Country girls, nice country girls. He wanted some action. Horny old bugger. We caught a cod. Engine broke down, going slow, get a blueback, keeper, three pounder, eat salmon that night. But I'd rather catch one big one. One big chinook, a tyee, a king. Bob Hope bitching at me all day in that irritating voice. I'm looking for this ledge, I'm looking for this ledge with a depth finder. Jigged, buzz-bombed, mooched, nothing. Tried a new lure, a silver one I found in Dad's tacklebox.

(Now it's Bartender #3 half-listening, a guy in a muscle shirt. I think the bartenders must take shifts with Laszlo, then go hide back in the cooler.)

ZING! GOT IT! Laszlo mimics a fishing rod and a sudden strike on the line. ZING! He doesn't finish the fishing story. He smokes non-stop. I have another Greyhound. Maybe they don't draft players who punch their coaches. Maybe there's a secret agreement, rules they don't tell you about. I'm bitter (wormwood, wormwood). I'm starting to feel like saussurite, like schist, like stone.

A stoned voice bellows in the direction of the jukebox: "PLAY SOMETHING . . . BY SOMEBODY . . . WHO KILLED THEM-SELVES!

This desire to be fucked up, and think it something special, something to be attained. That's rich. Ask my friend Ryan about dead guys. Ask a dead guy about getting fucked up. Ask if they're really happy.

All my friends are lawyers, Laszlo says. And the women are incredible! They work so hard they don't have time to meet anyone else. You want to meet great women hang out with lawyers.

Yeah. Like I really want to hang out with lawyers, Bartender #3 growls.

On TV the GM in the suit is helping the young hockey player pull on his new team sweater. It's too intimate. There is some awkward tugging at clothes, then embarassed smiles and camera flashes for the sports cards.

Who's this clown they pick? Who's this sack of hammers?

Some Swede faggot. A *foreigner*.

You on a team? Laszlo asks the muscled bartender.

Used to be. Same old used to be.

Now I recognize Bartender #3: a fantastically shifty forward with Tri-Cities. He had moves like a humpback salmon, and Pittsburgh was after him until he was submarined, blew out both knees big time. Good old Tom what's-his-name. They said he'd never walk again. Huge writhing scars each side of his knees. Twins. A suicide pass. Skate into the middle and CRANG! you flip over with a quicksilver crunching, then they carry you off, a sudden screeching pauper. Wheelbarrows of cash will alter anyone, but he's been changed by the cash he never got, by what could have been that draft year. He could have been the one under the blinding television lights, the one getting offered a million seven. Instead. Well instead he watches with me. Now Tom what's-his-name is a major drunk with rehab muscles. I'm not as shifty but at least my knees are okay. My knees are not too shabby. I cast a shadow, I get my back up, show up for every game. Buffalo could take me. The Jets. There's that windy corner. The Sharks. This sounds like *West Side Story*.

I'm going to drive up there to the property tomorrow. Come on along. Pick up my cousin and bullshit. Deli grub, some Heineken. Greenies. You like Heineken? No? The airport and take the speedboat across.

    Laszlo has told three different bartenders about the speedboat.

    Laszlo asks, How does that bear joke go again? Let's see. Bartender tells the bear he can't serve him because he's on drugs. This part. I can never remember. Drugs. What drugs. You help me, yeah. Oh, the *barbiturate*. The bar-bitch-you-ate! Ya ya. Ha ha. That's a good one.

    The two women do not share Laszlo's love of the bear joke.

    We're lucky, you know, Laszlo says to the women, that place up island. Played our cards right. Cheap locals can go jump in a lake. If they knew anything they'd be somewhere else, right? Road goes around pretty little bay. Speedboat. No waiting. Catch a big one. No tackle we'll take care of you. Little general store not far. Good beef jerky. If we don't have it you don't need it. That's what they say on their sign. They don't have it you don't need it. That's their hick philosophy, their London School of Economics approach to local yokel marketing. Road goes around nice little bay. See the smooth golden stones at the bottom. A beautiful place. We own it. It's ours.

Lizard King Jim Morrison says Hello. Jim Morrison says he loves me. Morrison says he wants to know my name. The jukebox decides what to play. And the big screen shows the famous footage: Big surly Eric Lindros refuses the sweater. He stares off, dark mad eyes and curly hair. A thick neck, a bull. He'll never sign with this team. Maybe they called his name but that doesn't mean they own him, that doesn't mean he's their *property*. He refuses their blue uniform, their lovely stone city, their scheming owner. In this hexed process, this amateur hour crapshoot, here's what I wish to know, to *divine*: who has the real power and who is the victim? That's what I have to learn, even though I already know the truth.

Wait until Lindros is on the ice, the young man says to Bartender #4. He'll pay then. Someone'll stick him good. Get his bad knee.

I say nothing. They shouldn't talk like that. I've seen too many torn-up knees. Hurt!? Are you fucking kidding? Un-fucking-believeable. Anterior cruciate; that's the worst. It digs into my stomach just thinking of ruined knees.

Just how many bartenders are back there? Do they have a bartender *pool*? There are more bartenders than customers.

Everyone thinks Lindros is a greedy arrogant asshole but meanwhile the team's owner is mulling over juicy offers of $75 million U.S. for the franchise. The Quebec owner will sell in the night; the owner will hustle the team out of Canada with a tearful press conference. The owner will cry all the way to the bank. Who's the greedy asshole then? What did our pal Peter Pocklington get for selling Gretzky to Los Angeles, for selling a person, a *human being*? $20 million? (For he is an honourable man.) Thanks for destroying the Oilers, *Peter.* And how much money does the crooked meatpacker owe the Alberta government right now? He's in so deep they can't touch his house of cards, his dead pigs and stuffed sausages and offal, his slit-throat palace over the river valley. So the players are greedy? The players are arrogant? Give me a break. Get real.

No one gives me a break. No one gets real. Instead they draft a dead guy. In fact they draft Ryan, my friend from Salmon Arm. His last night on earth we were riding in what journalists would later refer to as the death car. I was passed out in the backseat. Ryan was in the passenger seat. Then I woke up in the ditch, in the rhubarb where the world was utterly different. Green water was pouring out of the upside-down radiator, burning me. The power pole was in three pieces, its line sparking. Ryan's head rolled across the gravel road, his brain still sending messages, questions, trying to find out what's wrong. I took off my wet shirt and hid my friend's head. I was afraid to pick it up so I just covered it with my shirt. What would you do? The car looked like modern sculpture, the driver still curled inside it like a foetus. Not a scratch on me, though my teeth were chattering and my hair was steaming. My friend's head: pebbles and dust stuck on it. And this brain of mine. Then some kind of gleaming milk truck came by and the driver said Jesus. And the big club must not know he's dead. If Ryan was alive he'd laugh. Here they are throwing away a pick on him before they'll draft me.

I have watched the drunken screen for hours, eating the past, wrapping my head in it and my eyes complain at the images, at the labour; my eyes are shifting right out of focus. Can't they make a big screen that doesn't kill you?

I am one of God's creatures but no one is taking me. Not the

253

Lightning in Tampa, not the Panthers. Not the Jets. Not the San Jose Sharks. They're taking hundreds of snipers, killers, muckers, headcases, piranhas, plumbers, pretenders. They call out polyglot Latvian names at the silver microphone. They don't care about my plus-minus, they don't care about my Grade 8 blues records or sensitive feelings or that I move like silt and stick like glue. What about the San Diego Gulls or Las Vegas and that Russian guy named Radek Bonk? This is a great name for a player. Bonk! Pass me the puck! Hit him, Bonk. Bonk him! Marty McSorley was going to sign with Las Vegas, play in the desert. I'd play in the desert. I can't go back to the fucking last-place Cougars. I know I'm *this* close to making it but the Cougars have dragged me down, they've buried me, made me invisible. In a seething minute you are made to pay for your geography, for being in the snake-bit boonies; the center doesn't hold for *you*.

I'll have to try my luck as a free agent. Some good players aren't picked but they make it later as a walk-on. They force the issue, bull their way in the door. Courtnall, Joey Mullen, Dino Ciccarelli, Adam Oates. It happens. Brett Hull wasn't taken until the 117th pick, and Fleury was 166th his year. Nemchinov didn't go to New York until the 244th pick overall in 1990. Now he has a Stanley Cup ring. Every Cup team has its free agents, its "difficult" players. They made it, crawled out of the ooze. You hear their names: a mantra repeated. There's a free-agent camp somewhere in the States; the scouts look you over, look inside your head, see what you've got. Courtnall has it made in the shade now, big money, owns restaurants and a spiffy log cabin on a cliff over the crashing ocean. Douglas fir and ferns and fishing boats in the harbour where the whales come in to rub. A view. This is Geoff, not Russ. Russ was drafted first round and he married a movie starlet; Russ Courtnall has no idea what it's like to be invisible, to wait all day and be slowly made crazy, to want to punch out a guy named Laszlo. I'm so close, so close to treasure. Is it a litmus test

Russ? No. It's not a litmus test. Just look inside your rolling head, the head and source of all your son's distemper.

I wish the woman with dark eyes hadn't left. Why does one person seem different and necessary? I chose to interpret the angle of her neck, slurred messages the speed of blood inside her unknown neck and uncertain smile, her teeth and her lips with the darkest darkest lipstick. I watched the draft while I watched her eyes move, her brain shift into an uncertain smile, and I knew she was leaving just then to become a bus window or a blur in the rain in the raw city of colours, just as I knew I would not be drafted, as I knew they would take a dead man before they would take a player who clocked a coach.

On the Cougars Geoff punched anyone who touched his little brother Russ. I bet now both brothers bomb around in righteous speedboats, ocean their blue and white freeway while a pretty woman from Hollywood naps down in the V-berth. She is waiting for you and you are waiting for her. You are waiting to catch a big one. You stand wide-legged at the wheel and gaze at the sky over arbutus trees and your hair slides back in the salt breeze. You think your head is attached to your shoulders. Expensive sunglasses protect your eyes, zinc your fair skin, for you cast a shadow, you are the paragon of animals, you have connected the dots. Frantic lawyers and children clamour for your signature, your autograph; children and lawyers shout out your name in the sonic echoing arenas, in Inglewood, in Florida, in United Centre, in General Motors Place.

There is money moving out there, green as anti-freeze, green as absinthe, and everyone has a chance at it. Take this from this, if this be otherwise.

That's the *system*. You think they are going to change it just for you?

Bodies of Water

Cynthia Flood

GREEN, SCRUFFY, SPREAD OUT with park on three sides and mountains behind, the soccer field lay vacant before Charlie, who waited. Drake's Defenders and the Bayview Blockbusters would arrive soon.

Charlie supposed that the Drake, his son Graham's school, must be named for Sir Francis Drake; there wouldn't be any reason to call a school after a bird. The school's sign read simply *Drake,* hand-carved on a mossy board obscured except to the knowing by the sitkas that droop along that stretch of Marine Drive. Calling on his West Vancouver customers, his mind reviewing deadbolts and alarm fittings and electronic systems, Charlie always glanced at the sign, because of Graham—but the Drake also took him right back to the East End pub with the strippers. "This week Miss Peaches Pet," promised the turquoise neon outside, "see her to believe her." Why would anyone not believe?

Charlie liked driving through the East End, familiar since childhood, east towards home. Chinatown thinned out to the arched curving bulk of Rogers' Sugar. The Inlet shone behind railcars, containers, towering orange cranes. On his way home, Charlie sometimes dropped in at the Drake. He had a couple, watched some TV. Old Francis stood up there in oils above the bar, showing off his plumy hat, smiling faraway. Crossed swords were mounted beside the explorer; the strippers threw bits of clothing up to hang on the hilts.

Once in a while there were Drake's Nights, inauthentic swashbuckling and hear ye hear ye and a cocktail called Drake's Dram. Charlie liked the regular nights. In their breaks during the happy hour show, Sandy and Marcia, two of the regulars, often sat with Charlie. They all talked about work and kids, weather, car problems, the Canucks. The girls talked about their boyfriends. Coming out later into the grey littered parking lot, Charlie felt deeply single. Occasionally, Marcia or Sandy would come on to him, in a friendly manner. Charlie sighed and drove home.

At the Drake, a gravelled drive curled under more sitkas to bring the green panel truck (Reliance Security Systems, Home/Office/Industry) carrying Charlie and Graham up to a half-moon of lawn and a set of panelled front doors. This was always on Mondays, eight-thirty a.m. sharp, first bell at eight-thirty-five, prayers at eight-forty-five, skirts for the girls, ties for the boys. Graham jumped out, pulled up his kneesocks. Charlie slid into the departing line of BMWs and Mercedes. (The quantity of blood was startling.)

Charlie Mann's son Graham was eight. He was in Grade Three, doing fine, although Language Arts was not his forte. "That's typical for a boy," said his mother, Kay, and so, she said, were his well-developed large motor skills. Charlie thought it was great that Graham had made the junior soccer team. He also thought Graham talked fine. The custody agreement worked in well with the soccer, because Graham spent weekends with his father and the games were early on Saturdays.

Charlie came as early as he could to whatever playing field was scheduled, arriving before either team or the ref or any parents. Smoking, he sauntered about and saw the mist rise from the green. He watched the roving cats, the swooping hunt of the herring gulls, the dew evaporating on the bushes. Several of the Vancouver fields offered spectacular prospects of the North Shore. Sometimes the mountains were only a gigantic density, a pressure the eye sensed behind the grey *pointilliste* veils. On other days they were sharp and thin, like metal cut with tinsnips.

This northern vista always pleased Charlie. Over there was the house where Graham lived, Monday through Friday, with Kay and Ken. Charlie knew the road there well. He knew it from the long dip down McGill by the race track and New Brighton Park to the soaring bridge, to the loading docks gritty with grain dust on the farther shore, to the off-ramp that spun him east then west, to the steep pull of Keith Road and the treed streets going up the hillside beyond: residences. However, Charlie no longer drove by that house night after night to stare at the bedroom windows. He was past that stage.

Cars gradually clotted the rim of the soccer field. Invariably on the other side from where Charlie stood appeared Kay's car; Yellow Jellybean, Graham called it. Charlie could not always pick Kay out of the distant people, but Graham's red hair was immediate. At half-time, the boy ran across the field to his father, carrying his quartered orange in one hand and his grabbed backpack in the other. Charlie slung the nylon contraption over his shoulder, liking its weight, the bulk of the jeans and shirt and school uniform and books packed neatly inside, by Kay. Sometimes, in the second half, Charlie watched the yellow car moving away along the edge of the playing field. The black and white sphere of the soccer ball spun alongside. (The blood's colour also surprised— such a bright red.) At game's end, Graham came running to Charlie again, and they were off together into their weekend.

Graham was a good-looking child. Charlie thought he knew this himself, but he was also told so by other soccer parents, by shoppers when he and his son went to the 7-11 for milk or a video, and by the guys at Reliance when he and Graham went with a bunch of them to the hockey game. Looking at his son, Charlie thought, "Well, looks, they're not all that matters." Then, "I guess that's about all Kay and me had going for us," and then, "It could make things easier for him, that's for sure." Kay had said simply, "Gorgeous, isn't he?" So was she. At least Charlie supposed she still was, though he no longer saw her up close. There was no longer any need for him to look down at her short trim frame, her curly blonde crown. Only her brisk telephone voice came near him sometimes, making arrangements about Graham.

After his son had made the soccer team, Charlie laughed as he watched the practice sessions. He had a bit of a time explaining that to Graham, but how could he not laugh? The girls and boys all clustered around the ball, clung there as a solid group, so that spectators only occasionally glimpsed a rolling patch of black and white. The ball was a beetle amid bunched stalks of moving legs.

"Open it *out!*" roared the coach, and explained the game again.

Charlie and the other parents watched, with interest or love or impatience or anger, as the design of the game declared itself through the diminishing confusion of the children's moves. The players learned to pass, to block, to turn. They learned to plan. They understood. They played. The clusters dispersed. Forming and reforming, players moved like fish in an invisible tide, streaming over the green, while waves of cheering matched their flow. Now the ball was free to accept the kick in full. Whizzing, it spun, zig-zagged, flew low, jumped hard, stopped, swerved, slid in a slow unexpected trickle just there, inside the goal. Exultation, shouts, tears.

Charlie himself wasn't hard to look at. Kay had made him say so, in the happy early days. "Say it, Charlie! You know it's true.

'I'm a good-looking man.' Say it!" He mumbled it out and then kissed her, kissed her. Now, in the homes where Charlie installed complex alarm systems to guard silver and cats and electronic playthings, women often communicated their desire to take Charlie Mann off to the master bedroom right now, to suck and lick and fuck with strangers' intensity. Sometimes, even as Charlie stood on the doorstep and saw the woman looking at the company badge on his bomber jacket, he knew the invitation would be offered. And Kay had even wanted to marry him, even before he got this steady job. She *asked* him. He said *Yes*. Now, Charlie just shook his head.

On the soccer field, the parents watched intensely. Some cheered, rushed, exhorted, yelled at the ref, screamed wordlessly. By game's end, these red-faced adults had sore throats. Their small players slumped silently in the passenger seats of departing cars. Charlie, on his own as much as possible, jogged up and down the field to keep Graham in view. Sometimes he saw Kay pacing in parallel. (The blood looked so fresh and bright, running.) Sometimes another parent, almost always a mother, started a conversation; Charlie liked these chats, but never began them.

One of the Blockbusters was a lively dark-haired girl, chunky as Graham was wiry. Her eyes were like blackberries. Her father, alone, brought her to the games. Though he called out, occasionally and precisely—"To the wing, Angela! Jolly good!"—and ran, this parent, like Charlie, did so by himself. He wore a formal camel-hair coat. His expression reminded Charlie of something; all season, when he looked at that big pale man, Charlie had felt something trying to find a door in his head.

Charlie was dark and Kay was fair, and so they had this red-haired son. Kay had researched the genetics of it, told Charlie— he'd forgotten now. But by then things were no good. Things were bad, though they both loved the baby, felt their love for him throughout the apartment, even when they were silent in anger or shouting in it. Mostly Kay shouted. Charlie was better at silences.

He got the job with Reliance when Graham was six months old. The marriage had always bewildered him. Kay was from money. How could it work? He had been amazed when she showed up at City Hall where he waited with his grandmother's gold band. *Darling* sloped faintly on its inner surface. Kay *wore* it. Mrs. Mann, she was, for several years. As the baby slept nearby, Kay and Charlie made love. Loving Graham made sex sweeter, for sex had made him—even as other things grew worse.

Kay and Charlie were both noisy in bed, criers and moaners. From their apartment in the rickety West End building ("It's perfect," Kay said, "half-way between where I come from and where you come from"), they could hear their neighbours beside and below whenever they coughed, slammed, flushed. Months passed before Charlie realized that their love must be audible two floors down. For a while, attempts to be quiet became a comic enhancement of sex. Once, when Graham was still a baby, Kay's cry in orgasm was followed in a second by Graham's startled waking cry—followed in turn by laughter, by the milky comfort of the breast, by sex again for Kay and Charlie when the baby slept once more. The couple separated when Graham was three, divorced as soon after as possible. Kay's remarriage was immediate. Charlie had not known a woman since.

"Gray darling." Charlie overheard Kay's voice to Graham, in the background of a recent phone call. "Gray darling, I want you to. . . ." Why did *Gray darling* make him think of Angela's father, the big pale man? The memory, if that's what it was, didn't feel good. The Defenders met the Blockbusters only once a month or so, so opportunities to look at the man were few.

The Saturday following that phone call, he and Graham had had hamburger-and-fries lunches, gone to the movies, walked in Stanley Park to see if the duck babies were out swimming yet, ordered in pizza (double cheese and extra sauce), and spent the evening watching TV and playing *Risk*. A standard Saturday.

Graham had not done well at the game, pouted at bedtime. Charlie turned the conversation to the Defenders' win, and Graham cheered up, but later he called out to his father, drowsily, from the darkened sleeping alcove off Charlie's livingroom. Alarmed, Charlie saw the glitter of tears on the boy's cheeks.

"Dad, I don't want to be Gray Mann, a gray man. Tell Mummy."

Two words. So easy.

"Talk about it in the morning, Graham cracker." The nickname was as old as the child, who smiled and closed his eyes. Charlie hugged his son, already softening into sleep. (Most of the blood flowed from the left nostril. The bridge was distorted.)

Gray. Charlie could see how Kay would like it. Her new husband was Ken, Ken-doll. Kay and Ken. Kay and Gray and Ken. Yes, he could see it, sadly. He couldn't yet reach the link with Angela's father, but the feeling came through now: sadness, water. A sad beach. As a kid, he'd gone with his folks to Saltspring Island. Now, a week later, Charlie still hadn't got up the nerve to talk to Kay about the nickname she wanted for the child that the child didn't want.

Every Saturday and Sunday night, Charlie sat by Graham and watched him sleep. He thought about not very much, for a long time, while the TV crackled behind him and the digital clock twitched. This pleasure had been born unexpectedly in Charlie shortly after Graham's own birth, when the new father spent hours by the cradle, his large hand flat along the baby's back. "Like fishing, except you're not there to catch anything," he tried to explain to Kay.

"He doesn't need you to do that, Charlie." But Charlie needed to. Kay didn't get it, either, when he tried to explain to her that he could not steal expensive window locks and a front door lock from Reliance, his new employer, to make her feel safer in the break-in-prone West End.

"I can't do it, Kay," Charlie said repeatedly, and then, "They could still break in, anyway." He also said, "We can't afford it." Finally he said, "I can't afford it."

Charlie still loved to look at the sleeping Graham, at the perfect outflung arm, the jaw's soft skin, the feathered trim of the eyelids. Sometimes he could count the pulse in the boy's throat. Later, stretched in his sleeping bag on the floor, Charlie knew that his child slept, safely, only a few feet away. The child lay in the same patch of the world's darkness, safe, safe as no lock or key could make him. This knowledge made Charlie feel as if good food were pouring into the hungriest part of himself. Only making love with Kay had brought satisfaction near this. Charlie never touched himself on the weekends, though on week nights he was a regular.

Today spring rains had softened the field, so the white line gave easily beneath Charlie's heel. The kids would be coated with mud by game's end. (The blood on the cheek was mixed and smeared with brown.) Not a warm day, either—a chill bright March. Poolings of water shone on the field, silver blending with the green. The door in Charlie's mind opened.

The roof of the beach shack on Saltspring Island had a false front. Behind this lay teenage Charlie, peering between the cracks of the dark brown salty boards as the English couple sauntered towards the beach, she in her fur coat, her blonde hair pinned up, he with the cigar. Through the salt air, the smoke went up like a thrown ribbon, flat and curling. The photographers kept pace. *Who are they?* Who were they, Charlie wondered now. Movie stars? Just bloody rich? Behind them, not with them, walked the *baby boy,* thought teenage Charlie, but now he guessed four, or five. The child wore those English short pants, in tweed, and brown lace-up shoes, and a brown tweed jacket. A striped tie. *Dwarf suit.* He walked along, alone, looking after his parents, who did not turn, and the child did not lower his head, though spouting oysterholes and blue mussels and feathers and stones and crabs' legs and deer bones were all about him on the sand.

Then an older woman appeared, stepping quickly past the photographers towards the little boy, calling him—Charlie could not hear the name—till he turned, and the cameras bit and the child's lips began to do what was wanted: curl, smile. Then and now, Charlie winced. "No no!" cried the woman, shooing the newsmen off, "no, it's just us." She stroked his hair. *Who's she?* Nanny, Charlie supposed now, governess, daddy's secretary.

Then the boy broke from her and walked on, alone, past Charlie's hideaway and the invisible line past which the dune grasses grew no longer. He went on to the open beach. He went on and on. The couple did not turn. The outgoing tide had filmed the mile of sand with shining; the long slope lay brilliant, a fluent mirror, heaped and streaming with seawrack. Over the waterscape moved the tall adults, doubled below, and far behind them came the short enduring figure of their son. A long way out, islets of broken rock protruded. *Poor fucking little bastard.* Charlie thought so still, thought he would die if ever he saw such a look on Graham's face.

Now the Yellow Jellybean shone in the distance. Charlie saw Graham's hair. Kay's car drove away, followed by Ken's gray Volvo. Charlie frowned.

Shortly before the final break-up, Charlie had done what he had said he could not do. He stole locks. He hid the heavy stolen boxes in the bedroom closet. He did not tell Kay they were there. Lying awake in the early mornings of their last days under the same roof, Charlie knew the cardboard cubes and their metal innards were useless. After Kay left, after Kay left with Graham, after his wife and child had left, Charlie took the locks right back to Reliance.

That kid should come back up the beach, stop going after them, they don't care. Come back up and play.

Here now was Angela's father, pale, solemn, solid like his daughter, parking the BMW near the Reliance truck, nodding embarrassed recognition at Charlie. Here was Angela, scrabbling through her backpack, turfing out pajamas and schoolbooks and jeans on to the gravel. Shortly, her Dracula t-shirt disappeared beneath a sweater, and that beneath the Blockbusters' red and blue stripes. She whirled round to present her finished self, and smiled merrily at Charlie.

"It's cold!" she called.

All Angela's sleeves and seams and necklines needed a good parental pull to straighten them out; Charlie knew exactly how the fabrics would feel under his fingers. The big man just stood looking, and might as well have carried a placard saying *I Love Her.* Rumpled and waving, Angela ran off. How this lively creature would have cheered that abandoned boy when he came back up the beach, would have held hands and run with him in the salty wind, shown him the spouting and the bones and the stabbing oyster-catchers, taught him to feel the anemones, to race the little bustling crabs and whip the kelp about like a torero. . . .

The whistle blew. Charlie looked towards the Defenders. Graham waved. The ball began to move.

At half-time the score was tied at three. Parents were already hoarse. The sun gave off real heat now, and Charlie tucked his jacket under his arm and smiled at the big man, for Angela had got a goal. (Charlie was grateful for the judgement of the Defenders' coach, that Graham was not goalie material.)

"Mummy's gone with Ken to get stuff for a party tonight," snapped the boy as he came off the field, sour-faced. He dumped his bag at Charlie's feet and turned his back on his father.

Charlie fingered the straps of the backpack while he thought of what to say.

"Well, she can't be at every game, you know, Graham cr . . ."

His son's shoulders hunched up. Angela and her father were walking towards them.

"Why not? You are," shouted Graham. "I hate that dumb nickname." He ran ten paces away and stood sucking his orange quarters. Charlie dropped the backpack.

"What's wrong with him?" asked Angela, her voice thick with fruit. She had none of her father's English accent.

"Angela," warned the big man.

"S'all right," Charlie said. "Bit upset." Here it was, the dulling pain that came whenever Graham showed his wounds. In his chest first, and then throughout his frame, there was a heavy weighted sinking, a heaviness like thick congestion, like molten metal congealing. Once again, Charlie tried to think what he and Kay could have done other than divorce, but his mind had struggled with this so many many many times that it practically cried at the prospect of another attempt.

"He plays very well," Angela's father said loudly.

Graham came back. Charlie looked down at his short trim frame, his red curly crown.

"John Murdoch," said the big man. They all shook hands and laughed. Murdoch seemed unfamiliar with laughing. Charlie remembered that when he had first laughed after the separation, all the muscles had felt strange.

"Too hot now," Angela said, giggling.

Her father helped her to strip off her team shirt and the sweater underneath and to put the team shirt on again.

"We have the same t-shirt!" Graham pulled up his green and black stripes to reveal Dracula.

"Your mother gave you yours, didn't she, Angela?" said Murdoch fondly.

Angela poked her father in the stomach. "Why do you always call her *your mother? Say Judy.* That's her *name."*

"He does it too," said Graham eagerly, pointing at Charlie, "he calls her *your mummy,* but her name's Kay."

The whistle blew.

"My mum does it too. Does yours?" asked Angela, as the two children walked away.

"Yeah, all the time," said Graham. "Why do they? It's so dumb."

They ran, while the whistle blew again and the gulls screamed. The children's shapes, obscured by their baggy shirts and shorts, were emphatically female and male. Over their heads the herring gulls flew, random, concentrating. Why did you never see baby gulls? Graham had asked this. Charlie had no idea. Graham had also asked if what his teacher had said was true—that people's bodies were ninety-five percent water. Charlie didn't know that, either; the figure sounded high, to him.

The ball was rolling fast and red-headed Graham was running hard. Another Defender got in place to receive his pass. Graham's leg flexed and straightened. Charlie heard the *thuck* of connection, watched the ball rush level through the air, saw Angela move out. Slipping on the wet grass, she took the fast ball full on her nose and cried out once.

The quantity of blood startled. Its colour also surprised. Such a bright red! Running, it looked so fresh. Most flowed from the left nostril. The bridge was misshapen. On the cheeks, the blood was brown-smeared. The muddy ball had left a pattern, like a woodblock print, on Angela's forehead.

Graham and Charlie Mann, Angela and John Murdoch seemed alone in the middle of the empty wash of green. Murdoch lay on the muddy ground. Angela rested her bloody head on his left arm, while with a big checkered handkerchief held in his right hand he wiped her face. Graham knelt by Angela and cried, "Angela, I'm sorry, are you all right?" Over and over, over and over. Angela snuffled bubbly blood. The tears jumped out of her eyes as if powered by springs, bounced off her cheeks into the wet green grass.

Charlie knelt helpless by Graham, his hand tight on the boy's shoulder.

"You didn't mean to, Grady," Angela said wetly. "S'okay." With a sighing shudder, she took the handkerchief from her father, wiped, looked at the mess. "Yuck."

"Press that to your nose, Angela. Press." The big man's voice shook. He was paler than pale.

Graham shook off his father's hand, pulled the Reliance bomberjacket out from under Charlie's arm and put it awkwardly over Angela's upper body. Charlie leaned back. John Murdoch looked at him. Strings of pain ran between the two men.

Angela put her fingers to the bridge of her nose. A little gristly crunch. Graham's face went clammy white. "Hell," and Charlie shoved his son's head roughly down, held it. "You're fainting. Okay in a minute, get your blood back." John Murdoch's hand passed over the red curls, back to the black ones on his arm.

Charlie's mind showed him the face of the remembered boy on the beach. He thought, *I must turn back.* How long was it since he had lain with his head on a woman's arm?

People stood round them now.

"Deviated septum, likely," said the Blockbusters' coach. "Don't worry, sir, she won't scar."

"Wasn't I just saying that mixed games aren't really suitable for this age?"

"Can Angela play the rest of the game?"

Graham straightened up, looking less like flour paste.

"Wow! Lookit the blood!"

John Murdoch picked up his child and rose.

"None of this is to the point," he said. "Angela will return to the team as soon as possible."

Charlie wanted to hold and be held. He wanted to hear the joyous cry of another, not just his solitary muffled sound.

"See you at practice, everyone," said Angela, and took the handkerchief away from her face so her team-mates could see. Her nose bled freely. Then she pressed close to her father, who held her tight. Charlie picked Graham up.

"See you to the car, John," he said, and to the ref, "Graham'll be back in a minute."

268

By the time the fathers and the safely carried children reached the field's edge, the ball was in play again, looping and rolling in its black and white, while running feet scarred the green and mashed it up into mud. John Murdoch's handkerchief was scarlet. Kay always put tissues in Graham's pack, so Charlie got a big folded wad for Angela, now enthroned on the front passenger seat with cushion, car blanket, and seat belt.

John shook Graham's hand. "We all do things that end up hurting other people," he said. "You're a good boy."

"Bye, Grady. See you."

"Bye, Angela. See you at practice."

The girl and her father drove off.

That night, after pizza, Charlie said to Graham, "Phone Kay. Tell her."

"Okay Dad." And to his mother the boy said, "Grady," after the great kick and Angela and blood and deviated septum and almost fainting and his goal after returning to the game (though the Defenders lost). "Grady. That's what I'm going to be, Mum. Not Graham cracker any more. Not Gray."

Charlie heard the solidity of the child's tone. Behind it, he knew the mother's silence—her surprise—her wondering—*Where does this come from?* Because he had known Kay's flesh, he knew how she would answer, in due time: "Well hello, Grady." She would mean it too, abide by it, even though she would also think it was too Irish, think maybe when Graham grew a little older a further abbreviation might be possible . . . .

Charlie thought of telling Sandy and Marcia about Grady, of telling the guys at Reliance. He smiled and yawned.

As soon as his son lay still in the sleeping-bag on the floor, Charlie slid into his own bed. Drifting, he thought of driving through Vancouver's East End, all the way through to the Second Narrows bridge, which killed eighteen men in its making and throws itself so gracefully on to the further shore. Charlie thought

269

of the northern abutment of the bridge, where roads incline east and west and north. Here the traveller could choose, could even choose to describe a loop and turn back again.

Report on the Nanaimo Labour School

John Harris

IN AUGUST I GOT A FREE TRIP to Nanaimo. Nanaimo is one of my favourite towns. It has a seedy downtown area with lots of hotels and small shops where old hippies sell used books, brass beds, nickleodeons and hand-made guitars. The houses are all made of wood and are large and drafty. A doctor will live in one, a motorcycle gang in the next one and someone nearby will have a goat tethered to a tree. People who are into lawns, patios, Volvos and small dogs have abandoned Nanaimo for newer suburbs up and down the island. Tourists go in one end and out the other. They are into swimming, fishing and shopping centres, and a town with a pulp mill in the harbour and a coal mine in the past doesn't interest them. The town of Nanaimo has tried to capitalize on its historical past by putting a giant lump of coal in the centre of its downtown park. There is a plaque saying that this lump of coal was grubbed out of a tunnel that extended five miles out under the ocean bed, and there is a map of the tunnel. However, the lump of coal has not been a major attraction. Kids climb on it and get dirty. Nobody wants to think about people working, sweating, suffocating and being buried alive under tons of rock and water. Battles between unions and bosses are not as interesting as battles between armies. As compared to the bathtub races, which do attract crowds to downtown Nanaimo for one drunken weekend each summer, Nanaimo's historical past is a dead-end.

However, Nanaimo has played a major role in my own life. A year after I got married, I went to Nanaimo to be interviewed for my first teaching job. I was at UBC at the time, a scant twenty-two years old, with a wife and one kid, and I was busy at a summer job as a research assistant. A kindly professor wanted me to concentrate on writing my Master's thesis instead of sweating it out as usual on the Vancouver waterfront, where all the polish laid on me in eight months of graduate school was erased in four months of running two-hundred-pound sacks of flour into the holds of Russian freighters. Every second word was "fuck" and I pronounced "po-em" as "pum." So I spent four hours a day lying in the sun on the clipped lawns of UBC, transferring the professor's marginalia from the 1848 edition of Coleridge's *Complete Works* into the 1964 edition. An exciting lady from the east, who happened to be the chairperson of an English department out there, came to visit the professor. It turned out that she had just terminated some poor soul for neglect of duty due to alcoholism, and she needed a replacement fast. She couldn't interview me on the spot, however, but invited me to breakfast with her on the following day at the Port O' Departure Hotel in Nanaimo. I went over there, ate bacon and eggs and got hired.

Years later, at that same Port O' Departure, with Brenda, who loved my stories, I (inadvertently) started a chain of events that terminated my marriage.

It occurs to me now, too, that my father was present on both of these historical occasions. On the first, he happened to be on his way up-island to Tahsis, where the International Longshoremen's and Warehouseman's Union was organizing. We crossed on the ferry together and he dropped me off at the Port O' Departure. The lady from the east invited him to join us for breakfast but he said that he never ate with a lady. At the time I thought this was rather droll and likely to affect my Career Opportunity but the lady seemed to find his comment charming. On the second occasion my father, by then retired, was on his way home from a fishing trip. He noticed an announcement that I was reading at the college and he dropped in to see me. He didn't come to hear my stories; he thought (and still thinks) they are shit. The next day, we took a long walk, had dinner, and went to see a play with Ian, an old friend of mine who had set up the reading. He had written the play for the B.C. Centennial, about Captain Cook and his men and how they spread syphilis to the indians. Ian's wife was the star, which seemed to explain to my father why the ravishing lady in the Marlene Dietrich costume would marry the dishevelled weirdo who liked my stories. Later on, as a matter of fact, after my wife kicked me out, my father got the idea that it was Ian's wife who had slept with me at the Port O' Departure. There was a hint of admiration in his anger. At any rate, during that time in Nanaimo with my father I was shaken and distracted by my experience with Brenda. My father recognized that something was wrong. When we said goodbye he reminded me that my main purpose in life was to look after my wife and kids, advised me not to drink when away from home and gave me a couple of shirts which didn't fit him any more because he was, he said, shrinking.

My father didn't turn up during my last trip to Nanaimo, and nothing portentous happened. In a way I wish something had, and in a way not, as usual. I was in Nanaimo on business. I went to a labour school, as a representative of our little faculty union, to study the recent changes to the labour code, hear about the situations at other colleges, and practise handling grievances. This is not the most interesting way to spend a weekend, but it isn't as bad as it might seem, and I was going to Vancouver anyway to pick up Connie who was flying in from Guatemala.

I arrived in Nanaimo early in the day. It felt great to be near salt water again. Sometimes I imagine myself buying a small hunk of sea-front on Sechelt or a Gulf Island somewhere but I remember from various boy scout camps that it rains like hell around there. Mainly, though, what stops me is that the whole area is a retirement colony for artists. They water roses, cut driftwood, build shacks with lots of windows, do interviews with the amiable idiots who host CBC talk shows, and produce endless amounts of shit until they are finally bored shitless with roses, driftwood, scenery, silence and the CBC and go back to the city to get a job. At that point their art, if any, improves significantly.

I drove straight from the ferry landing to the college to register for labour school. I was assigned a room in residence and told to come to a plenary session that evening, where we were going to exchange information on the labour scenes at our respective colleges. I dumped my stuff in the room and phoned Ian and arranged to meet him later in the bar. Then I walked downtown, had coffee and read all the newspapers. Then I found three bookstores and combed through them. I made it into the bar by three o'clock with a bag full of books to read. I was on my third beer and book when Donna walked in.

She didn't see me at first and I was too surprised to say anything. I hadn't seen her for two years. She wasn't much for writing letters; so far as I knew, she was still in Kamloops. She was obviously just finished her day in the finance company. She was dressed conservatively but sexily as required, and she had that haggard look on her face that comes from spending a morning writing up loans for people who will never be able to pay them back but will likely pay interest for years, and an afternoon making collection calls to people who swear and threaten various parts of her anatomy. When she finally saw me she ran right over and I got a warm hug and kiss that, I imagined, lingered significantly beyond the merely affectionate. She sat down and ordered her usual double vodka and soda and we settled in happily to fill one another in on the past two years and complain about our jobs.

At six o'clock Donna's boyfriend arrived and if he was not overly happy to see me, he didn't show it. He is getting used to our platonic relationship. He wants to get married but Donna is not ready yet though they have been living together longer than most people stay married. Then Ian arrived. He and Donna got into a serious discussion about theatre. He was wondering if her company would finance a production but she didn't think so, not even if she were in it, unless of course Ian had a paid-off house or something to use as collateral. Ian admitted that he was in hock up to his eyeballs due to heavy support payments to two kids from two previous marriages and to his immediately-previous ex-wife who was in acting school. Donna suggested that, given the circumstances, his chances of getting a loan from anyone were as good as hers of becoming an actress. Ian thought her chances were not as bad as that. Finally, I proposed that we go and eat. The plenary session was already half over anyway. Hopefully, the other rep from the college had dutifully arrived to deliver the news.

Ian took us to a Mexican cafe. There we met some friends of his from the theatre and a couple from up north who knew Harvey and were already finished their enchiladas but came over to drink their coffee with us. The guy is a coroner. He told us that he was taking skin-diving lessons because a lot of his work on the island involves drownings. For example, they had recently fished up a Fisheries department diver who had apparently got caught in some weeds and, in the process of hacking himself out, had cut his airhose. His partner was busy on the other side of the pontoon and by the time he missed him, he was dead. But the RCMP said they figured the dead guy had been fucking his partner's wife and there had been a fight at his house the weekend before. "The cops didn't notice anything unusual and I doubt there was," said the coroner, "but I'd sure as hell like to see for myself."

We stayed at the cafe until midnight, and then went our separate ways. Both Ian and Donna and her boyfriend wanted me to stay over, but the last time I stayed at Ian's I got flea-bites. Ian always got to keep the dogs from his previous marriages. I doubted I'd sleep well at Donna's, for various reasons, not the least of which was the coroner's story and its possible application to my own case. Besides, I felt guilty about missing the plenary session. If I made it back to residence that night, I could be sure of getting to the morning sessions. I arranged to go to Donna's for dinner on the following day. Ian dropped me off at the college and gave me tickets to the next two plays in the local festival. He said that these were final performances and there would be parties afterwards at his place.

Next morning, I got up early and walked some paths in the college forest. Then I joined the labour school group for breakfast. There were two people from each college in the province and they were all standing around drinking coffee and babbling happily while they waited for breakfast. These are my colleagues and I feel great affection for them—for this group in particular because they work hard for the union. When we started in this business we were all very young and now we are growing old together, gracefully I think. We have all survived as teachers and that takes a good deal of imagination, and we have created a union that takes care of our professional concerns and sometimes even our salaries. Of course, while I always feel warm and secure when I am with my colleagues, I also feel that I am childish compared to them and don't quite deserve to be taken seriously, trusted with any great responsibility, or cared for as well as I am.

I was wondering what had happened at the plenary session. A lady from Dawson Creek hugged me and said she loved my story about the strike at my college but wasn't I a bit hard on faculty? I started to worry about the effect of this story, which had gotten fairly wide circulation in a popular, slightly leftish journal. I started to wonder if they had discussed my story at the plenary session. Maybe I broke one of the ethical guidelines. Maybe they passed a motion that I would only find out about later when the minutes were circulated.

The fact is, I don't know my colleagues very well. Though I love them, I have trouble relating to some of their concerns. I've never been able to attend the regular TGIF beergartens sponsored by the union. To me, drinking beer in the college would be like fucking in a mortuary. I don't even drink coffee in the college. Also, my colleagues love to have cocktail parties, backyard bar-becues, Christmas dinner-dances, New Year parties, retirement parties (where the retirer is presented with condoms, Rhino Horn and Grecian Formula), indoor beach parties in January and pro-fessional development events to talk about New Approaches to Teaching. I have to stay away from all these things. I am not inter-ested if $200 kiddie seats are being stolen from the back seats of Volvos, if there is too much chlorine in the pool at the fitness centre, if there is a growing tendency for daycare workers to fuck children or if computers are useful in teaching composition.

On the other hand, I am always willing to vote more money to the Faculty Fun Seekers. I attend all union meetings and I have been a shop steward or member of the executive for as long as I can remember. Once, in a crisis situation, I became president and ran the union with, I think, some success. At that time the incum-bent president, who had originally beaten me out in the election for the position by a vote of 90 to 6, suddenly took a job in the new administration of our new principal. Our principal is a very energetic (some say "charismatic" and others "psychotic") man who was making massive changes at the time as part of his new mandate. Because of all the turmoil and paranoia, I and my ex-ecutive were able to rule by decree and levy unprecedented sums

277

of money. We used the money to hire a lawyer who was a friend of the brassy young psychologist who was treasurer at the time. The lawyer turned out to be very good at his work, and so did the brassy young psychologist. We launched a number of actions under the Labour Code and wrapped a few ropes around the principal. We started the union on its present course of creative belligerence. Because of all this, I gained a lot of credit which I have been frittering away ever since.

After breakfast, we all got down to a serious study of the Labour Code. It was great to participate again in the idealism and enthusiasm of my colleagues. My colleagues are very professional. They possess and communicate the technique and technology that keeps things going. They further believe that this knowledge contributes to progress. They fight hard to be allowed to communicate this knowledge in the best way. You can mess with the salaries of my colleagues, but if you mess with class sizes, course content and departmental committees you are asking for war. Pensions are also sacred, but nobody's perfect.

As an example of the faculty attitude towards professional concerns, we believe that fifteen hours of lecturing per week, and class maximums of forty-five are not conducive to the exchange of information. When five office hours, twenty or more hours of preparation and marking, and another few hours of meetings are added to this, it is easy to see that faculty will be too irritable and irresponsive to teach. Of course they will do their best, but demoralization will slowly set in. They will start reading the textbook to their classes, using last-year's tests and writing rude comments on student papers. They will fall behind in research and publication and lose their love for poetry, math, science, etc. Eventually they will have mental breakdowns, drink excessively, or bumhole their students. My colleagues will use every trick in the book to prevent this from happening.

They are fairly good at these tricks. As professionals, they are patient, systematic and can produce copious amounts of standard English either verbal or written. However, they have one major weakness. They believe that everyone is educable. They would deliver briefs on the fifteen-hour lecture week to Adolf Hitler. If Adolf was confused or seeking information they would give him the same assistance they would give to Anne Frank. In other words, they have great faith in the redeeming power of reason and will do nothing to counteract it. They reasonably argue that the only way to foster reasonable behaviour is to be reasonable. To yell, swear, kick back, hate and plot complicated revenge is to play into the enemy's hands. What they sometimes fail to recognize is that their faith is also a vested interest that shades the fact that they do not have rationality entirely wrapped up. There are many fields of human behaviour like sex, friendship, love, money and even education where rational guidelines are often open to question or even despaired of. When my colleagues wander into these areas, they can be confused, overconfident and/or gullible.

This is not a complaint. If you can't believe in reason, what can you believe in? God? Mother Nature? Country? Love? Art? Karl Marx? George Washington? Don't make me laugh. Keep these in your dreams and they will do wonders and never get dirty, but when you are awake, think. Learn the best technique. Learn the proper behaviour. When I'm having my appendix out, do you think I want a politician or poet snapping on the rubber gloves? Am I worried about the state of the world? The nurse in the green mask is an angel. The doctor is God. Reason is my rock. However, I am weaker than my colleagues. I lack patience. I advocate the low blow. Hopefully I will grow out of this attitude in the not-too-distant future.

During that morning I learned what changes had been made by the slightly rightist fuckfaces who run the province and how these changes would likely affect grievance procedures. We were discussing these and other issues when I suddenly felt as if my bowels were being blown up by a bicycle pump. I barely made it to the washroom in time, and then I couldn't get out. It was the Mexican food. During the coffee break, the leader of my seminar group tracked me down. "Is that you?" he asked from the other side of the door. I told him what was wrong. He went back to the classroom and got my folder as well as all the information sheets that he was about to use in the next session. He shoved them under the door. "Read sections 93 and 125 of the code," he said, "and answer all the questions on the green sheet." This is an example of how understanding and accommodating my colleagues can be.

I spent the rest of the day in the washroom or at a nearby cafeteria table. I read through all the labour school material, the local student newspaper and one third of *Crime and Punishment.* By the time my bowels were settled, the labour school was shutting down for the day. I washed up and went off to Donna's for dinner. Of course, I couldn't eat or drink anything. I talked Donna and her boyfriend into coming to the play. After the play the cast had a party at Ian's. Ian took Donna and her boyfriend in hand and introduced them to everyone. I acted very responsibly and left early for my room. I couldn't drink anything anyway. I waved goodbye to Donna who was having a spirited conversation with one of the female leads. She smiled sadly at me and very gracefully blew me a kiss.

I slept well that night except I was awakened for a while at about 2 AM when some of my colleagues came in and crowded into the next room for a nightcap and some sandwiches. Fortunately for me, there were some visiting Japanese students on the floor above us and their group leader came down with the custodian and shut them up. I got up early and showered and was back in the college forest in time to walk the complete circuit and read about all the plants and fungi at each nature stop. When I got back down to the main campus, the cafeteria was still not open. I sat on a bench in the sunshine with the lady from Dawson Creek who told me gleefully that there would be some very sore heads at today's seminar.

Late that afternoon, the labour school closed except for some speeches from our executive that were scheduled for the next morning. My colleagues were meeting downtown for dinner but I was not up to eating. I phoned Ian but he wasn't in so I decided to go for a walk along the seawall. I'd walked that wall years ago with Brenda and I remembered how we paused for long periods to watch the boats coming and going. Then I remembered with even greater vividness how, the night before that, we'd walked away from the reading together discussing poetry, how we'd suddenly melted into one another's arms, how lost I was in her dark, naturally curly hair, how we'd made our way to the Port O' Departure, how slim she was, almost weightless, how her small breasts hardened when I kissed them, how her legs tightened around me and then (of course) how relatively ineffectual I seemed to be between recurring waves of panic, and finally how good it was to sleep warmly beside her and wake up now and then to see her peaceful face in the dark. I hoped she was still in love and loved, her breasts still hardening to someone's kiss. Then I thought about Connie and how long she'd been away, and how brown she'd be, her hair bleached by two months of tropic sun.

By the time I reached the end of the seawall my ass, scoured by yesterday's diarrhoea, was burning. I had to take a taxi back to Ian's. The play was great, and so was the party though I wished Donna were there to add a touch of real drama. When I got back to residence there was a note on the door telling me that, due to the number of delegates leaving that evening, the speeches scheduled for the next morning were cancelled. I was free to do whatever I wanted.

I lay down on the bed and started reading the Labour Code. I was disappointed.

Ivory Chopsticks

Danielle Lagah

NELL WASN'T CHINESE, not *really*. At least, that's what Popo
was always telling her. "Not even half," she'd say, the round jowls
of her cheeks quivering. "Only one quarter." She'd grip pieces of
Nell's fawn-blond hair between her thick fingers, examine the color
with a certain deliberateness. "Look like your mother."

It was true. At thirteen, Nell was already taller than Popo, and
fair. Cream-cheeked. Her mother, Lynette, had married in, *sort of*,
falling for the bad seed of the family, the one who'd been born
well after Popo's husband died. The Chinese son with green eyes.
"Only half," Popo would say, "He was the accident." It was a difficult subject, one she chose not to discuss further. But Nell was
proud of her father's rare looks, his pale skin and deep black hair.
She enjoyed the surprise of the gift shop clerks on Keefer Street
when he bartered with them in perfect Cantonese. Her father, Jin
the Accident. And Nell had his eyes: clear, green.

So she was only a quarter, not even *half*. Most of the time it
was okay, it was fine. She was allowed to talk to boys at school,

see movies rated 'R' with her friends on Fridays. She made her cousin Peggy jealous by wearing bright eyeshadows, spread thickly in the creases of her lids.

Every last Tuesday of the month was Dinner, when Popo would book the upstairs at Ocean Dragon on Fisgard for the family. It was always the same; Popo sitting under the silk-embroidered dragon banner on the rear wall of the restaurant. She came invariably in brown mink and gloves, smelled strongly of something Lynette called "mothballs." Nell and Peggy would play with the lazy susan in the center of the big round table, making a mess of the porcelain dishes of sesame seeds, bottles of spicy oil and soya sauce, until their mothers hissed.

And then the food would come, plates of strange steaming meats and tureens of soup, bowls of bright vegetables. After that there was honey cake, and sometimes red packets of lucky-money—crisp five dollar bills folded in half. Once, when Nell was younger she'd grabbed a money packet before dinner was finished, eagerly tearing it open.

"I think you have never heard of King Chou," Popo'd said loudly, her eyes fixed on Nell.

Nell had dropped the money on the table and pushed it away from her, but too late.

Popo continued in a voice loud enough for the downstairs customers to hear. "He want to eat only with chopsticks of ivory. So greedy. His wife worry what this would bring, and she was right. Five year later King Chou had gardens filled with meat and he bathe in a lake of wine. So he lose everything." Popo poked the air with her thick finger, nodded her head at Nell. "You remember this."

Tonight, her father couldn't find parking. He drove up and down Fisgard, back and forth through Chinatown's carved gates, the engine of the Cutless Supreme running hot. They were late; the rest of the family would be at Ocean Dragon already, waiting for their arrival.

"We could park in the pay lot," Lynette said, in the backseat with Nell. "Just this once."

In the passenger seat Popo folded her arms over her chest, thick mink coatsleeves sandwiched together. "No *pay lot*," she said. "Too much money."

It wasn't really to do with money, they knew. It was more an issue of principle. Popo felt it was her *right* to park along the main street for free. She'd been here before the parking meters and parkades had gone up, after all. She'd been here when Chinatown was new, when she had a hired car that took her to the Dart Coon Club for mah jong, when Fan Tan Alley was a place most non-Chinese didn't go.

Nell had often stood in the rear exhibits of Fan Tan Gift and peered into the large barred-off hollow in the brick wall, where they'd replicated a scene from an old Chinese gambling parlor. A mannequin bookie in a dusty grey fedora, money and old brown wine jugs strewn about, a broken wood and glass opium pipe. The first time she'd seen it she was seven; her mother had read out the handwritten information card on the wall. *Scenes like this were found all over old Chinatown. These are genuine artifacts, please do not stick hands through bars.* Since Nell had gotten older, she'd heard whispers about Jin's father from the rest of the family—that he'd been a bit of a drinker, a fighter. That he'd met Popo outside a Chinese gambling house.

Nell frequently tried to imagine how it happened, a younger, slimmer Popo sneaking away from her house-in-mourning, gloveless, minkless. She stumbles into the alley and Jin's father is there, leaning against the wall. His pale lips on a jug of liquor. Or maybe he's in a fist fight, first one punch, then another, boxing style. Helpless against martial arts. And Popo is there, kneeling down, dabbing the blood from the corner of his bright green eye. Maybe, maybe.

Her father drove further up Fisgard, past Quan Lee's Grocery, past the aging Chinese school Nell didn't have to go to—not like Peggy—past the police station. Parked cars lined the street on both sides. "We'll have to park on Herald," her father said, and they all waited for Popo's response.

She sighed raggedly, uncrossed her arms. "If you say," she said.

Her father pulled over just outside of the Herald Street Café. Nell and her mother climbed out of the back, Nell opened the door for Popo.

They walked slowly across the street, Nell lagging slightly behind. There was a new apartment complex along this block, a three-storey brick unit with rounded doorframes, garden patios on each unit. Nell imagined you could probably see all the roofs of Chinatown from the top floor, see the shape of Fan Tan Alley as it wound between the buildings like a dark stripe, black snake.

They were almost to Fisgard when Popo stopped very suddenly, leaning on her cane.

"What is it, Mom?" Nell's father put his arms around Popo's shoulders. "Are you feeling tired?"

She let Jin and Lynette help her to a street bench where she sat, breathing in, puffing out. Nell watched her father's worried looks. After a few seconds, Popo stood up. "It's okay," she said. "We should eat now."

Aunt and Uncle Wo, Peggy, and Great Uncle Ling-Ling were already seated at the big round table, watching as Nell's mother helped Popo ascend the restaurant stairs. Aunt Chow stood and pulled Popo's chair out dutifully, nodded at Peggy.

"Go and help your grandmother."

"No need," Popo said, puffing as she took the last step. "Too late now anyway."

They had bird's nest soup, served in teacup-sized bowls, the dense

285

broth filling the restaurant with a delicate odor. Nell had been warned by her mother how much it cost, sixty-five dollars a bowl, so she sipped at it slowly, spreading the salty gelatin over her tongue. Peggy kicked her leg under the table and whispered, "It's made with *real* bird's nests, you know. Sooo gross." Nell noticed Peggy hadn't touched her soup, and she wished they could send it back to the cooks and ask for sixty-five dollars instead.

Aunt Wo asked Nell how school was going.

"It's too bad that Jin didn't send you to Chinese classes with Peggy this year," she said, loud enough for Popo to hear. "Peggy is doing *very* well." She turned to her daughter. "Ask Popo how her day was in Cantonese."

"M-*om*." Peggy folded her arms and slumped down in her seat, the back of her black ponytail staticky against the chair fabric.

Aunt Wo sniffed, played with the strand of cultured pearls around her neck. "Popo pays a lot of money for your language lessons, young lady. Now sit up and ask her."

Across the table, Popo took a pigeon bone out of her mouth, added it to the pile on her sideplate. "Why you not want to speak Chinese, Peggy? Always your mother ask you. Always you say no."

Peggy fiddled with the buttons on her purple shirt, then mumbled a few words.

Popo smiled broad, her brown lips pulled tight. She went back to her pigeon, crunching noisily.

"I'm learning French," Nell said. "At school. We can talk about the weather now, and all the days of the week. And we can conjugate *avoir* and *etre*." She said these last words with flourish, mimicking the thick accent of her French teacher.

Popo grabbed a plate of oyster mushrooms, spooned a few on to her noodles, grunting. Nell felt her mother's hand on her knee.

"Do you know the story of Lu Tzi?" Popo said, looking at Nell. Peggy giggled.

Nell felt panic begin to rise in her stomach. The bird's nest soup swished around inside her, heavy. She stared at the table.

"There was a famous beauty named Hsi Shih," Popo continued, her voice rising. "She have bad heartburn, so all the time frowning. But in the village also was a very ugly girl, Lu Tzi. She think Hsi Shih look very beautiful when she frown, so she too put her hand like this," Popo put one hand up to her chest, the gold and jade ring on her middle finger gleaming under the restaurant lights. "And she frown in front of everyone. But when the village people see her, they run away or laugh." Nell felt her mother's hand on her knee begin to squeeze. She sat very still.

"Poor Lu Tzi. She admire Hsi Shih's frown, but not know why it is beautiful." Popo leaned back in her chair and nodded at Nell. "This is good lesson for you, I think."

Nell could feel her face burning all over, cheeks and nose, forehead. Her eyes tingled. She watched her father touch Popo's arm lightly.

"Mom," he said, clearing his throat, "I think that was a bit hard."

Popo raised her eyebrows at this. "If no one will teach her, how she learn then?"

Nell shoved her hands in her pockets as she wandered down Fisgard, cold air drying the tears on her cheeks. It was getting dark; neon street signs cast red and pink glows on the sidewalk. They weren't coming after her, not even her mother, because of what she'd said to Popo. So what.

The markets were getting ready to close; men in blue aprons were busy hauling crates of *gai lan* and oranges back inside. She watched them, their hands tossing bundles of bok choy into metal carts, wrapping twist ties around bags of clams. Calling out to each other in Cantonese. Their voices floated darkly inside her head, the few words she understood flashing like bright fish: *we, I, she, no*. Swimming away.

287

At Quan Lee's she stopped, craned her neck to look up at the second floor windows of the Dart Coon Club. Vague shapes moved inside, silhouetted against the smoke-stained damask curtains. She'd been up there once, a long time ago, when there was a party for Chinese New Years. She remembered the smell of it—cigars and strong perfume. And the noise—so many people talking, laughing. The clicking of mah jong pieces, the clink of crystal glasses on wood tables. She'd been scared of the four-foot bottle of Johnny Walker Red that stood in the corner, the dead rattlesnake that lay in a coil at the bottom. "It's supposed to have curative powers," her father had said while she cowered behind him. And Popo, she remembered. So different that night, so full of energy. She'd let Nell sit on her lap at the mah jong table for a few minutes, let her help tie the bundles of lettuce and twenty dollar bills for the parade dragon to the hooks outside the windows. But still, it had been Peggy that all the Chinese ladies smiled at, patting her fine black hair with their smooth hands. "My granddaughter," Popo'd said, beaming, "She look like me, don't you think so?"

Nell looked away from the windows, kept walking. At Fan Tan Alley she turned, ran her hand along the dirty brick as she moved past the backdoors of cafes and stores now locked up for the night. At the rear entrance to Fan Tan Gift she stopped for a few seconds, picturing the mannequin bookie standing inside in the darkness, dusty grey fedora pulled down over his face. Maybe all the ghosts of old Chinatown were in there too, hovering among shop souvenirs and guide maps.

At the end of the alley, Nell emerged into the light of Pandora street. She headed towards the public washroom in Market Square where she would touch up her makeup. Dust pink shadow across the lids of her green eyes.

North America, South America

Marilyn Bowering

THERE IS JUST ENOUGH LIGHT from the porthole to write by. A bottle of claret stands on the table. Mosquitos press round in clouds, and the rats scuttle in droves from one end of the ship to the other, their sharp claws penetrating the sheet that covers Crosby's body.

Cockroaches gnaw at the dead man's toenails. When the lamps are lit, the cabin grows dark with flies.

It is as though we have slipped hemispheres. The decks are slippery with dead insects, mould greens the food and the damp walls, the sheet over Crosby's body displays a map of spores.

Here—with me—in this room with Crosby's remains, the unseasonable heat fosters miasma—an unreal country of immense regions, tangled vines and creepers, decaying flowering shrubs, gigantic forest.

"I'm sorry if I woke you," Crosby said that first time I shook him from his nightmare. His nightgown was wet with sweat though the boards beneath my feet cracked with ice.

Let me say at once that he was good with the Indians. We expanded our trade up coast, sailing the Inside Passage to Rupert and back, stopping at Bella Bella to take on lumber. The missionary, Lafferty, came on board. He was a thick-set, honest man. I liked him, but Crosby shied away.

We sailed back to Bella Bella in December. A light snow swirled over the ground and wolves howled from the shore at night. The air was dry: it seemed to shatter in the Northern Lights and the sky become a vague sea of shifting colour. When the moon rose, its light spilled cool and clean across the Harbour. I said to Crosby, "You can almost hear angels sing," though from the fort came the cries of the Indians at their festival, and Lafferty's voice raised above in notes cold as iron, hymn on hymn.

We knew exactly where we were as the ship settled at anchor.

Crosby had no nightmare that night. I woke him early. Lafferty and the Indian, Titus, waited in the canoe. He was to go with them to King's Island on a shooting expedition while I saw to the fitting up and repairing of the ship.

I said goodbye. We handed down Crosby's small dog, Roger, which accompanied him everywhere, then Crosby lowered himself after. He slipped into the well of the ship's shadow.

When they emerged onto the grey morning sea, the red cedar of the canoe was a slash in the water. I remember that, and that my thoughts were clear, clean like the night before, like a fast river.

By the afternoon they were on the island. They beached the canoe and tied the dog to a tree. Somehow, Crosby became separated from the others. He had picked up a game trail. He thought Lafferty and Titus were close behind him—but their guns remained silent.

He continued on, following a narrow, dragging trail. It was as if—even though he had not fired a shot—a wounded animal pulled itself along on its belly ahead of him.

The sun lowered behind the ledge of the island. Crosby called to his companions, but his voice deadened on the wall of the forest, the tangled labyrinth of salal, marsh and dense fir.

Meanwhile the others had returned to the canoe and made camp a few yards from the shore. They had no tent, but they put up a boat sail as a windbreak against the cold that blew across the snow-flecked waters. Cloud, portentous as avalanche, lowered, their firelight flickered dimly.

Lafferty and Titus unloaded provisions—100 lbs of flour, plus bacon and other items; and the ammunition and firearms: a doubled Enfield rifle, both barrels of which were loaded, and a double shot-gun, one barrel loaded with No. 4 shot. After eating they lay down to sleep, Titus a little distance away towards the shore. The dog, Roger, remained tied to a tree.

Night drew in, the wind blew, ice hung and chimed in the trees; but for Crosby, lost in the forest, there was no quieting down. Instead the trees came alive with birds that sported in the branches: he saw the green, yellow and purple of their feathers. Monkeys showered earth and stones and seeds down upon him. He heard the hiss of serpents on the path, and the blood-freezing cry of alligators from the depths of a swamp; every avenue he tried was blocked by tremendous vines: he found himself, indeed, in the midst of that nightmare which had so long distinguished his sleep. Still, somehow, he controlled his thoughts. He knew this poisonous region of the mind. He was confident that with dawn he would emerge unscathed. Though he still saw and felt and heard these horrors, he perceived a way through them, a dim world of shadows behind the jungle, an intimation of the daylight world, and he held to that thread and followed it.

Thunder and lightning flashed, the artillery of heaven played and rain poured down, flooding the forest. For hours at a time he struggled through a tepid, slow-moving river of mud. Yet he kept on, though the monkeys mocked and the serpents dropped from the trees as he travelled the continent of his imagination.

A little before dawn he arrived back at the camp. The dog whined with pleasure to see him. Lafferty woke up and greeted him. The men conversed for a few minutes and then lay down to rest with the rifle and the gun between them, the dog at Crosby's feet.

An hour or so later Crosby was awakened by a loud report. He did not raise himself up, but turned his head cautiously and saw his poor companion, the missionary, roll over, and after giving one great groan, expire. At the same time the gun sounded again, and Crosby was struck through the left thigh.

He managed to lie still, though the snow on the blankets over his leg foamed pink. Immediately there was another shot. This time, the ball passed right through his left thigh and lodged in his right. The middle finger of his right hand was also smashed and part of the palm shot away.

He could hear the cracking of twigs, the burst of seaweed on sand as the culprit, Titus, ran along the shore, taking the now empty rifle and gun with him.

Blood flowed freely from Crosby's wounds, and joined in a river and tributaries that ran down to Lafferty's body and pooled in the warm hollow where a few moments before, the sleeping man had lain.

A few snowflakes melted on the body. Crosby felt faint, but managed to take out his revolver. In about half an hour, Titus returned. Crosby fired off three shots, but each missed him.

For four days the Indian hovered nearby with an axe, watching for an opportunity to kill Crosby. But every time he approached, the dog was on the alert and gave the alarm. Eventually hunger forced Titus to leave the island.

Crosby lay in a helpless state in a species of timeless torpor, with the deadman's head touching him, the eyes wide open. The only articles within reach were the pistol ammunition, and some sugar. Upon the latter, and some moisture obtained by sucking snow from off his blankets, Crosby existed.

The dog could not get at the provisions which were stored away in a box, but during the day he would run down to the shore to eat mussels, then immediately return to Crosby. He never appeared to sleep, but was always on watch. He barked furiously when wolves ventured near, or in the daytime when crows circled low over Lafferty's body.

At the end of the second week, a terrible gale blew up. Trees crashed like rotten fencing at the edge of the forest. Branches littered the sea-shore, the sea foamed high up the beach, lapping at the dead man's feet.

The storm raged throughout the day, and as it did, a sweet, sickly stench seemed to gather in and rise from the soaked earth, to coalesce in a still fog over the camp. Crosby could see almost nothing other than the dog, Lafferty's body, and the occasional lick of foam as a wave crept to the foot of his blankets.

He could still hear the crashing of limbs and the wild workings of the wind, but in the camp itself, all was in abeyance.

Suddenly, from out of the branches overhead dropped a huge boa. It encircled Crosby's body in its folds and drew itself tighter and tighter. The dog edged away in fear, whining and quivering, as the serpent slowly crushed Crosby's chest. There was an oily sheen on the serpent's skin, a rainbow of light that mesmerized Crosby even as the life ebbed out of him.

Then, more quickly than the beat of a bird's wing, a mountain lion sprang out of the fog and crouched at Crosby's side. It seized the head of the snake in its mouth and bit it through. Crosby swooned away. When he awoke, he found the coils of the boa slackened around him, but emerging from them were swarms of small snakes that clustered to his eyes and nostrils. They nursed through his clothes into the warmth of his chest and groin. They sucked at his skin, raising blots of red.

Crosby told me all this in a tremorless voice, though I noticed a shadow—fleeting as the meeting of raindrop and river—pass through his eyes.

In the interval, Titus had returned to Bella Bella. One day, when he was out hunting with a companion, an Indian called Tom, he confessed what he had done. He said that he had not killed Crosby outright, but that he believed he had shot him through the stomach, and that he was doubtless dead by this time. He suggested to Tom that they return to King's island and retrieve the cache of provisions that had been left behind.

On the 17th night after Crosby had been wounded, Tom and Titus reached the island. The dog gave the alarm. Crosby drew his revolver and shot, and the Indians ran.

The night was clear and calm: the stars spurted orange, green and white. Crosby could hear the Indians' rapid breathing as they stood on the beach. Once Titus realized that Crosby was still alive, he wanted to make a bolt for it, but Tom wouldn't let him. He called out to Crosby that their intentions were friendly, that he would shoot Titus if Titus tried to harm Crosby, that they would return Crosby to his people for a ransom.

He was in a pitiful state when we found him. Both his feet and legs were frost-bitten, and for the final three or four days he had lain in water. His legs were so thin that he could span his thighs with the fingers of one hand. The wound through his thigh was open. When we poured water on it, it escaped through the aperture on the far side.

The Indians killed Titus.

After telling his story, Crosby did not speak further of his experience. He regained his health and resumed his work among the Indians with whom, on the whole, he re-established good relations. His nightmares did not resume, and I assumed that he had fully recovered.

One evening, however, after he had retired to bed on the ship when we were again anchored at Bella Bella, there came a cry from his quarters. On reaching his cabin, I found him in the midst of convulsions. His face was fixed in a grimace, the lips drawn back from the teeth in the expression of an animal at bay. An orange-bellied snake lay on the pillow near his face. Its tongue flicked in and out and then it slithered into the nest of Crosby's blankets.

I could not find out who among the crew had played the cruel joke—Crosby's nightmares had been common knowledge. No one would admit to the deed, and Crosby developed a virulent fever, and died.

Lafferty's successor said a service over the body, but I was determined to take it to his friends on the lower coast for burial. Since then, however, there has been no wind. The very currents of the sea seem to have changed their courses so that there is no means of our leaving this harbour.

The men are falling ill in the unaccustomed heat. A thick fog obscures the coastline, and the cries of the Indians on shore are mixed with the whistling of strange tropical birds. I wipe the perspiration from my forehead, and try once again to write the necessary letter to Crosby's family. I would send them some article of his, a memento, but the stench of decay has penetrated everything.

I hear the cries of the men as they lie down to their troubled sleep. Some few of them wait for me to leave the cabin: they have conceived the idea that Crosby's body is harmful.

The Indians call to the sailors from shore. Some of them have paddled their canoes near to our bows. They cry out that they were wrong to kill Titus. They ride beneath the ship in the mist, their war canoes open up shadows over the sea; they throw stones into the black mouths of these shadows.

Crosby's dog stands unmoving on deck. He has not eaten or drunk since Crosby's death. At night he sounds a howl across the harbour, and the dissonance of a jungle answers back.

Fishing Veronica Lake

Stephen Guppy

IN JUNE OF 1961, WHEN I WAS fifteen years old, my stepfather, Clyde Cateret, decided to teach me how to fly-fish. Clyde
had been living with us for four years by that time, he and my
mother having met in the summer of '57 when Clyde was on a
fishing trip up in Vancouver. He was a gentle and even admirable
man, I suppose, though the word that best describes him—as he
seemed from my adolescent's perspective, at least—is *absent*. Not
that he ever neglected us, went off with friends when he should
have been at home or played around with other women: it was
Clyde's *attention* that was missing, not his presence in our home.
He loved my mother, I'm sure of that, and I believe that he tried in
his way to love me, but there were two things he'd loved longer
and better: electronic gizmos and fishing. Clyde's mind was on
one or the other of these two subjects most of the time he was
awake, and the thoughts he had about them took all his attention.
His characteristic facial expression was that of a man listening
very, very carefully to some faint, barely audible sound off in the

distance. A distracted look. An absorbed look. A look that shut things out.

Clyde had been offering to teach me how to fly-fish ever since he'd started up with my mother. For reasons that are no longer clear to me—if indeed they ever were—I'd always found excuses to refuse him. This time, however, my mother left me no choice.

It happened like this: We were cleaning up the dinner things— Mom was washing, I was drying—when Clyde wandered into the kitchen with the *Post-Intelligencer* dangling from one hand and his meerschaum, which was unlit, cupped in the other. He walked up behind us and stood between me and Mom, gazing out the window with his usual distracted look and tapping the stem of the pipe against the chrome trim that ran around the counter. He stood there for quite some time, ignoring us, while Mom went right on asking me about how things were going at school, whether my friend Jamie Seevers had recovered from his bronchitis, all the usual stuff that mothers ask their children. We allowed Clyde the privacy of his mind, which he seemed to need more than anything else we could give him, and made no attempt to include him in the conversation.

"Going to clear up tonight," he said finally. "This wind should chase the rain away. Be a beautiful morning for fishing."

I knew this statement for what it was—a cue, an invitation— but I ignored it. I wasn't going to fish with Clyde, and I didn't want to argue. It was best, I'd decided years before, to pretend I didn't know what my stepfather was suggesting, to let the moment slip away and hope he'd take the hint. Clyde, having made the offer, stood staring out at the cloud-streaked evening sky a moment longer, then cleared his throat, inserted the stem of the pipe between his teeth, and turned away, rustling his paper.

Mom shot me an angry look, lips pressed hard together. She jerked her head toward Clyde's back. I knew I had no option.

"Going out after the big one, Dad?" I said, looking straight into my own blurred face reflected in the plate that I'd just finished drying.

There was a long pause while Clyde took his pipe out of his mouth and examined the pipestem for blockages.

"Think I might, Sonny," he said. "Think I just might, at that. We could head out along about six, if it suits you." Then he headed for his study, and I went back to wiping the plates. At five forty-five the next morning, we were on our way to Veronica Lake.

My stepfather was an electrical engineer, a Double-E from Michigan State: the classic Illinois prairie boy with a talent for wiring up gizmos. Years after he died, I found out that he'd worked on the experiments that led to the discovery of the transistor, and that he'd been recruited by one or two of the earliest of the semi-conductor firms that were starting up in the Santa Clara valley. Plenty of engineers of his generation had gone on to ride the big waves of microwave technology and consumer electronics, but Clyde had chosen, for whatever reasons, to stay in the calm, placid waters. He'd spent his working life at the Nuclear Reservation in Danforth, Washington, devising monitoring systems for the canisters of nuclear waste.

Danforth, as you probably know, is in the south-eastern corner of the state, near the bend in the Columbia River. It was a one-horse, one-industry sort of place in the early 'sixties: the drive-in was called Nukie's (it's now the site of a Burger King), the mascot of the high school football team was a freshman dressed up as a mushroom cloud, there was a street called Plutonium Cresent. You get the idea. In 1961, in Danforth, there was nothing particularly remarkable about working in a nuclear plant or a disposal site for radioactive materials: we rarely mentioned or thought of the risk; we were marching straight into the future, and the rest of the world seemed obsolete.

I remember something that took place the previous year, when

I was still in junior high school. It was a film about nuclear power. A man with a grey suit and a crew-cut stood up at a blackboard, just as if he were one of our teachers. He held up a basketball. It was a Voit, I remember, exactly like the one I had at home. *In the future*, he said, *a piece of radioactive material no larger than this basketball will light up a city the size of Chicago. There will be no more need for expensive dams, no necessity for using coal or oil to power turbines. Everything will run on electrical power, provided by a nuclear reactor.*

The film made me think of another film I'd seen, a horror movie I'd gone to with some friends a few weekends before. In that film there'd been a boy who'd seen a spaceship come to earth. It had landed in a farmer's field a couple of miles from his house. No one else had seen the spaceship land, and no one, not even his parents, would believe him when he told them what he'd seen. In the spaceship was an alien brain, a disembodied head with a bulging cranium encased in a plastic sphere. The brain was the centre of an alien plot to make slaves of the earthlings and take over our world. By the end of the movie, everyone except the boy had been captured by the creatures from space and transformed into a zombie. The power that flowed from the alien brain controlled them.

There are six thousand lakes in Washington state. There are glacial lakes, the unearthly blue of gemstones, that you can only get a look at from an airplane, seep lakes formed by runoff, man-made lakes backed up by hydro dams, ponds you could throw a rock across that go so far down into bed-rock no diver has ever touched bottom. My stepfather's favourite trout-fishing spot was a small lake you could only reach by driving half an hour on a pot-holed gravel road and then half an hour more up a power-line. It had, of course, an official name that you could find, if you wished, on the government geographical surveys, but to the fly-fishing fraternity it had always been known as Veronica Lake. Some wit,

I guess, had christened it: half the lake was obscured by cliffs from the access point a couple of hundred yards downhill from the power-line; you could see one half of the lake from your car, but a stand of jack pine, green as trees in daydreams, hid the other half from view.

Veronica Lake, I knew, was some kind of actress. Clyde told me the rest of the story as we drove, how she'd worn her blonde hair so that it fell over one eye, covering half of her face. "The original woman of mystery," Clyde said. "How could any man possibly resist her?"

Clyde's car was his one indulgence, other than his precious split-cane flyrods. It was a Studebaker Golden Hawk, long and sleek with snazzy fins. It was two-tone gold, had white-walls, and went a million miles an hour. We were travelling on gravel by quarter to seven. The Studie's lush suspension made the pot-holes disappear, and even the narrow dirt road—two ruts in the grass, to be more accurate—beside the power-line seemed reasonably smooth. Just after seven that morning, I was looking at Veronica Lake.

I was used to getting up early—basketball practice was at seven all winter, and in the spring I liked to get a run in before sitting down to breakfast—but the cold air rising off the lake made me homesick for my bed. I took off my basketball runners and pulled on the rubber waders Clyde had borrowed from someone at work. Clyde handed me a trout rod, one of his half-dozen spares, and we started down the hill towards the water. I was wearing the blue-plaid mackinaw that I wore to do chores around the yard, and my mother had dug up an old wool toque that I believe had belonged to my father, but I could still feel the breath of that lake on my skin.

My rod, the rod Clyde lent me, was, I now know, an H.L.Leonard Duracane Standard; I keep it at the cabin now and still use it on occasion. It was long, light, and whippy; when I held it, it felt like a living thing, some terrified or energetic animal that wanted to be

300

free of my grasp. The reel was a good one as well, I suspect; I looked for it among Clyde's things when he died, but I never came across it. It made, I remember, a satisfying clicking sound when I tentatively played out line and had the straightforward but precise and subtle feel of a Mercedes or a Nikon F1. I balanced Clyde's trout rod carefully and made my way down the slope. In a moment, I was walking into water. I could feel the cold climb my legs through my boots, jeans, and long johns; it was like the way exhaustion can wash through your body when you lie down after a five-mile run or a particularly hard-fought game. I fought it the way you have to fight that kind of exhaustion sometimes, bending my knees in the heavy boots to feel my body working and telling myself that I'd done plenty of harder things than wade in a lake to catch trout.

Clyde had entered the lake further away from where we'd left the car than I had; I glanced his way a couple of times to see how he went about casting, but both times he looked up with a reassuring smile the moment I turned my head, so I went back to trudging around in the water. I had no idea what to do with a fly rod. I played out some line from the reel until it looped down almost to the level of the lake, an operation I'd seen, or imagined I'd seen, fisherman perform in the movies or on the TV. This done, I lifted the rod like a buggy-whip and flailed it at the surface of the lake. My technique, I realized to my embarrassment, was more likely to deafen a fish than to catch one, but the trout-rod felt clumsy and wild in my hands and the balance of it seemed to work against me. I suppose I must have splashed the front of my shirt pretty good and sent the fly nowhere in particular except a yard or two downstream. I didn't, at any rate, get my line caught in the trees.

My stepfather let me try a few abortive casts, and then he made his way toward me, walking parallel with the lakeshore.

"It takes some getting used to," he said. "You have to develop a feel."

He put his rod down on the grassy slope and stood beside me, holding my arm with one hand and guiding my rod with the other while I tried another cast. I breathed in Clyde's unmistakable smell—his canvas vest, tobacco, the woodsy scent of his soap—and felt myself pull away. He took his hand off my arm and stepped back a foot or so while he described the fluid motion I should use to control the rod. If he noticed the fact that I'd cringed from his touch, there was nothing in his voice to show it.

Standing behind me with his back to the undergrowth that lined the shore, Clyde explained the conventional roll-cast, telling me how to angle the tip of the rod a bit below the horizontal, strip line from my reel and feed it out with my line hand while moving the rod tip back and forth until I'd piled up some line on the water. I did all this awkwardly, I'm sure, but my stepfather just kept talking, his voice in that absolute stillness like the voice of my own subconscious mind. *Lift your forearm, Son,* he told me. *Keep it straight out in front of your shoulder. Bring the rod up to the vertical and let the line come to rest. Now . . .*

I snapped my wrist as he'd told me, saw the long loop of line catching fire in the sunlight, saw the fly go out to the edge of things, through the brilliance of the sunlit lake, through the clear air, into shadow. It was a sloppy enough cast, I'm certain, but in spite of my clumsiness with rod and line, I felt for that brief instant some connection between my casting arm and the vague, inarticulate darkness at the centre of the lake. I wanted so much for the trout to leap, flashing like a comet's tail, from the tableau of reflected trees and glassy greenish shadows that I almost believed I could see it: it was there, made of atoms of shivering light, as perfect and as fugitive as I was. After two hours of casting, I caught my first fish, a sleek ten-inch cut-throat that thrashed like a spasming muscle in my hand as I jiggled it loose from the barb of the hook. I felt what I suppose all first-time fishermen feel: sorrow for the beautiful, alien thing I had taken from its element, and satisfaction at my ability to conjure this life from the lake. My stepfather, by this time, had landed a pair. He continued to spool out his slow, graceful casts, his rod arm whipping the split-cane rod tirelessly from vertical to horizontal, his line, incandescent in the sunlight, describing brief parabolas and complex epicycloids. I thought, as I rested my aching arm between casts and watched him, of the twitching phosphor sine-wave on the screen of the oscilloscope he kept above his workbench—the workbench where he tied his flies and wired up hi-fi sets and experimental colour TVs.

Buried deep beneath the porous ground of the Danforth Nuclear Reservation, there are 828 radioactive beagles. The dogs are in a cylindrical vault, encased within six-inch thick stainless-steel walls, sunk forty-seven feet beneath the surface. Nearby, in an identical storage tank, one of several others in that particular tank farm, is every single drop of piss and turd those beagles ever took. There are just over sixteen tonnes of radioactive beagle waste in total. The beagles were used in an experiment to test the effects of radioactivity on animals—and ultimately on humans. They were exposed to radiation in carefully-measured doses, and the effects of the exposure were observed and recorded. Then the dogs were bred and the incidence of birth defects noted. When the experiment was deemed complete, the beagles were destroyed.

There are also entire freight trains buried out at Danforth, as well as cores from the reactors of nuclear submarines and bulldozers that had been used to move radioactive waste. In the opinion of some physicists, the tank farms at Danforth may very well be the last surviving artefact of mankind on this planet, as by the time the plutonium and other radioactive matter in those subterranean tanks becomes inert, the human race will almost certainly have become extinct.

We packed up our rods a few minutes after noon. Clyde packed

303

the few trout we'd caught into a cooler, and we started on our way back to town.

"Hungry?" Clyde asked.

I was famished. Clyde turned up a side-road and then angled the Hawk into the gravel lot in front of a road-side cafe. The place was as unprepossessing as you'd expect a little one-room diner hidden out in the backwoods to be, but there were close to a dozen cars and trucks out front, and we could smell the bacon frying the minute we got out of the car. The place was full of fishermen, most of them wearing canvas vests and the same sort of squashed hat that Clyde wore, and there were two or three guys in hard-hats who may have been loggers or worked construction. The waitress, who was bottle-blonde and fortyish, was weaving between the tables and the counter, balancing stacks of pancakes on those heavy white stone-wear plates you always see in places that serve good plain food.

"Any action, Clyde?" one of the fisherman said as we made our way to a vacant table.

Clyde held up three fingers.

"Cut-throat?"

My stepfather nodded.

"Hope you left a few for the rest of us," another man said.

"One or two still up there, I'd imagine," Clyde told him.

"Any sign of her?" a third man asked. He winked at his companions.

"No sir, not a ripple," Clyde said.

No sign of *whom*, I asked my stepfather after the waitress had brought us our menus and filled our cups.

"Veronica Lake. It's an old joke," Clyde said.

We waited in silence for our orders to come up. I was tired by then; my legs had begun to ache at the calves, presumably from walking in water. I was hungrier than I could remember having been for some time. I'd ordered a stack of pancakes, hash browns, bacon, and two eggs over easy. Clyde had the same, without the pancakes. When he'd had a few sips of black coffee and poked his eggs around on the plate a bit, he took off his horn-rimmed glasses and lit a cigarette. Without his glasses, his eyes looked weak and unfocussed. He stared across the crowded room toward the open door.

"What matters about fishing a lake," he said, pausing to place his Winston on an ashtray with the same peculiar precision of movement that he brought to tying flies and building hi-fi's. "What matters about fishing a lake is that everything is hidden. You can't see the various textures in the water, as you can when you fish a river. In a river, there's fast water, holding water, eddies and riffles. There's slicks and runs. Boulders rearranging the current. You can see what you're up against, pick the most likely spots. Fishing lakes is different. Nothing moves. There are no clues."

The waitress brought a fresh pot of coffee from the kitchen and, without asking, re-filled our cups. A couple of the fisherman left, raising their hands to Clyde, who nodded briefly and took a drag on the Winston.

"You have to learn to look at the lake, that's the secret," he continued. "Watch where the may-flies congregate. Look for drop-offs and shoals beneath the water. Changes in reflected light, the way it strikes the surface."

I worked away at my pancakes, my only contribution to the conversation an occasional nod of assent. I was feeling, I guess, uncharacteristically at ease with my mother's husband; the aspects of his life I knew about—fly-fishing, electronics, working at the atomic plant—which had always seemed so uninteresting to me, the duties and preoccupations of a nondescript adulthood, had acquired a sense of mystery and significance in my mind. I wanted him to speak to me about his life, the work he did at the Nuclear Reservation, who he'd been before my mother and I had met him. He continued, however, to talk about trout-fishing until I'd mopped up the last of my breakfast, and then he straightened up in his

305

chair, put his glasses back on, and signalled the waitress for our cheque.

In the summer of 1956, the government decided to fire up the reactor at Danforth without benefit of filters to see if they could track the radiation as it travelled on the wind. The idea behind this plan of theirs was logical enough. The Soviets had nuclear plants in Siberia and Urkutsk, and they apparently gave little thought to the effects of radiation. Few of their nuclear facilities had filtration systems of any sort, and they were constantly emitting high levels of radiation, which the operators of the Soviet plants simply allowed to disperse on the wind. By tracing the radioactive air as it travelled across the Siberian tundra, it was thought, the Americans would be able to locate the Soviet plants and to assess their capabilities. To accomplish this with any accuracy, of course, they first had to know how rapidly wind-blown radiation might disperse and decay. To do this, they ran the reactors at Danforth without filters and followed the wind in cars that were equipped with Geiger counters. It was my stepfather's job, I've only recently discovered, to design these monitoring systems for the cars. I have no idea if he actually participated in any of the infamous "green runs," but he was sometimes away for days at a time in connection with various projects, so it's possible that he may have been directly involved. I imagine him, anyway, driving north toward the Canadian border with the dark-suited men from the AEC, following the path of the radioactive dust like Bushmen staying under a raincloud, the Geiger counters chattering in the unmarked Chevrolet.

On the drive back to town Clyde was silent. I prattled on about things I'd done at school, bragging a bit about exam scores and touchdowns I'd scored or almost scored with the football team the previous autumn. We descended toward the highway, passing from gravel road to narrow asphalt backroad, the Golden Hawk gaining momentum as the surface over which we were travelling improved. Before long, we were back on Route 17, cruising through arid scrublands toward the river and our home. The fatigue I'd been ignoring ever since our trip had begun possessed me, and I leaned back against the plush seat and let myself drift away. I was nearly asleep when my stepfather starting talking, and I listened in a kind of stupor as he told me about his work.

"At the plant," he said, "we're lake-fishing most of the time. Or someone is, anyway. Casting out across the surface when they don't know for sure what's underneath it. Looking to hook the big ones. All that power, free as air."

I remembered the brain in the science fiction film. The basketball that lit up a city.

"The trouble is, when you work like that," Clyde continued, "you don't know what might happen. You could hook the biggest trout you ever saw. Or a saw-toothed pike. Or snag bottom. A fellow I know hooked a corpse once. Guy just like him, in an L.L.Bean vest, floating dead in Veronica Lake."

In an hour, we were home. Clyde gutted and cleaned the trout while I went upstairs for a nap, and I guess we must have had them for dinner, though I have no memory of our having done so. I do remember thanking Clyde for taking me out fishing, telling him I'd had a good time, which was true, and making plans to go fishing again. In a couple of weeks, however, I'd landed a job pumping gas at the Danforth Esso, and then there was school and football. In the spring, I'd found a girlfriend, and I was spending most of my free time over at her place, playing Bobby Vinton records on her parents' new hi-fi and pretending to work on our homework. After that, there were other girls, sports, summer jobs. I never went fishing with my stepfather again.

Twenty-five years later, when Clyde Cateret was living in a shared room at a retirement home near Danforth, as absorbed in the business of dying as he'd once been in building his hi-fi sets or tying flies at his bench in the basement, I would listen to him try to describe the visions he had seen in his dreams. He would begin to speak incoherently about how he'd been walking through a valley full of terrible malformed creatures. He would describe the trees, the fields of grass, the fireweed nodding gently in the sunlight. Then he'd slowly start to talk about the dogs he'd seen, packs of dogs that wandered around the hayfields. *Little dogs*, he'd say to me, *some with paws like flippers. Brown and white beagle dogs, covered in lesions. Some with marks like terrible burns. Some with four eyes or five eyes or eyes split like berries. Some dogs born without legs. Some dogs with too many.*

I thought he was senile, and to some extent I guess he was. Several of the people he'd worked with had died years before, of leukemia and thyroid conditions. Clyde himself had had two operations, and he would die of lymphoma when he was seventy-one years old. The three years he spent in the retirement home, after my mother had died and I had moved north into Canada and allowed myself to forget him except for a visit every summer, he passed in a fog of memories, conversing with the shadows of his past.

When my stepfather died, I drove south for the funeral. With my mother gone, there was no one there with whom I could share my feelings. Some men from the nuclear plant were there, as well as some fellows with whom Clyde had sometimes gone fishing. I recognized a few of them and accepted their condolences in the numb, inarticulate way one does on these occasions. I saw them, predictably, through the eyes of the teenaged boy I'd been when they had come to the house with my stepfather, and their white hair and aged-looking faces seemed the result of a catastrophe or terrible illness rather than the natural and predictable product of age. It was as if I had been keeping a photograph of them in my

308

memory, and it had been damaged by immersion in water or partially burned in some fire.

A lot has been written and said about rivers, but far from enough about lakes. In the thirty-three years that have passed since that morning in 1961, I've thought about lakes a great deal. There's a number of good lakes near my home here on Vancouver Island, and my son and I fish rainbows every month it doesn't snow. There's one in particular that reminds me a little of Veronica Lake. You see the main body of water from the logging road, right there below you, but the rest of the lake, nearly half of it, is obscured by a heavily-forested outcrop of land. My son and I hike through thick salal across that outcrop to do our fishing. We could fish just as well, I suppose, from the more accessible end of the lake, or for that matter from the nearby lake on which we have our cabin, but I tell myself that the fishing is better in that hard-to-get-at spot, even though I know it probably isn't. There's an odd satisfaction, though, in working through the undergrowth to stand at that mud bank and cast out into glacial run-off. I say nothing to my boy about my reasons for choosing this particular place to fly-fish, though I've told him the story of Veronica Lake the actress, of course, and observed his look of bored incomprehension just as Clyde must have noticed mine three decades before. We stand together and far apart in the green light of cold mountain water, the chill aching clear through our trousers and boots, and hurl our weightless, shining line out toward the far, dark centre. The surface of the water is still; the trees and hills and clouds or sunlit skies on the lake are mere reflections. There is nothing in what my boy and I see to reveal to us what may be out there, muse or fury, dream or nightmare. Still, in our blindness, we cast out our lines. The hidden world is always the right world.

Fresh Girls

Evelyn Lau

CAROL IN THE BATHROOM, HOLDING her hair with one hand and a mascara wand with the other, her face lopsided in the mirror on the medicine cabinet. Her face floating alongside cherry-red mouthwash, dental floss, old razors. Carol fixing her honey hair and saying, "You don't think I'm neurotic, do you? Do you?". . . coming out into the living room with the zipper teeth of the makeup bag between her fingers, smiling a girl's smile. She's twenty-four— same age as Jane at the massage parlor, bowing her head in the hallway when she thought no one was looking, after that old guy left. Looks like he took more than he paid for. Jane ran an escort agency at twenty, now she's washed up, sits in the back room all day waiting for a faithful regular while the other girls come and go. More blondes these days, making up their pale eyes at the table, smoking the other girls' cigarettes, reading trash. Jane watches. She's starting to get a curl to her lip, like she knows too much, but she's not bad-looking in regular clothes, when she changes into a sweater and jeans to buy soup or cigarettes or condoms down the street. She's got freckles on her shoulders, sort of cute. Looks better when she washes her makeup off, but in work gear—the blue eyeliner, the tight white dress with the chiffon thing along the neck that she ribbons into her hair—Jane looks worn out. Yeah, even though her room is the one with the little pink rosebuds on the shade over the lamp by the bed.

Carol's not like that, she hasn't done it long enough. Sitting on the floor, poking at herself with the needle, smearing a trickle of blood with the back of her hand onto her thigh, onto that dress she's borrowed from somewhere, a purple mini with flowers. Pretty legs, hair falling into her eyes; she's not even sweating, though she's been poking for the last twenty minutes. She's even made one up for me, it's sitting on the overturned cardboard box Mark calls a coffee table. Pale gold liquid and then the squirt of her blood in the syringe, like a curly hair. I look at it, look back at her, wait to get desperate enough.

"Mark, I need five bucks for pantyhose," Carol says.

She looks up and the lamplight hits her face and her hair and the hardwood floor. They're all the same color, honey, and her eyes blink and her teeth show and Mark goes scrambling. She's one of those you can't turn down, you can smell the freshness on her, like she just took a shower and dusted off with baby powder. Like she just took a walk through a forest. Monica will hate her; chain-smoking and bitching in the back room, one leg up on the arm of that ancient couch, magazines and science-fiction books and romance novels with torn-off covers stacked behind her. Eating chicken soup out of a cup and pulling at her styled bangs in the mirror on the table; tinted so blonde she's gone gray in parts, the parts that aren't shimmering with Grease in the light.

"New girls, they come; new girls all the time," Monica mutters, exhaling angrily. "How am I supposed to make a living? Tell me. First you, then the redhead, then that skinny blonde, she's got an accent too, my God! How am I going to get business? Not so many men, I have to sit here all afternoon, waiting and waiting . . ."

Monica's red lips pucker with hatred, and then the doorbell rings and she puts her feet in high heels, pulls at a curve of hair in the hall mirror, grabs up condoms. She knows he'll want a new girl, whoever he is. The men can tell the ones who've been here long, they smell like the back room, five ashtrays operating at once and the taste of packaged soup on their tongues.

Monica, too, looks not bad when the day's over and she's changed into a man's shirt and little pink shorts, examining her face in the mirror in front of me, carefully wiping off the last of the foundation and brushing out her hair before leaving to pick up her kid. She makes it my turn to clean the bathroom, though, and for a moment I hate her. It's easy to turn to hate behind the boarded-up windows of this place, each room with its lamp dusty with red light so everyone looks good, even sometimes a man, so pale and smooth on the bed it's like being with a baby, its face not yet formed.

"Thanks, Mark," says Carol.

She's rounding the hallway, a package of pantyhose from the grocery store down the street in her hands, her face a bright dazzle. She turns to me and grins for a minute.

"Hey, isn't it weird walking down the street when you're stoned? Like, it's like everyone knows, and they can all tell, and you're scared you're showing it somehow, like they can tell just by looking at you. They all look at you funny, except for the guy who whistled at me. He was standing on his balcony. He was real cute, I wonder why girls can't whistle at guys too? And there was this cop car down the street, the cop inside looked at me real funny . . ."

She's tearing open the package and chattering, but I hardly notice, my arm is turned up on the couch, Mark is telling me to pump my hand and saying "Good, good girl, that's it, there it is," and I'm leaning back against the back of the sofa real fast, tasting

312

the taste of it come up in my throat, like silver or copper or one of those metals, and that slivered feeling all along the back of my neck and shoulders, where it'll hurt the next morning.

At the massage parlor I spend a lot of time in the back room too, but that doesn't matter, I have other people. There's a doctor, for example, who calls me every few weeks from Medicine Hat, Alberta. "I want to fuck your pussy all night," he says, and then he flies down for some physicians' conference and I find him on his hotel bed, waiting. He looks at me after I come back from the bathroom with half my makeup gone and smiles and says, "You're still pretty," as if he expected somebody else to be behind the face I put on for him.

To him, and others, I'm still in my Lolita years, but I have a birthday coming up soon. I'll be twenty and what then? The back room is getting too small, and even the owner's tiring of the pretty girls with their daddy complexes curled up next to the desk where he balances the books and takes half their money; the girls who pull up their skirts and tuck their naked legs beneath them on the chair and fiddle with their long curly hair, pouting—"So, Daddy should I get it cut? I was thinking maybe I'd get it cut next time, all these split ends, look . . . " while they dangle a waterfall of gorgeous hair in front of him. Everyone wants to be pretty for Mario, he takes their money and lets them sit in the back room when they get old, twenty-four, twenty-five. Lets them eat chicken soup and buy condoms for the other girls and take in a few hairy, smelly regulars wearing checked pants and bad ties. Mario's wife comes in then with her freckled legs, wearing a red dress, tilting her head to one side and saying "No, don't cut it, that'll be bad for business," and the girls lid their eyes and put on older mouths, the kind of mouths that say contempt and knowing, but they say, "Well, okay," and Mario continues to work hard over the ledgers.

But to some men I'm still a baby girl. That's what he calls me, the rich old man in his apartment with the blackened windows, "Baby Girl," he says, "You're still a Baby Girl," and I think I've never heard words so sweet. He calls me nights when he's drunk. He never touches me, that one, only wants me to sit on his silk-covered couch in that incredible room with one wall nothing but a mirror, like a pond of ice, and the grand piano with red roses in a crystal vase on top. The old man in his blankets smokes Silk Cuts and asks me to light the oil lamp on the table. I turn it up too high, so the flame swirls a black mark onto the ceiling. He's getting worse. One night when I go to pee I see he's vomited up his dinner in the toilet, cut green beans floating in the bowl with rice or some gelatinous white substance; he hasn't bothered to flush the toilet. But he likes his Rusty Nails the way I make them—clumsily, "Like a woman," he says, "women never know how to make drinks." I bring them in to him sloshing over the side of the glass, half a cup of Drambuie, half a cup of Scotch, no ice, spilling over. He smiles weakly and looks at me in the mirror and says I look good or bad, pick a week, I turn around and smooth some swatch of material over my belly and say, "I'm getting fat," and he says "Yes," and then "No, no, you're perfect, you're just a Baby Girl." And I swell inside, a golden feeling.

"I like you," he says, "that's a real compliment, I don't usually like anyone."

But the cab drivers chuckle when I leave, clanging the iron gate behind me: "That old guy's quite a character, you know, he's got working girls coming out of his apartment most every night."

I know. I know about the girl who comes over from the top massage parlor in town, how she lies in the chaise longue and what he does to her. But he never does anything to me and that's good enough. Nights I sit by the phone waiting for him to get drunk so he'll call me, and I can go down to the secret address via certain cab drivers, tripping through the maze of gates and gardens and the exclusive apartments he lives in. He'll be drunk and fiddling with the grandfather clock in the hallway, offering me a drink and telling me to make it myself. As long as I listen 'til three, four in the morning and give him a sleeping pill before I leave, I stay on his good-girl list, and sometimes he even calls me afterwards and leaves messages on my machine.

"I'm sorry, Baby Girl, I don't remember anything that happened last night, we didn't go to bed, did we?"

And I call him back and reassure him, "No, everything's still the way you want it, pure."

Pure as coke, as the driven snow. I know all the dealers in town, they all hold meetings at Mark's place, the English guy with the crooked tie who swings golf clubs at me and says over and over, "You sod, you sod," and takes out little green scales to weigh my purchase; the Japanese guy in his designer sweaters with the yellow pills ten times as strong as morphine who watches me and waits for me to come down and call him, with his mercenary eyes and his Jag always parked just around the corner. They all have my number.

But then I have theirs. The old guy's the best. When I say around midnight, as I always do, that I have to leave, he tugs at me with his little white claw and says, "No, please stay, please. I'll give you another two hundred, will you stay?" And then before his lip can curl back on itself, before he gets reflective and serious and says, "This is sad, isn't it, when you think about it, it's sad me calling you down here and paying you to listen to me," I run into the other room and find his checkbook. Some nights I have to fill it out for him; he puts it down and looks at me with deer eyes and that wan smile and says, "I can't, I'm too drunk," and I fill it out and then guide his hand to the place where he has to sign, crook-edly. And I take the check, plus the stash of twenty-dollar bills he's lined up for me on the kitchen counter on my way out. And give a little cheer as I run past the gardens and through the three gates to the marble elevator, because I've done it again, I'm still his Baby Girl.

315

So it doesn't matter about the back room, though yes, I have what one could call expenses. And a Baby Girl name, like Jane's, that will follow me pathetically from birthday to birthday. I never wanted to get older like ordinary teenagers, I knew there was nothing up there to look forward to except smelly old regulars and a parade of new girls, sixteen, seventeen, coming in illegally through the doors of every massage parlor in town and crowding me out. Days of humiliation, sitting in the back room sifting through an old *Vogue,* answering the phone, accompanying the girls to the vault where they drop half their money. Watching with a tired smile like the one Jane has on her lips these days, fussing with the ribbon in her hair, her tummy starting to round out under the tight white dress. They're my only family, Mario and the changing girls' faces, and the johns who ring the doorbell and grope at my stockings in the rooms upstairs where I go with a kit of condoms and jelly and baby powder, and a porn video to excite them into spending the fifty-dollar bills in their wallets if my naked body isn't enough.

Carol's ready, she's got on her high heels and she's waiting, nervous, beside me on the sofa. She doesn't have to say anything for me to know she's only done it a few times.

"Like, I'm not really sure about this," she whispers, plucking at her skirt. "Mark told me this guy is really nice, some Chinese guy, but, like, do I kiss him? Are you supposed to kiss them?"

"Well, I do," I say. "If you want to be special, you do too, because most girls won't," but by this time Mark's come out of his stupor on his end of the couch, and this Chinese guy is coming down the hallway with a big moon face.

Mark says, "This is Carol . . ." and Carol's face dims, and next thing I know she's in the kitchen, dragging Mark, and I can hear her saying, "Please, I need a fix before I go into the bedroom, please, Mark, don't do this to me, I thought you were my friend. I feel like you don't care, you won't listen to me, I don't even know this guy, just give me one fix before I go in."

And him saying "No, come on, Carol, don't be stupid, he'll know you're stoned, he says he only likes clean girls, girls who've never done drugs."

And I'm left alone with this guy in the living room. He stands there. I smile sweetly at him.

"You want a seat?"

"No, no, I'm sitting all day. In the office." He keeps standing there, toying with something in his jacket pocket, looking around with his lids lowered. He gives me a swift look, I cross my legs.

"Are you clean?" he says.

"Oh, sure," I say, keeping up that smile. "I never touch drugs, I don't even smoke."

It's true, that last bit, I quit a year ago.

"Good, you sound like a nice girl." He can hear Carol's voice from the kitchen, and he turns to me and says, "What about you, are you . . . ?" His voice is hesitant, the kind I like, the kind I can use. "I'll pay one hundred . . . ."

"No," I say, laughing. I've worked hard all week, I'm loaded. "No, sweetheart, I'm on vacation. But Carol will do you."

I can hear Mark pushing her into the bathroom, giving up, and the john and I wait in the living room, him standing silently beside me, too nervous to fidget, and me swallowing the taste of chemicals and grinning into the middle distance until Carol comes out, her face shining, her eyes like disco balls, silver and spinning. She grabs me and whispers that she needs a condom, then disappears with the john into the bedroom, and Mark is waving a come-hither needle at me from the bathroom doorway.

It seems like days later that Carol emerges from the bedroom and I catch a rear view of the Chinese guy as he pads naked into the bathroom, but it can't be that long because she's only just coming down off the fix that Mark gave her.

317

"So, how'd it go?" I ask her, the way Jane asked me my first day at the massage parlor, when I came back from my first customer, holding a sealed envelope for the vault for Mario. "Was he okay?"

I don't remember how I answered, that first time, but Carol says nothing. Her eyes are muddy and they glance off me like it hurts to look straight at me, and she crosses the hardwood floor and steps out on the balcony. The sun is starting to come out, I can see the lemon light mixed with pink and blue around the edges of the curtains, I hear Mark in the bedroom getting comfortable on the bed that's just been vacated.

"Carol?" I say, but I can just make her out on the balcony, fumbling for a smoke, and I sink back into the cushions and pick up the needle she had left for me on the coffee table. And she stays out there like that for a long time, still and gray against the railings, and I know for a fact it's not because she likes sunrises.

Diamond

Wayde Compton

I belong irreducibly to my time. —Frantz Fanon

I HAD PASSED THROUGH a quarter century, and finally my vision was going. I blamed it on reading. There were signs at the University warning you about everything from date rape to late capitalism, but nothing that said anything about reading yourself blind. I was trying to get used to the glasses, but they caused the worst sort of nightmares from the very start. My optometrist claimed it was a normal phenomenon as one gets used to a prescription. At the end of the day there were times I was rendered so dizzy and in such pain that I threw up.

But while reading I came to learn the names of all nine Muses: Calliope, Clio, Erato, Euterpe, Melpomene, Polyhymnia, Terpsichore, Thalia, and Urania. I also learned about the Scylla and Charybdis, which sounded familiar when I heard them mentioned in lecture. I realized my mom had told me about the sea monster and the whirlpool when I was a little kid. She'd turned the old myth into a children's bedtime story.

All my friends when I was a kid were mixed like me. Our parents were interracial couples, as they say, and us Civil Rights babies, I guess. Back in those days, the mixed couples stuck together. It was still freaky as hell in the early seventies, I imagine, to see a black man and a white woman pushing a pram with a nappy-headed kid flaunting its golden skin to the world. Brazen. Birds of a feather, as they say.

So the mixed couples flocked together playing cards, and us, their children, fought over who got to play Lando Calrissian in the backyard.

I once saw my mother cuss out a young white hippie woman. The woman was walking up the street towards us with her mixed baby. Baby had little golden dreads growing out like caterpillar fern tendrils. My mom, who don't know from dreads, castigated the woman something fierce, saying, 'When I married a black man I made damn sure I knew how to comb a black child's head. You have no excuse for letting that poor child walk around, head all knotted up. Are you out of your mind?' In Mom's day, you had to fight tooth and nail for every inch of respect. They were looking for excuses and you best not be giving them any.

I came to learn the names of all three Furies, too: Alecto, Megaera, Tisiphone.

I bumped into one of those old friends, mixed progeny, a good buddy of mine I had kept up with only through the odd encounter and mostly rumour. He lived in the sticks now, in Delta, apparently. His name was Cameron, and he had always been a smart and unusual guy. Last I'd heard he was fronting a Marxist punk rock band called Hammer and Sickle Cell Anemia, and dating a white girl who played bass in an all-girl hardcore band. But when I walked into A&B Sound, there he was, the picture of hip hop.

We soul shook.

'Sup? I ain't seen you in ages, nigga! Whatcha bin doin'?'

I filled him in, we caught up a bit. Turns out he was a DJ now, had a gig coming up at The Quarter. He passed me a handbill with a slick and dizzyingly cartoonish design. Said,

Featuring DJ T-Rope, N.W.N. (Niggas With Négritude), DJ Osiris, Grand Master Narrative and the Tenuous Ten, and DJ Parataxis

'Which one is you?'

'I'm DJ Osiris. I know, there's one in every city in North America, but whatcha gone do. Sounds too cool!'

'Osiris. The god, right?'

'Dass right. Pan-Africanism, home, that's where I'm coming from these days. The Afrocentric shit. The funky dialectic. You get to study much of our own stuff up at that school?'

'No. None at all.' It was true. I felt embarrassed, here in the presence of Osiris, about how little I knew of Africa.

'Yeah, well, it wasn't until I *left* school that I started to learn things. Like Plato and Aristotle and those motherfuckers stole all their shit from Egypt. A thief culture, that's what the West is. Everything that ain't nailed down, they take. Check it.' He rifled through his backpack and produced a book with an amateurish graphic of a pyramid on the cover. 'I'm learning to read hieroglyphics, man. That's the kind of cultural shit I'll get into in my MCing, if I ever get some money together. Right now I'm just DJing, but I'm trying to polish my voice, my delivery. You know, get the skills up. I need to get paid, is what I need. Got ta get paid, is what I got ta get.'

We stared at each other for a bit. I didn't remember him ever talking like this when we were kids, this accent.

'Well, I'll see you later . . . .' I hesitated, not sure if I was supposed to call him Cameron or Osiris. 'I'll try to check out your show.'

'Later,' said my new old friend, and we knocked fists, and he left.

As soon as I got to the club I realized I'd left my ID at home. I was always doing this. The pants I usually wore out to clubs didn't have a back pocket, so I would take my money out of my wallet, put it in my front pocket, and leave the wallet at home. Half the time it wouldn't occur to me to bring my ID, or that I'd get carded at twenty-five. When I arrived, the doorman was propped up on a wobbly stool, wobbling and counting the heads streaming by with a little metal clicker.

'ID,' he said to me, and only me, even though the three girls ahead couldn't've been a day over fifteen.

'I left my ID at home. Look, man, I'm twenty-five years old.'

'I need to see some ID.' He didn't even look me in the eye. More probable minors breezed by while he arbitrarily singled me out.

'Listen, I really am twenty-five. I can prove it. Would an eighteen-year-old know all nine Muses? There's Calliope. Clio, Erato, Euterpe. Melpomene. . . . '

He turned and looked at me. 'What the fuck are you talking about?'

'The Muses. You know, the ancient Greek goddesses of the arts, the daughters of Zeus and Mnemosyne, the. . . . '

He stood up, and his stool fell over. He was easily six inches taller than me, a face as blank as paper. 'Are you fucking with me, you piece of shit?'

'No, man, I'm trying to prove to you that I'm over eighteen. I'm studying Brecht. I know who Devo are. I owned a Rubik's Cube. I can locate a clitoris on a woman. What more evidence do you need?'

Before he could pull my arms off, Osiris peeped his head out of the front door and saved me. 'Nigga, getchyo ass in here. My set's coming up.' And to the doorman, a simple 'He's with me' even absolved me of the cover.

322

It was like stepping inside a rattle: the dancers in their gear, the players laying back, the homegirls hip-shaking. We skirted the floor, bought pints at the bar, and then made our way to a little stage up against the back wall. The platform was surrounded by people jackin it up. The current DJ was in position before the wheels, needles centripetal on the vinyl. I marvelled that this place was so thick with sound you had to wade through it, and all that sound passed through a tiny piece of diamond on the end of a needle, on the end of an arm, on a turntable, on a table, on this stage. Some dude leaning against the wall said to Osiris, 'You up next, O.'

'They just trying different people out tonight,' Osiris said to me. 'Five or six motherfuckers are here. Comin from all over . . . .'

Osiris's voice trailed off. He became distracted by the current DJ's cutting. A craftsman observing a colleague, I observed. I could tell O was nervous and probably hadn't been doing this long. He turned away while the current DJ grooved, and started stretching like a man up to bat. He was talking at me a mile a minute, sort of rambling.

'All sorts of shit kept from us. All sorts of shit. Bitch-ass white dude asked me today why if Africans are so into the drum, the talking drum and all that shit, why there are so few rock drummers who are black? *Maybe cause we don't get down to that Geddy Lee-Rush-stadium rock shit, motherfucker.* Ain't like my dad was beating bongos at the dinner table, peckerwood. White people in this city are so backward. Can't even get their racism right. Technology is our thing, why ain't it? I don't play no goddamn drums. I *program* the fuckin hell outta shit, though. Why we gotta be so *earthy?* Stupid backwater crackers. You know, they ain't cornered the market on technology. Hell, no. Every time you stuck at a red light bitchin bout, "I'm gonna be late for work," just think, a black man's shit is fucking you up. Brother named Garrett Augustus Morgan invented the motherfuckin traffic lights, man.'

'I didn't know that . . . .' I could feel a headache coming on. I touched my temples with my fingers and rubbed them in a circular motion.

'Of course you didn't know that. Ever wonder why they're red, yellow, and green? Colours of the Ethiopian flag, man. Garrett Augustus Morgan was a righteous inventing motherfucker. Think they want you to know shit like that? Naw, go bang a fuckin drum, jungle bunny. Don't think about doing anything that'll last longer than a few vibrations in the air. Anyway, whatever. Say, tell me some shit you're learnin about at school, home. Take my mind off this. I'm stressed out up here. Shit, this place is packed.'

I started to tell him about how I'd been doing some reading on my own, stuff about blacks in west coast history, the gold rush days, the first influx of us, but the music was so loud it seemed like my voice was being whisked away the moment it left my mouth. I could barely hear my own words, except as they vibrated inside my head. The club boomed. It felt like a giant was picking up the club and dropping it on the ground over and over again in four four time. Squeals of synth and sampled horn gasped at me humanly, unbearably. My mind balked. My vision crumpled. I held onto a column and downed my beer. A migraine was clearly arising. 'The Egyptians invented beer,' I heard a voice say, but it wasn't DJ Osiris; he was already in front of the turntables for his set.

He must've hit the right nerve; there was a floor rush as soon as his first few beats broke out. Bodies started bobbing and bearing into me on all sides. I was swept out onto the floor. The bass buzzed in my skull, vibrated up inside my teeth. A speaker was just above my head; I could feel wind emanating from the cones. My heart paradiddled. There was just the pulse and ebb of each boom of bass and residual crack of manufactured snare:

WOOM BOOM CRACK
WOOM BOOM CRACK

In succession, cessation, succession, my friend's Afrocentric cut flowed like blood from the speaker above me, wailing, a voice chopped, saying, sort of singing,

New Af ri ca—
Ne wAfri ca—
New Af rica at tackin ya

and the boom bloomed into the next subsequent crack like I imagined a round from a Kalashnikov would sound. My eyes tore open with water. Through each succession of blur, the darkness, the spinning, the lights, the smoke, the colliding, the limbs, the dreads, the glasses, the tears, the drink, the woom, the boom, the crack, I saw the edges of the room, a box beneath the ground, a basement with concrete walls, with exposed pipes, with a vague floor on which white kids spun like dreidels, breaking, locking, popping, windmilling, spinning counter-clockwise.

And his hands, brass, curved into each title of vinyl as he replaced one record, then another, holding up the vibe, straddling ecstasy and vengeance, pulling back tracks, cutting, retracing steps, thefts. I could barely see the vinyl spinning on the steel through what felt like blood welling behind my bruised eyes. There was glitter.

He lifted a record up from its place on the turntable, holding it gently with both hands as if it were the most fragile and precious thing he'd ever touched. The deafening roar of time rushed by as through a door the size of a year and tore into sediment. Tears ran down my face, chest, soaked me, tugged at my ankles like a current. I reached out to steady myself. Everything, everyone, was moving, bouncing up and down. Shadows teemed. Just then, my glasses were swept off my face in a single, sharp, staggering blow.

The Last Time We Talked

Ron Smith

LARRY SITS ACROSS FROM ME AT LUNCH and I know he's thinking much the same as I am. What the hell's happened to this guy over the last sixteen years?

He takes a sip from his water and then watches the ice cubes swirl around the glass. I'm taking in my usual overdose of caffeine, spiked with too much sugar and cream. At least I've quit smoking.

He's asking himself the obvious things: Do I look as bad as he does? Do I look as old? I know I haven't lost as much hair or put on as much weight. He's thinking: The guy's a lard ass. And his wife, what about his wife? She was attractive back then. What's she look like now? Could she possibly look as tired, as worn down as he does? He's asking himself about my wife, my Annie, which kind of pisses me off.

I look at my hands. No calluses. My hands are soft and pink, fleshy, and my life line forks in the middle of my palm. I used to move around the squash court like a tomcat. Now I can't roll off my couch without feeling winded. I admit it, I'm in rotten shape.

There's nothing subtle about the way we look at each other. Sixteen years will do that to your perspective. I look, but I don't see. This is not someone I know, not quite. I watch him closely. I want to see more than some physical similarities to the memory I'm dredging up. Hell, I have enough trouble with the picture I see of myself when I look at the wedding photograph Annie keeps on the mantlepiece.

But Larry and I had been good friends. When we went for a beer after an hour of squash, we always had something to say to each other. Small talk mostly, about sports or music. Occasionally, when one of us needed help, we'd confide in the other.

As I say, we were friends. When the four of us played Canasta and drank gin into the early hours of the morning—well, there wasn't a topic that made any one of us blush. I'm hoping that history will help get us over this initial shock.

How's Carla, I ask.

He sucks in some air, looks me straight in the eye and says nothing. He drops his gaze to the menu and recites the entrees, as if I'm retarded.

I had talked to Carla two nights earlier, shortly after I'd arrived at the detox centre. I checked in, got the schedule for meals and sessions, and then the lecture on curfew and booze from a short, stout woman who made it clear I wasn't going to jerk her around. Her eyes were huge. All the rules were for my benefit, she pointed out.

I agreed. I assumed this would show I was going to be cooperative. Receptive to the therapy.

After I'd unpacked my gear, I sprawled out on one of the three narrow beds in the room. I studied the ceiling and thought, this is not going to be easy. This is prison. With day passes handed out at the discretion of the warden I'd just met. And worst of all, I'd volunteered myself for this experiment. So far I was lucky, no one had showed up to share my room. Or toilet and shower. This would be a bonus, to be on my own. When I broke into the sweats, I could deal with my demons alone. The idea of sharing my paranoia with someone else made me feel unclean. Besides, I figured if I could stand two weeks of looking at the photo wallboard someone had used to decorate the room, I'd probably survive the cure.

Everyone had insisted I try therapy. Group therapy, for Christ's sake. I don't much like talking about myself, at least not about the intimate stuff. And especially not to a bunch of strangers. Still, I knew as well as anyone else that I needed to get my life back on track. The last two flashes of temper had scared the shit out of me. Smashing crockery was one thing, but when you started to grab family around the neck, well, crazy came to mind. That's what hurt. The striking out. Wondering if I might bust someone's head open.

The ceiling was made up of two hundred and sixteen, one foot by one foot tiles. I tried to calculate the dimensions of the room but I'd never been much good at math. Then I lay perfectly still and listened to my breathing. As my chest rose and fell, I thought about phoning Larry and Carla. I tried to understand the connection between my counting, my breathing, and them, but I couldn't see one. What a waste of time, I decided. The mind just works that way sometimes.

Larry and Carla had moved from the city up to this small town on the Sunshine Coast a few months after Annie and I moved to Vancouver Island. Larry had landed some work on a new television series. Before that he had done some free-lancing on major films. But the work was intermittent and this series promised something more steady. The script called for a small seaside town with an active harbour. Larry discovered Gibsons. At least the producers credited him with the discovery. And that was enough to guarantee him employment for as long as the show ran.

Just before we left, Carla had become seriously ill. After a couple of weeks of tests, no one seemed able to diagnose her problem. The doctors advised hospitalization. Still no one knew what was wrong with her. We could see the lesions developing up and down her arms and legs but no one could stop them. The wounds spread and grew. They turned dark brown and then black. They looked like craters in her skin. She had been so beautiful, Annie said. Specialists were flown in from the Mayo Clinic and some place in Florida. Nothing changed. We visited her a few times in hospital, but the sight of her turned my stomach. Annie's, too, although on the last visit I was surprised when Annie bent down to the bed and held Carla in her arms. The two of them rocked back and forth. Whispering. Sobbing. Annie stroking Carla's hair. Once we'd settled on the Island, the separation grew into silence. Neither Annie nor I had the words.

Later we heard Carla had been released from St. Paul's and they had moved. Here. When I suggested to Annie that I might look them up, she had said, Are you sure? Do you think you should? After all this time? Christ, Axel, she might have died! It's been sixteen years! What will you say to Lar if she's dead?

Sorry? I had asked, a little too sarcastically.

Annie had made a fist.

I'll tell him I'm sorry. What else would you have me say?

Annie had been right. Getting up the nerve to make the phone call had been harder than I thought it would be.

I climbed off the bed, put on a clean shirt and made my way to the office. Three men and a woman sat in the large stuffed chairs in the common area on to which all the rooms faced. The woman said something about taking chances but the context was lost on me. One of the men smiled in my direction as I walked by, but all I could think about was the phone call. The warden sat behind her desk. She looked downright unfriendly. Her hair was grey and knotted up in a bun at the back.

I rapped lightly on the doorjamb and said, Excuse me. Have you got a phone?

We both stared at the phone on her desk.

There are pay phones in the entrance, she said. All clients are required to use the pay phones.

I turned and looked down the hall. I could see the phones in their little cubicles but no phone books.

Sorry to bother you again, I said, but I don't have the number.

She squeezed her lips tight, reached into a drawer and placed a phone book on her desk. Her chubby hand rested on the cover. These have a way of walking out of here, she said. So it doesn't leave the room. Understand?

I nodded. Charmer, I wanted to say.

I had stewed over the thought of making this phone call for a couple of weeks. Now I had to fight to get the number. I flipped through the pages to the M's. I half expected not to find the name. But there it was. L.J. McCormack. And the number. Perhaps it was a coincidence. I had never known Larry's middle initial. This could be somebody else altogether. The name's not that uncommon, I thought.

The warden placed a pen and pad of paper in front of me. I wanted to tell this sweetheart to mind her own business. I wanted to tell her that making off with a phone book was not exactly my idea of big-time crime. Instead I wrote down the number.

Thanks, I said, and pushed the book towards her.

Good luck, she said.

I looked at her and grinned. How did she know? For a few moments I thought she could see right through me. I hated that. She could see my fear. I didn't like that. What if Carla was dead?

As I walked down the hall I wondered what the hell I was afraid of. I always feel uneasy about making a phone call and getting the wrong party. Sure I know I can hang up and no one will be the wiser. Yet when I hear a voice at the other end of the line that I don't know, I always get flustered and blurt out some silly apology, as if I've busted in on a couple making love. As if I've committed a crime. I know I've made the call. That's the point. And no matter what I do, no matter how I explain it to myself, or what I say to the person at the other end, if I dial a wrong number, I feel like I've made a damned fool out of myself. Annie says that's stupid. No one will remember, even if they know.

But I would, I say. I'd remember.

The phone had rung eight times.

Hello.

A woman answered.

Her voice paralyzed me. I wanted to hang up. I'd hoped Larry would answer. Chances were I'd recognize his voice. I couldn't remember what Carla's voice sounded like. Whoever the woman was she sounded tired. I'd probably wakened her.

Hello, she said again.

Is this the McCormack place? I asked.

I felt stupid. What did I expect? I'd just looked up the number. But was it the right McCormack? And was this Carla?

I mean, I said, is this the L.J. McCormack who works in film and television?

Did, the voice said. Used to. Doesn't anymore.

The line went quiet. And then the voice spoke, the mouth a little closer to the phone.

Who is this, anyway?

Carla had always been feisty. This was a good sign.

Axel Sterne, I said.

Axel? I could hear her hesitate before she said, Axel, you asshole, it's ten-thirty at night!

Carla?

Who were you expecting?

I don't know, I said. I don't know who I expected.

How was I supposed to tell her what I was thinking? I couldn't just say, So you're still alive, are you? Annie and I thought you might be dead. My free hand waved in the air as if I were batting away each silly thought that popped into my head.

What? she said.

Well, you know how it is these days? With marriage and all?

You and Annie still together? she asked.

Yes, I answered. I felt like I was cheating. I couldn't tell her about the packed bag I'd found in the closet of the spare room. How I'd gone down to the basement and punched a hole in the wall of my office. I couldn't speak of the ultimatums.

How is she?

Fine, I said. I wanted to tell her that Annie hadn't changed, hardly at all. That she still had the deep dimples when she smiled. And the same long blonde hair with bangs. I wanted to tell her that Annie still played opera on the stereo when she vacuumed and dusted. That she was as generous as ever. That she liked the island, the isolation. That in spite of me she was at ease with her world.

Who would have thought, I heard her say. Jesus, Axel, we must be the only ones on the bloody planet who are still on our first marriages. She laughed. And it ain't from want of trying to leave, she said. God knows. Right?

I wondered what she meant. Was she referring to her illness? Or had she heard something about Annie and me? The road we'd travelled the last three years had been pretty rough.

So, what did you think? she asked again. Maybe you thought Larry might have found himself a younger woman? Or maybe you thought I was dead? Did you think I was dead, Axel?

I could hear her breathing at the other end of the line. She sounded asthmatic.

Did you?

No, I said quickly. No. None of those. I don't know what I thought. The lie seemed the wise way to go. Easier. I turned and looked through the bevelled glass of the entrance. Moonlight filtered through the tall firs and lit the rose garden with a blue glow. It was a cool light for such a warm summer evening. The pathway leading to the Tea House looked mysterious and forbidden.

How are you Carla? I asked.

I'm fine, Axel. Just fine, she said. Nice of you to ask. I get around as best I can. You know how it is? We get older. She laughed. Right?

She stopped talking. Then I heard her moving. I heard the rustle of cloth.

She said, I was lying down when you phoned.

Sorry, I said. You should have told me. I didn't mean to wake you. I guess I wasn't thinking. I didn't check the time.

You didn't wake me, she said. I'm glad you called. I still have to rest a lot. Sometimes I have to lie down for days on end. You know what it's like when you can't move? Nothing will stay still.

I could hear her laughing and wheezing at the other end of the line.

She said, Then I get this overwhelming urge to move. God I hunger to move. To run. Or, better still, fly. I'd like to walk in space. Do you know what I mean, Axel? Not to have to depend on anything or anyone for help? That's what I wish for when they tell me I have to rest. I want to move. Not lie here like I'm a goddamn corpse.

That doesn't sound so good, I said.

We all need our beauty rest, Axel. Some just need more than others. At least that's what they tell me. She laughed again. Her voice softened when she said, It's good to hear your voice, hon. How are you doing?

I'm all right, I said. What else could I say? I said, I'm almost fifty. Remember when we used to joke that we'd be lucky if we made it to fifty?

Yes, she said. You were going to come to some dramatic end. In a racing car or at the top of some godforsaken mountain in the middle of the Himalayas. Good Christ, Axel, you used to get dizzy climbing a ladder.

This time when she laughed, she also snorted. Carla was enjoying herself at my expense. The sounds she made with her nose annoyed me.

I remember, I said, I remember. We were just kids. Give me a break. Anyway, unless I get hit by lightning, which seems about as likely as some quack writing me a prescription for whiskey, I'll be fifty in two months. Less a couple of days. But who's counting.

When I finished talking I could hear movement at the end of the line, but I sensed no one was listening. Carla, I said, you there? No one answered. Shit, I said. Carla, don't play games with me. Answer me, you hear? Larry? I pressed the phone into my ear until it hurt. Larry, you there? What's going on? Larry, answer me, I yelled. I turned to see the warden look out of her office down the hall towards me. She put a fat finger to her colourless lips and disappeared.

Part of me wanted to shout into the bitch's face. Up close. The other part of me was beginning to panic when I heard Carla say, Larry's asleep, Axel. It's late. We have separate rooms.

Where the fuck you been? I said.

I had to move, she said. Larry and I sleep apart so I won't wake him. My hours are quite irregular. And, as I told you, I need to move. I'm fine now. Besides, Larry has to go into the office in the morning.

What office? I asked. What's he doing these days?

The car dealership, she said. Didn't I say. She paused. Sorry, Axel, I thought I told you. Larry's a partner in a car dealership.

I thought only politicians owned car dealerships, I said. I knew as soon as I spoke I was going to say the wrong thing. Annie was always telling me I couldn't find a pair of feet large enough for my mouth. I tried to kill the snide tone but Carla picked up on it.

Cute, Axel, she said. Cute. Where you staying?

I twisted the phone cord around my fingers. I'm at the Redwood Center, I said.

The detox place? Carla said. I could hear the surprise in her voice.

Not to worry, I said. I'm in the advanced stages of cure. I'm really here for the R&R. I wanted to joke about it but the jokes were all stale.

You're a boozer, Axel, she said. If you're staying at the Redwood Center, you're a boozer. There is no cure, Axel. You just can't drink.

No, I said. I know that.

I wanted to tell her that I hadn't had a drink now for a month. At the beginning, the days blurred into one another a bit. I wanted to tell her about my mood swings. It was the mood swings I couldn't control.

Axel, she said, you need to talk to Larry.

Why is that? I asked. But I got the sense she was thinking of something else.

He can help you, she said. Believe me. He can help you, she said.

I wanted to ask her what special knowledge Larry had, but she said, I got to go Axel. It's late. I'll tell Larry you're here. He'll call and arrange to meet with you. I'd like to come along but I don't think they'll let me out. Not at the moment. She sounded breathless. Distant.

Carla, I said. But I heard the click at the other end of the line. Outside, the moon was half hidden behind a bank of cloud. The path was barely visible. Shadows moved like animals stalking the garden. For the first time in a long while I felt vulnerable. Afraid.

That had been two nights ago.

335

Since then I'd been to three sessions conducted by the warden, Mrs. Phyllis Staunton. She was tough, but I found I could open up to her. She didn't pry. She didn't nag or accuse. That's what I disliked the most. The accusations. With her I found myself talking, telling her things I'd never revealed to anyone else.

Annie and I always ended up screaming at each other. Insulting each other. Soon I was throwing things. Grabbing people. Hitting people I loved.

Phyllis said that was often the way we were. Men who drank. I'd be that way, she said, until I got the bug out of my brain. Nothing excused my behavior, she said, but it might help me to understand myself. To know that I was ill. I had to get rid of my guilt. This was the kind of shit I'd always figured was liberal double talk. Weakness mistaken for sickness. But I was at the point of revising that view.

When Larry phoned and asked me out to lunch, Phyllis went all soft at the mention of his name. This short, chunky woman who wore a grey wool suit on the hottest of summer days actually flushed in the cheeks when she heard the name of Larry McCormack.

Then she stammered that while normally contact with persons external to the programme was discouraged during the first week, of course I could have the afternoon off—that an afternoon with Mr. McCormack would do me a world of good. That there were few men as fine as Mr. McCormack.

And after all he has been through, she said.

The way she spoke, I thought I was going to lunch with a saint.

We have ordered lunch.

From the terrace I look out to the bay. Two sailboats ride at anchor. Larry hasn't said much since he gave me the tour of the dealership. I'm impressed. It's a sizeable operation. A lot of responsibility, I say, although I still find it hard to believe that any-

336

one I know could be hawking cars for a living. I'd always thought of it as a profession for desperate men. He stares at me and I can only retreat to the bay and mountains beyond.

When I swing my head back, Larry is still studying me as if I'm a goddamn specimen on a slide. So I continue turning and look into the window at our reflection. Truth is, Larry looks a lot better than I do. He has a Latin complexion, a black beard which is peppered with just the right amount of grey, and a head full of silver hair. He's tall and has no gut to speak of. The tan slacks and blue and green checked sports shirt fit him as though a tailor's life had hung in the balance. He exudes confidence. Perfection. I feel anxious, keyed up, ready to spring. Then I see his lips move. I turn and look at the table in front of him.

You listening? he asks.

I nod.

Do you beat up on Annie? he says.

I want to protest. This is nuts. I didn't come out to lunch to be interrogated about my private life.

Do you? he insists. One thing I now remember about Larry is that he can be relentless.

Yes, I say. I mean, I used to. I haven't in a while, I say.

And the kids? he says. You do have kids?

Yes, I say.

Well? he says.

I give him a puzzled look. I want to divert his attention away from wherever he's taking us. When I look at him, his eyes give me the creeps.

Do you smack them around, too? he says.

I was crazy then, Lar. I didn't know what I was doing. I love them all, I say.

I'm about to crack. I can feel the tears in my eyes. I'm tempted to order a beer. I used to tell myself that one beer was not like an ounce of whiskey. I used to be able to divide my life up like that. Into parts.

337

I say, More often than not spanking them was a matter of discipline. A way of keeping order in the household, I say.

Don't bullshit me, Axel, he says. Don't try to con someone who's been there.

We stare hard at each other. I want to tell him to get out of my face. He's beginning to smother me. There is an edge to his voice. My legs feel numb.

I turn away. I watch a gull swoop down and pull a shell out from between the rocks and barnacles.

After you moved, he says, after you moved, it took the doctors another two years to diagnose what was wrong with Carla. Her skin would turn and then heal. Turn and heal. They found out that her circulatory system hadn't developed properly. Blood wasn't getting to her hands and feet. Then the problem extended to her arms and legs.

The gull lifts off the ground, flies to thirty, maybe forty, feet.

He says, Then came the surgery. Four major surgeries on her nervous system. They needed to kill the signals being sent by the brain to the nerves that control the blood supply. Four major operations over two years. Three were relatively successful. She still needed to lie down, though. That's the only way her heart would pump blood to her whole body. And when she was lying down the pain subsided. But the fourth operation didn't work. Lesions kept appearing on her left arm. And they were growing larger and becoming infected.

The gull faces into the prevailing wind, glides and drops the shell. I hear the smack on the rocks, like a fist on flesh, and then watch the bird drop out of the sky to the beach, its beak pulling the guts out of the broken shell. I've always been squeamish. I want to tell him to stop. I've heard enough.

But he continues. The infection she has right now, he says, covers an area about this size. He uses his index finger to draw an imaginary line around his shoulder and down his chest. He traces back and forth over the line where Carla's breast would be.

Jesus Christ, Lar, I say. I had no idea.

She could die at any time, he says.

What confuses me is that I can hear no remorse, no distress in his voice. I'd be a basket case if it were Annie.

The sun pushes up above the trees. Soon we're feeling the full blast of the noonday heat.

How do you deal with it? I ask. Everything I'm thinking sounds trite.

Carla taught me. He pauses and folds his table napkin. Precisely, from corner to corner. We're dealt a hand, he says. Right?

I nod.

We can't change that hand, either. You understand? The timer's on.

That's a little too fatalistic for me, I say.

Don't be stupid, Axel. Listen to me. Listen carefully.

I want to run. Larry's mad. I want to tell him my fate is to run when I hear this kind of talk. But I'm stuck in my seat.

He says, After Carla's last operation I looked forward to see what my prospects were. I saw *nada*. Only a lot of suffering. And I looked backwards to see if I could figure out what I'd done to deserve this. To love someone as much as I do and then to have to watch her in this kind of pain, well that was more than I could bear. So I drank. I began and ended my days with gin. That was easy. Gin was something, the one thing, I could count on.

What happened? I asked.

I quit, he says.

You quit, I say. Just like that! You quit. What am I supposed to do, get down on my knees?

I live from day to day, he says. No magic.

Swell, I say. The breeze has picked up off the water. I can feel the perspiration drying on my forehead. Is that it? Is this all Phyllis's guru has to offer?

And Carla? I ask. What about Carla?

He smiles. Well, every so often, he says, I take a pillow and place it over her head. Usually in the morning, after coffee, just before I head off for work.

What? I say.

When I press down, he says, she wakes up. She thrashes her legs and arms around a bit. Then in a muffled voice, she says, That you, Lar? Honey, that you? Yes, I say, yes it is dear. And she says, Tempted again are you? Then we both laugh. A belly full of laughs, he says.

You're sick, I say. This is morbid stuff, Lar. People are committed for talking like this.

Then she tells me, not today. All right, Hon? Someday sweetie, she says to me. Someday. But please not today, she always says.

He is on the verge of crying. Up in the trees the crows are talking to each other. I remember one day, when Annie and I arrived home, seeing two crows at the top of our driveway, one with its wing spread over the other.

Do you know what you're saying? I ask.

Yes, he says. Yes I do.

What? I say.

Love, he says.

But I can't figure if what he's said is a question or an answer.

A Kind of Fiction

P.K. Page

VERONIKA SAW THE OLD WOMAN fall. She couldn't pre-
vent it. She was as helpless as if she were falling herself. She felt
with excruciating clarity the old woman's foot slip inside her shoe,
saw her pitch forward, extend her arms, and crash down the steps.
Slow motion. The sight was horrifying.

Veronika was there when the old woman lay extended on the
driveway. 'If I can get her up,' Veronika thought, 'we'll know how
badly she is hurt—whether or not she needs to go to emergency.'
Veronika didn't like the responsibility. Wasn't sure she would know
what to do if the old woman's leg were broken, or her collar bone
or hip. Wasn't this the sort of thing that happened to old bones?
They grew brittle and cracked.

And these must be old bones. Veronika guessed her to be in her
late sixties. She watched as the old woman slowly pushed herself
into a sitting position; noticed the quite beautifully set moonstone
ring on her engagement finger. Veronika thought the old woman
behaved as if she were entirely alone in the world—unobserved.

As if the driveway on which she had fallen led only to an empty street in an empty city. In fact, except for Veronika, there *was* no one about. The old woman looked dazed. Veronika wondered if she had suffered a slight concussion or a small stroke for she didn't seem to be aware of Veronika.

She was talking to herself. 'Hurt,' she said, and then, 'Badly?' she asked herself as she stretched each leg—her stockings in ribbons. Her expensive shoes were Italian, Veronika thought. She felt she had seen her before somewhere. At the symphony or on the bus. Veronika couldn't be sure which, and as she continued observing she felt the old woman had a slightly familial look. Would her mother have looked like that if she had lived so long?

The old woman rubbed her shins and then, slowly again, got to her feet, shrugged her shoulders, turned her head from side to side, testing. Veronika noted the excellent cut of her coat.

She noted again that the old woman seemed unable to see her. Didn't want to see her perhaps. Who enjoys such moments of humiliation? Veronika watched her take a step, then another, and set off down the street, slow, but very erect.

*

It was some months before Veronika saw her again. Actually saw her. She had dreamed of her often enough and thought of her daily. Had become quite disproportionately preoccupied with her. She was leaving an afternoon concert. Alone. Using a cane. And moving carefully. Veronika wanted to speak to her, but as before the old woman didn't seem to see her, seemed in fact to give her powers of invisibility. Powers she didn't necessarily want.

Veronika followed, on the verge of speech, but somehow silenced. What could she say? 'I've seen you before?' 'I hope you're OK?'

Preferably, perhaps, 'Did you enjoy the concert?' Less personal. But Veronika knew the old woman had enjoyed the concert, had a feeling for this music as she herself did. Perhaps the old woman had played the violin in her youth, even performed the difficult Beethoven B flat quartet they had both just heard. Veronika felt she knew what the old woman had thought of the performance. Could she, by some form of thought transference, get into the old woman's mind? If she were to say, 'What did you think of the *presto?*' would the old woman reply that it should have been played faster? Veronika thought she would.

Even so, she felt it would be an impertinence to speak to her. There was a kind of inviolability about the old girl—an impenetrability, perhaps. Veronika felt she actually knew the old woman from the inside—knew her self-containment, knew it was not an aloofness, as many might think, but a mask for a too-warm nature which, in her own best interests, she had to control and direct.

Who were her friends? Veronika wondered. Elderly women, for the most part, as women usually outlive men. Gardeners, probably. Or were they faceless companions found on the Internet? It would not surprise her if the old woman had a computer. Even though most of her generation hadn't. She looked, in a kind of a way, contemporary.

Veronika, lost in her ruminations, suddenly realized that the old woman had disappeared, or that she had misplaced her, the way she misplaced papers on her desk. She must have caught a bus, or picked up a cruising cab, for she was nowhere on the street, though she had been in full sight only minutes before.

So easily and completely had she disappeared that Veronika began to wonder if she had imagined her. But why, under heaven, would she imagine such a person? Surely if she were capable of inventing, she would have invented the perfect companion—male, antic, musical; someone who would make her laugh, pour her a drink when she was tired, draw her a bath. No, she could not, would not, have invented her.

She had read somewhere that characters in fiction very often took on lives of their own, got out of hand and surprised their creators. She had never quite believed that. But she was in no position to argue now. For that was exactly what was happening. The old woman was a kind of fiction, one she could not erase from her mind, one who was absorbing more and more of her time and thought. One who had a provenance. A history. And Veronika knew it, was privy to it in some way she could not understand but which interested her deeply.

Perhaps she should see a shrink, Veronika thought, in parenthesis. For surely this was not a normal preoccupation—but then, what was?—get right down to it. Just *exactly* what was?

Veronika knew the old woman was comfortably off—or had been once, at any rate, before inflation. And married—most certainly. But what did he do—the husband? Veronika questioned briefly. Was he not away most of the time? That perhaps accounted for the children—a girl and a boy. Outrageous children. The girl had been stage-struck since her first school play and, to everyone's surprise had, in her teens, been cast in a production of *Hair,* mainly because—it was commonly thought 'that girl would do anything!'—she had been perfectly willing to stand on stage bare naked, something her mother had not been overly enthusiastic about, but neither had she been exactly shocked or critical, having known her daughter 'from the egg', as it were. Unlike Trik, who had been affronted—darkly affronted. Their son, on the other hand, was a right-wing journalist and that she had found far harder to contend with. It hadn't occurred to her that rebellion would take such a form. Rebellion was surely a swing to the left, or so it had been in her day. So when he had supported the extreme right— publicly, in his column—she had had difficulty discussing it with him. And when his columns became bigoted, prudish, fundamentalist even, it was painful for her—exceedingly painful, as if she herself had made a humiliating *gaffe.*

Jimmy had been quieter than Sylvie—taken to books as other

boys take to baseball, despite Trik's valiant efforts to play catch with him, take him camping. That male-bonding that had become so popular and, in some way, so phony. Not that Trik had been phony. He had genuinely wanted to play with his son, but Jimmy had other interests. He wanted Superman comics, but more than those, he wanted children's histories about the fur trade or the wreck of the Titanic. They thought he might take a history major but he took political science and got a night job on a newspaper while still at college. They hadn't worried about Jim the way they had about Sylvie. He was unlikely to take drugs or stay out all night or do any of the things that Sylvie was almost certain to do—once, at any rate.

But neither child had turned out quite as expected—not for *her,* Veronika, for what could *she* expect?—but for the old woman and her dead husband who had dreamed it differently. And now that Trik was dead—yes, Veronika said, that was the husband's name without any doubt—it was not the first time she had said it—now that Trik was dead and she couldn't discuss it with him, or look at it with his objectivity, for he was discerningly objective in the realm of ideas—it was difficult indeed. Although, Veronika thought, the old woman had lived long enough to have seen much diversity in her life and was sufficiently knowledgeable to know how huge the gene pool was, she felt sure that—what? Her mind was wandering.

Veronika, on her way home, and walking along dreamily in her fiction-writing mode—(a mode she had never explored before, and why now? she asked herself)—knew all this about the old woman, and more, even more, when she could keep her mind on it. That was the key—keeping her mind on it—as members of the family created themselves for her, seemingly as fast as they could. She was in no way their puppeteer, their activator, could not have changed a hair on their heads—although Sylvie had done so over

345

and over, dying her blond hair black or red or green—and now she was never to do so again. Dead—flying too close to the sun, drag racing, of all things. Suddenly Veronika shook with sobs. As if Sylvie were her child—bright, gilded, now ash-blackened and gone. Unbearable. She thought of her at kindergarten, like quick-silver on the green grass, so far ahead of all the others. Had she been programmed for attention? Needing it so badly and getting it wherever she went. Shining. Buttercups, she thought. And couldn't bear it.

Veronika wept unashamedly as she walked, burdened by grief—the loss of Trik, of dazzling Sylvie—who had stamped her feet as a child when they called her Syllie—Jimmy's attempt at her name. Veronika felt suddenly weak, barely able to walk, and her head was flooded with them all, such a crowd walked with her—Trik, beloved Trik, and silver Sylvie and Jimmy, poor, poor Jimmy whom she loved—indeed, loved dearly, but loved from the stone heart he had created for her—and why? Oh why? Oh why?

She was dizzy and almost falling, her face wet from weeping. They jostled her—Trik and the two children—Sylver Diamond (stage name); James Ormond (by-line). She had not invented them—Trik, Jimmy and Sylvie—or their real names—Patrick, James and Sylvia. Those were their legal names, their baptismal names. She knew them all as if they were members of her family. But the old woman—the old woman had been nameless. Veronika felt so weak she had to lean against a railing for support. She wondered if she were ill, gravely ill. Then suddenly as if struck by lightning, she knew the old woman's name. It was Veronika. Veronika Sylvia Ormond. Her own.

Silent Cruise

Timothy Taylor

SHEEDY WAS A METICULOUS handicapper. He had a CD-ROM library of past performances and an index of tracks with pictures and lay-out diagrams. He downloaded race results off the Internet directly to the Psion palm-top computer he favoured track-side.

Dett was prostrate before the altar of a more compulsive method entirely, the mechanics of which he didn't understand or question and about which Sheedy respectfully did not ask. And yet, they needed one another.

In the Fat Choy Lounge at 13:01 Saturday September 6, 1997, Dett was engaged in the habitual translation of analogue detail into digits. It would be impossible for Dett to be in the Fat Choy on a Saturday, or anywhere else on any other day of the week, without yielding to the delicious impulse: the sixth day of the week in a place named with the sixth and third letters of the alphabet, waiting for the third race.

Sixes and threes, two sets.

"What are you getting in the third, Dett?" Sheedy was asking, pecking at the tiny black palm-top. The overhead TV was providing Cantonese analysis of a race that ran at 12:43 in Santa Anita. Around the subterranean Fat Choy, Chinese men (23 of them) in patched grey cardigans and battered hats were fanning their forms up and down, beating them silently into their palms, conducting as the timbre of their luck resounded faithfully in the replay.

Dett looked down at his program. The third race at Hastings Park had a post time of 14:23 with 12 horses running. The 14, the 23 and the 12 linked themselves to the sequence of sixes and threes—Dett visualised this in three dimensions, the multi-coloured numbers re-clustering like evolving DNA—each addition reconstructing the predictive significance of the strand.

These were Dett's numbers. Spools of digits, a numeric cascade inspired by every ambient detail. A "bit-snow," as he came to think of it, that had alarmed him only once. He had played the ponies since high school, betting a combination of handicapped picks and selections made through the sifting of these compulsive numbers. But in second year university—Dett was studying mathematics—he found himself losing, all at once, plunging below the payout of random picks. There were ancillary problems, he was failing his exams.

He couldn't fault the handicapping. His own spill of numbers had increased in manic intensity to the point that they emitted a noise. He was driven to numeric fixations unlike anything he'd seen: the day of the week on any date in Julian or Gregorian history? Despite a compulsion to solve this problem, a compulsion that lasted in full flower for many months, eliminating friendships, disturbing professors whose lectures might be interrupted, it wasn't particularly relevant to any of his courses. The question wasn't on any of his finals.

His Non-Parametric Methods professor took him aside at the

end of second year. A tobacco-stained Irish mathematician whose advice had been compacted down in Dett's memory to a single string of words: " . . . the most unusually gifted student does not necessarily succeed . . . "

Indeed, he flunked third year. And although the noise eventually abated, the obsession to precisely calendarize everything calmed, he still invested some time researching Repetitive Word Disorders which he learned were clustered under Obsessive Compulsive Disorders, themselves a strain of Thought Disorder. Was he sick?

It was true the numbers tumbled ceaselessly, and his various personal and academic embarrassments satisfied the requirements of the Diagnostic and Statistical Manual of Mental Disorders, which stated that obsessions must be "intrusive or inappropriate." But Dett didn't think the American Psychiatric Association's catalogue of disorders captured his mental action in total. On occasion his numbers persisted in sprinkling a pattern of meaning across the situation at hand (mostly at the track where they had thankfully resumed their function). If bit-snow were a sickness, then he had grown to like the numeric frost on his mental peaks, it was a key feature of his personal topography and screw the APA anyway.

Sheedy never asked about it directly. It was enough that at a crucial moment he sensed a facility soft-wired into Dett's cranial gore, and on that uncharacteristic, un-handicapped hunch had picked Dett to fill a vacant Financial Analyst position for which the advertisement had expressly stated "MBA required."

"You have second sight," Sheedy said during the second interview. Dett remembered that he was wearing a hand-me-down suit of his father's from the Eaton's Pine Room.

Second sight, second interview, second-hand suit. Dett asked Sheedy to repeat himself.

"Second sight," Sheedy said for the second time. "You see shadows behind the numbers, which is rare."

He could never have predicted this. 13 months of unemployment living in a friend's basement next to a thicket of home-grown. 64 applications. 19 first interviews. 18 polite rejection letters. One lonely second interview and this strutting Vancouver Stock Exchange peacock in a bottle green suit actually understood his numbers.

"You like the ponies?" Sheedy asked him.

It had been good to get out of that basement on his own terms.

Sheedy sent him on the Securities Course, basic training for financial analysts, brokers and investment dealers. It had been 47 years since anybody scored 100%, you just didn't get everything right in this world.

Dett got everything right.

Sheedy took his new protégé to Hy's Steak House to celebrate. Sent Dett staggering home early with a pound of beef and a half bottle of Chilean cabernet sloshing around his gut. Dett was thinking: 100% every 47 years. 100, 47, 100, 47. 1997-47 makes 1950. Today was January 13th, so back-calculating the day of the week he established that January 13, 1950 was a Friday.

Friday the 13th. He liked that. The last idiot-savant had nailed it on Friday the 13th.

Fat Choy is Chinese for Good Luck.

"Who do you have in the third?" Dett asked back to Sheedy now, sitting across the lino-top table in the smoky track-side lounge.

Sheedy straightened his gold tie against his French blue shirt, shot cuffs out the sleeves of his Prince of Wales double breasted. He had a distinct Boss aura despite being a Little Man. (He inspired in Dett the auto-thoughts *proportional* and *lifelike*.) Black brush cut. Black eyebrows. Olive skin and a straight nose to match his straight teeth which were also very white. He walked everywhere like he was pissed off, shoulders hunched, legs and arms straight. The MBAs who worked at Sheedy-Mahew called him Bucky Badger after the mascot of his Wisconsin alma mater.

"Got spanked by Bucky this morning," someone would say.

"Yeah he looked pissed," would come the response.

"A badger is always pissed, you know that, I know that…"

So it ran.

"A Little Risk," Sheedy said now, the palm top having endorsed one of the favourites.

"Ooooh. Ballsy," Dett mocked gently.

They were the only suits in the Fat Choy, ever. This was where Sheedy brought his hot prospects for a couple of laughs before signing up a new account. Dett rode data-shotgun from time to time. The two of them would drive out to the track in Sheedy's leased metallic green Porsche Carrera 4. Dett would run the conventional numbers for the client, establishing base confidence in the firm. But Sheedy also knew Dett could run his stranger numbers and pick a winner on occasion, and if he picked one of Sheedy's hot prospects onto a winner—a placer, a shower, anything that demonstrated Sheedy-Mayhew was also a *lucky* firm— well then Sheedy could pitch any woo known to man. Sheedy could wax the sale.

"Who is it?" Dett asked.

"Andrew Xiang for the third race. I need second sight."

"And you like A Little Risk?" Dett asked, scanning the program.

"I do," Sheedy answered, squinting at his six-inch screen.

"Does Andrew know the ponies?" Dett asked, changing tack.

"A little gaming itch, like you or me, nothing big time. You want another?" Sheedy produced a money clip from which he delicately extracted a twenty.

Dett got Sheedy his drink. Southern Comfort and coke, no ice. "But Andrew isn't a new account," he said as he sat down again.

"Have a drink for Chrissake," Sheedy said, staring at the empty table in front of Dett.

Dett shrugged. "It's only one o'clock."

"Fuck one. We gotta have some fun sometimes. You're not having fun?" This was classic badger, displaying a small wound for emotional leverage. Dett thought all the blood that had cumulatively seeped from Sheedy's wounds over the nine months he'd been at Sheedy-Mayhew wouldn't moisten the pecker on a Brazilian needle-tip mosquito. But Sheedy was also recently divorced (again) so now he was going to riff on How Important It Was To Just Have Fun Once In A While until Dett broke down and had the drink.

"What're you having?" Sheedy said when Dett returned with his glass.

"Southern Comfort and coke," Dett said. "No ice, boss."

Sheedy laughed, and reaching a manicured hand across the table he gripped Dett tightly by the back of the neck.

"We're having a good year," Sheedy said, and here Dett found himself staring into his mentor's cold brown eyes with a pound of Rolex clicking audibly in his right ear.

"Bre-X," Dett said. He wasn't above reminding Sheedy once in a while that he had counselled selling the infamous gold stock a full month before the geologist went airborne, falling only slightly faster then the share price eventually did.

"You're the best. How much do I pay you?" Sheedy said, releasing him.

"Not nearly enough, but let's not talk about it here," Dett said.

"I'm just asking because you look so raggedy-assed all the time."

"This is Armani," Dett said, touching his lapel and recalling the sticker shock.

"You take your own action I hope, take care of yourself with the things you learn," Sheedy said, between sips.

"I take care of myself," Dett said. It was true. Information trickled through and you didn't need much to beat the house.

"And I facilitate this," Sheedy said.

"You do," Dett said, wishing to move on. "I was asking why

we're trotting Andrew Xiang out here when he's already a client. Are we selling something hard?"

Sheedy grimaced slightly and leaned forward again.

"OK," he said, pressing his palms together in front of him. "We have to . . . evacuate somebody."

"Liquidation sale," Dett said.

"Not a liquidation sale," Sheedy said, lowering his voice. "Christ don't even think that, our seller is still very liquid."

"So who fucked up?" Dett asked, thinking: one of the MBAs.

"The seller is *my* client," Sheedy answered.

Dett regarded his boss who just briefly pushed a hand through his black hair, straightened his shoulders and gathered himself. Sheedy only had a few clients and they were all guys who lived on very quiet properties in the hills around Whistler and paid commissions in cash.

"Remember Jimmy ?" Sheedy asked. "He has to leave the country. It's legal."

Jimmy was one of those clients. When money or signatures were required he flew down from Whistler in a chartered heli-jet. He had an impenetrable sleepy expression and a discordant predilection for angry expletives like 'cock-sucker' and 'whore'. On the one occasion they met, in connection with a deal Dett was working on, Jimmy had shaken his hand limply and said only: "Sheedy mentioned you. So let's put this whore to bed then, all right?" He pronounced it Hoo-Er.

"So sell the stuff," Dett said to Sheedy now. "What's the deal?"

"The shares in concern won't trade openly until the fall by which time he has to be out of the country. The fall is too late, by then he'll be banned in Vancouver and probably everywhere else."

"A private sale then," Dett said.

"A mandatory sale," Sheedy answered, staring intently at Dett. "He has over four hundred thousand tied up here and he wants his cash."

"Best-efforts," Dett said, shrugging.

"You're not hearing me," Sheedy said. "We sold him these shares and he was more than a little reluctant at the time. But he trusts me, understand? Now he has to do a runner on 48 hours notice and I have to produce his cash."

"Is he threatening you?" Dett said.

"He doesn't have to," Sheedy said, shaking his head. "We are fucking hooped here Dett."

"I see it," Dett said, imagining the quiet phone call that Sheedy had received at home last night. It wouldn't have been Jimmy calling either, some associate nobody had ever heard of before. "It's critical we move on this..." Words of elaborate politeness.

"There's an upside, naturally." Sheedy tried to lighten the tone. "Double commission. Undying loyalty of the client's friends. All that shit."

"Fantastic."

"Hey," Sheedy said. "You and I have done this before. Your brains, my good looks."

"So what do we have here?" Dett asked.

"A couple of months ago we took Jimmy deep into two positions. If we unload even one of them he'll be happy," Sheedy said. "You feel like selling some healthcare or some technology today?"

Dett pretended to look out the window, as if the answer to this question lay somehow in the weather. High light blowing cloud, cool and pleasant. It meant nothing.

Sheedy swung his case onto the table, tore open the Velcro side pouch and produced the fax-smeared stock exchange fact sheets.

"This is all I get?" Dett asked, incredulously. A prospectus was normally six pounds of paper. If Dett was going to do numbers, conventional or otherwise, he preferred more of them. It inspired him, he waded into them and paddled around.

"What do you want?" Sheedy said. "Xiang knows these companies up the yin-yang. We need second sight today, so pick me the winner. Health care or technology. And a horse in the third. I gotta take a leak." And here he snapped shut the palm top, slid it into a side pocket of his suit, de-perched from his chair and stalked off to the johns.

Dett glanced down at what Sheedy had left for him on the table.

Commerce-Net provided Internet marketing solutions. Yawn. Who didn't? Expected to open at $3.80 in late November. Zero revenue. Zero track record. About the only thing Commerce-Net had were some "channel partners" as they were known, heavy hitters like Microsoft who backed the technology without a direct investment. When Dett had skimmed to the bottom of the sheet he got to the phone numbers. CEO Bertie Perkins could be reached at 1-888-555-0000. Who picked a number like that? Dett closed his eyes. 3.80, 0, 0, 18885550000. It all flattened out and left him in a single void place.

Halox Inc. was developing a bowel cancer marker which, if it were picked up by one North American hospital in one hundred would make everyone connected with the company a millionaire— legitimate investors, Sheedy's drug dealer clients, nieces and nephews of the CFO. Of course, at the moment Halox was hacking and bunting it's way through the bush-leagues of level two clinical trials. This would be considered Still a Long Way From The Show. Another zero going public with zero. Pure speculation.

Dett looked around the room, his eyes red from the smoke of the endless collective Fat Choy cigarette, some foul brand these old guys favoured.

Three minutes to the first post here at Hastings Park. Sheedy would be at the window putting down a hundred on whatever horse the palm top picked to win. Sheedy bet all nine races every time, an indiscriminate strategy that lost him about 20% a year. Dett knew that random bets and the barest trace of luck would get him into the same tax bracket.

Sheedy once said to Dett: "When my old man went to the ponies, the stands were full of honest people and the game was totally crooked. You could actually play a game like that."

Exactly. Dett folded up the Halox and the Commerce-Net papers and went outside and watched the changing odds on the board across the stretch. Rumsey favoured in the first at lean odds of 8:5, which Dett took as emblematic of how the game had diminished. All these hard-core track guys scanning the same numbers, picking the same winners, same losers with the same information. It was hard to win any money in this environment without second sight, something that could cast a shadow behind the numbers the handicappers had factored down to value zero.

So now Dett looked around himself and the nearly empty asphalt yard, not yet littered with torn betting slips as it would be over the next hours and he started spontaneously counting heads. 26 people on the benches. 18 people at the fence. He averaged the people in the grandstand with a sweeping glance. One person per ten seats.

Rumsey was at the pole, position number one. The heavy favourite according to the form, which said "Rumsey is the one-to-beat." Dett thought: horse number one, the one to beat, over 1 1/16 miles.

He won by one-and-a-half lengths.

"Did you have that action?" Sheedy asked him after Dett had descended again into the Fat Choy Lounge.

"Did you?" Dett asked back.

"You had it you fucker, why didn't you tell me?"

"You didn't ask."

"I'm slumping," Sheedy said, staring at his little screen, entering the results.

"He was the favourite," Dett said.

"Who picks a favourite? You can't make any money doing that."

"Most people pick the favourite," Dett said. "That's what makes them favourites. You just have to bet a whole lot."

Sheedy made a mental calculation. "I'm thinking at 8:5 I would have had to bet about three hundred grand to get us out of our little situation here."

Which brought to mind Jimmy packing crates for the midnight float-plane south of the border. Glued to his cellphone, waiting for news on the matter of his available cash. "Hey Eddie, did we get a call from that broker down there?" "Nothing yet." "Well you phone that cock-sucker and rattle his fucking chain."

"Do you want another drink?" Dett asked Sheedy now.

"Naaa," Sheedy said and looked at his watch which Dett already knew read 1:43 PM. Ten minutes to the second post. "So what is it, health care or technology? I like technology myself. I met Bertie Perkins at a trade show once. Sharp guy, respected. Xiang will know that."

"Commerce-Net and Halox," Dett said. "They might as well be identical."

"I'm not talking fundamentals, I'm talking gut."

"Either way they're zeroes, Sheedy. Total specs. I would advise a client to buy based on how much long-shot money they had to piss away."

"If I wanted MBA answers at a time like this, I would have brought an MBA to the track with me," Sheedy said.

"Sorry," Dett said. "This is not a fuzzy logic problem."

"Which one can be sold more easily, then?"

"Same answer," Dett said.

Sheedy flopped back in his chair. "Maybe you need the drink," he said. "You need to loosen up."

"You're not listening."

"Talk."

"We sell him both. He knows the companies so he knows they're both spec zeroes. We tell him it's a hedge, like betting a box, two horses to finish, any order. The Internet breaks up, people will still get colon cancer. The marker tests come up blank, you always

357

have the Net. Technology-healthcare. Optimism-pessimism. Shoot him some of that stuff."

Sheedy went up and got the drinks.

"Will this work?" he asked, sitting down.

"Christ Sheedy, I can't promise. We've done it before, I can say that much."

"Un-hoop me, I can say that much. Do you have my horse in the third?" he asked. "We're going to need that horse."

"I'm waiting for it," Dett said. "But I'll get one."

"What about the second race?" Sheedy asked him.

Dett just shook his head. He was going to sip this drink and think about nothing and then go over to the parade ring and have a look at the runners in the third.

"Come on, give me a pick on two," Sheedy said. "I need a win here."

Dett sighed. Outside, he looked across the track up high to the blue mountains opposite and breathed in deeply. 11 horse field. Horses six and five were the favourites. 6 plus 5. 5 plus 6.

Sometimes he didn't need a big pool of numbers.

He went inside.

"Springhill Billy," he said to Sheedy.

"Horse number one?"

Sheedy bet a hundred and Dett went track side in time to see the horses pass the grandstand. Grey Lightening by a head on Springhill Billy.

"Interesting," Dett said out loud.

Springhill Billy was holding third at the half way point.

"Fade baby," Dett yelled.

Springhill Billy was sixth in the stretch, and seventh at the wire by seven lengths.

"What the fuck was that?" Sheedy said when he sat down. "The thing sprang a leak."

"Sometimes you just bet a hunch."

"Everything you bet is a hunch," Sheedy said, face back over the palm-top. "Number six won."

"And five?" Dett asked.

"Showed," Sheedy said, looking up suddenly, "How are you feeling partner?"

"Don't sweat it," Dett said. "We saved the win for the third race."

"I sincerely hope so," Sheedy said.

Andrew Xiang was standing at the top of the steps for several minutes before Dett spotted him.

"Do you guys like this place?" he asked when he sat down and had a look around himself.

Sheedy shot a look over at Dett.

"I like it," Dett said, taking the tag.

"Why not sit in the clubhouse? You can get a sandwich up there," Andrew Xiang said.

Sheedy was on his feet, "That's a good idea. Let's go."

"These guys are the only real bettors left," Dett said, looking around himself as he got up, as if he were seeing the room for the last time.

"Quirky," Andrew said, still seated. "I wonder who'll be betting down here after they all die of lung cancer."

"Hey, it's the Fat Choy room, maybe they won't die," Sheedy said.

Andrew Xiang laughed.

"It has to be the room," Dett said. "You never see the old guys anywhere else."

It turned out they could get sandwiches at the Fat Choy bar.

"Do you wager Mr. Xiang?" Dett asked. The use of Mr. might have been spreading it a bit thick. Andrew was only a few years older than Dett and although he had a lot of money he didn't have what Sheedy called "a roasted fuck of a lot of money."

"Andrew. Sure I like to bet."

"I'm losing today," Dett said, avoiding Sheedy's curious gaze.

"Too bad, who did you like in the second?" Andrew asked.

"Number one, Springhill Billy," Dett said.

"He faded," Andrew said, wincing sympathetically. "I listened in the car. Long shot though, I can relate. It's hard to make money against your old guys here."

"You're exactly right," Dett said. "The game has changed. More professional and yet harder to play. Bigger house take, narrower odds. It's tough."

"That's business right there though, isn't it," Sheedy was leaning forward on the table now, picking up Dett's leave. "Bigger house. Competition. You know what I'm saying?"

"It's true," Andrew said.

"I find myself betting the box more," Sheedy said, warming up. "Cover myself off a little."

"How is it going today?" Andrew said, smiling broadly. He knew the answer already.

"Well, I'd like to be up on the day, if you understand what I'm saying."

Now Andrew was laughing. "I thought you might want that," he said.

Dett excused himself. Sheedy was at stride, talking about three-horse boxes now. Dett figured he might as well go over to the parade circle. 15 minutes to the third post, time to listen to those numbers, time to take a slow walk in a flurry of bit-snow.

Crossing in front of the grandstand it occurred to Dett that the scary part was the thought that it might stop snowing all at once. Even researching Repetitive Word Disorders he hadn't actively wished the bits to stop. He always had a sense of how the silence might ring on and he imagined what mental fixations might fill such a void.

With two scratches there were ten horses running, which suggested immediately three significant numbers: The One, the Ten, and the difference of nine.

Dett watched the grooms leading the horses out of the pad-
docks and around the small dirt parade ring. It wasn't his habit to
note the beauty of a horse but Dett couldn't deny that they were
all exquisite. A chestnut. A grey. A muscled one, a lithe dancer.
Long of body, high of haunch. Was it femininity people saw, Dett
wondered, or masculine power? The meekness in the slow step or
the wildness in the eye?

Ten horses walking slowly in a circle. Ten glistening coats. Ten
horses and One would win. Nine losers. With the scratches, the
ninth horse was now Silent Cruise.

He found him in the parade. Silent Cruise was a deep mahogany,
muscled and powerful. His head tossed. He appeared impatient.
Silent Cruise wore deep purple silks, Dett noticed, a kingly
colour.

He glanced at the racing form. Silent Cruise was picked to win
and to place by the two race columnists.

He walked back slowly towards the Fat Choy. Pausing briefly
in front of the grandstands, he wondered how long the track would
survive with nine out of ten seats empty. One seat in ten.

The One in Ten. The empty nine. Those numbers again.

Sheedy surprised him.

"Sheedy," Dett said. "Where's Andrew?"

"Still downstairs," Sheedy said. "Pick please."

One in ten was all he was getting. One in ten and the nine left
over. That integer string plus an image of a favoured horse with a
rich royal purple silk. Horse number nine.

"Silent Cruise will at least show," Dett said. "Get him to take
Silent Cruise."

"Show?" Sheedy asked.

"It's a safe bet and I'm getting it hard," Dett said. "It rings for
me. Drop Silent Cruise on the table with absolute confidence like
you never thought of another horse. And make a deal about putting
down some of your own money."

"I need a winner," Sheedy said.

"No we don't Sheedy," Dett said. "We need to show luck which means we have to Be In The Money. There's more luck picking a show and showing than there is picking a win and getting beat by a neck."

Sheedy became a very serious badger.

"It's not going well down there," Dett said, interpreting the look.

"He thinks they're both dogs," Sheedy said. "I mean real dogs. He hasn't made his final decision yet but I don't feel good about this. If we don't show him something amazing in the third, I think he may walk away from both of these stocks."

Sheedy's cellphone bleated.

"Damn," Dett said, looking away.

Sheedy stood adrift on the sloping asphalt.

"You have to take it," Dett said.

"Hello." Sheedy said, and Dett retreated a few yards. Now Sheedy was nodding, cellphone to one ear, left hand up and over his other ear to block out the track noise, to make sure he caught the quiet words, the quiet non-specific words spoken across the insecure cell frequencies. Words which Dett imagined stringing themselves along the issues of "our agreement" and "the paper concerned" and "the cashflow aspects of the situation."

1 in 10 in 1 in 10.

Sheedy clicked the phone shut, pocketed it and stood for a second with his hand on his lips.

"Our guy?" Dett asked, consciously drowning out his numbers.

"We have to pull something out here," Sheedy said.

"Lower the price."

Tough-looking women on quarter horses were escorting the thoroughbreds down to the gate, the jockeys standing in the stirrups, the wind rippling the silks. The squat working horse and the thoroughbred side-by-side highlighted the rare beauty of the racer, high-strung creatures prancing and skittering next to their serene companions. As Silent Cruise passed—the deep shining brown, the vivid purple—the thoroughbred laid his head piteously against the neck of the smaller horse as though seeking a reprieve. It brought to mind how young they were, all of them, the equine equivalent of the 14 year old super-model backstage with her teddy bears.

Sheedy was talking: "...totally wrong signal to lower the price at this point."

Dett flashed on something Sheedy had said earlier. The undying loyalty of the client's network of friends which suggested the obvious downside corollary.

"These really are dogs aren't they?" he said, as it dawned on him.

Sheedy paused and stroked his small, symmetrical chin.

"Commerce-Net lost both its channel partners in some legal dispute this morning. Microsoft is going to sue. Halox is a fucking placebo. The word is that the trials are completely flat."

"Christ Sheedy," Dett said.

"These puppies are going to sewer on Monday when it hits the street. Jimmy has to be out." Sheedy's speech slowed. "He simply will not take a four hundred grand hit the same week he's doing a runner and leaving a dozen houses behind."

"When were you going to tell me this?" Dett asked.

"I wasn't," Sheedy said. "Did you want to be privy?"

He had a point, and he also looked more than a little scared now. "Wax this sale for me Dett and your efforts will not be forgotten."

"And him?" Dett asked, nodding his head towards the Fat Choy.

"Fuck Xiang," Sheedy said, the badger was back in an instant. "Don't even ask that question. If it wasn't him it would be some other loser, like on every bet you and I ever made together. You were born knowing this shit. That's why we're a team."

Sheedy stalked off a few yards, hands stiffly at his side. Wounded. Then he stalked back.

"Now give me my winner," he said.

Dett wasn't sure that he had ever used numbers to consciously screw somebody before. On the other hand, he'd never been forced to.

One in ten then, he thought, at the moment of truth this is all I get? A string of 1's and 10's which might be mathematically expressed as (1, 10, 1, 10, 1, 10...)

1, 10, 1.

January 10, 1901 let's say. Well January 10, 1901, as it happened, was a Thursday.

10, 1, 10.

October 1, 1910 was a Saturday.

Thursday to today, Saturday. A 3 day spread.

Today and the holy number 3.

3rd letter = C.

Saturday and a C.

S. C.

SC.

Silent Cruise.

"This is insane," Dett said, and it seemed to his ears like he was speaking from inside a steel drum.

Sheedy was waiting impatiently.

"There is no rigour in this," Dett said.

"Has there ever been?" Sheedy asked.

"Silent Cruise," Dett said, by way of an answer.

Sheedy was appraising him. "You said Show before."

"Silent Cruise is the One in Ten, Sheedy. It's what I'm getting."

Sheedy faced him squarely. "Don't you start guessing on me."

"He's the One," Dett said simply. "The One in Ten."

"Who's the jockey?" Sheedy asked, digging in his pocket for a racing form. Mysticism was one thing, but corroboration never hurt.

Dett gave him the name, having checked.

"Same guy who rode Rumsey to win in the first," Sheedy said, handicapping aloud and liking the result. And with that, the decision made, he turned and marched back towards the Fat Choy

364

room. 10 yards off he stopped and turned. Yelled back: "Are you watching out here?"

"Where else?" Dett said.

Sheedy was back in 145 seconds with Xiang. Dett had counted the seconds. 143, 144, 145…

"This is much better," Andrew Xiang said. "I can actually breath out here."

Sheedy squinted in the milky sunshine, a little out of breath from trotting in to the windows and making the last minute bet.

"Did you make your bet?" Dett asked Xiang.

"I got a tip," he said. "You have to bet on a tip."

"Silent Cruise," Sheedy said, leaning in as if to deliver this information to Dett.

There was the gunshot sound of the gates slamming open and in an instant Dett could feel the vibration in his soles.

"Here's to Sheedy's luck," Andrew Xiang said. "Here's to mine."

Dett turned back to the track in time to feel the breeze as the horses hurtled past towards the first turn. Canadian Diamond and Haida Bells, stirrup to stirrup. New Blazer was third by half a length on Silent Cruise.

"Come on now. Come on now," Sheedy was chanting quiet encouragement to the jockey from just over Dett's right shoulder.

Into the back Canadian Diamond and Haida Bells pulled away to one-and-a-half lengths, and the pack squeezed up on New Blazer and Silent Cruise.

"He's flattening out. Don't let him flatten out now. Take him in. Come on, take him in."

Entering the straight the four had again pulled free by a length, and Silent Cruise was moving confidently to the outside on New Blazer.

Thunder to the soles of my feet, thought Dett, his mouth unable to open. Thunder in my empty insides. Thunder you beautiful beautiful thing. Thunder home baby. The One in Ten.

"Ride him home," Sheedy was screaming now. "Ride him home. Come on. Take him in. Take him home." And there was an instant after Sheedy said this that Silent Cruise moved on Canadian Diamond and Haida Bells, in third just half a length off the leaders. But it was only an instant, and then Dett could see that the horse was going down.

"Ride him. Ride him," Sheedy was pouring out his final supplication.

Ten yards off the wire Silent Cruise abruptly fell, half a ton of horse crashing chin first into the dirt. His jockey spilled over his head and into the track, curled already in a defensive ball. Haida Bells ran into the tangle of legs and hooves and also fell, her rider sprawling through the rails and onto the infield turf.

The field surged past. Tulista from fifth to win, followed by Canadian Diamond and A Little Risk.

Haida Bells surged to her feet, swayed, staggered and cantered away. Eyes spread wide and white froth streaming from her nostrils. Silent Cruise struggled on his side, then rose.

From down the grandstand fence, Dett registered a woman's shout. Disembodied. The words released into a hovering silence: "Don't look Maggie," she cried. "Don't look."

And Dett did turn away, pushing his back sharply to the track. And from this swivelled position he noted how Sheedy stood defeated. The crumpled basketball leather of his cheeks, the false pearl of his tiny teeth hanging dryly beneath a thin bloodless lip. Andrew Xiang stood blank-faced, wooden next to him.

Dett turned back to the track. Silent Cruise was standing on three legs, staring slightly upwards without comprehension. His front right leg was shorn off almost cleanly twelve inches above the hoof and from his bloody leg protruded a stump of bone. The hoof and fetlock were still connected by a visible sinew, and the piece flopped brokenly onto the dirt as Silent Cruise looked for footing, weakly finding none, only the emptiness under his right foreleg and what must have been the eclipsing pain of contact between open bone and earth. As the crowd surged to the rail around them, Dett felt a complete silence descend into his insides.

While the horses galloped in, the track crew circled the damaged thoroughbred, their calm ponies sidling in obediently around the staggering racer, penning Silent Cruise against the inside rail. A rider dismounted and took Silent Cruise by the bridle, holding his head as he reared tentatively, losing strength, and then he was helped down to his side. Around him rose the wall of ponies and crew, backs to the crowd, shoulders and flanks together. A wall of respect, thought Dett, although through the legs of the horses he could still make out the needle, and the operation that was quickly performed. A tractor pulled a covered trailer onto the track, and the crew held up a blue tarp in front of the dying thoroughbred as he was loaded. A very slight heave of the flank was the final thing Dett saw.

Dett looked around himself numbly. The two thrown jockeys were on their feet. Fragile as the very elderly, supported by crew. One had made it to the grandstand fence and now stood, muddy circles around the eyes, leaning and shaking. Sheedy and Xiang were gone.

Dett walked back to the Fat Choy in silence.

"No, I like that pick Sheedy," Xiang was saying. "Thanks very much."

"How much did you bet again?" Sheedy was asking, laughing falsely.

"250 dollars."

"I went down a hundred myself."

Dett watched this jocular exchange, staring at Sheedy and seeing the re-animated fear under his waxy pretence of humour. Even now, Dett knew, Sheedy was trying desperately to find his angles, to return the conversation to Halox. To Commerce-Net. Counting on Dett to assist in re-aligning the conversation on the axis of the sale.

Dett thought only that Sheedy had walked away from track side, Silent Cruise down and the results in. And he imagined walking away from Sheedy in the moment of his breakdown, imagined vividly the enraged badger hurling abuse at his retreating back.

"I liked that horse," Dett said.

There was a polite silence as the two men regarded him.

"He was coming on," Xiang said finally. "What can you say? It's racing."

"Running fourth," Sheedy said shaking his head. Disappointed with the dead horse's performance.

"Third," Dett said.

"A Little Risk would have caught him. You could see that, which I mean as no disrespect to your pick," Sheedy said.

Xiang chuckled. "I figured it was Dett's pick," he said. "People are always taking credit for their employee's work."

Sheedy made an insincere face like *Guilty, what can I say?*

"You picked the one to die," Xiang said, looking over at Dett.

"An interesting skill," Sheedy said, preparing to riff.

"I thought Silent Cruise would win," Dett said, cutting off Sheedy and returning Andrew's stare.

"You don't handicap at all," Xiang said.

"Nine times out of a ten," Dett returned, "handicapping is a crock of shit. The punter is gone and there's no one left to take advantage of."

"In your view."

"In my respectful view Mr. Xiang, yes."

"And your method instead?"

"I prefer," Dett said, "interpreting the insane pattern of my own numbers."

Sheedy was wincing behind an open palm.

"I am sincerely impressed with that," Andrew Xiang said, nodding slowly as if he had just figured something out. "It's brave and rare."

Sheedy couldn't watch this anymore, and leaned forward, palms pressed tightly together. "Could we return to the matter at hand?"

"I can't help you guys," Xiang said quietly.

"Help me?" Sheedy said, flushing and going rigid.

"I'm just not interested in either," Xiang continued calmly.

"Fine," Dett said.

"Fine," Sheedy said, nodding vigorously up and down, his face heating visibly.

Xiang raised his shoulders and smiled. "I suppose there is one way I *could* help you."

Sheedy was beginning to vibrate with escalating badger rage but he stayed in his chair.

Andrew Xiang leaned across the table and whispered. "Get out of Halox. Get out of Commerce-Net."

It was Dett's turn to freeze. He knew.

"Bad news on both," Andrew said. "Obviously I can't say what precisely, but if you have clients long on either, I would back away. Since I won't buy yours, you should know I'm not shitting you. End of help."

And here Andrew Xiang left.

Dett didn't say a word all the way out to the car. The sale had been dead before it started and Sheedy hadn't seen that at all.

Sheedy riffed on a simple hostile theme, time and the sexual preferences of Andrew Xiang: "Waste of my fucking time. Faggot wasted my fucking time." All the while walking rigidly, hands in his pockets, jaw thrust out, head jerking from side to side as he scanned his memorized client list for the Plan B sucker.

Dett was flooded with images. Silent Cruise in the stretch, gaining on the leaders, the envelope of his spirit like a sonic boom through the air and soil and echoing off the far hills. Approaching the wire, veins all over the thoroughbred's body had bristled under the mahogany surface, marbling his hide.

"Gilbert Bligh maybe," Sheedy said when they got to the car.

I turned back, Dett thought, standing silently at the passenger door. I turned back to the sight of his breakdown, to the sight of his pain. Was there a trace of disrespect in watching Silent Cruise die? In not leaving him with the track crew and work ponies, in the company of his own?

"What do you think of Gil Bligh?" Sheedy repeated, louder.

Or had the fall pushed the duration of the race out beyond its strict borders? Would it then have been disrespectful to turn away, to treat wire results as the entirety of the event itself?

"Answer me!" Sheedy shouted and he thumped his hand on the Porsche's roof, which brought Dett's eyes sharply up from the green surface.

"What's the question?" he asked.

"We are emphatically not out of this yet, you hear me?" Sheedy was yelling at him from what might have been a great distance. His voice came through a kind of static. A static bristling with a thousand digits, rising to the surface of Dett's sub-conscience. 1's and 10's. 9's and other shadowy figures.

"We were punished," Dett said, hardly hearing his own words.

"Give me a freakin break," Sheedy said, angrily popping the locks.

"I actually got that horse. I *got* it."

"Oh yes," Sheedy said, stepping away from the car, circling with his head lowered, arms rigid and balled in fists. And then after two or three circles, when his fury hit some glass-breaking pitch, he looked up and screamed across the car: "I've been meaning to *thank you for that.*"

"Those *were* the numbers though. Those were the real numbers."

"Evi-fucking-dently," Sheedy said, spit flying from his lips and speckling the metallic green surface between them.

"The One in Ten," Dett said. "One in Ten."

"Shut…" Sheedy had to back away from the car again and circle. He couldn't complete the sentence.

"One is the full number," Dett went on. "The number that eliminates the other. The One that casts the shadow across the remainder."

Dett felt a delicious impulse rise within him as he continued. "The numbers 1, 9 and 10 can give us various dates in the 20th century," he said. "Like, say, September 10, 1901; October 9, 1901; January 10, 1909; October 1, 1909; January 9, 1910; and September 1, 1910. That's Tuesday, Wednesday, Sunday, Friday, Sunday, Thursday."

Sheedy continued to circle, now making a noise from his throat that sounded like a leaf blower. His arms were still stretched down at his sides but his fingers were spread as widely as he could. He might have been psyching up to break bricks with his head.

"But all along it was only the 9 I needed," Dett went on, oblivious. "9, 9, 9…September 9, 1909 was a Thursday! A Thursday Sheedy. The 3 day spread. It corroborates."

This all burst from him in a hail of internal applause. He thought it must have been like this to crack the Weirmach encryptions. A room full of jumping, hugging bodies and flying bits of paper.

"The remainder was 9 and I didn't understand it. 9 was the empty set, the left out number. 9 was the shadow. I was shown the shadow and we used it wrong, we tried to fuck someone over and the numbers fucked us back. It is so beautiful."

Sheedy continued to circle, his Samurai cry rising, cresting, then fading off into a plaintiff ululation of grief which itself wound down after a minute or two.

"Get in the car," Sheedy said finally, his face drained. "We have work to do…"

"So beautiful…" Dett was saying to an audience of billions of digits which swarmed in appreciation.

"… phone calls to make, markers to pull in, numbers to run … "

"You're wrong about numbers," Dett said, and a brief silence descended in him. "You think numbers are bits and pieces."

Sheedy put his elbows on the roof of the car. Leaned his face into his hands.

"Numbers," he said, his voice muffled. "You see, Dett, you swim in a sea of friggin numbers. You float in a data cloud, my young friend."

And here Sheedy lifted his head from his hands, fixed red eyes on his protégé and held up a single quivering finger to emphasise his point.

"And that Dett is a *good thing*. That makes all the molecules in your universe the same thing, little snips of data, numbers, digits, bytes. You have the building blocks and you can put them together one way and you have an interest rate swap. Another way and you have a derivative based on the price of Argentinean Black Angus testicles. A third way and you have the Argentinean Black Angus testicle itself. It's data. *Your* data *your* world. There isn't an MBA in a fucking thousand who is as stripped clean as you. I hired you because I envy you."

"You're still wrong," Dett said. It was amazing to him how insight, when it arrived, threw a brilliant light across every particle in the universe. "Numbers are perfectly analogue," he announced. "Not bits. Not pieces. Perfectly analogue."

"We're both going to be bits and pieces if you don't get in the car," Sheedy said. Then he climbed into the Porsche and slammed the door, which in a car of this price and parcelled engineering, produced a sound like: Snick.

But Dett couldn't hear most of this anyway. The gentle cascade of his numbers had started again and grown to a thunderous noise, the numerals spilling out of him like some kind of anchor chain, screaming and clanking as the linked steel integers fell into the depths. 1 in 10 in 1 in 10 in 1 in 10 in 1 in 10 in 1 in 10.

It still had a new car smell, this Porsche 911 Carrera 4 which could do 0 to 60 miles per hour in about 4 and ½ seconds flat. But these were meaningless numbers to Dett at the moment, who was busy pondering, musing, smiling, thanking the great host of numerals that arrayed themselves around him on a never-ending, seamless plane.

9, 9, 9 . . . I would just like to *thank* the number 9.

Dreamland

Carol Windley

IN INDIA, LILLIAN'S HUSBAND shot and killed a tiger. She did not herself witness this event and found it difficult to imagine her husband, an austere and proper man, intimately involved in that uncompromising moment of blood and passion when the tiger took the shot into its living body. But it was happily conceded by everyone who had been on the hunt: the tiger belonged to Lillian's husband. Its skin was displayed on the polished floor of the house they occupied in Madras State. The tiger's skull was unexpectedly small and innocent; its eyes were gold-coloured glass, blind. Lillian sat with her feet resting on the tiger's back as she read or sewed. Secretly, she asked it to carry her away from here, to the hills, to the far-off mountains.

For nearly twenty years Lillian and her husband lived in India, most of the time in Madras State. They had four children, all boys. At about the time that Lillian could count on the fingers of one hand the years left until her husband's retirement from the Indian Civil Service, he invited her to his office and showed her a map spread out on his desk. The map was of Canada, a country about which Lillian knew absolutely nothing. Her husband pointed to a dot of land on the left hand side of the map.

"This is where we are going," he said.

Lillian didn't understand. She placed her hand on a corner of the desk to steady herself, to keep from falling into the cold painted waters, from catching her hair and dress on the jagged edge of the ochre land mass. Her husband began to talk about annual rainfall, mean temperatures, temperate climates, the benign influence of certain ocean currents. He spoke of the mystery, the beauty of the northern rain forest, of which he had lately read, and in fact heard, from various sources. And the silence, he said. And the distance, the enormous, incontestable distance from India, the India of the British Raj, of which he had had more than enough.

"But we are going home," said Lillian, meaning home to England.

"We are not 'going home,'" her husband said. Then he tapped the map sharply with his finger. "We are going here. This will be our home," he said.

He seemed to gloat; he looked ferocious, and triumphant. Lillian thought: the soul of the tiger has entered his soul. She felt afraid of her husband, not, perhaps, for the first time. As soon as she had returned to the house she went straight to a table in the sitting room where she kept writing paper and a pen. She wrote her husband's name quickly on a scrap of paper, then burned the paper in a brass censer that hung in the sitting room and was meant to be only decorative. But she put it to use. The flames consumed her husband's name and in this way she removed him from her mind.

That was in India, in 1919, and now it is one year later and Lillian and her children actually inhabit the place on the map. It is where they live. They are on the west coast of an island that is itself on the extreme west coast of Canada. They live in a fishing village of perhaps two hundred people or less. Her husband brought them here and then he returned to India alone, to finish up the three years until his retirement. He went back to India and left Lillian and the boys here as if this were an entirely reasonable thing to do. "You will be safer here than anywhere," he told Lillian repeatedly. "The boys will be happier here than anywhere else," he said. This new life would make men of them, he said.

While he was with them he had a house built on a piece of land at the edge of the inlet waters, a tall house of wood with a steep roof and two rooms up, two rooms down. He had some furnishings shipped from Victoria by boat: a table and chairs, a sideboard, a bookcase, a wood-burning stove, which he proceeded to install himself. He unpacked his books, including Homer's *Iliad*, Darwin's *Descent of Man*, a volume entitled *Principia Mathematica*. He spoke of the time when he would return, and how he would sit in a chair by the window undisturbed reading these books. He nailed the tiger skin hastily to the wall, not minding what he damaged.

During the long days of rain that ensued the tiger glowed like a lamp, like the Indian sun at dawn, only beginning to attain its true brilliance. In Lillian's estimation the tiger's face appeared less blind, less innocent, as if adversity was pushing it toward some new and interesting truth.

Her husband stayed for six months in all. In early December he left on the mail boat, in a storm. The mail boat had to go along the open coast, which could be rough and dangerous at any time of year, in any weather. She stood on the dock watching the boat as it plunged into the waves and at last she called out her husband's name. The name was torn from her, a great cry for help, for assistance of some kind, and she was for a moment appalled at the sound. But the wind was fierce; no one heard her. *He* certainly didn't hear her. The mail boat was swept into the rain and fog and soon it was obscured.

There is no road out of this village. There is Lillian's house and after that there is nothing much, only a rough trail leading into the bush. At first everything she sees offends her eye: the ugly twisted pines, the straggly cedars, dead snags, blackened stumps where land has been partly cleared and then abandoned—visions of despair, of desperation. Some days she thinks the constant rain and fog will surely destroy her. And then the west wind starts up, chilling her to the bone and making her feel somehow vagrant, dispossessed. Her boys seem to exult in the wind, as they do in everything here. They climb trees, wade in the sea, throw rocks at one another, hide on her when she calls them. They are being made men of, she supposes. She stands listening, watching at the place where the trail leads off into the woods. No one lives there. It is an absence, an absence of life, of all but the most dangerous, elemental forms of life. She can see that it bears no relationship whatsoever to the milder forests of England and certainly none to the light-filled dry tumbling vastness of India.

No one Lillian has spoken to in the village can tell her who made this trail, or when, to what purpose. It is simply there. As a diversion, almost against her better judgement, she begins to follow the trail into the forest. Underneath the trees she sees a surprising number of plants: sword fern, salal, thimbleberry, water hemlock and a species of frail wild lily, the name unknown to her. She begins to make a project of naming as many of these plants as she can, and to make sketches of those she cannot yet name. All that first spring and summer she does this, drawing pages and pages of wet inky ferns, the fronds translating themselves wilfully into mouths, eyes, the palms of hands; human features that delight Lillian, although she cannot decipher their meaning, or identity.

At night when her boys sleep, Lillian gets up from her bed and travels again down this trail, feeling her way in the dark. She is blind, her eyes full of a wonderful innocence. This is the night and

377

she is in it, like a creature of the forest, a small animal. She feels, she knows, that this is a foolish practice, walking here by herself at night, but she cannot give it up, must not give it up. She feels the danger beating against her ribs like her heart, although more robust and sustaining. Easily she could lose her way, easily fall, tripping over a vine or tree root. And there truly are wild animals out here, dangerous animals. The village is rife with stories of encounters between men and bears and mountain lions. She chooses to discount these stories. Nothing in this forest is in the least interested in her. It even amuses her to imagine her husband's consternation, if he were called back from India simply because his wife had lost herself in the forest, in the night, and had been gobbled up by a bear. What does *his* discomfort matter to her, however? What does any of it matter? She is a small forest animal, padding down the trail, snuffling and whistling. Impossible to tell just where Lillian leaves off and the damp night air begins.

As well as the tiger skin there are several other objects brought all the way here from India. There is a collection of brass vessels of different sizes, the largest nearly three feet tall. Lillian likes to fill it with ferns and branches and wild flowers she gathers out in the bush. As a result, the house smells persistently, and not unpleasingly, of damp earth. Upstairs in her bedroom is a plain sandalwood box with a hinged lid in which she keeps her hairpins and combs. These are her own belongings, her possessions. She bought them herself, over the years, at market places in India. She went shopping in a rickshaw pulled by one of the servants. The rickshaw flew over the street, its wheels humming. There was a time when Lillian felt it wrong to be pulled along in this way, by another person, who might, after all, resent being used in this way. Her husband had laughed and said, "Oh, don't be ridiculous, Lillian," and so, after awhile, she thought only of the wind on her

378

face, a sense of flight arranged for her pleasure, and now she misses it, she misses all of it. She misses India.

In the marketplace, beggars held out their hands. Her husband warned her, "You will only encourage their indolence." That was the way he looked at it. To her the beggars didn't seem indolent; they seemed rigid with intent and purposefulness. Their hands were lean and dark, sinewy and warm with the stored energy of the omnipresent sun. She gave them money, as much as she could spare. Her husband hated weakness, poverty, sickness. Once he pointed urgently to a dark shape huddled in a gutter and said, "Can you tell, is that a child or a monkey? Can you see which it is?" He had been very agitated.

She said, "Oh, a monkey," but the truth was, from where they were standing, it was impossible to be sure. Her husband was a Tax Collector; he took money from the Indian people and gave it to the ruling English. That was how it worked. It was an important position her husband held, but he was, at least in this case, a realistic man. He said the taxes were paying for some very fine meals and elegant homes. "Could India survive on her own, however?" He doubted it. "Look at Mohandas K. Gandhi, for one example," he said. "And the trouble he is causing."

An incident occurred in India. Lillian went into her dresser drawer for something, a lace collar to wear with her dress. She pulled her hand out just in time. Nestled in her folded petticoats and clean handkerchiefs was a scorpion. One of the servants had plainly hidden it in her drawer to hurt her, to kill her possibly. Shaking with anger and fear, she told her husband, and he assembled the servants on the veranda at dusk. The sun was a red disc spinning on the rim of the earth. Her husband went up and down the line of servants, saying, "Above all else, I expect you to be open, honest, above-board. Play fair with me and I will play fair with you." He wore a white suit, a white hat; he was a tall man, dark-complexioned, with dark eyes. Later, he took Lillian aside and said that it was her job as mistress of the household to see that this kind of thing did not happen again. It was obvious to him, he said, that she did not have the respect of the servants. "Less daydreaming, Lillian," he said. "And more attention to the task at hand."

There is one more thing from India here in this new house on the inlet, and that is the brass censer in which Lillian had burnt her husband's name. She cannot precisely remember packing it in her trunk before leaving India, but here it is, somewhat tarnished it's true, but still beautiful, a lovely object, hanging from a hook in the front room. One morning, in a reflective mood, she dips her finger into the bowl of the censer and brings it out coated with a fine white ash. Her husband's name. She puts her finger to her mouth to lick it clean, then stops. In the pantry she scrubs her hands clean with a bar of soap, lathering her arms to the elbows. His ashes, she thinks. How awful, what a thing to do. In her mind, for a moment, it is as if her husband has died and she has desecrated his remains and now he is speaking to her, shouting at her from an omniscient position: Do you see where your daydreaming gets you, my girl? Your indolence? You will do anything, won't you?

Toward the end of the second year, she writes to her husband: I cannot tell what season of the year it is anymore. There is one long season, cold and wet, every day the same. You cannot imagine the monotony, or how it weighs on the spirit.

Her husband replies: "Last week I was forced to stay in a village stricken with disease. I am now dosing myself with quinine water. In addition, a rather brutal murder has occurred here, a Hindu-Muslim quarrel, I suspect. Every day the same, Lillian? Oh dear, oh dear."

A pod of killer whales swims into the inlet. The whales are in a frenzy, leaping high into the air, sending up great plumes of white spray. The entire village has turned out to watch from the shore, from the wharves. This has never happened before, everyone tells Lillian. The whales careen wildly; the villagers call out Oh! as if they were at a circus. Wind ripples the furiously churning surface of the water; clouds race past the mountains; everything is happening at once. Lillian drags her sons close, closer to the water's edge. You may never see a sight like this again, she tells them, as excited as any of the others. A rumour spreads, that this is an omen, that this strange behaviour on the part of the whales means something, good luck or bad. A man near Lillian says it has nothing to do with luck, it is the whales being whales, it is nature. Yes, Lillian says; yes indeed; nature. Then she thinks: The whales are in love. In love with the sea, the sky. It is too much for them, they cannot contain the energy of their love. She feels sympathy for the whales; they could easily annihilate themselves for this love; they have lost all sense of danger.

She thinks also of the tiger, her tiger, alive and floating through the green and gold air of the mountain slopes, its prey below on the ground, and the tiger's paws flexing, its claws unsheathed, its eyes burning with love, for itself, and the object it so desires: the prey.

Lillian walks out into the land at night, where no one else has the courage to go, and she finds it surprisingly peaceful, dark, muted. It is like walking into a pleasant dream. Then she thinks, No, her dreams are not always pleasant; sometimes they frighten her. Sometimes she wakens with a cry and realizes that she is alone, she is alone on what seems the edge of the world; beyond the walls of her house there is only the sea and then nothing. That incomprehensible absence. She can't get back to sleep; how could she sleep, she is too wrought up. She lies awake and listens to the wind, to the rain, to the sea. On the whole she would rather not sleep; she would rather be out there in the forest, playing a sort of game with fate. If I stumble and fall, she thinks. If a mountain lion leaps from a tree, snarling, its teeth bared. Nothing will happen, she tells herself. I am all right, she says. One more step, and then one after that. The ground underfoot is slick, uncertain. And there is the smell of dank vegetation, of death, she thinks. She is brave; unmindful. She walks on.

It occurs to her now that of course it was the children's ayah who put the scorpion in her dresser drawer. The ayah didn't like Lillian; she gave her sidelong glances, full of meaning. She spoiled the children, feeding them candies and hot Indian food, stroking their hair with her plump scented hands.

The ayah was there on the evening Lillian's husband reprimanded the servants over the issue of the scorpion. The ayah stood slightly apart from the others, as if wishing to disassociate herself from the matter, and from her condition of servitude. She was not the same as the other servants, her posture seemed to say. In the warmth of the setting sun her face was rosy, swollen. Lillian's husband went up and down, lecturing. "One of you is responsible," he said, "beyond doubt." The ayah was very pretty standing there, her hands meekly clasped.

Lillian thinks how strange, how very strange, that only now, years later, on the opposite side of the world, is she able to clearly recognize in the ayah's combined attitudes of submission and apartness not innocence, but guilt.

Her husband taunted her. Before they left India, he said to her, "There is no society out there, you know. No English society, church teas, fancy dress balls, all that nonsense. You'll be on your own, out there."

"I was never all that much interested," she had said, although she had enjoyed the fancy dress balls, the impromptu theatre. In any case, her husband had been wrong. In the village there are men and women from England, immigrants, like Lillian, anxiously running their hands over the walls of moist air to see if it is real, this prison, this small place they have come to. Wearing gumboots they wade through mud to play mah jong around kitchen tables; they sing songs together, and dance, and toast one another with glasses of sherry. At the end of all this entertainment, they stand and sing "God Save the King," their mouths alive, biting with great vigour into the words "victorious," "glorious." The English in diaspora, Lillian thinks. It is the same everywhere. She does not join in the singing, but watches the energy of the open mouths with interest. She is amazed that the words still have meaning for these people, not only these words, but any words at all. Any spoken words. For her, words have become as vague and formless as the mist that wreathes the mountainsides. She begins to avoid social occasions; she develops a most unlikely habit of running to hide when people walk down the road to visit her. She hides in her garden, behind the trunk of a cedar tree, or she runs into the house and locks the door. Anything she or anyone else might have to say seems suddenly pointless, irrelevant. (Quite, quite irrelevant, she hears her husband's voice saying, in her mind.) She is a small animal, solitary, making her way down a trail no one else dares to take.

Of course, she isn't an animal. She is Lillian, with her sketchbook and her pen and ink, getting it all down on paper, recording the shapes, the mysterious, scarcely apprehended shapes and forms that green growing plants can take. As she draws, she is fascinated to see human features behind the branches, mixed in with the vining stems and fleshy leaves, appearing magically, independent of her pen. The corner of an eye, the tip of a nose, a full, pouting lower lip.

Even the tiger is there, his black stripes boldly visible against the delicate tracery of a sword fern. The tiger makes her smile. He is arrogant, indifferent, strutting on the paper: did you intend to forget me? he asks.

383

Lillian ventures further down the trail than she has ever gone. She plunges on and on through the bush. She scratches her hand on a branch; pauses to pull her skirt impatiently free of a thorned vine. Then she arrives at an open place, unlike anywhere else. She has an idea, from studying maps of the area, and from hearing people talk, that she has come to the mudflats, where the sea at last wears itself out and becomes engulfed by the land. The ground is marshy, like a peat bog, and the water is everywhere shallow and blue and motionless. Tall, bearded grasses grow along the shore. A blue heron stands one-legged not far from her. Everything is quiet and seems consecrated to this singular moment. Lillian sits down on a log and places her sketchbook open on her knee. Will she find her way back? she wonders. Will her sons notice that she's been gone for an unusually long time? It is July and surprisingly hot. She is wearing a wide-brimmed hat tied under her chin with a scarf, to shade her eyes. It is, in fact, a hat she wore many times in India, while engaged in just such an activity as this: sketching the indigenous flora and fauna of the land. She draws a long curved line meant to represent the heron's long neck, which ought to look graceful but is instead strangely clumsy, unmanageable. She turns to a fresh page. Behind her in the bush there is a noise, as if something, an animal, is creeping up on her to have a better look. She doesn't turn around.

Her husband said to her before he went back to India, "I suppose you will forget me once I am gone." He had been at the window looking at the inlet, at the small dark islands that rose abruptly out of the water. She wanted to tell him that it was too late, she had already forgotten him, she had forgotten his name; she had written it down and let it be consumed by fire. Instead she said, "The children might forget you. Three years is a long time to a child." He replied that it was her responsibility to see that they did not forget him. Then he began unpacking his books, telling her that she must encourage the boys to read these books, it was important that they read and exercise their minds. "I will write to them," he said. "A letter for each child, every month."

Of course, even after all this time the boys have not forgotten their father, although they mention him less and less as the weeks and months go by. And even after reducing it to a fine white ash, Lillian remembers her husband's name. She hasn't spoken it aloud since the day he left on the mail boat, but she does remember it. No, the irony is that it is herself she has forgotten. Her self, her physical presence, seems to have become amorphous; parts of her float through the cedar forest; parts of her catch on dead snags. Her husband said, "The great beauty of this place is that you can make anything you want out of it. No one has really discovered it yet. It is a sort of dreamland, waiting. You can make what you want out of it. That's what I want. That's exactly what I want."

He spoke with such enthusiasm; he so badly wanted his dreamland away from the rest of the world, away from India, away from the ancient populated parts of the world. But Lillian knows what her husband does not know, even yet: that the land makes what it wants of you. The land is not clay waiting to be shaped; it is a monster already formed, with claws and a hungry mouth. A shiver runs down her spine. She can sense something behind her, although commonsense tells her nothing is there. She is alone and at any moment she can get up and begin the walk back.

She draws, curving a slender grass stem deliberately across the clean white page. Her hand moves quickly, forming a latticework of sea grasses bending as if swept by a fierce wind; only there is no wind. Behind the grasses elusive human features appear, shy, diffident. They lack an identity, although it seems to Lillian they might at any moment assume one. She sees an ear, then the open palm of a hand. The fluttering edge of a scarf; the brim of a sun hat much like the one she has on her head. And an eye, wide, surprised; knowledgeable.

Cortes Island

Alice Munro

LITTLE BRIDE. I WAS TWENTY years old, five feet seven inches tall, weighing between a hundred and thirty-five and a hundred and forty pounds, but some people—Chess's boss's wife, and the older secretary in his office, and Mrs. Gorrie upstairs, referred to me as a little bride. Our little bride, sometimes. Chess and I made a joke of it, but his public reaction was a look fond and cherishing. Mine was a pouty smile—bashful, acquiescent.

We lived in a basement in Vancouver. The house did not belong to the Gorries, as I had at first thought, but to Mrs. Gorrie's son Ray. He would come around to fix things. He entered by the basement door, as Chess and I did. He was a thin, narrow-chested man, perhaps in his thirties, always carrying a toolbox and wearing a workman's cap. He seemed to have a permanent stoop, which might have come from bending over most of the time, attending to plumbing jobs or wiring or carpentry. His face was waxy, and he coughed a good deal. Each cough was a discreet independent statement, defining his presence in the basement as a necessary intrusion. He did not apologize for being there, but he did not move around in the place as if he owned it. The only times I spoke to him were when he knocked on the door to tell me that the water was going to be turned off for a little while, or the power. The rent was paid in cash every month to Mrs. Gorrie. I don't know if she passed it all on to him or kept some of it out to help with expenses. Otherwise all she and Mr. Gorrie had—she told me so—was Mr. Gorrie's pension. Not hers. I'm not nearly old enough, she said.

Mrs. Gorrie always called down the stairs to ask how Ray was and whether he would like a cup of tea. He always said he was okay and he didn't have time. She said that he worked too hard, just like herself. She tried to fob off on him some extra dessert she had made, some preserves or cookies or gingerbread—the same things she was always pushing at me. He would say no, he had just eaten, or that he had plenty of stuff at home. I always resisted, too, but on the seventh or eighth try I would give in. It was so embarrassing to go on refusing, in the face of her wheedling and disappointment. I admired the way Ray could keep saying no. He didn't even say, "No, Mother." Just no.

Then she tried to find some topic of conversation.

"So what's new and exciting with you?"

Not much. Don't know. Ray was never rude or irritable, but he never gave her an inch. His health was okay. His cold was okay. Mrs. Cornish and Irene were always okay as well.

Mrs. Cornish was a woman whose house he lived in, somewhere in East Vancouver. He always had jobs to do around Mrs. Cornish's house as well as around this one—that was why he had to hurry away as soon as the work was done. He also helped with the care of her daughter Irene, who was in a wheelchair. Irene had cerebral palsy. "The poor thing," Mrs. Gorrie said, after Ray told her that Irene was okay. She never reproached him to his face for the time he spent with the afflicted girl, the outings to Stanley Park or the evening jaunts to get ice cream. (She knew about these things because she sometimes talked on the phone to Mrs. Cornish.) But to me she said, "I can't help thinking what a sight she must be with the ice cream running down her face. I can't help it. People must have a good time gawking at them."

She said that when she took Mr. Gorrie out in his wheelchair people looked at them (Mr. Gorrie had had a stroke), but it was different, because outside the house he didn't move or make a sound and she always made sure he was presentable. Whereas Irene lolled around and went *gaggledy-gaggledy-gaggledy.* The poor thing couldn't help it.

Mrs. Cornish could have something in mind, Mrs. Gorrie said. Who was going to look after that cripple girl when she was gone?

"There ought to be a law that healthy people can't get married to someone like that, but so far there isn't."

When Mrs. Gorrie asked me to go up for coffee I never wanted to go. I was busy with my own life in the basement. Sometimes when she came knocking on my door I pretended not to be home. But in order to do that I had to get the lights out and the door locked the instant I heard her open the door at the top of the stairs, and then I had to stay absolutely still while she tapped her fingernails against the door and trilled my name. Also I had to be very quiet for at least an hour afterward and refrain from flushing the toilet. If I said that I couldn't spare the time, I had things to do, she would laugh and say, "What things?"

"Letters I'm writing," I said.

"Always writing letters," she said. "You must be homesick."

Her eyebrows were pink—a variation of the pinkish red of her hair. I did not think the hair could be natural, but how could she have dyed her eyebrows? Her face was thin, rouged, vivacious, her teeth large and glistening. Her appetite for friendliness, for company, took no account of resistance. The very first morning that Chess brought me to this apartment, after meeting me at the train, she had knocked at our door with a plate of cookies and this wolfish smile. I still had my travelling hat on, and Chess had been interrupted in his pulling at my girdle. The cookies were dry and hard and covered with a bright-pink icing to celebrate my bridal status. Chess spoke to her curtly. He had to get back to work within half an hour, and after he had got rid of her there was no time to go on with what he'd started. Instead, he ate the cookies one after another, complaining that they tasted like sawdust.

"Your hubby is so serious," she would say to me. "I have to laugh, he always gives me this serious, serious look when I see him coming and going. I want to tell him to take it easy, he hasn't got the world on his shoulders."

Sometimes I had to follow her upstairs, torn away from my book or the paragraph I was writing. We sat at her dining-room table. There was a lace cloth on it, and an octagonal mirror reflecting a ceramic swan. We drank coffee out of china cups and ate off small matching plates (more of those cookies, or gluey raisin tarts or heavy scones) and touched tiny embroidered napkins to our lips to wipe away the crumbs. I sat facing the china cabinet in which were ranged all the good glasses, and the cream-and-sugar sets, the salt-and-peppers too dinky or ingenious for daily use, as well as bud vases, a teapot shaped like a thatched cottage, and candlesticks shaped like lilies. Once every month Mrs. Gorrie went through the china cabinet and washed everything. She told me so. She told me things that had to do with my future, the house and the future she assumed I would have, and the more she talked the more I felt an iron weight on my limbs, the more I wanted to yawn and yawn in the middle of the morning, to crawl away and hide and sleep. But out loud I admired everything. The contents of the china cabinet, the housekeeping routines of Mrs. Gorrie's life, the matching outfits that she put on every morning. Skirts and sweaters in shades of mauve or coral, harmonizing scarves of artificial silk.

"Always get dressed first thing, just as if you're going out to work, and do your hair and get your makeup on"—she had caught me more than once in my dressing gown—"and then you can always put an apron on if you have to do the washing or some baking. It's good for your morale."

And always have some baking on hand for when people might drop in. (As far as I knew, she never had any visitors but me, and you could hardly say that I had dropped in.) And never serve coffee in mugs.

It wasn't put quite so baldly. It was "I always—" or "I always like to—" or "I think it's nicer to—"

"Even when I lived away off in the wilds, I always liked to—" My need to yawn or scream subsided for a moment. Where had she lived in the wilds? And when?

"Oh, away up the coast," she said. "I was a bride, too, once upon a time. I lived up there for years. Union Bay. But that wasn't too wild. Cortes Island."

I asked where that was, and she said, "Oh, away up there."

"That must have been interesting," I said.

"Oh, interesting," she said. "If you call bears interesting. If you call cougars interesting. I'd rather have a little civilization myself."

The dining room was separated from the living room by sliding oak doors. They were always open a little way so that Mrs. Gorrie, sitting at the end of the table, could keep an eye on Mr. Gorrie, sitting in his recliner in front of the living-room window. She spoke of him as "my husband in the wheelchair," but in fact he was only in the wheelchair when she took him out for his walk. They didn't have a television set—television was still almost a novelty at that time. Mr. Gorrie sat and watched the street, and Kitsilano Park across the street and Burrard Inlet beyond that. He made his own way to the bathroom, with a cane in one hand and the other hand gripping chair backs or battering against the walls. Once inside he managed by himself, though it took him a long time. And Mrs. Gorrie said that there was sometimes a bit of mopping up.

All I could usually see of Mr. Gorrie was a trouser leg stretched out on the bright-green recliner. Once or twice he had to make this drag and lurch along to the bathroom when I was there. A large man—large head, wide shoulders, heavy bones.

I didn't look at his face. People who had been crippled by strokes or disease were bad omens to me, rude reminders. It wasn't the sight of useless limbs or the other physical marks of their horrid luck I had to avoid—it was their human eyes.

I don't believe he looked at me, either, though Mrs. Gorrie called out to him that here I was visiting from downstairs. He made a grunting noise that could have been the best he could do by way of a greeting, or dismissal.

There were two and a half rooms in our apartment. It was rented furnished, and in the way of such places it was half furnished, with things that would otherwise have been thrown away. I remember the floor of the living room, which was covered with leftover squares and rectangles of linoleum—all the different colors and patterns fitted together and stitched like a crazy quilt with strips of metal. And the gas stove in the kitchen, which was fed with quarters. Our bed was in an alcove off the kitchen—it fitted into the alcove so snugly that you had to climb into bed from the bottom. Chess had read that this was the way the harem girls had to enter the bed of the sultan, first adoring his feet, then crawling upward paying homage to his other parts. So we sometimes played this game.

A curtain was kept closed all the time across the foot of the bed, to divide the alcove from the kitchen. It was actually an old bedspread, a slippery fringed cloth that showed yellowy beige on one side, with a pattern of winy roses and green leaves, and on the other, bedward-side stripes of wine red and green with flowers and foliage appearing like ghosts in the beige color. This curtain is the thing I remember more vividly than anything else in the apartment. And no wonder. In the full spate of sex, and during its achieved aftermath, that fabric was in front of my eyes and became a reminder of what I liked about being married—the reward for which I suffered the unforeseen insult of being a little bride and the peculiar threat of a china cabinet.

Chess and I both came from homes where unmarried sex was held to be disgusting and unforgivable, and married sex was apparently never mentioned and soon forgotten about. We were right at the end of the time of looking at things that way, though we didn't know it. When Chess's mother had found condoms in his suitcase, she went weeping to his father. (Chess said that they had been given out at the camp where he had taken his university military training—which was true—and that he had forgotten all about them, which was a lie.) So having a place of our own and a bed of our own where we could carry on as we liked seemed marvellous to us. We had made this bargain, but it never occurred to us that older people—our parents, our aunts and uncles—could have made the same bargain, for lust. It seemed as if their main itch had been for houses, property, power mowers, and home freezers and retaining walls. And, of course, as far as women were concerned, for babies. All those things were what we thought we might choose, or might not choose, in the future. We never thought any of that would come on us inexorably, like age or weather.

And now that I come to think of it honestly, it didn't. Nothing came without our choice. Not pregnancy, either. We risked it, just to see if we were really grown up, if it could really happen.

The other thing I did behind the curtain was read. I read books that I got from the Kitsilano Library a few blocks away. And when I looked up in that churned-up state of astonishment that a book could bring me to, a giddiness of gulped riches, the stripes were what I'd see. And not just the characters, the story, but the climate of the book became attached to the unnatural flowers and flowed along in the dark-wine stream or the gloomy green. I read the heavy books whose titles were already familiar and incantatory to me—I even tried to read *The Betrothed*—and in between these courses I read the novels of Aldous Huxley and Henry Green, and *To the Lighthouse* and *The Last of Chéri* and *The Death of the Heart.* I bolted them down one after the other without establishing any preferences, surrendering to each in turn just as I'd done to the books I read in my childhood. I was still in that stage of leaping appetite, of voracity close to anguish.

But one complication had been added since childhood—it seemed that I had to be a writer as well as a reader. I bought a school notebook and tried to write—did write, pages that started off authoritatively and then went dry, so that I had to tear them out and twist them up in hard punishment and put them in the garbage can. I did this over and over again until I had only the notebook cover left. Then I bought another notebook and started the whole process once more. The same cycle—excitement and despair, excitement and despair. It was like having a secret pregnancy and miscarriage every week.

Not entirely secret, either. Chess knew that I read a lot and that I was trying to write. He didn't discourage it at all. He thought that it was something reasonable that I might quite possibly learn to do. It would take hard practice but could be mastered, like bridge or tennis. This generous faith I did not thank him for. It just added to the farce of my disasters.

Chess worked for a wholesale grocery firm. He had thought of being a history teacher, but his father had persuaded him that teaching was no way to support a wife and get on in the world. His father had helped him get this job but told him that once he got in he was not to expect any favors. He didn't. He left the house before it was light, during this first winter of our marriage, and came home after dark. He worked hard, not asking that the work he did fit in with any interests he might have had or have any purpose to it that he might once have honored. No purpose except to carry us both toward that life of lawnmowers and freezers which we believed we had no mind for. I might marvel at his submission, if I thought about it. His cheerful, you might say gallant, submission.

But then, I thought, it's what men do.

I went out to look for work myself. If it wasn't raining too hard I went down to the drugstore and bought a paper and read the ads while I drank a cup of coffee. Then I set out, even in a drizzle, to walk to the places that had advertised for a waitress or a salesgirl or a factory worker—any job that didn't specifically require typing or experience. If the rain had come on heavily I would travel by bus. Chess said that I should always go by bus and not walk to save money. While I was saving money, he said, some other girl could have got the job.

That was in fact what I seemed to be hoping for. I was never altogether sorry to hear it. Sometimes I would get to my destination and stand on the sidewalk, looking at the Ladies' Dress Shop, with its mirrors and pale carpeting, or watch the girls tripping downstairs on their lunch break from the office that needed a filing clerk. I would not even go inside, knowing how my hair and fingernails and flat scuffed shoes would tell against me. And I was just as daunted by the factories—I could hear the noise of the machines going in the buildings where soft drinks were bottled or Christmas decorations put together, and I could see the bare lightbulbs hanging down from the barnlike ceilings. My fingernails and flat heels might not matter there, but my clumsiness and mechanical stupidity would get me sworn at, shouted at (I could also hear the shouted orders above the noise of the machines). I would be disgraced and fired. I didn't think myself capable even of learning to operate a cash register. I told the manager of a restaurant that, when he actually seemed to be thinking of hiring me. "Do you think you could pick it up?" he said, and I said no. He looked as if he had never heard anybody admit to such a thing before. But I spoke the truth. I didn't think I could pick things up, not in a hurry and out in public. I would freeze. The only things that I could pick up easily were things like the convolutions of the Thirty Years' War.

The truth is, of course, that I didn't have to. Chess was supporting me, at our very basic level. I didn't have to push myself out into the world because he had done it. Men had to.

I thought that maybe I could manage the work in the library, so I asked there, though they hadn't advertised. A woman put my name on a list. She was polite but not encouraging. Then I went into bookstores, choosing the ones that looked as if they wouldn't have a cash register. The emptier and untidier the better. The owners would be smoking or dozing at the desk, and in the secondhand stores there was often a smell of cat.

"We're not busy enough in the winter," they said.

One woman said I might come back in the spring.

"Though we're not usually very busy then, either."

Winter in Vancouver was not like any winter I had ever known. No snow, not even anything much in the way of a cold wind. In the middle of the day, downtown, I could smell something like burned sugar—I think it had to do with the trolley wires. I walked along Hastings Street, where there wouldn't be another woman walking—just drunks, tramps, poor old men, shuffling Chinese. Nobody spoke an ill word to me. I walked past warehouses, weedy lots where there wouldn't be even a man in sight. Or through Kitsilano, with its high wooden houses crammed with people living tight, as we were, to the tidy Dunbar district, with its stucco bungalows and pollarded trees. And through Kerrisdale, where the classier trees appeared, birches on the lawns. Tudor beams, Georgian symmetry, Snow White fantasies with imitation thatched roofs. Or maybe real thatched roofs, how could I tell?

In all these places where people lived, the lights came on around four in the afternoon, and then the streetlights came on, the lights in the trolley buses came on, and often, too, the clouds broke apart in the west over the sea to show the red streaks of the sun's setting—and in the park, through which I circled home, the leaves of the winter shrubs glistened in the damp air of a faintly rosy twilight. People who had been shopping were going home, people at work were thinking about going home, people who had been in the houses all day came out to take a little walk that would make home more appealing. I met women with baby carriages and complaining toddlers and never thought that so soon I'd be in the same shoes. I met old people with their dogs, and other old people, slow moving or in wheelchairs, being propelled by their mates or keepers. I met Mrs. Gorrie pushing Mr. Gorrie. She wore a cape and beret of soft purple wool (I knew by now that she made most of her own clothes) and a lot of rosy face coloring. Mr. Gorrie wore a low cap and a thick scarf wrapped around his neck. Her greeting to me was shrill and proprietary, his nonexistent. He did not look as if he was enjoying the ride. But people in wheel-chairs rarely did look anything more than resigned. Some looked affronted or downright mean.

"Now, when we saw you out in the park the other day," Mrs. Gorrie said, "you weren't on your way back from looking for a job then, were you?"

"No," I said, lying. My instinct was to lie to her about anything.

"Oh, good. Because I was just going to say, you know, that if you were out looking for a job you really should fix yourself up a little bit. Well, you know that."

Yes, I said.

"I can't understand the way some women go out nowadays. I'd never go out in my flat shoes and no makeup on, even if I was just going to the grocery store. Let alone if I was going to ask somebody to give me a job."

She knew I was lying. She knew I froze on the other side of the basement door, not answering her knock. I wouldn't have been surprised if she went through our garbage and discovered and read the messy, crumpled pages on which were spread out my prolix disasters. Why didn't she give up on me? She couldn't. I was a job set out for her—maybe my peculiarities, my ineptitude, were in a class with Mr. Gorrie's damages, and what couldn't be righted had to be borne.

She came down the stairs one day when I was in the main part of the basement doing our washing. I was allowed to use her wringer-washer and laundry tubs every Tuesday.

"So is there any chance of a job yet?" she said, and on the spur of the moment I said that the library had told me they might have something for me in the future. I thought that I could pretend to be going to work there—I could go and sit there every day at one of the long tables, reading or even trying my writing, as I had done occasionally in the past. Of course, the cat would be out of the bag if Mrs. Gorrie ever went into the library, but she wouldn't be able to push Mr. Gorrie that far, uphill. Or if she ever mentioned my job to Chess—but I didn't think that would happen either. She said she was sometimes afraid to say hello to him, he looked so cross.

"Well, maybe in the meantime . . . ," she said. "It just occurred to me that maybe in the meantime you would like to have a little job sitting in the afternoons with Mr. Gorrie."

She said that she had been offered a job helping out in the gift shop at St. Paul's Hospital three or four afternoons a week. "It's not a paid job or I'd have sent you to ask about it," she said. "It's just volunteer work. But the doctor says it'd do me good to get out of the house. 'You'll wear yourself out,' he said. It's not that I need the money, Ray is so good to us, but just a little volunteer job, I thought—" She looked into the rinse tub and saw Chess's shirts in the same clear water as my flowered nightgown and our pale-blue sheets.

"Oh, dear," she said. "You didn't put the whites and the coloreds in together?"

"Just the light coloreds," I said. "They don't run."

"Light coloreds are still coloreds," she said. "You might think the shirts are white that way, but they won't be as white as they could be."

I said I would remember next time.

"It's just the way you take care of your man," she said, with her little scandalized laugh.

"Chess doesn't mind," I said, not realizing how this would become less and less true in the years ahead and how all these jobs that seemed incidental and almost playful, on the borders of my real life, were going to move front and center.

I took the job, sitting with Mr. Gorrie in the afternoons. On one little table beside the green recliner there was spread a hand towel—to catch spills—and on top of it were his pill bottles and liquid medicines and a small clock to tell him the time. The table on the other side was stacked with reading material. The morning paper, last evening's paper, copies of *Life* and *Look* and *Maclean's,* which were all big floppy magazines then. On the lower shelf of this table was a pile of scrapbooks—the kind that children use at school, with heavy brownish paper and rough edges. There were bits of newsprint and photographs sticking out of them. These were scrapbooks that Mr. Gorrie had kept over the years, until he had his stroke and couldn't cut things out anymore. There was a bookcase in the room, but all it held was more magazines and more scrapbooks and a half shelf of high-school textbooks, probably Ray's.

"I always read him the paper," Mrs. Gorrie said. "He hasn't lost his ability, but he can't manage to hold it up with both hands, and his eyes get tired out."

So I read to Mr. Gorrie while Mrs. Gorrie, under her flowered umbrella, stepped lightly off to the bus stop. I read him the sports page and the municipal news and the world news and all about murders and robberies and bad weather. I read the letters to the editor and the letters to a doctor who gave medical advice and the letters to Ann Landers, and her replies. It seemed that the sports news and Ann Landers roused his interest the most. I would sometimes mispronounce a player's name or mix up the terminology, so that what I read made no sense, and he would direct me with dissatisfied grunts to try again. When I read the sports page he was always on edge, intent and frowning. But when I read Ann Landers his face relaxed and he made noises that I took to be appreciative—a kind of gurgling and deep snorting. He made these noises particularly when the letters touched on some especially feminine or trivial concern (a woman wrote that her sister-in-law always pretended that she had baked a cake herself, even though the paper doily from the bakeshop was still under it when it was served) or when they referred—in the careful manner of that time—to sex.

During the reading of the editorial page or of some long rigma-role about what the Russians said and what the Americans said at the United Nations, his eyelids would droop—or, rather, the eyelid over his better eye would droop almost all the way and the one over his bad, darkened eye would droop slightly—and the movements of his chest would become more noticeable, so that I might pause for a moment to see if he had gone to sleep. And then he would make another sort of noise—a curt and reproving one. As I got used to him, and he got used to me, this noise began to seem less like reproof and more like reassurance. And the reassurance was not just about his not being asleep but about the fact that he was not at that moment dying.

His dying in front of my eyes had been at first a horrible consideration. Why should he not die, when he seemed at least half dead already? His bad eye like a stone under dark water, and that side of his mouth pulled open, showing his original, wicked teeth (most old people then had false teeth) with their dark fillings glowering through the damp enamel. His being alive and in the world seemed to me an error that could be wiped out at any moment. But then, as I said, I got used to him. He was on a grand scale, with his big noble head and wide laboring chest and his powerless right hand lying on his long trousered thigh, invading my sight as I read. Like a relic, he was, an old warrior from barbarous times. Eric Blood-Axe. King Knut.

> *My strength is failing fast, said the sea king to his men.*
> *I shall never sail the seas, like a conqueror again.*

That was what he was like. His half-wrecked hulk of a body endangering the furniture and battering the walls as he made his momentous progress to the bathroom. His smell, which was not rank but not reduced to infantile soap-and-talcum cleanliness, either—a smell of thick clothing with its residue of tobacco (though he didn't smoke anymore) and of the enclosed skin that I thought of as thick and leathery, with its lordly excretions and animal heat. A slight but persistent smell of urine, in fact, which would have disgusted me on a woman but which seemed in his case not just forgivable but somehow an expression of ancient privilege. When I went into the bathroom after he had been there, it was like the lair of some mangy, still powerful beast.

Chess said I was wasting my time baby-sitting Mr. Gorrie. The weather was clearing now, and the days were getting longer. The shops were putting up new displays, stirring out of their winter torpor. Everybody was more apt to be thinking of hiring. So I ought to be out now, seriously looking for a job. Mrs. Gorrie was paying me only forty cents an hour.

"But I promised her," I said.

One day he said he had seen her getting off a bus. He saw her from his office window. And it wasn't anywhere near St. Paul's Hospital.

I said, "She might have been on a break."

Chess said, "I never saw her out in the full light of day before. Jesus."

I suggested taking Mr. Gorrie for a walk in his wheelchair, now that the weather had improved. But he rejected the idea with some noises that made me certain there was something distasteful to him about being wheeled about in public—or maybe about being taken out by somebody like me, obviously hired to do the job.

I had interrupted my reading of the paper to ask him this, and when I tried to continue he made a gesture and another noise, telling me he was tired of listening. I laid the paper down. He waved the good hand toward the pile of scrapbooks on the lower shelf of the table beside him. He made more noises. I can only describe these noises as grunts, snorts, hawkings, barks, mumbles. But by this time they sounded to me almost like words. They did sound like words. I heard them not only as peremptory statements and demands ("Don't want to," "Help me up," "Let me see the time," "I need a drink") but as more complicated pronouncements: "Christ, why doesn't that dog shut up?" or "Lot of hot air" (this after I'd read some speech or editorial in the paper).

What I heard now was "Let's see if there's anything in here better than what's in the paper."

I pulled the stack of scrapbooks off the shelf and settled with them on the floor by his feet. On the front covers were written, in large black crayoned letters, the dates of recent years. I flipped through 1952 and saw the cutout newspaper account of George VI's funeral. Above it the crayon lettering. "Albert Frederick Arthur George. Born 1895. Died 1952." The picture of the three queens in their mourning veils.

On the next page a story about the Alaska Highway.

"This is an interesting record," I said. "Do you want me to help you start another book? You could choose what things you want me to cut out and paste in, and I'd do it."

His noise meant "Too much trouble" or "Why bother now?" or even "What a stupid idea." He brushed aside King George VI, wished to see the dates on the other books. They weren't what he wanted. He motioned toward the bookcase. I brought out another pile of scrapbooks. I understood that it was the book for one particular year that he was looking for, and I held each book up so that he could see the cover. Occasionally I flipped the pages open in spite of his rejection. I saw an article about the cougars on Vancouver Island and one about the death of a trapeze artist and another about a child who had lived though trapped in an avalanche. Back through the war years we went, back through the thirties, through the year I was born in, nearly a decade beyond that before he was satisfied. And gave the order. Look at this one. 1923.

I started going through that one from the beginning.

"January snowfall buries villages in—"

That's not it. Hurry up. Get on with it.

I began to flip the pages.

Slow down. Go easy. Slow down.

I lifted the pages one by one without stopping to read anything till we reached the one he wanted.

There. Read that.

There was no picture or headline. The crayoned letters said, *"Vancouver Sun,* April 17, 1923."

"Cortes Island," I read. "Okay?"

Read it. Go on.

> CORTES ISLAND. Early Sunday morning or sometime late Saturday night the home of Anson James Wild at the south end of the island was totally destroyed by fire. The house was at a long distance from any other dwelling or habitation and as a result the flames were not noticed by anyone living on the island. There are reports that a fire was spotted early Sunday morning by a fishing boat going towards Desolation Sound but those on board thought somebody was burning brush. Know-

ing that brush fire posed no danger due to the wet condition of the woods at present they proceeded on their way.

Mr. Wild was the proprietor of Wildfruit Orchards and had been a resident on the island for about fifteen years. He was a solitary man whose previous history had been in the military service but he was cordial to those he met. He was married some time ago and had one son. It is believed he was born in the Atlantic Provinces.

The house was reduced to ruin by the blaze and the beams had fallen in. The body of Mr. Wild was found amongst the charred remains burnt almost beyond recognition.

A blackened tin thought to have contained kerosene was discovered within the ruins.

Mr. Wild's wife was away from home at the time, having on the previous Wednesday accepted a ride on a boat that was picking up a load of apples to be transported from her husband's orchard to Comox. She was intending to return the same day but remained away for three days and four nights due to engine trouble with the boat. On Sunday morning she returned with the friend who had offered her the ride and together they discovered the tragedy.

Fears were entertained for the Wilds' young son who was not in the house when it burned. A search was started as soon as possible and before dark on Sunday evening the child was located in the woods less than a mile from his home. He was wet and cold from being in the underbrush for several hours but otherwise unharmed. It appears that he took some food with him when leaving the house as he had some pieces of bread with him when found.

An inquest will be held in Courtenay into the cause of the fire which destroyed the Wilds' home and resulted in the loss of Mr. Wild's life.

"Did you know these people?" I said.

Turn the page.

August 4, 1923. An inquest held in Courtenay on Vancouver Island into the fire that caused the death of Anson James

Wild of Cortes Island in April of this year found that suspicion of arson by the deceased man or by person or persons unknown cannot be substantiated. The presence of an empty kerosene can at the site of the fire has not been accepted as sufficient evidence. Mr. Wild regularly purchased and made use of kerosene, according to Mr. Percy Kemper, storekeeper, Manson's Landing, Cortes Island.

The seven-year-old son of the deceased man was not able to provide any evidence about the fire. He was found by a search party several hours later wandering in the woods not far from his home. In response to questioning he said that his father had given him some bread and apples and told him to walk to Manson's Landing but that he lost his way. But in later weeks he has said that he does not remember this being the case and does not know how he came to lose his way, the path having been travelled by him many times before. Dr. Anthony Helwell of Victoria stated that he had examined the boy and believes that he may have run away at the first sight of the fire perhaps having time to lay hold of some food to take with him, which he has no recollection of now. Alternately he says the boy's story may be correct and recollection of it suppressed at a later date. He said that further questioning of the child would not be useful because he is probably unable to distinguish between fact and his imagination in this matter.

Mrs. Wild was not at home at the time of the fire having gone to Vancouver Island on a boat belonging to James Thompson Gorrie of Union Bay.

The death of Mr. Wild was ruled to be an accident due to misadventure, its cause being a fire of origins unknown.

Close up the book now.
Put it away. Put them all away.
No. No. Not like that. Put them away in order. Year by year.
That's better. Just the way they were.
Is she coming yet? Look out the window.
Good. But she will be coming soon.

There you are, what do you think of that?

I don't care. I don't care what you think of it.

Did you ever think that people's lives could be like that and end up like this? Well, they can.

I did not tell Chess about this, though I usually told him anything I thought would interest or amuse him about my day. He had a way now of dismissing any mention of the Gorries. He had a word for them. It was "grotesque."

All the dingy-looking little trees in the park came out in bloom. Their flowers were a bright pink, like artificially colored popcorn.

And I began working at a real job.

The Kitsilano Library phoned and asked me to come in for a few hours on a Saturday afternoon. I found myself on the other side of the desk, stamping the due date in people's books. Some of these people were familiar to me, as fellow borrowers. And now I smiled at them, on behalf of the library. I said, "See you in two weeks."

Some laughed and said, "Oh, a lot sooner," being addicts like myself.

It turned out that this was a job I could handle. No cash register—when fines were paid you got the change out of a drawer. And I already knew where most of the books were on the shelves. When it came to filing cards, I knew the alphabet.

More hours were offered to me. Soon, a temporary full-time job. One of the steady workers had had a miscarriage. She stayed away for two months and at the end of that time she was pregnant again and her doctor advised her not to come back to work. So I joined the permanent staff and kept this job until I was halfway into my own first pregnancy. I worked with women I had known by sight for a long time. Mavis and Shirley, Mrs. Carlson and Mrs. Yost. They all remembered how I used to come in and mooch around—as they said—for hours in the library. I wished they hadn't noticed me so much. I wished I hadn't come in so often.

What a simple pleasure it was, to take up my station, to face people from behind the desk, to be capable and brisk and friendly with those who approached me. To be seen by them as a person who knew the ropes, who had a clear function in the world. To give up my lurking and wandering and dreaming and become the girl in the library.

Of course, I had less time for reading now, and sometimes I would hold a book in my hand for a moment, in my work at the desk—I would hold a book in my hand as an object, not as a vessel I had to drain immediately—and I would have a flick of fear, as in a dream when you find yourself in the wrong building or have forgotten the time for the exam and understand that this is only the tip of some shadowy cataclysm or lifelong mistake.

But this scare would vanish in a minute.

The women I worked with recalled the times they had seen me writing in the library.

I said I had been writing letters.

"You write your letters in a scribbler?"

"Sure," I said. "It's cheaper."

The last notebook grew cold, hidden in the drawer with my tumbled socks and underwear. It grew cold, the sight of it filled me with misgiving and humiliation. I meant to get rid of it but didn't.

Mrs. Gorrie had not congratulated me on getting this job.

"You didn't tell me you were still looking," she said.

I said I'd had my name in at the library for a long time and that I'd told her so.

"That was before you started working for me," she said. "So what will happen now about Mr. Gorrie?"

"I'm sorry," I said.

"That doesn't do him much good, does it?"

She raised her pink eyebrows and spoke to me in the high-falutin' way I had heard her speak on the phone, to the butcher or the grocer who had made a mistake in her order.

"And what am I supposed to do?" she said. "You've left me high and dry, haven't you? I hope you keep your promises to other people a little better than your promises to me."

This was nonsense, of course. I had not promised her anything about how long I'd stay. Yet I felt a guilty unease, if not guilt itself. I hadn't promised her anything, but what about the times when I hadn't answered her knock, when I'd tried to sneak in and out of the house unnoticed, lowering my head as I passed under her kitchen window? What about the way I'd kept up a thin but sugary pretense of friendship in answer to her offers—surely—of the real thing?

"It's just as well, really," she said. "I wouldn't want anybody who wasn't dependable looking after Mr. Gorrie. I wasn't entirely pleased with the way you were taking care of him, anyway, I can tell you that."

Soon she had found another sitter—a little spider woman with black, netted hair. I never heard her speak. But I heard Mrs. Gorrie speaking to her. The door at the top of the stairs was left open so that I should.

"She never even washed his teacup. Half the time she never even made his tea. I don't know what she was good for. Sit and read the paper."

When I left the house nowadays the kitchen window was flung up and her voice rang out over my head, though she was ostensibly talking to Mr. Gorrie.

"There she goes. On her way. She won't even bother to wave at us now. We gave her a job when nobody else would have her, but she won't bother. Oh, no."

I didn't wave. I had to go past the front window where Mr. Gorrie was sitting, but I had an idea that if I waved now, even if I looked at him, he would be humiliated. Or angered. Anything I did might seem like a taunt.

Before I was half a block away I forgot about both of them. The mornings were bright, and I moved with a sense of release and purpose. At such times my immediate past could seem vaguely disgraceful. Hours behind the alcove curtain, hours at the kitchen table filling page after page with failure, hours in an overheated room with an old man. The shaggy rug and plush upholstery, the smell of his clothes and his body and of the dry pasted scrapbooks, the acres of newsprint I had to make my way through. The grisly story that he had saved and made me read. (I never understood for a moment that it was in the category of the human tragedies I honored, in books.) Recalling all that was like recalling a period of illness in childhood when I had been willingly trapped in cozy flannelette sheets with their odor of camphorated oil, trapped by my own lassitude and the feverish, not quite decipherable messages of the tree branches seen through my upstairs window. Such times were not regretted so much as naturally discarded. And it seemed to be a part of myself—a sickly part?—that was now going into the discard. You would think marriage would have worked this transformation, but it hadn't, for a while. I had hibernated and ruminated as my old self—mulish, unfeminine, irrationally secretive. Now I picked up my feet and acknowledged my luck at being transformed into a wife and an employee. Good-looking and competent enough when I took the trouble. Not weird. I could pass.

Mrs. Gorrie brought a pillowcase to my door. Showing her teeth in a hopeless, hostile smile, she asked if it might be mine. I said without hesitation that it wasn't. The two pillowcases that I owned were on the two pillows on our bed.

She said in a martyred tone, "Well, it's certainly not mine."

I said, "How can you tell?"

Slowly, poisonously, her smile grew more confident.

"It's not the kind of material I'd ever put on Mr. Gorrie's bed. Or on mine."

Why not?

"Because—it—isn't—good—enough."

So I had to go and take the pillowcases off the pillows on the alcove bed and bring them out to her, and it did turn out that they were not a pair, though they had looked it to me. One was made of "good" fabric—that was hers—and the one in her hand was mine.

"I wouldn't believe you hadn't noticed," she said, "if it was anybody but you."

Chess had heard of another apartment. A real apartment, not a "suite"—it had a full bathroom and two bedrooms. A friend of his at work was leaving it, because he and his wife had bought a house. It was in a building at the corner of First Avenue and Macdonald Street. I could still walk to work, and he could take the same bus he took now. With two salaries, we could afford it. The friend and his wife were leaving some furniture behind, which they would sell cheaply. It would not suit their new house, but to us it seemed splendid in its respectability. We walked around the bright third-story rooms admiring the cream-painted walls, the oak parquet, the roomy kitchen cupboards, and the tiled bathroom floor. There was even a tiny balcony looking out onto the leaves of Tatlow Park. We fell in love with each other in a new way, in love with our new status, our emergence into adult life from the basement that had been only a very temporary way station. It would be featured in our conversation as a joke, an endurance test, for years to come. Every move we made—the rented house, the first house we owned, the second house we owned, the first house in a different city—would produce this euphoric sense of progress and tighten our connection. Until the last and by far the grandest house, which I entered with inklings of disaster and the faintest premonitions of escape.

409

We gave our notice to Ray, without telling Mrs. Gorrie. That raised her to a new level of hostility. In fact, she went a little crazy.

"Oh, she thinks she's so clever. She can't even keep two rooms clean. When she sweeps the floor all she does is sweep the dirt into a corner."

When I had bought my first broom I had forgotten to buy a dustpan, and for a time I had done that. But she could have known about it only if she let herself into our rooms with a key of her own while I was out. Which it became apparent that she had done.

"She's a sneak, you know. I knew the first I saw of her what a sneak she was. And a liar. She isn't right in the head. She'd sit down there and say she's writing letters and she writes the same thing over and over again—it's not letters, it's the same thing over and over. She's not right in the head."

Now I knew that she must have uncrumpled the pages in my wastebasket. I often tried to start the same story with the same words. As she said, over and over again.

The weather had turned quite warm, and I went to work without a jacket, wearing a snug sweater tucked into my skirt, and a belt pulled to its tightest notch.

She opened the front door and yelled after me.

"Slut. Look at the slut, the way she sticks her chest out and wobbles her rear end. You think you're Marilyn Monroe?"

And "We don't need you in our house. The sooner you get out of here the better."

She phoned up Ray and told him I was trying to steal her bed linen. She complained that I was telling stories about her up and down the street. She had opened the door to make sure I could hear, and she shouted into the phone, but this was hardly necessary, because we were on the same line and could listen in anytime we wanted to. I never did so—my instinct was to block my ears—but one evening when Chess was home he picked up the phone and spoke.

"Don't pay any attention to her, Ray, she's just a crazy old woman. I know she's your mother, but I have to tell you she's crazy."

I asked him what Ray had said, whether he was angry at that.

"He just said, 'Sure, okay.'"

Mrs. Gorrie had hung up and was shouting directly down the stairs, "I'll tell you who's crazy. I'll tell you who's a crazy liar spreading lies about me and my husband—"

Chess said, "We're not listening to you. You leave my wife alone." Later he said to me, "What does she mean about her and her husband?"

I said, "I don't know."

"She just has it in for you," he said. "Because you're young and nice-looking and she's an old hag.

"Forget it," he said, and made a halfway joke to cheer me up.

"What is the point of old women anyway?"

We moved to the new apartment by taxi with just our suitcases. We waited out on the sidewalk with our backs to the house. I expected some final screaming then, but there was not a sound.

"What if she's got a gun and shoots me in the back?" I said.

"Don't talk like her," Chess said.

"I'd like to wave to Mr. Gorrie if he's there."

"Better not."

I didn't take a final look at the house, and I didn't walk down that street, that block of Arbutus Street that faces the park and the sea, ever again. I don't have a clear idea of what it looked like, though I remember a few things—the alcove curtain, the china cabinet, Mr. Gorrie's green recliner—so well.

We got to know other young couples who had started out as we did, living in cheap spaces in other people's houses. We heard about rats, cockroaches, evil toilets, crazy landladies. And we would tell about our crazy landlady. Paranoia.

411

Otherwise, I didn't think of Mrs. Gorrie.

But Mr. Gorrie showed up in my dreams. In my dreams I seemed to know him before he knew her. He was agile and strong, but he wasn't young, and he didn't look any better than he did when I had read to him in the front room. Perhaps he could talk, but his talk was on the level of those noises I had learned to interpret—it was abrupt and peremptory, an essential but perhaps disdained footnote to the action. And the action was explosive, for these were erotic dreams. All the time that I was a young wife, and then, without undue delay, a young mother—busy, faithful, regularly satisfied—I kept having dreams now and then in which the attack, the response, the possibilities, went beyond anything life offered. And from which romance was banished. Decency as well. Our bed—Mr. Gorrie's and mine—was the gravelly beach or the rough boat deck or the punishing coils of greasy rope. There was a relish of what you might call ugliness. His pungent smell, his jelly eye, his dog's teeth. I woke out of these pagan dreams drained even of astonishment, or shame, and fell asleep again and woke with a memory I got used to denying in the morning. For years and years and surely long after he was dead Mr. Gorrie operated in my night-life this way. Until I used him up, I suppose, the way we use up the dead. But it never seemed to be this way—that I was in charge, that I had brought him there. It seemed to be working both ways, as if he had brought me there, too, and it was his experience as much as it was mine.

And the boat and the dock and the gravel on the shore, the trees sky-pointed or crouching, leaning out over the water, the complicated profile of surrounding islands and dim yet distinct mountains, seemed to exist in a natural confusion, more extravagant and yet more ordinary than anything I could dream or invent. Like a place that will go on existing whether you are there or not, and that in fact is still there.

But I never saw the charred beams of the house fallen down on the body of the husband. That had happened a long time before and the forest had grown up all around it.

Acknowledgements

"Shiners" reprinted from *Bad Imaginings* (©1993), by Caroline Adderson, published by The Porcupine's Quill. Reprinted by permission of the publisher.

"Being Audited" reprinted from *The Rain Barrel* (©1994), by George Bowering, published by Talonbooks. Reprinted by permission of the author.

"North America, South America" by Marilyn Bowering printed by permission of the author.

"Diamond" reprinted from *49th Parallel Psalm* (©1999) by Wayde Compton, published by Arsenal Pulp Press. Reprinted by permission of the publisher.

"Dirty Blue Collar" by Jenny Fjellgaard printed by permission of the author. Title taken from a line in Gary Fjellgaard's "Colour of Your Collar" by permission of the songwriter.

"Bodies of Water" reprinted from *My Father Took A Cake To France* (©1992) by Cynthia Flood, published by Talonbooks. Reprinted by permission of the author and publisher.

"Revisionism and Lesser Sorrows" by D.M. Fraser reprinted from *West Coast Review* 18:3 (©1984) / Pulp Press by permission of Stephen Osborne, literary executor of D.M. Fraser's estate.

"Measuring Death in Column Inches (*a nine-week manual for girl rim pigs*)" reprinted from *All the Anxious Girls on Earth* (©1999) by Zsuzsi Gartner, published by Key Porter Books. Reprinted by permission of the author.

"Fishing Veronica Lake" by Stephen Guppy reprinted from *95:Best Canadian Stories*. Reprinted by permission of the author.

"Report on the Nanaimo Labour School" reprinted from *Small Rain* (©1989) by John Harris, published by New Star Books. Reprinted by permission of the author.

"Ucluelet" reprinted from *The Watery Part of the World* (©1988) by Maria (Gladys) Hindmarch, published by Douglas & McIntyre. Reprinted by permission of the author.

"After the Season" reprinted from *Spit Delaney's Island* (©1976) by Jack Hodgins, published by Macmillan of Canada. Reprinted by permission of the author.

"Righteous Speedboat" by Mark Jarman is reprinted from *New Orleans Is Sinking* (©1998) by permission of Oberon Press.

"Ivory Chopsticks" by Danielle Lagah printed by permission of the author.

"Fresh Girls" reprinted from *Fresh Girls and Other Stories* (©1993) by Evelyn Lau, published by HarperCollins. Reprinted by permission of the publisher.

Contributors

Caroline Adderson's story collection, *Bad Imaginings* (1993), was a finalist for the Commonwealth Writers Prize and the Governor General's Award, and won the Ethel Wilson Fiction Prize. Her novel, *A History of Forgetting* (1999), was nominated for a BC Book Prize.

George Bowering, a prolific writer with over forty titles, has twice won a Governor General's Award, once for poetry, *The Gangs of Kosmos* and *Rocky Mountain Foot* (1968), and another time for the novel, *Burning Water* (1980). Among his books of short fiction are *Flycatcher & Other Stories* (1974), *A Place to Die* (1983), and *The Rain Barrel* (1994).

Marilyn Bowering has written several books of poetry, including *Autobiography* (1996), a finalist for the Governor General's Award and the winner of the Pat Lowther Award. Her two novels are *To All Appearances a Lady* (1989) and *Visible Worlds* (1997), which was chosen for a BC Book Prize and shortlisted for Britain's Orange Prize.

Wayde Compton has published in numerous literary magazines, and his book, *49ᵗʰ Parallel Psalm* (1999), was a finalist for the Dorothy Livesay Poetry Prize.

Jenny Fjellgaard's story, "Searching for Recognition / Re-cognition," won second prize in fiction in the Alternative Writing and Design Contest and appears in *Netherwords* (2001).

Cynthia Flood, winner of the Journey Prize and the National Magazines' Gold Award for fiction, has published two books of stories, *The Animals In Their Elements* (1987) and *My Father Took A Cake To France* (1992). Her first novel, *Making A Stone of the Heart*, will be published in 2002.

D.M. "Don" Fraser wrote two books of stories, *Class Warfare* (1974) and *The Voice of Emma Sachs* (1983). *Prelude*, Volume 1 of *The Collected Works* (1987) and a novel, *Ignorant Armies* (1990), were published after his early death in 1985.

Zsuzsi Gartner is an award-winning journalist and fiction writer. Her first book, the collection of stories titled *All the Anxious Girls on Earth* (1999), was nominated for the Ethel Wilson Prize.

Stephen Guppy's fiction has appeared in his collection, *Another Sad Day at the Edge of the Empire* (1985), as well as in *The Journey Prize Anthology,* and two editions of *Best Canadian Stories*. His third book of poetry, *Understanding Heaven*, is forthcoming, as is a second collection of stories, *The Work Of Mercy*.

John Harris has written two critical monographs, a travel book called *Tungsten John* (2000), and two story collections, *Small Rain* (1989) and *Other Art* (1997).

Maria (Gladys) Hindmarch has published three books, *A Birth Account* (1976), *The Peter Stories* (1976), and *The Watery Part of the World* (1988).

Jack Hodgins' books of fiction include his early story collection, *Spit Delaney's Island* (1976), and such novels as *The Invention of the World* (1977), *The Resurrection of Joseph Bourne* (1979), and *Broken Ground* (1998). He has also written *A Passion for Narrative: A Guide for Writing Fiction* (1994). Hodgins has received the Canada-Australia Prize, the Ethel Wilson Award, and the Governor-General's Award.

Mark Anthony Jarman, the author of the novel, *Salvage King Ya!* (1997), and story collections, *New Orleans Is Sinking* (1998) and *19 Knives* (2000), has won the Maclean-Hunter Prize in Creative Nonfiction two years in a row. His short fiction has been included in *The Journey Prize Anthology* and in *Best Canadian Stories*.

Danielle Lagah's work has appeared on CBC Radio's *Out Front*, in literary journals, and in *Breaking the Surface* (2000).

Evelyn Lau has written *Runaway: Diary of a Street Kid* (1989), *You are Not Who You Claim* (1990), winner of the People's Poetry Award, *Oedipal Dreams* (1992), nominated for the Governor General's Poetry Award, two collections of short fiction, *Fresh Girls and Other Stories* (1993) and *Choose Me* (1999), the novel, *Other Women* (1996), and *Inside Out: Reflections On A Life So Far* (2001).

Murray Logan's collection of thirteen short stories, *The King of Siam* (1998), was a finalist for the Danuta Gleed Literary Award.

Annabel Lyon's stories have appeared in many literary magazines and have been collected in *Oxygen* (2000), nominated for the Danuta Gleed Literary Award.

Shani Mootoo's works include *Out on Main Street & Other Stories* (1993), a novel, *Cereus Blooms at Night* (1996), which was nominated for the Giller Prize, and a book of poems, *The Predicament of Or* (2001).

Alice Munro's more recent books of short fiction include *The Moons of Jupiter* (1982), *The Progress of Love* (1985), *Friend of My Youth* (1990), *Open Secrets* (1994), and *The Love of a Good Woman* (1998). Her work has won numerous prizes, among them The National Book Critics' Circle Top Fiction Award, the Giller Prize, and the Governor General's Award three times.

P.K. Page is the author of more than a dozen books. A two volume edition of her collected poems, *The Hidden Room*, was published in 1997. In addition to winning the National Magazine Award, the Canadian Authors' Association Literary Award, and the Governor General's Award for her poetry, Page received the Hubert Evans BC Book Prize for her memoir, *Brazilian Journal* (1987). Her stories have been gathered in *A Kind of Fiction* (2001).

Liza Potvin won the Edna Staebler Creative Non-Fiction Award for her book, *White Lies* (1992). Her stories have appeared in many literary journals, winning the *Quarry* Best Short Story Prize (2000) and the *Zygote* Best Fiction Award (2001). Her forthcoming book of stories is titled *Flights of Gravity*.

Kevin Roberts has written three plays, twelve books and chapbooks of poetry, two collections of short stories, *Flash Harry & The Daughters of Divine Light* (1982) and *Picking the Morning Colour* (1985), plus a novel, *Tears in a Glass Eye* (1989). His most recent book of poems, *Cobalt 3* (2000), was shortlisted for the People's Poetry Award.

Eden Robinson's book of stories, *Traplines* (1996), a *New York Times* Notable Book of the Year, was awarded the Winifred Holtby Prize. Her novel, *Monkey Beach* (2000), nominated for both the Governor General's Award and the Giller Prize, won the BC Book Prize.

Ron Smith has written three works of poetry, *Seasonal* (1984), *A Buddha Named Baudelaire* (1988), and *Enchantments & Other Demons* (1995). "The Last Time We Talked," originally published in *The Bridport Prize Anthology* (England), is part of Smith's story collection, *What Men Know About Women* (1999).

Linda Svendsen's work has appeared twice in the *O. Henry Prize Stories* and three times in *Best Canadian Stories*. As a screenwriter, Svendsen has adapted Margaret Laurence's *The Diviners* and scripted *The Sue Rodriguez Story*. Her collection of interlinked stories, *Marine Life* (1992), was nominated for an *L.A. Times* Book Prize, and has recently been produced as a feature film.

Timothy Taylor has received both the Journey Prize and a National Magazine Award for his short fiction. His stories have been included in *Best Canadian Stories*, *Coming Attractions*, and three times in the 2000 *Journey Prize Anthology*. His novel, *Stanley Park*, was published in 2001, and his first story collection, *Silent Cruise*, will appear in 2002.

Madeleine Thien's work has appeared in several literary journals, *Best*

Canadian Stories, and *The Journey Prize Anthology*. The manuscript for her collection, *Simple Recipes* (2001), won the 1998 Asian Canadian Writer's Workshop's Emerging Writer Award.

Audrey Thomas has written over 20 radio dramas for the CBC. Her books of fiction include *Mrs. Blood* (1975), *Intertidal Life* (1984), *Goodbye Harold, Good Luck* (1986), *The Wild Blue Yonder* (1990), and *Isobel Gunn* (1999). She has received the Marian Engel Award, the Canada-Australia Literary Prize, the W. O. Mitchell Literary Prize, and the Ethel Wilson Award three times.

Carol Windley's story, "Dreamland," received First Prize in the CBC Radio Literary Competition. Her collection of short fiction, *Visible Light* (1993), was nominated for the Ethel Wilson Fiction Prize and the Governor General's Award and won the Bumbershoot-Weyerhaeuser Publication Award. Her novel, *Breathing Under Water*, appeared in 1998.

Terence Young's first collection of poetry, *The Island in Winter* (1999) was shortlisted for both the Gerald Lampert and the Governor General's Awards. *Rhymes With Useless* (2000), his collection of short stories, was a runner-up for the Danuta Gleed Literary Prize.

About the Editor

Keith Harrison studied at UBC, California (Berkeley), and McGill. He has published four novels, *Dead Ends*, *After Six Days*, *Eyemouth*, and *Furry Creek*, and a collection of short fiction, *Crossing the Gulf* (Oolichan, 1998). His novels have been nominated for the Books in Canada First Novel Award and the QSPELL's Hugh MacLennan Fiction Prize, and his short fiction has won the Okanagan Short Story Award. He teaches English and Creative Writing at Malaspina University-College, and lives on Hornby Island, BC.